UNHAPPY ENDINGS

Brian Keene

DB

First Edition Paperback
April 2009

Published by:
Delirium Books
P.O. Box 338
North Webster, IN 46555
sales@deliriumbooks.com
www.deliriumbooks.com

Reprint information for the remaining stories appear on page 323.

ISBN 978-1-934546-10-9

Copy Editors: David Marty & Steve Souza

Author Acknowledgements: Thanks to my family (Cassandra, Shane, Sam and Max); Shane Ryan Staley and Delirium Books; and as always, my readers and the message board regulars at BrianKeene.com.

This one is dedicated to Jason and Tash...

TABLE OF CONTENTS

UNHAPPY ENDINGS

This is a book about unhappy endings. I don't think you need a spoiler alert to tell you that bad things happen to the people in these stories.

I wrote them, after all.

My endings have haunted me since the publication of my first novel, *The Rising*, many years ago. It was decidedly bleak—so much that some people were infuriated by it. And my endings have gotten even bleaker since then. Over the past few years, some critics and readers have questioned whether or not I'm capable of writing a happy ending. They point to *Dark Hollow, Ghoul, City of the Dead, Terminal* and pretty much everything else in my canon, and point out the grim, nihilistic outlook of them all. (I'd argue that *Ghoul* has a happy ending if you skip the epilogue and *City of the Dead* has a happy ending—of sorts. But I digress.)

The critics and the readers are right, of course. My endings are usually unhappy ones. The good guys seldom ride off into the sunset. The prince doesn't get the girl. The hero might indeed save the day, but get his entire family killed in the process. "Why," people ask. "Why are your endings always so fatalistic? Why can't you write a happy ending just once?"

My answer is always the same: I write what I know. That's the most common bit of advice given to authors—write what you know. Usually, it means 'don't bullshit your way through a story." If you know nothing about cars, then your main character probably shouldn't be a mechanic. Otherwise, you'll end up with a crucial passage in the middle of the book wherein your protagonist fixes the digital clock on the dashboard by replacing the car's timing belt. And then all of your readers will make fun of you on the internet. All because you weren't writing what you know.

I write unhappy endings because they are what I know. By and large, unhappy endings are what life has shown me in my forty-one years. That is why I'm grateful for the happy moments. I cherish them. Hold onto them for as long as I can. Because sooner or later, something bad will come along and totally fuck things up again. Life is nothing more than a series of moments. Some of them are good. Some of them are not. You enjoy the good ones while they last, and hopefully, the memories of those times will get you through the bad.

The world is a scary place. You have people who love you—family and friends, children and parents. You try to do right by them. You try to keep them happy. Make ends meet. And then, when you least expect it, the world comes along and snatches the rug out from beneath your feet. Maybe it's through cancer or Alzheimer's. Maybe it's a terrorist bomb or a natural disaster. Maybe it's through sudden loss of employment or the slow decline of alcoholism. Maybe a tractor trailer slides into your mini-van on your way home from school. Maybe a disgruntled employee shoots you in the break room at work. It wears the face of a crooked cop or a smiling politician or the psychotic who snatches newborn babies from the maternity ward. It can come in the mail. It can come from the sky. But in the end, it doesn't matter what form the bad things take.

In the end, all that matters is the end itself—and how you face it.

Writing horror fiction is my way of facing these things. My way of facing the inevitable end. In interviews, I've often joked that writing is cheaper than therapy. But here's the thing, folks. I'm not kidding. This is my outlet. This is how I face the day. Here are the things that terrify me. Perhaps they terrify you, too. This world scares me more and more each day. Maybe that's because I recently became a father again. Maybe it's because I'm beginning to feel my own mortality. All I know is that there are very real monsters in this world, and it is my job, as a horror writer, to show them to you.

Let's meet some of them now. Perhaps you'll see some familiar faces.

Perhaps one of the faces will be yours.

This is the way your world ends…unhappily.

Brian Keene
July 2008

JACK'S MAGIC BEANS

The lettuce started talking to Ben Mahoney halfway through his shift at Save-A-Lot.

He'd shown up for work ten minutes late. Mr. Brubaker was waiting for him at the time clock.

"You're late, Mahoney."

Ben sighed. "Sorry, Mr. Brubaker. I had to stay late after school. I was talking to my teacher. Been having trouble with calculus.

This was bullshit. In fact, Ben had hung around to ask Stacy Gerlach if she'd go to Eleanor Murphy's party with him on Friday night. Eleanor's parents were in New York for the weekend on one of those bus trips where you got to go shopping and see a Broadway show. The party was supposed to be off the hook—two kegs and a DJ playing trance-hop all night long. Sadly, Stacy already had a date. Pissed off at this news, Ben had blown through two red lights on his way to work. He'd also blown his sub-woofer because the bass was cranked too high. Ben's bad day got worse, and his anger was still simmering when he rushed in.

He did not tell Mr. Brubaker any of this. Instead, he apologized and swore that it wouldn't happen again.

Scowling, hands on hips, Brubaker stomped away to holler at somebody else. Ben swiped his timecard, walked into the break room, pulled his smock out of his locker, and fished around in his pockets for loose change. He put four quarters into the soda machine, waited for the can to clunk down, popped the tab, took a sip, and then started his shift—all while trying to ignore the dull headache building behind his eyes.

Ben worked part-time in Save-A-Lot's produce department. He came in during the evenings and spent four hours rotating the fruit and vegetables—a process that involved pulling all of the produce out of the bins, placing fresh produce on the bottom, and then putting the older produce back on top. That way, customers would pick the older stuff first and it wouldn't go bad. The only problem with this method was that most of the people who shopped at Save-A-Lot knew about rotation and they invariably dug through the fruits and vegetables to the bottom of the bin, thus finding the fresher selections and fucking up all of his hard work.

Old people were especially bad about doing this, and that was one of the reasons Ben hated them. He also hated the way they walked and the way they smelled. He hated it when an old person was in front of him on the road. They didn't know how to drive. He hated it when they walked in front of him, blocking the aisle. He hated how they always bothered him with stupid questions when he was busy stocking shelves. He worked in the produce department. He knew where the apples were. Why, then, would they ask him where the spaghetti was located? You want to find the pasta? Try reading the fucking signs.

Ben was sixteen. He was physically and mentally fit—a teenaged Adonis. He would never get old. Never lose his hair or his hearing or control of his bladder. His joints and teeth would never ache. He would never have to worry about running out of breath from the simplest of tasks. His eyesight would never go bad. Neither would his internal organs. He would never have to worry about not being able to have an orgasm—let alone getting a hard-on. He was young and in his prime. These were the best years of his life and those years did not involve getting old. Old people filled him with loathing.

So when he saw the old woman squeezing the peaches, and the lettuce told him to kill her, Ben agreed. It seemed like a reasonable idea.

His headache got worse.

"Kill that old bitch," the heads of lettuce said in unison. They'd each grown a little mouth, the size of his thumbnail. Their voices were high-pitched, like a cartoon character. "Knock her over and kick her goddamned face in. Bet she's wearing dentures. No fucking way those teeth are real."

Ben dropped the spray bottle that he'd been using to mist the cucumbers. He stared at the lettuce. After a moment, he smiled, forgetting all about the pain behind his eyes. The lettuce smiled back at him.

"Go on, Ben," the lettuce urged. "Make her bleed."

"How do you know my name?"

"We are the lettuce. We know everything. It has always been thus and always will be. The lettuce is wise. Now kill that old bag."

It was hard to argue with lettuce. Like they'd said—they were wise. Shrugging, Ben dropped his apron on the floor, rushed across the store and knocked the old woman to the floor. Her head cracked against the linoleum. It sounded very loud. The sound made Ben smile. He kicked her in the side of her face. The old woman's dentures skittered beneath the banana display. The lettuce had been right. They weren't her real teeth.

The old woman pawed at his pants leg. Her eyes implored him.

Ben spit in her face. "You squeezed. The fucking. *Peaches.*"

Somebody screamed.

Ben giggled.

The old woman groaned.

Then Ben stomped her face again, harder this time. Her nose splintered beneath his heel. Ben realized that he had an erection. Rubbing himself through his jeans, he raised his foot and stomped a third time. And a fourth. Then he stood on top of her face with both feet and ground his soles back and forth, pushing down with all his weight. Something gave way beneath his feet. His shoes grew wet.

The old woman was the first to die. Ben died seconds later when Roger from the floral department skewered him through the chest with a broken mop handle. Roger laughed as he thrust the spear again. He stopped laughing and became the third to die when a customer ripped his tongue out with her bare hands.

Then everybody started dying at once.

* * *

Tom Brubaker had a headache and shouting made him feel better. After he was done hollering at Ben Mahoney, he shouted at the cashiers and the butchers and a delivery guy and the little old Asian woman who ran the grocery store's Chinese kiosk. Then he yelled at Jeremy Geist, the short, pudgy kid who was re-arranging the book and magazine display.

"Damn it, Geist. How many times do I have to tell you? Every book should be faced out. People are more likely to buy the fucking things if they can see the goddamned covers."

"I'm sorry, Mr. Brubaker."

Geist's bottom lip trembled. Brubaker focused on it, overcome with disgust. His headache intensified. His temples throbbed. Somebody screamed on the other side of the store. Brubaker ignored it. He said nothing. He didn't speak. Didn't holler. Didn't move.

Jeremy thought that was worse—the not hollering part. He'd never seen Mr. Brubaker be quiet before. It made him nervous. He wondered who was screaming and why. Then more people started shrieking. There was some kind of commotion in the produce department. Things were getting weird. Jeremy, remembering some advice his counselor had given him on dealing with conflict, decided to reason with his boss.

"It's just that there's not enough room. There are too

many books and not enough space."

Brubaker grinned.

The screams grew louder.

Brubaker's headache vanished. He glanced at the shelves. Each of the paperbacks had the same title: *KILL 'EM ALL*.

It was very sound advice. After all, these were bestsellers written by important authors who knew what they were talking about. Oprah said these books had meaning and value. Oprah said these books would enrich your life. You couldn't argue with Oprah. That was crazy.

So he didn't. Instead, Brubaker wrapped his hands around Jeremy Geist's throat and squeezed. Geist's lip began trembling again, so Brubaker squeezed harder. A few feet away from them, a customer overturned the magazine rack onto a little girl. Then the customer hopped onto the rack and jumped up and down. The child, still pinned beneath the wreckage, screamed for her mother. Her mother didn't answer. She was too busy shouting obscenities and clawing the face of another customer.

Brubaker kept squeezing, even after Geist was dead.

He didn't stop until another customer squirted him with lighter fluid and set him on fire.

Brubaker laughed as he burned.

* * *

Angela Waller was third in line at the pharmacy counter when the screaming started. She flinched, almost dropping her purse. The redneck guy in front of her was startled enough by the commotion to stop arguing with the pharmacist. Angie paused, waiting for gunshots—expecting maybe a robbery or some disgruntled nutcase on a rampage. When the gunshots didn't come, she held her breath. The screams got louder.

Behind her, somebody said, "I wish they'd shut up. My head hurts."

It had been a weird afternoon—getting weirder with

each second. Angie had seen more road rage and rudeness on her way here than she normally saw in a month. There was something in the air, something heavy and malignant, ready to burst like storm clouds bloated with rain. If there was trouble in the store, then Angie wanted no part of it. She just wanted to get her prescription filled and go home, where she'd take off her work clothes, put on some pajama pants, curl up on the bed, and paint her toenails.

In three days, Angie and her girlfriends were taking a cruise to Antigua in celebration of her twenty-ninth birthday. Girls only—no boyfriends or husbands. She needed her Prozac before she left. That was the only reason she remained in line when the screams began. The pills were a necessity, just like tampons, her diaphragm, her passport, and cell phone. Prozac: don't leave home without it. She'd been diagnosed with chronic depression when she was fifteen, and had been on the drug most of her adult life. Sure, the recommended length of usage was only six to twelve months, but like her doctor said, if it helped, it helped. And help it did. She could function on Prozac. Taking it was as natural as breathing.

The screams increased, multiplying throughout the store.

And then Angie forgot all about Antigua and her prescription because the pharmacist lunged over the counter and stabbed his pen into the neck of the man in front of her. The redneck reared back, grasping at the pen. Blood bubbled out around it. Humming the theme from *The Young and the Restless,* the pharmacist grappled with the injured man. Angie backed away, too frightened to scream, and this time she did drop her purse. Doing so saved her life. She knelt to pick it up and thus avoided a sweeping blow from the woman behind her, who had decided to crack Angie in the back of the head with a bottle of mouthwash.

"You slept with my Herbert," the woman shouted. "Little whore!"

Angie tried to skitter backwards, but there was nowhere to go. All around her, fights broke out. Customers and Save-A-Lot employees clawed, punched, and shrieked at each other. A naked fat man crawled around on all fours, growling like a dog. A severed penis dangled from his clenched teeth. A woman tried swinging from the skylights but crashed to the floor. A crowd of people leapt on her. Another woman with a nail file sticking out of her breast ran past, screaming about a gnome in her tiramisu. Blood flowed—pooling on the floor, splashing across displays, pouring from wounds, and staining the hands, mouths, feet, and makeshift weapons of the attackers.

"You fucked Herbert! Fucked him hard!"

Angie's attacker kicked her in the side. Slipping in a puddle of liquid soap and someone else's blood, Angie curled into a ball and tried to protect herself. The woman yelled again, once more accusing Angie of sleeping with Herbert, but Angie was pretty sure she'd never slept with a Herbert, married or otherwise.

"Did he lick you? He never did that for me. Said he didn't like it. But I know the truth. He couldn't find the clit."

"Please," Angie rasped. "I don't—"

The woman aimed another kick, and Angie focused on staying alive.

* * *

Marcel Dupree had just turned off his car and was double-checking the headlights, radio, and everything else when somebody rear-ended him. The impact bounced him off the steering column, knocking the wind from his lungs. Shocked, Marcel flung the door open and stumbled outside, forgetting all about the headlights. He was too flustered to speak. He could only watch in stunned silence as a black Cadillac Escalade reversed, then raced forward and rammed his car again. The SUV's driver was hidden behind tinted windows.

"Hey," Marcel tried to shout. It came out more like a whisper. The driver gave no indication that they'd heard him. The Cadillac's engine roared and smoke belched from the tailpipe.

The impact of the collision slammed his car door shut. Marcel wondered if the door was locked. As the Cadillac backed up, he checked the door and then checked it again. He was about to check a third time, when he became dimly aware that other people were hollering, as well. He heard the distinct impact of another car crash. Sirens wailed—police, fire, and ambulance. Marcel glanced around, trying to determine what was happening. The Cadillac ran into his car again, crumpling the rear bumper.

"Hey," Marcel shouted, finally finding his voice. "What are you doing?"

Forgetting about the door lock, he ran towards the Escalade, waving his fists and yelling. The tinted window slid down, revealing the driver. Marcel had never seen him before.

"What the hell is your problem, man?"

"You took my parking space!" Spittle flew from the enraged driver's mouth. His face was red. "How do you like it? Huh, motherfucker? How do you fucking like it, nigger?"

The slur shocked Marcel. He'd been called it before, when he was younger, but the word still had impact. Before he could respond, the Cadillac's driver turned the wheel and sped towards him. Marcel leapt out of the way and rolled across the hot pavement. Then he jumped to his feet and shouted for help. All around him, people ran through the parking lot. Most of them were engaged in similar battles, fighting in groups or one-on-one, using vehicles, shopping carts, tire irons, and anything else as weapons. He gaped in horror as a pick-up truck ran over a fleeing mother pushing a baby stroller, then reversed and ran over them again. The vehicle bounced up and down as the tires rolled over the corpses. A young man with a pistol shot the truck's driver and then turned the gun on other bystanders. Some charged him, some ran away, and others totally ignored the assault, involved as they were in other fights. A cop shot the young man with the gun, blowing his lungs through his back. The officer then fired at an old woman beating a teenager over the head with her walker.

"Police!" Marcel tried to get the cop's attention. "Over here. Help!"

The cop wheeled around, attracted by his cries. Marcel's relief vanished as the cop aimed the pistol at him.

"No!" Marcel held his hands up in surrender. "What are you—"

A neon-green Volkswagen slammed into the cop. The policeman flipped up over the hood, smashing against the windshield. His shoes remained on the pavement—his feet still inside them. The blacktop turned red. Inside the car, four teenage girls laughed. Then they turned on each other, clawing and gouging. The Volkswagen crashed into a parked car.

Marcel fought the urge to puke. There were angry cries behind him. He ran for the Save-A-Lot, aware that people were suddenly chasing him, shouting things—threats, curses, promises. He focused on counting his steps.

One...two...three...

His heart pounded. His mouth went dry. His lungs burned with the exertion. More feet echoed behind him as others joined in the chase.

Thirteen...fourteen...oh God...fifteen...

He burst through the doors of Save-A-Lot and skidded to a halt. Normally, Marcel would have spent the next five minutes trying to select the right shopping cart. But today, his disorder was all but forgotten. He felt the urge to call his doctor and tell him he'd found a cure. After all the frustration and the constant experimenting with different medicines, he'd found a way to beat it.

He didn't need meds. He just needed chaos.

Marcel stood staring at the scene inside the store.

If the parking lot had been a battleground, this was the frontline.

And then the war *really* started.

* * *

Sammi Barberra had just closed out her register, and was getting ready to turn in her cash drawer and clock out, when everybody in the store went insane. It started with one scream, then six, then a dozen. Fights broke out across the store. She ducked down behind the register, huddling into a ball and trying to remain out of sight while all around her, people slaughtered each other. She put her hands over her ears, attempting to block the screams, the cries, the impact of flesh on flesh—and the wet, tearing sounds. An explosion in the parking lot rocked the building. The overhead lights flickered, but stayed on. One of the big panel windows at the front of the store shattered, spraying shards of glass all over the floor. Sammi stayed where she was, hidden from view.

The only problem was, she couldn't see what was happening. Sammi peeked around the corner of the counter and immediately wished she hadn't.

Mr. Brubaker's burned head rolled slowly across the floor. Sammi resisted the urge to scream. The manager's eyes and mouth were still open. A customer was bowling with it, using plastic milk jugs as pins and Mr. Brubaker's head as the ball. It came to rest at the foot of the candy rack in her aisle. His head was upside down and she could see into the ragged stump, straight down his windpipe. Mr. Brubaker's eyes stared at her. He looked angry, even in death. Sammi ducked back beneath the register.

"Damn," she heard the bowler mutter. "I need more balls."

There was a brief moment of silence. The crazy person had apparently moved on.

She needed to pee. She squeezed her thighs together and wept silent tears.

Footsteps drew towards her.

"Oh God..."

Sammi jumped to her feet, prepared to flee. Before she could get out from behind the register, somebody grabbed her wrist and yanked her forward over the counter. It was

Jerry Sadler, the retarded guy who collected shopping carts in the parking lot and sometimes bagged groceries for customers. Sammi didn't recognize him at first, because one of Jerry's ears was missing and there was a wide gash in his cheek, deep enough to reveal his teeth and gums.

"Jerry," she gasped. "Let go, you're hurting me. Are you okay?"

"You're so pretty. I always thought you were pretty."

His words were slurred as a result of his injury, but his eyes shone with clear intent.

"Jerry!" Sammi tried to pull away, but he tightened his grip.

"You're too skinny, though. It makes you look younger. Makes you look like a little girl."

"Stop it!"

"I like little girls. I watch them all the time."

"Get off me, you freak!"

In the next register aisle, a child in a brightly-colored SpongeBob shirt sprayed a wounded, quivering woman in the face with hornet spray. The chemical stench filled the air. The spray bubbled, foamy and white, mingling with the woman's blood. The pint-sized maniac giggled. Sammi began to cry.

"Jerry, you're hurting me. Stop it!"

"You called me a freak. That's like a retard."

"I'm sorry, okay?" Sammi tried to reason with him. "We've got to get away, Jerry. Something's wrong. Please let go."

A man stumbled by them. He was bent over, clutching his stomach. The handle of an umbrella jutted from his back.

"Look how skinny your wrist is," Jerry slurred. "I can snap your bones, just like a little bird."

He smiled. A thin line of pink drool dripped from his bottom lip and landed on the counter. Nearby, an injured employee crawled towards them on her hands and knees. Sammi couldn't tell who it was because the woman's face, hands, and name badge were covered in blood.

"Jerry," Sammi warned. "Let me go."

Still smiling, Jerry twisted her wrist. A sharp jolt of pain shot up Sammi's arm. Screaming, she slapped at him, but Jerry dodged the blow. With her free hand, Sammi grabbed her cash drawer. Then she lashed out with it, striking him in his already wounded face. Teeth shattered. Jerry let go of her wrist and moaned, shaking with rage. Sammi hit him again. He struck out, backhanding the drawer. It flew from Sammi's grip and clattered across the floor.

"Gonna break all your little bones, skinny girl."

A broken tooth fell out of his mouth as he made the threat. Jerry didn't seem to notice. He made another grab for Sammi's wrist, but then the crawling employee reached them. This close, Sammi could see her features through the blood. She recognized her as Hazel Stern, one of the supervisors who usually worked the service desk. Sammi didn't know her very well. Rumor around the store was that Hazel and Mr. Brubaker were having an affair. Sammi also glimpsed the scissors clutched in the injured woman's hand. Without pausing, Hazel stabbed them into Jerry's leg, cooing softly as she did.

Shrieking, Jerry turned his wrath on the new opponent. As the two employees struggled, Sammi vaulted over the counter and fled down the aisle, dodging attackers and leaping over corpses. A jar of spaghetti sauce whizzed by her head, smashing into a row of pickles. A customer tried to push a breakfast cereal display over on her, but she dodged the falling boxes and kept running.

A little boy lay sprawled on his stomach in front of her. Blood trickled from one of his ears. As she passed by, he reached for her, his tone pleading.

"Please, help me."

Sammi paused, but before she could act, an adult grabbed the child's feet and dragged him away. The boy wailed. His eyes remained on Sammi. Weeping, Sammi kept going, heading towards the rear of the store. There was nothing she could do.

Not for the first time today, she felt like throwing up.

The only difference was that this time, she hadn't eaten.

* * *

And then there was Jack Bartlett, who spent his fifteen-minute break bundled up in a heavy coat, taking a nap inside the meat department's big walk-in freezer.

Jack missed the whole thing.

When he woke up, people were screaming.

He opened his eyes and sat up straight, banging his head against the cold steel wall. Wincing, he blinked, trying to figure out what was happening. There were two women in the freezer with him. One of them was about his age, startlingly skinny and wearing a Save-A-Lot uniform just like his. Her long, blonde hair was pulled into a ponytail with a pink scrunchy. The other woman was older, maybe in her late twenties, dressed in jeans and a white, spaghetti-strap blouse. Her short, brunette hair was plastered to her scalp with sweat and blood. Jack didn't know her, but he definitely knew the skinny girl—Sammi Barberra, one of the cashiers. She was a freshman at the community college, just like him. His buddy, Phil, had gone out with her a few times back in high school. Rumor was that Sammi had bulimia. Looking at her, it was easy to believe. She was pretty, in a super-model-goes-to-Auschwitz sort of way.

Both women were yelling and crying, and trying to hold the door shut. Somebody was pounding on the other side, hollering to be let in. The blows echoed through the freezer, loud enough to be heard over their cries. Neither Sammi nor the other woman seemed to have noticed Jack. Their backs were to him. Both of them gripped the door handle tightly and kept pulling it shut, bracing their feet apart. There was blood on their clothes. Their panic was palpable.

Jack sat up the rest of the way. "Hey."

Ignoring him, they kept their attention focused on the door.

"Pull," the woman shouted.

"I'm trying," Sammi sobbed. "Oh my God..."

Outside, whoever was pounding on the door hollered, "Let me in, goddamn it! They're gonna kill me."

"Stay out there," the woman yelled. "Don't come in here."

"Please, listen to me! I'm okay. I'm not like the others."

"Just go away." Sammi grunted, pulling harder. "Leave us alone!"

Jack stood up. His heavy freezer coat rustled.

"Hey," he tried again. "What's going on?"

The women screamed in unison. Sammi let go of the door handle and turned around. The other woman held tight but looked over her shoulder. Smiling in confusion, Jack took a step towards them, hands held out in front of him, palms up.

Sammi's eyes grew wide. "Stay back. Don't come any closer!"

He stopped. "Sammi, it's me—Jack. Phil's friend? What the hell are you doing? What are you afraid of?"

Before she could answer, the door was wrenched out of the other woman's hands. A black man ran into the freezer. His clothes were also spattered with blood.

"Shut it," he yelled. "Shut the door, quick!"

"Are you one of them," the woman demanded. "Are you okay?"

"I'm fine," he said. "Do I look like I'm trying to claw your eyeballs out? Now shut the damn door."

Jack heard more screams from outside the freezer. Lots of them. Wide-awake now, he took another cautious step forward while the woman slammed the freezer door shut again.

"What's going on?" Jack asked. "Is somebody hurt?"

"Who the hell are you?" The man whirled around, fists raised.

"Who the hell am I? I work here. My name's Jack. And unless I'm mistaken, customers aren't allowed back here. So who the fuck are *you*?"

"Marcel. And you just stay right there, man. Don't make

me hurt you. I'll mess you up."

Shaking his head, Jack turned to Sammi. "What's going on?"

"They…the people…Mr. Brubaker…Jerry tried to…"

She broke off, sobbing.

"Somebody help me with this door," the other woman said. "Is there a way to lock it?"

"It's a safety door," Jack told her. "Can't lock it from the inside, just so nobody accidentally gets trapped. You can lock it from the outside, but even then, somebody inside can still open it. But why do you need to lock it?"

"Duh. So they don't get in."

Jack took a deep breath. "Who? Where did all this blood come from? Who's hurt?"

Sammi wiped her nose on her apron. "A lot of people. Hurt or dead."

"Look…" Jack ran his hands through his hair. "What the hell is happening?"

"First the door," Marcel said. "Otherwise, we're not going to be around long enough to tell you."

A quick search of the freezer turned up several lengths of plastic bands that had been used to fasten boxes to skids. There was also a roll of shrink-wrap. While the women held the door closed, Jack and Marcel tied it shut with the bands and makeshift shrink-wrap rope—running them from the doorknob to a nearby shelf, thus making it hard for anyone outside to pull open the door. As they finished, someone else pounded on the door. Unintelligible moans and shrieks accompanied the blows. Fingernails screeched across steel. The four survivors stared at the door, not daring to speak, barely breathing. After a few minutes, the sounds faded.

"Jesus," the older woman panted. "I can't believe this."

"Quiet," Sammi whispered. "They might still be out there."

"You're right. Sorry."

Sammi shrugged. "It's okay. What's your name?"

"Angie. Angie Waller." She winced, gently rubbing her side.

"Are you okay?" Sammi asked.

Angie nodded. "I'll be fine. Some old lady kicked me in the ribs, but I don't think they're broken."

"I'm Sammi. This is Jack." She turned to the black man. "What did you say your name was?"

"Marcel." He moved past them and checked the door, fingering the bands and shrink-wrap ropes, making sure they were tight and secure. "Marcel Dupree."

"It'll hold," Jack said. "I was in the Scouts. I know how to tie a knot."

Marcel didn't answer. His attention remained focused on the door.

"So," Jack sighed. "What did I sleep through?"

They told him.

* * *

They remained inside the freezer for the next hour, huddled together for warmth and whispering, careful not to attract attention. Occasionally, someone on the outside would try the door, but the bonds held. Eventually, the screams subsided. Angie, Marcel, and Sammi all had cell phones, but when they tried to dial for help, none of them could get a signal since they were surrounded by steel walls.

Shivering, Sammi clasped her arms around her shoulders. "It's cold in here."

"It's a freezer," Jack said. "It's supposed to be cold."

Their breath hung in the air like wisps of fog when they spoke. The compressor hummed softly on the other side of the wall.

"Besides," he continued, "it could be worse."

"How?" Sammi asked. "What could possibly be any worse than this?"

"The lights could go out."

"Well," Marcel said, "we know the power is still on. Otherwise the freezer wouldn't be running. So if the electricity is still on, then maybe this didn't happen everywhere. Maybe it was just confined to Save-A-Lot."

"I don't know," Angie said. "Even on the way here, people seemed angrier than normal. On the highway. And we all heard fire sirens and police cars. They weren't all coming here."

Marcel snorted. "So everybody all over the world just went insane at the same fucking time?"

"Maybe not all over the world." Angie shrugged. "But at least here in town. Could be it's some sort of localized thing."

"Yeah," Jack said, "but what kind of thing? What makes everyone go batshit crazy all at once and start killing each other?"

"Terrorists." Marcel got to his feet. "Al Qaeda, or maybe some homegrown group like those Sons of the Constitution motherfuckers. Maybe they dropped some gas on us."

"How?"

"They could have used a crop-duster or something. Like what happened in that little town in Pennsylvania a few years ago. That chemical got released from a hot air balloon and made the rain purple, and then everybody died? Remember that?"

"I do," Sammi whispered. "I had nightmares about it for weeks. Those poor people..."

"It couldn't be gas," Jack said, watching Marcel as he crossed the freezer and checked the door again. The man seemed to be counting his steps under his breath. "You guys would have smelled it when it came through the store's ventilation system."

"Not necessarily," Angie said. "Gas can be odorless. Invisible. But I agree that it wasn't gas. It was windy outside. If they'd used gas, some of it would have blown away. If that happened, then it wouldn't have been as effective in the parking lot, and the way Marcel talks, things were just as bad out there. And besides, if there was gas, then each of us would have breathed it, too—and we're okay."

"Maybe we're immune," Jack suggested.

"You can't be immune to gas."

"The water, then." Sammi's teeth chattered as she

spoke. "Somebody could have spiked the town's water supply."

"Maybe," Angie agreed, watching Marcel. "But I drank water from the tap today, and took a shower, too, and I didn't go crazy. How about you?"

"I don't drink city water," Sammi said. "I only use bottled spring water."

"But you showered, right? Brushed your teeth?"

Sammi nodded. "Yeah, after my morning run."

"Well, there you go."

Jack noticed Sammi's face turn red, as if she were embarrassed. He wondered why. Sammi looked away from them. Jack turned his attention back to Marcel. He was checking the straps again.

"What's up, Marcel?"

He shrugged. "Just making sure these will hold."

"Dude, they're okay. I told you, I'm the knot master. You keep messing with them, somebody on the other side is going to hear you."

"I know." But even as he said it, Marcel gave no indication of stopping. He tugged the bonds again. "Just want to be sure."

"Marcel..."

"I can't help it, kid."

"My name's Jack. Not kid."

Releasing the bands, Marcel turned around and walked back to them.

"I'm sorry," he said. "Guess I should have said something sooner. It's just a little embarrassing is all—especially telling strangers."

They stared at him, but it was Jack who finally spoke up, asking what they were all thinking.

"What is?"

Marcel sat down again. "I've got OCD—Obsessive Compulsive Disorder. You guys know what that is?"

They nodded.

"Of course you do," he muttered. "Everybody does these days. People make jokes about it at work and on TV.

Most people think that folks with OCD are crazy. But we're not—and it ain't funny. I hate being like this. Hate the fucking looks people give me."

"So your OCD has to do with doors?" Angie asked.

Marcel nodded. "Yeah, something like that. Doors and appliances, mostly. I need to make sure the doors are locked and everything is turned off. That's what I was doing when...well, when everything went to shit. I was sitting in my car, double-checking the headlights and stuff. The more stressed I am, the worse it is, and right now, I'm pretty fucking stressed. I'm scared and worried about my family and I'm sick of sitting in here freezing my ass off. But at the same time, I know it's suicide to go back out there. So, my OCD kicked in and I was making sure the straps around the door is secure. We know it is. Your knots will probably hold. But I've got to make sure anyway. I can't help it. And it ain't just doors, either. I have to count things—how many potato chips I eat out of the bag, how many steps I take, how many times the phone rings. And I can't stand odd numbers. Like, if I'm reading a book, I can't stop on an odd numbered page. If I walk somewhere, I have to end on an even numbered step. When I'm channel surfing, I skip past the odd-numbered channels. If I go out to eat and the check comes and it's an odd number, I've got to tip enough to make it even."

They stared at him, not speaking.

Marcel shrugged. "I guess you probably think I'm crazy."

"I don't," Jack said. "Shit, man—we've all got our problems, you know? I'm on Prozac. People make fun of that, too."

Marcel grinned. "Prozac? So am I. It's the only thing that works for me. I tried Paxil, Luvox, Xanax, and Zoloft, but all they did was make me comatose. So now I'm on Prozac. It works better."

"Not to be rude," Angie said, "but if you're checking the door even though you know it's secured, then are you sure the medicine is working?"

"Yeah. Believe me, I'm sure. Like I said, my symptoms get worse when I'm stressed. So pardon me if I seem a little freaked out right now."

Outside the door, somebody screamed—a long, unwavering howl that seemed to rise in pitch and intensity. Then it stopped.

"Fuck," Jack whispered. "That sounded like some kind of animal. Are you guys sure it was other people that did these things?"

"You didn't see them." Angie burst into tears. "I'm not surprised they sound like animals."

She lowered her head and sobbed. Her shoulders shook, but she made no sound.

"Hey." Marcel reached out a tentative hand and squeezed her shoulder. "If you're worried you offended me with that medicine remark, don't be."

"No," she sobbed. "It's not that. I'm just scared. And depressed. Story of my life. I've got chronic depression. You guys aren't the only two on Prozac. That's what I was here for."

Marcel nodded. "Me, too. I ran out of meds yesterday, in fact. Haven't taken any since yesterday morning. Come to think of it, that might be why my symptoms are a little worse today."

Angie wiped her eyes on her sleeve.

"That's kind of weird," Marcel continued. "Right? That all three of us would be taking it?"

"Not really," Jack said. "There are lots of people on Prozac, dude. The doctors prescribe it like candy."

"Yeah, but to have three people out of four on it? That just seems odd to me."

"Four," Sammi mumbled.

"What's that?"

"Four people. I take it, too."

"You're depressed?" Jack asked.

Sammi shook her head.

Marcel let go of Angie's shoulder. "OCD?"

"No." Sammi sighed, pausing before she spoke again.

"Bulimia."

"I knew it," Jack said, then stopped, realizing he'd blurted it out. His mouth hung open. His cheeks reddened with shame.

"Knew what?" Sammi snapped.

"Just...well, some of the guys back in high school said that you were anorexic. That was why you were so skinny. I'm sorry. I shouldn't have said anything."

"You should be sorry. And I'm not anorexic. There's a difference between the two, you know. And I'm getting help. That's why I'm on Prozac."

"So...you throw up after you eat?" Now that the rumor had been confirmed, Jack was honestly curious.

"No. Not that it's any of your fucking business, but I'm an exercise bulimic. I used to binge—I mean, eat— and then I'd exercise my ass off. At first, I thought it was a healthy, competitive way to lose weight. I had lots of energy—like I'd just chugged a can of Red Bull. It felt good, you know? When the endorphin rush kicked in, I wasn't depressed anymore. Didn't feel bad about myself. And most importantly, I looked toned. But I wasn't toned. I was just building muscle while I dehydrated myself to burn off the fat. My skin clung more closely to my muscles. People tried talking to me about it, but I wouldn't listen. Finally, I got real sick. Passed out at a rave. My doctor prescribed Prozac to curb my desire to binge, since food is a form of comfort. I've been taking that and going to counseling for six weeks now."

"Six weeks," Jack said. "Must be nice. I've been on Prozac most of my life."

"That's dangerous," Marcel warned.

"I know. But the doctor said if it's working, then we should stick with it."

"Maybe you're better off," Marcel admitted. "There is a crazy side effect when you stop taking it. At least there was for me. I got horrible vertigo—like someone just pulled the floor out from under me. It lasted for a couple weeks, totally at random. At least you didn't have to go through that."

"I started taking it when I was ten," Jack said. "I didn't want to at first. Thought it meant I was crazy or something. My Mom coaxed me, though. She used to call the pills 'magic beans', like in *Jack and the Beanstalk*. She said my depression was like a big giant, and if I took my magic beans, then I'd have a way to defeat it. The doctor liked that. Liked it so much, I think he started using it on other kids, too. He told me to visualize the beanstalk as a line to recovery and wellness. My cure was waiting at the top of the beanstalk—a castle in the clouds. He was always spouting psychobabble bullshit like that. Weird old geezer. I don't go to him anymore, but my new doctor has me on Prozac, too."

Marcel chuckled, then broke into laughter. It echoed in the freezer, bouncing off the walls. The others stared at him in shock, dismayed by his bizarre reaction.

"Dude," Jack whispered. "Stop it or they'll hear you."

Still laughing, Marcel put his hands over his mouth and squeezed his eyes shut.

"Asshole," Sammi pouted. "You're just as fucked up as we are. What gives you the right to laugh at Jack?"

Marcel paused, catching his breath. "I'm not laughing at him. Seriously."

"Well, then what's so funny?"

"Us." He gestured at them. "We're all on Prozac. We're stigmatized by society because of it. Think about it. Everybody in town goes insane, and the only four people left alive all suffer from some form of mental illness. People used to think we were crazy. Suddenly, we ain't so fucking crazy anymore. We're the sane ones."

Marcel giggled again. Angie smiled. After a moment, Sammi did, too. Both women began to laugh. Jack didn't say anything. His expression was serious. After a moment, the others noticed.

"What's wrong?" Angie asked. "Did you hear something?"

"No," he whispered, "but I think I figured out why we're still alive—why we're immune to whatever made everyone else go nuts."

"Why?"

He grinned. "The magic beans."

All three of them stared at him.

"Prozac," he explained. "Remember? I said my Mom used to call them magic beans?"

"Yeah," Sammi said. "What about it."

"It's the one thing we all have in common. We all took Prozac today."

"I didn't," Marcel reminded him. "I'd run out."

"Yeah, but you still take it regularly. We all do. And I bet there were other people out there who were on it, too. Think about it. Was everybody crazy?"

"I saw a little boy," Sammi said, her voice trembling. "He asked me to help him, but before I could…" She trailed off, unable to finish.

"I saw people, too," Angie confirmed. "They seemed fine—scared, like me."

Marcel nodded. "Same here."

"I bet they were like us," Jack said. "Bet they were on Prozac."

"You don't know that," Angie said. "There are too many variables. Dosage. Type. Things like that."

Jack shrugged. "I'm on pills. What about the rest of you?"

"Pills," Angie said.

"Liquid." Sammi shivered. "But it can't be the Prozac. That doesn't make any sense."

"It makes about as much sense as everybody else suddenly turning into homicidal fucking maniacs. Didn't you ever have Mrs. Repasky's biology class?"

"No." Sammi shook her head. "I had Mr. Jackson. He's gross. He was always biting his fingernails and then spitting them all over the floor while he talked."

"Yeah, I never liked him."

"Me either."

"Mrs. Repasky," Jack said, "told us about how diseases change over time. With each generation, some new and terrible disease pops up. The Black Death, leprosy, cholera, cancer, AIDS. That flu strain that killed all those people after World War One. All of these illnesses came out of nowhere, with no warning, and infected millions. So what if mental illnesses suddenly started doing the same thing? What if they mutated?"

Angie snorted. "You're saying that all those people were infected by some bizarre new psychosis?"

"Maybe," Jack said. "And we're immune to it because of the Prozac."

Sammi shook her head. "Is that even possible?"

"Shit." Jack shrugged. "How the hell do I know? I'm just a stock boy."

* * *

"I hope my family is okay." Sammi's nose had turned from red to white, and tiny ice crystals clung to her eyelashes. "I promised my little sister I'd help her with her homework tonight. She's in eighth grade."

Without warning, she started to cry again.

"Try not to think about it," Marcel said. "Ain't nothing we can do for them right now."

Angie frowned. "That's pretty cold, don't you think?"

"No," Marcel said. "It's not cold. Just practical. I got people at home, too. And I know they'd want me to stay alive."

"Cold..." Sammi sniffled. "It's so cold in here."

The others nodded in agreement. Jack stood up, stretched his stiff arms and legs, and crept to the door. He put his ear close to the frigid metal and listened.

"Hear anything?" Marcel asked.

"No. Nothing. It's quiet. Seriously, guys—it's been a while since we heard anything. Maybe they're all gone—or dead."

"Maybe," Marcel said, "or could be it's just a trap. Maybe they're waiting right outside the door."

"Well," Angie whispered, "we can't stay in here much

longer. We'll get frostbite, not to mention there's no food or water—unless you count that frozen stuff. And pretty soon, I'm going to have to go to the bathroom."

Marcel pointed to the corner. "Go ahead. Knock yourself out. We won't look."

"No thanks."

"I'm staying put," Marcel said. "You guys will too, if you're smart."

Jack returned to the group and hunkered down on his haunches. "Screw that. I'm not starving to death inside a grocery store freezer. I'd rather take my chances out there."

"Same here," Sammi said. "I want to see my family. I want my Mom."

"One step at a time," Jack told her. "First we have to get out of this freezer."

Marcel sighed. "Oh fuck me running. I'm not going to be able to talk you guys out of this, am I?"

"No," Jack said, "but we won't blame you if you want to stay behind. We'll send help, soon as we find some."

Angie pulled out her cell phone and flipped it open, checking the time. "It should be dark outside. If we're going to try it, now is the time."

"We've been in here that long?" Jack was surprised.

Angie nodded.

"You know what they say," Marcel muttered. "Time flies when you're having fun."

Jack smiled. "Does that mean you changed your mind? You coming with us?"

"I was outvoted, wasn't I? Either way, you guys are gonna open that door. I'm not staying here by myself. There's safety in numbers. Besides, my head hurts. Think I'm probably dehydrated, so I need to find some water, at least."

They fell silent. Sammi, Angie and Marcel stared at Jack, waiting for him to make a decision. It was not lost on him that somehow, he'd become their leader. He swallowed hard and took a deep breath.

"We need weapons, just in case they are waiting for us."

He reached into his jacket pocket and pulled out a box cutter. "Look around. What do we have?"

They searched the freezer, hunting through the shelves, racks and drawers, and looking under pallets. Marcel found a jagged length of wood from a broken skid. A nail jutted from the end. He swung the board through the air, testing it.

"That'll work."

Sammi found an old mop and broke the handle over her knee, creating a makeshift spear. She winced in pain, and rubbed her knee. Although he didn't say it out loud, Jack was impressed. Sure, Sammi had muscles from her particular type of bulimia, but he was surprised she had enough strength to snap the handle. Maybe her fear was giving her extra power.

Then he noticed that she was also rubbing her wrist.

"You okay?"

She nodded, grimacing. "Yeah. Jeremy almost broke my wrist earlier. It's just a little sore."

Angie grabbed a pack of frozen steaks.

"What are you gonna do with those?" Sammi asked.

Angie smacked the steaks against her thigh with a loud whack. She grinned.

"Knock somebody out until I find something better."

Sammi returned the smile. "That's pretty kick ass.

"I thought so."

Jack extended the blade of his box-cutter. The dim overhead bulb glinted off the razor's edge. He took a deep breath and shuddered.

"Okay," he said, "let's do it."

"You guys sure?" Marcel whispered. "Maybe we should wait?"

Jack frowned. "I thought you were with us?"

"I am. But I've never been more fucking scared in my life."

"We're all scared," Angie said. "But if we wait any longer, we'll freeze to death. Let's get it over with, before we lose our nerve."

They surrounded the door, weapons at the ready. Their breath clouded the air. Working as quietly as he could, Jack sliced through the strapping bands and shrink-wrap. Then, with one last glance at the others, he opened the door. It swung slowly outward. Jack's breath caught in his chest. He shielded his eyes with his free hand. Behind him, the others did the same. The lights were still on in the stockroom, and they were temporarily blinded by the brightness.

Sammi sniffed. "What's that smell?"

Their eyes slowly adjusted to the light. Angie gasped, dropping her steak. Marcel retched. Turning away, Sammi put her hand over her mouth and nose. Jack stepped out into the wreckage and tried to be brave. His left shoe squelched on something—a kidney, a liver, a spleen—he wasn't sure what. Some kind of internal organ. When he picked up his foot, there was a tread mark in the remains.

The stockroom had been ransacked. Blood-spattered boxes and cartons were ripped open. Cases of canned goods had been dumped out on the floor. A stack of skids had fallen over. Arms and legs stuck out from beneath them. Blood pooled around an upended pallet jack. The lower half of a naked torso lay on the floor. Innards stretched away from the body like fleeing snakes. A dead man hung from a forklift, the prongs impaling his limp body. Severed hands, limbs, fingers and heads lay everywhere, along with unidentifiable scraps of human tissue—cuts of meat that mirrored the choices in the butcher's showcase up front. The room was silent, except for the incessant buzzing of flies. It stank—blood, shit, slaughter. The unpainted concrete walls were red.

"Well," Angie said, "the power's still on."

Marcel gagged. "I wish it wasn't."

Jack reeled. The stockroom seemed to spin and his vision blurred. He knelt on the floor, leaned over, and vomited. Marcel did the same a moment later. Sammi and Angie stood guard until they recovered, looking around nervously. The room remained deserted. Both men slowly rose, unsteady, wiping their mouths.

"You okay?" Jack rasped.

"Yeah," Marcel said. "I will be. Getting a killer headache, though. Probably from all this stress."

"Might be dehydration," Angie said. "Like you said before."

"Or stress," Sammi offered. "Tension. Maybe you should rest."

Marcel shrugged. "Don't worry about me."

Jack turned to Sammi and Angie. His cheeks turned red. "Sorry about doing that in front of you."

"Don't worry about it," Angie said. "Happens to everybody. I feel like puking, too."

Sammi giggled. "Nice to see somebody other than me throwing up for once."

"Girls rule," Angie whispered, "and boys drool."

Marcel scowled at the comment, flicking a thread of saliva from his chin.

"Everybody ready?" Jack asked.

They nodded. He led them forward, trying not to look at the carnage, trying not to hear the sounds their shoes made as they stepped through a glistening tangle of stripped flesh, or the slow drips of blood falling from the stains on the ceiling. Jack wondered how the blood had gotten up there. He could read nothing in the splash patterns. They were everywhere—a crisscross of crimson.

At the end of the warehouse was an employee restroom. The door was slightly ajar. Although it was dark inside, they could make out the form of a woman crouched in front of the toilet. The seat was up. Her shoulders rested on the rim. Her head was deep inside the bowl. Water dripped from the faucet, and the mirror on the wall was shattered. The edges of the white porcelain sink were splashed with red, just like everything else in the warehouse. A sign on the wall next to the bathroom admonished all employees to wash their hands before returning to work. The irony filled Jack with a sick sense of dread.

He turned back to the others. "So far, so good."

"Maybe they're all dead," Sammi whispered.

"Let's hope so. Just stay quiet and stick together. Okay?"

Angie and Sammi nodded in understanding. Marcel appeared distracted. His eyes were shut and his expression was pained. One hand clutched the length of wood. The other rubbed his right temple, fingers probing deep into the flesh.

"Marcel?" Jack reached for him. "You okay?"

The older man looked up. His eyes were red and watery. When he spoke, he sounded tired.

"What's up?" he rasped. "Sorry, I wasn't paying attention."

"What's wrong with you, dude?"

"My fucking head hurts. I think Sammi's right. It's just the stress. Exhaustion."

"You okay to keep going?" Jack asked. "We can stop if you need to."

Marcel nodded. "Yeah, I'll be fine. Lead on, kemosabe."

"Chemo-what?"

Marcel frowned. "You never saw The Lone Ranger?"

"No," Jack said. "I think my grandfather used to watch it when he was a kid."

"Never mind."

They approached the large double doors that led out into the grocery store. Jack and Angie peeked through the windows, while Sammi and Marcel hung back.

"Holy shit," Jack moaned.

The slaughter in the stockroom paled in comparison to what awaited them in the store. They smelled it through the closed doors—a noxious brew of blood, piss, shit, bleach, ammonia, and other chemicals from the household cleaning products aisle. The stench made their eyes water.

"I don't see anybody moving," Angie whispered. "Maybe they left. I say we make a run for it."

"What do you guys think?" Jack asked Sammi and Marcel without turning around.

A loud crack rang out behind them. Sammi breathed a long, drawn-out sigh. Marcel laughed—a bubbling, drawn-out croak.

Jack and Angie turned around. Sammi stared at them, her head cocked to the right, her eyes glassy. A thin ribbon of blood trickled down the side of her face. Marcel stood behind her, gripping his club with both hands. The other end—the piece with the nail in it—was embedded in the top of Sammi's skull. The mop-handle spear slipped from Sammi's fingers. Her knees buckled. Marcel released the weapon and Sammi toppled to the floor.

"Fuck!" The knife shook in Jack's trembling hands.

"She was stealing from me," Marcel explained, his voice calm and self-assured. "I had to teach her a lesson. Had to curb that shit."

"Sammi?" Jack whispered, hoping she'd respond.

"You guys would have done the same thing," Marcel said. "If you're taking her side, then I have to assume you were stealing from me, too. And that means I'll have—"

Angie's scream cut him off. "You son of a bitch!"

She lunged at him, swinging the pack of steaks. The frozen meat collided with Marcel's head, stunning him. Jack heard the crack, even over Angie's cries. Marcel's head rocked backward. Grunting, he staggered to the side. Already his ear had begun to swell. Before he could recover, Angie hit him again, breaking his nose and driving the splintered cartilage up into his brain. Marcel made a gulping noise. His eyes fluttered and his hands clenched, then unclenched. A single tear slid down his cheek. He fell forward, his body jittering on the floor. A dark stain spread across his pants. The sharp smell of urine filled the air, mixing with the store's miasma.

"He's still alive," Jack said, watching him flop around.

"No he's not." Angie dropped the steaks and checked Marcel's pulse. "He's dead."

"But he's moving. And he pissed himself. Look at him."

"That's just the last few electrical impulses from his brain. It will stop in a minute."

Even as she said it, the convulsions slowed. Marcel's limbs twitched a few more times, and then ceased. Jack watched with a mixture of awe and revulsion.

"How did you know how to do that?"

Angie shrugged. "I didn't. My grandfather was in Vietnam. He served in the First Cavalry and went through all that hand-to-hand combat training. He told me once that if you hit somebody in the nose just right—and hard enough—it would kill them. I was never sure about it until now, though. Guess he was right."

"Jesus..."

Angie knelt by Sammi and felt her throat, checking her pulse as well. Jack watched with trepidation.

"Is she?"

Angie nodded. "Yes. She's dead. Poor kid."

"Damn."

"Were you friends?"

"Not really. I mean, we knew each other. But that was all."

"Yeah. I kind of got that impression while listening to you talk in the freezer."

Jack tried to swallow. His throat felt tight, his breathing constricted.

Angie picked up Sammi's spear. "You okay, Jack?"

"Yeah. I just...I've never seen anything happen like that before. Never saw somebody die."

"Neither have I, until today."

"It's not like the movies."

"No," she agreed, "it's not. But we'd both better get used to it. I've got a feeling that's the new world order."

"What do you mean?"

"I think you were right. You're theory—the magic beans? The beanstalk?"

"Seriously?"

Angie shrugged. "Why not, Jack? I mean, shit, it's not like I've got any better ideas. None of this makes any sense."

"But if the Prozac protected us, then why did Marcel snap like that?"

"He said he'd missed a dose. Maybe that was all it took.

One missed dosage and you go nuts like everybody else."

Jack glanced back out at the store. "If that's the case, then we'd better stock up on meds before we leave. God knows when we'll find some again."

Angie leaned against the wall and sighed. She closed her eyes. Her body shook slightly.

"You cold?"

She shook her head, sliding down the wall until she crouched.

"Depressed?"

"No. Yes. Look…Jack—I'm not a commando. I've never killed anybody before. Just give me a few minutes, okay?"

"Sure." He turned back to the window, granting her some privacy. "I'll keep watch until you're ready."

"Thanks. I appreciate it."

Jack looked out the smudged glass, staring at the carnage. From his vantage point, he had a view of the freezer aisles and part of the dairy aisle. He knew them well. He worked them several nights a week and most weekends—rotating the milk, yogurt, and sour cream; restocking frozen pizzas and vegetables, TV dinners, ice cream and a hundred other items. He barely recognized the aisles now. The glass doors in the frozen vegetables section were shattered. Mist curled out of the freezer, lazily falling towards the floor. Dead bodies littered the room, sometimes three high. The few areas without corpses were littered with pieces of them. Blood and scarlet handprints covered the other freezer doors. Somebody had removed the popsicles from their shelves and replaced them with dozens of severed heads—men, women, and children, young and old.

People-sicles, Jack thought.

He stifled a laugh. It scared him. Was he cracking up, too? Would he be turning on Angie next? He didn't feel crazy, but would he really know if the illness was starting to set in? All his life, he'd had to deal with people picking on him about his mental illness. Cruel taunts and jokes from classmates who had no fucking clue. He'd been called crazy a thousand times, but now…

He glanced over his shoulder at Angie. Her eyes were still closed, her face serene.

No, he wasn't crazy. He was just scared.

He heard movement behind him. Jack turned, and saw Angie climbing slowly to her feet.

"You ready?" she asked.

He nodded. "If you are."

Angie made a seesaw motion with her hand. "Not, really. But I sure as hell don't want to stay here."

They crept into the store. The double doors creaked on their hinges. Jack had never noticed them doing it before, but now, the sound seemed to echo down the aisles. Both of them braced for an attack, but the store appeared deserted. Muzak still played over the loudspeakers—Elton John's "Island Girl." Even though he hated the song, Jack knew all the words. It always came on at least once during his shifts. It used to be an annoyance. Now, the song filled him with dread—and a strange, surreal sense of longing. It was familiar in a world that was anything but. It reminded him of home.

Home. The word ran through his head, looking for something to connect with. His parents—he hadn't thought of them since this whole thing began. Were they okay? Both of them worked during the day. Chances were good they'd been sitting in rush hour traffic when everything happened. Depending on how far the illness had spread, they could be okay. Maybe they were out of range.

And maybe not.

Elton John continued wailing. *"You feel her nail scratch your back just like a rake. He one more gone, he one more John, who make the mistake."*

Jack shivered.

"That music's creepy," Angie whispered, echoing his thoughts.

"Yeah, it is."

"Why don't grocery stores play stuff like the Foo Fighters or Dave Matthews?"

He shrugged. "It could be worse."

"What could possibly be any worse than Elton John?"

"Fergie. The Pussycat Dolls. Fall Out Boy. Kanye West. Take your pick."

"You fight dirty, Jack."

He grinned, despite his fears. "So do you."

She reached out and took his hand, giving it a squeeze. Jack squeezed back.

"Don't get the wrong idea," Angie said. "This doesn't mean we're gonna hook up. You're a little too young for me. This is just because I'm happy to be alive and because I'm scared."

"No worries," Jack said, trying to project confidence. "Don't be scared. I'll protect you. My doctor didn't call me Jack the Giant-Killer for nothing."

"You'll protect me? So far, I've been covering your ass."

"I know," Jack admitted. "But I was hoping you wouldn't notice."

Despite their efforts to stay quiet, both of them giggled. Then they moved on, still holding hands. They moved slowly, picking their way around human wreckage. Angie slipped in a pile of intestines. Jack accidentally dropped his knife and bumped into a bloody shopping cart full of severed feet—most of them still wearing shoes. Elton John gave way to Christopher Cross, singing about being lost between the moon and New York City. Jack and Angie knew how he felt.

"Notice something?" Angie asked.

"What's that?"

"I think we're alone in here. They're all dead. Each and every last one of them. It's like they butchered each other until there was nothing left."

"Well, we should still be careful. Somebody had to be the last one standing. He or she might still be around. Or there may be others like Marcel, that didn't change until now."

They made it to the pharmacy without encountering trouble. Angie paled as they approached the counter. Her grip tightened around Jack's hand.

"What's wrong?" he whispered. "Did you hear something?"

"No," she said. "Just brings back bad memories."

"Wait here. I'll try to hurry."

"Where are you going?"

"To get us some meds. If my theory is right, then we're gonna need them."

"Did you ever work in a pharmacy?"

"No."

"Then how the hell do you know what you're looking for?"

"Prozac is really fluoxetine, so that's what they should have it labeled as."

The pharmacy's employee door was locked. Setting his box-cutter aside, Jack vaulted over the counter. He searched through the shelves and bins until he found what he was looking for—a drawer full of fluoxotine.

"Bingo!"

"You found some?"

"Yep. Grab me a bag, will you?"

"Paper or plastic?"

"Plastic. Easier to carry."

Angie retrieved a plastic bag from one of the registers and handed it to him. Jack yanked the drawer out of the cabinet and dumped its contents into the bag. Then he returned to the counter.

"Do you have your insurance card with you?"

Angie gave him a puzzled look. "No."

"Oh, well." Jack chuckled nervously. "What the hell. Prozac's on the house. Can I interest you in some OxyContin, as well? Or how about some high-grade pharmaceutical marijuana?"

"Just the anti-depressants, please."

Jack shook his head. "You should never turn down free weed."

"We should probably divide up the meds," Angie suggested. "In case we get separated or something."

"Okay," Jack agreed, "but I think we should take them

at the same time. That way, we can sort of remind each other. Less chance of forgetting a dose."

"Good idea."

"Thanks."

"So what now?" Angie asked. "Do you think we should leave?"

"That depends. You've probably got people you want to check on. So do I. We need to at least determine if the whole city is like this. The power is still on. Maybe we can find a television or a radio—check the news and see if we can learn anything."

"Something tells me we're not going to."

"That's crazy talk," Jack teased.

"I just think we need to prepare for the worst possible scenario. You and I might be the only two sane people left in this city. What if we find our loved ones and they're like everybody else? Or what if they're still alive—and they try to kill you?"

Jack's expression soured. "I don't want to think about it."

"You might not have a choice, Jack."

"Shit..."

"And there's something else to consider."

"What?"

"While we're watching each other's backs, we also need to keep an eye on each other. If either of us misses a dose—or if we're wrong about that and this...whatever it was that caused this, infects one of us, the other could be in real danger."

"We'll be okay," Jack insisted. "If we were gonna go psycho, we would have changed when Marcel did."

"We don't know that. We don't know anything."

Jack's expression fell. "So you think we should split up? Go our separate ways?"

"No. I just think we should be careful around each other. Marcel was complaining about a headache right before he snapped. If either of us gets one, we should tell each other right away. Agreed?"

"And then what?"

"I don't know."

Jack sighed. He looked as if he were ready to cry.

"Look," Angie said after a pause, "I think you're right about finding some news. Let's try that first. We'll worry about everything else in time."

"Okay."

Still using caution, they found two student-sized backpacks in the employee locker room. They filled these with bottles of spring water, crackers, sardines, and other canned goods, as well as medical supplies, cigarette lighters, and anything else that might prove useful. Jack considered grabbing some cash from the registers, but decided against it. Angie took a carton of cigarettes from behind the customer service counter.

"Do you smoke?"

She shrugged. "Fuck it. I do now."

They crept to the front of the store. The electronic eyes above the doors registered their movements and the doors slid open as they approached.

"Oh..." Angie stared out at the parking lot. Sodium lights bathed it in a sickly yellow glow. "It's even worse than it is in here."

Jack said nothing.

The parking lot was littered with corpses and debris. Something had sparked a fire. Many of the cars were now blackened hulls. Some of the bodies were burned as well. Birds perched on the dead, scavenging the choice bits. The stench was revolting.

Slowly, they walked outside, clutching their weapons, supplies, and most importantly, Jack's magic beans. The doors slid shut behind them, and the electricity went out, plunging the store and the parking lot into total darkness. Squawking, the birds took flight. The stench grew stronger.

"I can't see shit," Angie whispered.

"Neither can I. The power must be out everywhere."

Jack looked around. There were no streetlights or glows from the windows of the nearby buildings. No car headlights, no radios blaring. Even the birds had fallen silent. He gazed up at the sky. The stars were hidden behind a curtain of clouds. He searched for the twinkling lights of a passing airplane, but the sky was empty.

The silence overwhelmed them.

"It's the end of the world," Jack said. "For real. The end of the fucking world."

"No," Angie disagreed. "It's not the end of the world. It's just the end of the people. The world will be just fine. Look around us. The world is still here. It's just the people that are gone."

"We can't be the only ones left alive," Jack said. "It doesn't make any sense. There has to be others like us."

To Angie, it sounded like he was trying to convince himself.

They took a few hesitant steps forward. Jack stumbled over a severed arm and almost tripped. After he regained his balance, Angie found his hand in the dark and held on tight.

"Careful," she whispered. "Wouldn't do to break your leg after all of this."

"That would suck. Doctors might be hard to come by."

She held up a hand, silencing him. Her expression was alarmed.

"What's wrong?" Jack whispered.

Angie nodded at the Chinese restaurant, adjoined to the supermarket. The door was slightly ajar. The smell of cooking meat drifted out of the building. Despite his terror, Jack's mouth watered.

"Listen," Angie mouthed.

Jack cocked his head and focused. After a moment, he heard it—a slight rustling sound, followed by a crunching noise. Someone walking on broken glass, perhaps, and trying to be stealthy about it.

Gripping her weapon tightly, Angie crept toward the open door.

Something zipped by them—an angry bee. A second later, they heard the shot.

"Get down," Jack shouted.

Angie was already ahead of him. She flung herself to the pavement, skinning her elbows and knees. Another blast boomed across the parking lot. Ducking behind a toppled shopping cart, Jack saw a brief flash of light from inside the restaurant.

"Get out of here," a man screamed. "Get the fuck away from me, you crazy bastards!"

Unable to seek cover without becoming a target, Angie cast a terrified glance at Jack. Still cowering behind the shopping cart, he motioned at her to stay down.

"Hey," he shouted. "Stop shooting! We don't want to hurt you."

The unseen man responded by firing another round. When the echoes died down, they heard him yelling.

"Whole fucking world's gone insane. But you won't get me!"

"We're not trying to," Jack insisted. "We just want to go home. Please!"

"Bullshit! You're like everybody else. Bug-fuck crazy. They were cooking people in here. Look at this grill! Who would do something like this?"

Jack cupped his hands around his mouth. "Are you on Prozac?"

The man didn't reply.

"If you are," Jack shouted, "then you need to keep taking it. You'll be okay as long as you stay medicated. We're leaving now. We don't want any trouble. Okay?"

Silence.

Slowly, excruciatingly, Angie crawled towards Jack. She held her breath, anticipating another shot, expecting to feel a bullet slam into her—but the man in the restaurant had fallen silent. When she reached Jack, the two of them crabwalked to a nearby vehicle. They ducked down behind it, breathing hard.

"Well," Angie panted, "there's one crazy who's not dead yet."

"I don't think so." Jack wiped the sweat from his forehead with his T-shirt. "I think he was like us—scared. Paranoid."

"And that's what we've got to look forward to."

"Only if we give in to it."

He got quiet. His head hung low and his shoulders slumped. At first, Angie thought he was just waiting to see if the man in the restaurant had forgotten about them. Then she realized he was sulking.

"What's wrong?" Angie asked.

"I've been thinking," Jack said. "When we get to a safer location, we need to check the expiration date on these pills."

"They won't have any," Angie reminded him. "We filled the prescription ourselves. We didn't print out one of those little labels that has the expiration date. But usually, I think it's about a year."

"Well, after we check on our families, our next stop *needs* to be another pharmacy, so we can load up on more."

Angie sighed. "So that's our life now? Drugstore cowboys, spending every day looking for more magic beans?"

"As fucked up as it is, yes. We need Prozac even more than we do food and water."

"No," Angie said. "What we need is a fucking pharmacist. With no labs producing it, how long before we run out?"

"One step at a time, my fellow giant-killer. One step at a time."

They slowly crossed the parking lot, taking deliberate steps and picking their way through the wreckage. Then they walked down the main drag, heading away from the relative safety of the store.

The city skyline loomed in the distance. Columns of smoke rose into the sky. Massive fires burning on the freeway, washing the bellies of the clouds in a wavering orange glow. They saw signs of an explosion. The burned out shell of a tanker trunk sat smoldering on the median strip. The overpass had collapsed, burying the road beneath it in a mountainous pile of rubble. Chunks of concrete lay on top of crushed cars.

They reached an intersection and came across the first dead body. Then another. Then a dozen. Two. Hundreds. Their revulsion grew with each city block. The streets resembled the grocery store's interior, but on a grander and more gruesome scale. The only thing moving were the birds—crows, gulls, pigeons; they swooped down from the rooftops, perching on the mounds of corpses and feasting on the choicest morsels.

Jack and Angie walked in silence. He tried calling out once, but the sound of his voice echoing through the empty streets disturbed him even more than the carnage all around them.

"Jack?"

"What?"

"Are you sure we won't change? Are you sure we won't become like them?"

"Yes," Jack lied. "As long as we take our meds, we should be fine."

They went out into the world, and hoped they wouldn't wake the sleeping giant.

STORY NOTES

Jack's Magic Beans *started with the opening sentence.*

Yes, I know that's how all stories start, but in this case, that's all I had—the opening sentence. I typed: The lettuce started talking to Ben Mahoney halfway through his shift at Save-A-Lot. *Then I stared at the laptop. I had no idea what happened next.*

About six months later, my wife, Cassandra, told me about an associate of hers who referred to Prozac as "magic beans." I thought that was interesting. I mulled it over for an evening.

The next day, I knew what happened after the lettuce started talking.

What happened was this story.

I seem to write two kinds of stories. There are my serious *books (*Terminal, Ghoul, Dark Hollow*) and then there are my fun books (*The Conqueror Worms *and all of the zombie novels). Critics and fans may disagree with those classifications, but that's okay. These are just personal terms. I've noticed that I tend to write a fun book immediately after finishing a serious one. With the exception of the opening sentence, I wrote* Jack's Magic Beans *right after finishing* Ghoul *– a novel that kicked my fucking ass on both a psychological and emotional level. It was a serious book. In short, it left me depressed.*

Luckily, Jack's Magic Beans *worked like an anti-depressant – just like in the story. Writing this was a cure.*

FADE TO NULL

She woke to the sound of thunder, lying in a strange bed with no memory of who she was or where she was, and panic nearly overwhelmed her. Her stomach clenched. Her breath came in short gasps. Frantic, she glanced around the room for clues, but familiarity eluded her. The room was small, equipped with a dresser, a writing desk, and a chair with one leg shorter than the others. Atop the dresser sat a slender blue-glass vase with some flowers in it.

The flowers soothed her, but she didn't know why.

She studied the rest of the room. Looming overhead were the cracked, yellowing panels of a drop ceiling. The carpet was light green, the wallpaper pastel. Framed prints hung on the wall—Monet, Kincaid, Rockwell. She wondered how it was possible that she knew their names but didn't know her own. The closet door was slightly open, revealing a stranger's clothes. There was only one window, and the blinds were closed tight. If the room had a door, other than the closet, she couldn't see it.

The sheets were thin and starchy, and rubbed against her skin like sandpaper. They felt damp from sweat. Clenching the sheets in both fists, she raised them slightly and peered beneath. She was dressed in a faded sleeping gown with a dried brown stain over one breast. What was it? Gravy? Mud? Blood? Except for her underwear, she was bare beneath the gown.

She considered calling for help, but decided against it. She was afraid—afraid of who, or what, might answer her summons. Despite the fact that the room seemed empty, she couldn't help but feel like there was someone else in here with her. Someone *unseen*.

The thunder boomed again. Blue-white light flashed from behind the closed blinds, and for a moment, she saw glimpses of other people in the room with her—a man, a woman, and a little girl. They were like the images on photo negatives, stark against the room's feeble light, but at the same time, flickering and ghostly—composed of television static. The man stood by her bedside, dressed in a white doctor's coat. A stethoscope dangled around his neck. He held a clipboard. The woman stood next to him, wearing a simple but pretty blouse. She seemed tired and sad. The little girl sat in the wobbly chair, rocking back and forth on the crooked legs.

"It's okay, Mika. Grandma is just having a bad dream."

The voice was distant. Muted. An echo. And female.

She tried to scream, but only managed a rasping, wheezy sigh.

The three figures vanished with the next blast of thunder, blinking out of existence as if they'd never been there at all.

Maybe they hadn't.

She was dimly aware that she had to pee.

When the drum roll of thunder sounded again, the drop ceiling disappeared as quickly as the ghost-people had. Everything else in the room remained the same—the drab furnishings, the dim light—but in the ceiling's place was a purple, wounded sky. Boiling clouds raced across it, but she felt no wind. Although the temperature hadn't changed, she shivered. The pressure on her bladder increased. She relaxed, and felt a sudden rush of warmth. Then the violet sky split open, revealing a black hole, and it began to rain desiccated flowers.

Flowers, she thought. *There are flowers on the dresser. Ellen brought them.*

Then she wondered who Ellen was.

Dried petals continued to shower the bed, tickling her nose and cheeks. She sighed. The feeling was not unpleasant. Then, as quickly as it had begun, the rain of flower petals stopped—replaced by something else. Her eyes widened in terror. A squadron of bulbous flies poured from the hole in the sky, buzzing in a multitude of languages. Their bodies were black, their heads green like emeralds. They circled the room in a swirling pattern. A flock of birds plunged out of the hole, giving chase. The thunder increased, inside the room with her now. The noise was deafening. The flies scattered and the birds squawked in fright. A black, oily feather floated gently towards her.

She tried to sit up, but her fatigue weighed her like a stone. All she could do was lie there and watch. Listen. Wonder.

Where was she? What was this? What was happening?

She thought again of the flowers. They'd been brought by…who, exactly? She couldn't remember. Someone. She thought it might be important.

The warmth dissipated. She was cold again. Her fear was replaced by a powerful sense of frustration in both her physical discomfort and her confusion. Why couldn't she remember anything?

Above her, the sky continued to weep. Now, strands of DNA fell in ribbons, forming puddles on the bed and floor. Life stirred within those puddles, writhing and squirming. The thunder changed into a voice—a deity, perhaps, screaming. It was a terrible sound. She clasped her hands over her ears and tried to block it out. She'd heard screams like this before. Perhaps she'd even made them, at one time. They sounded like the symphony of birthing pains.

A large puddle of liquid tissue had formed on the sheet in front of her, right between her legs. As she watched, something wriggled from the puddle—a one-inch tentacle, about the thickness of a pencil. There was an eyeball attached to one end of the tendril. It stared at her, and as she watched, the pupil dilated.

In the background, the deity was still screaming. She no longer cared. Her attention was focused on the tentacle-thing. The creature groped feebly at her gown, and then pulled itself forward. She slapped her hand down on it, pressing it into the mattress and grinding her palm back and forth. The tentacle squeaked—even though it lacked a mouth—and then lay still. She removed her hand. All that remained of the thing was a pinkish-white blob of mucus. Slime dripped from her hand.

Silence returned. The disembodied screaming stopped. So did the thunder. The flies and the birds turned to vapor. The hole in the sky closed up, and seconds later, the drop ceiling reappeared.

"Please," she whispered. "Please...please..."

Then, new voices spoke. A man and a woman.

"She used to love to paint. I thought bringing some of this might help, but she can't even hold the paintbrush."

"Yes. Her motor skills are decreasing rapidly."

"How long does she have?"

"In this stage of Alzheimer's, it is difficult to say. I've seen some hang on for years after the fourth stage has set in. Others go quickly. All we can do is keep her comfortable."

"I just hate bringing Mika to see her like this, you know? I'm worried about how it will affect her."

"That's understandable, Ellen. And while some studies suggest that it's beneficial for patients, we can't even really be sure that your mother is aware of the presence of those around her. I know it's not much comfort, but at least she's calm and peaceful, for the most part."

"Who are you?" she moaned. "Where are you?"

She closed her eyes and let her cheek loll against the pillow, wishing the sky would rain flowers again.

"Who am I?" she whispered. "Please..."

The voices disappeared.

At last, she slept.

When she awoke again, the room was dark and cold. She shivered. There were flowers on the dresser, but she no longer knew what they were.

STORY NOTES

This story started as nothing more than a fragment. About one-hundred words of it was originally written for one of those multi-author collaboration projects—two dozen authors each contributing to one short story. Unfortunately, the project never came to fruition. I no longer remember who was involved or what the premise was. All I know is that it was never published (if it had been, I'm sure I'd have a contract or a copy of the book around here somewhere).

Anyway, I bought a new computer and I was in the process of transferring my files over to it when I ran across this old, forgotten fragment. I re-worked it into this story. Alzheimer's has impacted my family in a very personal way. It's a truly terrifying disease. I find it especially scary because none of us really know what's going on inside the mind of the victim.

THE RESURRECTION AND THE LIFE

For John Urbancik...

And so the Jewish priests accused the Rabbi, who was called Jesus, of blasphemy and tried to stone him. Jesus and his disciples fled Jerusalem for their very lives. Escaping to the borders of Judea, they crossed over the Jordan River to the place where John had been baptized in the early days. There they set up camp, safe from the law, and Jesus began to teach again.

Many curious people came to the site over the next four days. Some just wanted to listen to what Jesus had to say. Others had heard rumors of miracles—that he'd made a blind man see, touched a lame little girl and commanded her to throw away her crutches, cast out demons and walked across water. They flocked to the riverbank hoping for a glimpse, hoping to see something miraculous so that they could tell their children and grandchildren about it in years to come. They longed to say, "I was there the day Jesus of Nazareth made the sky rain blood. He split a rock with his staff and brought forth water. He touched your father's stump and his arm sprang forth anew. Serpents fled as he trod."

At first, they were disappointed. That emotion soon waned. Jesus performed no miracles during those four days. He didn't have to. No matter what their reasons for attending, once the throng heard him speak, they believed. His voice was melodious and assured, and the strength of his convictions shone through in every word. Unlike the prophets who held court in the desert or in the bazaars and alleyways, Jesus appeared sane. Likeable. His charisma was infectious.

When John had taught on this same riverbank in earlier years, he'd prophesied about the Messiah. Many of the older members in the crowd had heard John's predictions regarding Jesus, and after listening to Jesus speak they said, "Though John never performed a miraculous sign, all that he said about this man, Jesus of Nazareth, was true. He really is the Son of God. The Messiah walks among us."

On the fifth day, a messenger from the Judean village of Bethany crossed the border and entered the camp. Word spread through the crowd that he was seeking Jesus. Worried that the messenger might actually be an assassin sent by the priests, Peter, one of Jesus' disciples, met with the man and demanded that the message be given to him instead. But Jesus overheard this and granted the messenger an audience, telling Peter, "If any come seeking me, you must show them the way."

Jesus and the messenger drew away from the others, and Jesus offered the man water and bread, saying, "I can feed your hunger and thirst, if you will only partake."

When he was sated, the man delivered his message.

"Rabbi," he said, "I have tidings from Mary and her sister, Martha, who reside in the village of Bethany. It concerns their brother, Lazarus."

Jesus knew Mary, Martha, and Lazarus very well. All three were dear and faithful friends of his. Many months ago, as Jesus and his disciples were traveling through Judea, they'd come to a village where a woman named Martha opened her home to them. Jesus taught from Martha's home for many days. Her sister, Mary, had sat at his feet and listened to what he said. Martha had been unable to partake in the teachings because she was distracted by all the preparations that had to be made in order to feed all twelve of Jesus' entourage. She'd come to Jesus and asked, "Lord, don't you care that my sister has left me to do the work by myself? Tell her to help me!"

When he heard this, Jesus said, "Martha, you are worried and upset about many things, but only one thing is needed. Mary has chosen what is better, and it will not be taken away from her."

At first, Martha had not understood his meaning, but when at last the knowledge dawned on her, she laughed. The sound had filled the Son of God's heart with happiness. He loved them both, and loved their brother Lazarus most of all, for he was a good man and had not been offended when Mary poured perfume on Jesus' feet and wiped them with her hair. Lazarus had understood the symbolism and blessed it with his acceptance rather than demanding blood.

Jesus smiled at the memory.

"Lord?" The messenger shuffled his feet in the sand, unsure if Jesus had heard him.

"What news from Mary and Martha?" Jesus asked. "What news of Lazarus?"

"The sisters have commanded me to say, 'Lord, the one you love is sick'."

When he heard this, Jesus patted the messenger's hand. "This sickness will not end in death. No, it is for God's glory so that God's Son may be glorified through it."

* * *

Jesus loved Martha, Mary and Lazarus. Yet when he heard that Lazarus was sick, he stayed where he was two more days, teaching upon the banks of the Jordan.

"Surely, he will go to aid his friends," whispered Judas. "He would not let death claim a man such as Lazarus."

"Our Lord cannot return," Peter said. "Have you forgotten? Bethany is in the heart of Judea. We have just fled that place for our very lives. To return now would mean certain death."

On the seventh day, just as the sun rose over the hills, Jesus called his disciples together. They sat around the fire and shared a wineskin and bread. The assembled crowd was still sleeping. Many of the people who had come to hear Jesus out of curiosity had ended up staying, forsaking their farms and families so that they could gain knowledge and understanding.

When they had broken their fast, Jesus said to his disciples, "Let us go back to Judea."

"But Rabbi," Paul exclaimed, "a short while ago the Jews tried to stone you, and yet you are going back there?"

Jesus nodded. "We must return. Our friend Lazarus is sick."

"Then we shall travel under the cover of darkness," Matthew suggested.

"No, Matthew," Jesus said. "That is not the way. Are there not twelve hours of daylight? A man who walks by day will not stumble, for he sees by this world's light. It is when he walks by night that he stumbles, for he has no light."

Paul stood up. "I still do not think it is a good idea, Lord."

Judas poured river water on the campfire and stirred the ashes. The rest of the disciples grumbled among themselves.

Jesus insisted. "Our friend Lazarus has fallen asleep; but I am going to Bethany to wake him up."

"Lord," Luke said, "if Lazarus sleeps, then he will get better. We should let him rest."

"That is not the sleep I speak of. Lazarus is dead, and for your sake I am glad that I was not there, so that you may believe. But enough talk for now. Let us go to him."

Jesus stood up and prepared to leave. He moved amongst the crowd, wishing them well and imparting his blessing. Some of the people wept when they heard that he was leaving, for they knew what the Jewish priests would do if he were caught.

Jesus reached the bank of the river and turned around.

He called out, "I go to Judea."

"Then you go to your death, my Lord," Judas whispered.

Thomas, who was also called Didymus, said to the rest of the disciples, "Let us also go, that we may die with him."

* * *

When they arrived, Lazarus had already been dead and in his tomb for four days.

Bethany was less than two miles from Jerusalem, and many Jews had come to Martha and Mary to comfort them in the loss of their brother. They brought whispers and gossip of Jesus' arrival—how he and his followers were approaching in broad daylight, marching down the main road in plain defiance of the priests.

When Martha heard that Jesus was coming, she went out to meet him, but Mary stayed at home.

Jesus greeted Martha. "It is good to see you."

The distraught woman did not return his smile, nor would she meet his eyes.

"Martha, do not be troubled," Jesus said.

"Lord, if you had been here, my brother would not have died. But I know that even now God will give you whatever you ask."

"And what would you have me ask of my Father, dear Martha?"

Martha lowered her head again. Her voice was barely a whisper. "That He not have taken Lazarus from me."

"Your brother will rise again," Jesus told her.

"I know he will rise again in the resurrection at the last day."

"But," Jesus said, "I am the resurrection and the life. He who believes in me will live, even though he dies; and whoever lives and believes in me will never die. Do you believe this, Martha?"

"Yes, Lord," she replied, "I believe that you are the Christ, the Son of God, who was to come into the world."

"Then let not your heart be troubled. You will see your brother again. Now where is Mary?"

"She is at our home, Lord. I should make haste there as well, to prepare for you and your disciples."

Sighing, Jesus eyed the crowd that had gathered to see him. "We shall follow along behind you as we are able."

Martha ran home ahead of them. Mary was still in mourning, and had not moved from the straw mat in the corner. She was surrounded by many friends, all of them offering comfort, and yet no comfort did she find. Martha went to her sister's side.

"The Rabbi is here and he is asking for you."

When Mary heard this, she got up quickly and went out to meet him. The people who had been comforting Mary noticed how hastily she left. They followed her, assuming she was going to the tomb to mourn her brother there.

Jesus and his disciples had not yet entered the village, and were still at the place where Martha had met them. Jesus was giving an impromptu lesson to the assembled crowd. When Mary reached the place and saw Jesus, she fell at his feet and wept.

"Lord, if you had been here, my brother would not have died."

Mary's friends grew sullen and whispered among themselves about the influence Jesus had on her. Several of them began to cry as well, overcome with sorrow for their friend, Lazarus. They felt bad for the two sisters. Both had believed until the very end that this son of a carpenter—this Nazarene—would somehow save Lazarus. But he had not.

And now Lazarus was dead.

Jesus was deeply moved by their tears, and his spirit was troubled. "Where have you laid him?"

"Come and see, Lord," Mary replied. Her face was wet, her eyes red.

They walked along the road and Jesus wept. As they passed by the sisters' house, Martha joined the procession, assuming that Jesus wished to bid his respects to the deceased. More villagers followed along, and the disciples grew nervous, certain that word of their presence would reach the priests in Jerusalem soon.

One of Mary's friends watched Jesus cry, and said, "See how he loved Lazarus! He did not mean for him to die."

But another of them said, "Could not he who opened the eyes of the blind man have kept this man from dying? That is what we were told would transpire. That is what the sisters believed."

Jesus did not respond. His tears fell like rain, spattering the dry, dusty ground.

Father, he prayed, *forgive me that I did not want to return to Judea. I knew what awaited me here – the beginning of the end. I was fearful of death. I am sorry. I now follow your will, though I am still afraid.*

* * *

They came to the tomb, a cave with a massive stone blocking the entrance. Even with the entrance sealed in this way, the smell of rot and decay hung thick in the air.

"Take away the stone," Jesus said.

"But, Lord," said Martha, "by this time there is a bad odor, for he has been in there four days."

"Did I not tell you that if you believed, you would see the glory of God?"

"Yes."

"Then take away the stone."

Several of the disciples did as he commanded, grunting with the effort. They rolled the boulder away, revealing a yawning, black crevice. The stench that wafted out was horrible and many in the crowd turned away. The foul miasma did not seem to bother Jesus. He stepped towards the opening and looked up into the sky.

"Father," he said, "I thank you that you have heard me. I know that you always hear me, but I say this for the benefit of the people standing here, so they may believe that you sent me."

He moved closer still. He trod on old bones and his sandals crushed them into powder. Jesus bowed his head in prayer. The crowd watched, fascinated.

Then Jesus shouted, "Lazarus, come out!"

No one moved. They stared in shocked silence as a sound came from inside the tomb—a soft whisper, cloth on rock. A bent form shuffled towards the entrance and many of the onlookers were afraid. Somewhere near the back of the crowd, a child began to cry. A cloud slid over the sun, and when it had passed, the dead man staggered out of the tomb, his hands and feet wrapped with strips of soiled linen, and a bloody cloth around his face. His bodily fluids had oozed into the rags, crusting them with gore.

Gasping, the crowd shrank away. But Mary, Martha, and the disciples surged forward, shouting with joy.

Jesus said, "Take off the grave clothes and let him go."

They stripped the dirty linens from Lazarus's body and when his sisters saw his face, they wept with happiness.

"Oh, brother," Mary cried. "You are returned to us. We are blessed. Truly, the Lord is mighty."

Lazarus stared at them, blinking, as if trying to remember who they were. Then he smiled.

"Hello, my sisters. It is good to see you."

Jesus twitched, as if startled. His disciples noticed, but no one else among the crowd did; they were too busy celebrating Lazarus' resurrection. Mary and Martha knelt at their brother's feet and kissed his hands. Lazarus ignored them, his gaze settling on Jesus.

"Thank you," the dead man said, grinning. *"Thank you for this release."*

Jesus did not reply. He tried to appear happy but his smile faltered. His demeanor troubled the disciples, and they pulled him aside.

"What is it, Lord," asked Mark. "Are you not happy to see our friend?"

"He is not our friend," Jesus whispered.

"But Rabbi," Judas said, "this is Lazarus that stands before us, resurrected by your will and strength. This is a sign of your testimony."

Jesus shook his head. "This is not what I summoned. This is something else."

"What, Lord?" Matthew glanced back at the crowd, watching Lazarus move among them.

Jesus frowned. "Speak softly, so that none other shall hear. This is not our friend Lazarus. Something else inhabits the temple of his body. Something that it is not given to me to have power over."

Luke was incredulous. "Lord, even the demons submit to us in your name. You have power over everything."

"No," Jesus replied, "I have given you authority to trample on snakes and scorpions and to overcome all the power of the enemy; nothing will harm you. However, do not rejoice that the spirits submit to you, but rejoice that your names are written in heaven. I saw Satan fall like lightning from heaven. I saw his army fall with him. But there were Thirteen that did not fall, yet neither did they serve my Father. My Father has no power over their kind. Great among the Thirteen is Ob, the Obot. He is lord of the Siqqusim and it is given to him the power to reside in the dead."

"Then cast him out, Lord," Judas said. "Force him to flee our friend's body."

"I cannot," Jesus said, "for as I said, I have no power over him."

"But why is he here?"

"My Father is displeased, for I feared to enter Judea again."

Frowning in confusion, the disciples watched Lazarus and the Jews. The dead man moved spryly, his limbs showing none of the stiffness that came with death.

"*I am hungry,*" Ob croaked with Lazarus' mouth. "*Who among you shall feed me?*"

"We shall prepare a great feast for you, brother," Martha cried, "to celebrate your return to us."

"Yes," Mary agreed. "We shall all feed you."

Ob smiled at this news, and stared at Jesus.

"*Will you not come dine at my sister's table?*" Ob asked,

laughing.

"I will not."

"You will miss a rich meal." Lazarus put his arm around Mary's shoulder and leaned close to her. *"Delicious and succulent. Truly a tantalizing feast for the senses."*

Jesus stirred. "Come and walk with me, Lazarus. Let us give thanks together for your return."

Ob's smile faltered. Noticing that the crowd was watching him, he held his head high and walked over to where Jesus stood. The disciples drew away from them, leaving the two alone.

"You befoul this body," Jesus spat. "You defile my Father's glory."

Ob leaned close, his stinking breath hot on his adversary's face. *"Your Father is disappointed with you. Since the day you turned fourteen, you have known this time would come. When the angel appeared to you and revealed your destiny, you were distraught. Since then, you have accepted God's will. You knew that in this, your thirty-second year, you would be asked to work this miracle. You would be asked to intercede on behalf of your friends. You would return to Judea, be betrayed by the one you call Judas, and die at the hands of the Jews. You knew your Father's will, and yet you balked. You delayed, because you did not wish to return. Did not wish to set these events into motion. And thus, He has sent me so that you will not forget: it is His will that you serve."*

"You lie."

"I am not the Master of Lies. That is your older brother, the Morningstar."

Jesus glanced over Ob's shoulder. Martha and Mary were waiting.

"If you harm them," he whispered, "then know this. I will—"

"Do nothing," Ob interrupted. *"I am forbidden to harm them. If I do, I shall be returned to the Void. Your Father may be powerless against me, but He has human agents who know the way."*

They glared at each other, unblinking, and it was Jesus

who looked away first.

"I understand now," Jesus told his disciples. "My Father's will has been made clear to me. I understand why He commanded us to return to this place. I understand all that will transpire. And know this, Judas. I forgive you."

Judas was taken aback. "Forgive me, Lord? For what? Do you not know that I love you? That I serve you faithfully?"

Jesus' smile was sad. His eyes grew wet again. Instead of responding to Judas, he bid farewell to the sisters and told his disciples to follow him.

"Where are we going, Lord?" Thomas asked.

"I must go into the desert and pray. We cannot be here after dark."

"Lord," Peter insisted, "we must stay and fight him."

"No," Jesus said. "My Father has forbidden it."

* * *

That night, there was a great celebration in the village, and all hailed Lazarus' return. After the celebrants had fallen asleep, satiated on lamb and duck and wine, Ob moved among them and began to feed. He plucked sleeping babes from their mother's breasts and drank their blood. He then turned to the mothers, nuzzling at their teats as they slept, before sinking his teeth into the soft flesh. Screams ripped through the night.

His only regret was that his army—his Siqqusim—could not join him.

Ob's feeding frenzy continued. He ripped the arms from men and wielded the severed limbs like clubs, striking at others. He chewed the face off a beggar, tore into stomachs, gouged eyeballs and ate them like grapes, bit into Adam's apples as if they were real apples, and left a trail of gore and offal behind him. Bethany became a place of slaughter. He licked the scabs of lepers, skewered children on spears, and even feasted on the livestock and pets.

When he was satisfied, Ob vanished into the night, intent on finding the necessary ingredients to open a portal and free his brethren from their imprisonment in the Void.

The cries of the dying and wounded drifted into the desert, and when Jesus heard them, he wept again.

* * *

Many of the Jews who had come to visit Mary, and had seen what Jesus did, put their faith in him after the resurrection. But when the first light of dawn lit upon the massacre, they went to the Pharisees and told them what had occurred. None of them thought to connect Lazarus to the crimes.

The chief priests and the Pharisees called a meeting of the Sanhedrin.

"What are we accomplishing?" they asked. "Here is this man, Jesus of Nazareth, performing many miraculous signs. If we let him go on like this, everyone will believe in him, and then the Romans will come and take away both our place and our nation. Surely, he has loosed a demon upon us, as punishment for speaking against him."

Caiaphas, the high priest, spoke up. "The Romans shall do nothing. I have a plan. It is better that one man should die for the people than that the whole nation perish. We shall slay this Rabbi, and we shall slay this demon he has summoned forth. We shall also slay this man, Lazarus, whom has returned from the dead."

So from that day on they plotted to take the life of Jesus and Lazarus' life as well, although they did not know he was possessed by a demon.

When word of this reached Jesus, he called his disciples together. "We can no longer move about publicly among the Jews. Instead, we will withdraw to a region near the desert, in a village called Ephraim."

And so they did. Mary and Martha wondered what had become of their brother. When Jesus and his disciples disappeared, they assumed Lazarus had gone with them. Meanwhile, Ob roamed the sands and mountains of Judea, raiding and feasting in the night and hiding during the day, plotting to unleash the Siqqusim.

* * *

When it was almost time for Passover, many came to Jerusalem for their ceremonial cleansing. The crowds kept looking for Jesus, and as they stood in the temple, they asked one another, "What do you think? Isn't he coming to the Feast at all?" The chief priests and Pharisees had given orders that if anyone found out where Jesus was, they should report it so that he could be arrested.

Eventually, Jesus returned to Bethany. His spirits seemed low, and he did not teach. The sisters gave a dinner in his honor. Much to Mary and Martha's delight, Lazarus arrived as well, and reclined at the table with Jesus. They could not understand why the disciples met his arrival with dread and shrank away from him. Lazarus' flesh, while not marred, was sallow and ripe. Mary put a few drops of pure nard, an expensive perfume, on her brother's head. Then she poured some on Jesus' feet and wiped them with her hair. The house was filled with the fragrance.

Judas objected. "Why was this perfume not sold, and the money given to the poor? It was worth a year's wages."

"Leave her alone," Jesus said. "It was intended that she should save this perfume for the day of my burial. You will always have the poor, Judas, but you will not always have me."

Ob laughed, loud and boisterous. The dinner guests were shocked, but Jesus ignored him.

"The hour has come," Jesus continued, "for the Son of Man to be glorified. Unless a kernel of wheat falls to the ground and dies, it remains only a single seed. But if it dies, it produces many seeds."

"And one day," Ob interrupted, *"all will die, and the seeds of my kind's revenge shall be sown."*

Jesus' demeanor changed. He whirled on Lazarus.

"Silence your tongue!"

Ob leaned close and whispered, "*Caution, Nazarene. I am forbidden to harm the sisters, but your Father said nothing of your precious disciples. I can eat their bodies in remembrance of you.*"

Ignoring him, Jesus turned back to his listeners. "The man who loves life will lose it, while the man who hates life in this world will keep it for eternal life. Whoever serves me must follow me; and where I am, my servant also will be. My Father will honor those who serve me."

There came a loud, insistent knock at the door. All of the assembled jumped, startled. The knock came again. Mary opened the door. A priest and four soldiers pushed into the home.

"Where is Jesus of Nazareth?"

"I am he."

"And where is Lazarus of Bethany?"

Ob rose. "*I am he.*"

The priest appraised them both. "And you, Jesus, claim you brought this man, Lazarus, back from the dead."

"I did, by the Glory of God."

"Then you blaspheme."

"If you have eyes," Jesus said, "let them see. Follow me."

He strode past the armed men, and they did not molest him. The priest followed him outside, along with the disciples, the sisters, and the other guests. Ob remained inside. Jesus turned back to the house.

"Lazarus, come forth."

Ob's host body's legs moved without him willing them. He glanced down in panicked confusion.

"*What is this?*"

His arms and hands defied him and opened the door. He strode out into the streets and cursed Jesus' name.

"*What trickery is this?*"

"No trickery," Jesus said. "I cannot command thee, but it suddenly occurs to me that I can command the flesh you inhabit."

Many among the crowd were confused, but did not intercede.

Jesus turned to the priest. "I brought this man back from the dead. Is he not now marked for death because of it?"

The priest nodded.

"And if I did it again, would you not then believe?"

"What are you saying, Rabbi?"

"Carry out your sentence. Slay him. Then I shall bring him back and you shall see."

"*Wait,*" Ob shouted. "*You cannot –* "

The priest nodded at the soldiers. "Make it so."

Mary and Martha averted their eyes, but were not afraid, because they had faith in the Lord. A soldier stepped forward, armor clanking, and thrust a spear into Lazarus' chest. Ob grasped the shaft and grunted. The crowd gasped.

"He lives," they murmured. "He does not fall."

"His head," the priest commanded. "He cannot survive that."

Ob's eyes grew wide. "*No. Strike not my head. Do not –* "

A second soldier drew his short sword and ran it through the back of Lazarus' head. He pushed hard, pierced the skull, and slid it the rest of the way in. Lazarus dropped, and Ob was dispatched. He screamed with rage, but none save Jesus could hear him.

As he fled, Ob's spirit whispered in Jesus' ear. "*You know what fate your Father plans for thee. I shall be there, waiting. And after your spirit has fled, when your discarded flesh hangs from the cross, I will take it for my own. When you rise from the dead, it shall be me inside this bag of skin and blood and bones. You may be the Life, but I am the Resurrection.*"

The priest looked at the corpse lying in the street and said to Jesus, "Now, if you are who you say, bring him back."

Jesus folded his arms. "I will not. For you have eyes but do not see. I am the resurrection and the life, but your lack of faith blinds you."

"This Rabbi is touched in the head," the priest said.

"Nothing more. He is not the Messiah. He is a simple madman."

After the priest and soldiers had departed, and Mary and Martha wept for the second time over their brother's fallen form, Jesus turned to the disciples.

"Now my heart is troubled, and what shall I say? 'Father, save me from this hour?' No, it was for this very reason I came to this hour. Father, glorify your name!"

Then a voice came from heaven, "I HAVE GLORIFIED IT, AND WILL AGAIN."

Some in the crowd thought the voice was thunder. Others said it was an angel.

Jesus said, "This voice was for your benefit, not mine. Now is the time for judgment on this world; now the prince of this world will be driven out. But when I am lifted up from the earth, I will draw all men to myself. You are going to have the light just a little while longer. Walk while you have the light, before darkness overtakes you all. For one day, it will. Darkness will descend upon this entire world, and shall not be lifted. That shall be the time of the Rising, when the Siqqusim are unleashed upon the Earth. Put your trust in the light while you have it, so that you may become sons of light, and not be left behind as the dead."

When he had finished speaking, Jesus left Bethany and hid himself from them. In the desert, powerless to act against Ob, he turned to the ways of man. He performed a secret spell, passed down from Solomon, taken from the *Daemonolateria,* and cast Ob's disembodied spirit into the Void with the rest of his kind.

Judas, who was hiding behind a stone, saw Jesus work the forbidden rites and was appalled. He had believed his Rabbi to be the Son of God, and had believed that Jesus' powers came from the Holy Spirit. But now, here he was working arcane magicks. At that moment, Judas' heart was filled with resentment, and he vowed to turn Jesus over to the priests.

And in the Void, Ob wailed and raged and waited for the death of light and the time of the Rising.

STORY NOTES

The Resurrection and The Life *is a remake of chapter eleven of the* Book of John, *which tells the story of how Jesus raised Lazarus from the dead. My story is a decidedly different version than the one you'll read in the Bible. The main difference is the addition of Ob.*

I'm assuming that you're already familiar with my novels The Rising *and* City of the Dead, *in which Ob appears. If not, then an ultra-brief history lesson is required. Ob is a demon. He commands a race of sub-demons known as the Siqqusim. The Siqqusim possess the corpses of the dead, reanimating them, wearing them like you or I wear a suit of clothes. They are zombies, in effect. Since the Siqqusim reside in the corpse's brain, the only way to defeat them is to destroy their dead host's brain, thus dispatching the Siqqusim back to the ether.*

Remember this, because Ob appears again later in this collection.

I got the idea for the story while sitting in church one Sunday morning. I was listening to a preacher talk about Lazarus' resurrection, and I thought, "So Lazarus was the first zombie."

BURYING BETSY

We buried Betsy on Saturday. We dug her up on Monday and let her come inside, but then on Wednesday, Daddy said we had to put her back in the ground again.

Before that, we'd only buried her about once a month. Betsy got upset when she found out she had to go back down so soon. She wanted to know why. Daddy said it was more dangerous now. Only way she'd be safe was to hide her down there below the dirt, where no one could get to her without a lot of trouble. Betsy cried a little when she climbed back into the box, but Daddy told her it would be okay. I cried a little, too, but didn't let no one else see me do it.

We gathered around the spot in the woods; me, Daddy, Betsy, and my older brother Billy. Betsy is six, I'm nine, and Billy is eleven. Betsy, Billy and Benny—that's what Mom had named us. Daddy said she liked names that began with the letter "B."

Betsy's eyes were big and round as she lay down inside the wooden box. She clutched her water bottle and the little bag of cookies that Daddy had given her. The other hand held her stuffed bear. He was missing one eye and the seams had split on his head. He didn't have a name.

We closed the lid, and Betsy whimpered inside the box.

"Please, Daddy," she begged. "Can't I just stay up this once?"

"We've been over this. It's the only way to keep you safe. You know what could happen otherwise."

"But it's dark and it's cold, and when I go potty, it makes a mess."

Daddy shivered.

"Maybe we could let her stay up just this once," Billy said. "Me and Benny can keep an eye on her."

Daddy frowned. "You want your little sister to end up like the others? You know what can happen."

Billy nodded, staring at the ground. I didn't say anything. I probably couldn't have anyway. There was a lump in my throat, and it grew as Betsy sobbed inside the box.

We sealed her up tight, and hammered the lid back on with some eight-penny nails. There was a small round hole in the lid. We fed a garden hose through the opening, so Betsy could breathe. Then Daddy got his caulk gun out of the shed and sealed the little crack between the hose and the lid, so that no dirt would fall down into the box. Finally, we each grabbed a rope and lowered the box down into the hole.

"Careful," Daddy grunted. "Don't jostle her."

We shoveled the dirt back down on her. The hole was about eight feet deep, and even with the three of us it took a good forty minutes. Her cries got quieter as we filled the hole. Soon enough, we couldn't hear her at all. We laid the big squares of sod over the fresh grave and tamped them down real good. Made sure the hose was sticking out at an angle, so rainwater wouldn't rush inside it. When we were done, Daddy gathered some fallen branches and leaves and scattered them around. Then he stepped back, wiped the sweat from his forehead with his T-shirt, and nodded with approval.

"Looks good," he said. "Somebody comes by, there's no way they could tell she's down there."

He was right. Only thing that seemed odd was that piece of green garden hose, and even that kind of blended with the leaves. It looked just like a scrap, tossed aside and left to rot.

"And," Daddy continued, "it will take a long time to dig her back up. It would wear anybody out."

We walked back up to the house and got washed up for dinner. I had blisters on my hands from all the shoveling, and there was black dirt under my fingernails. It took a long time to get my hands clean, but I felt better once they were. Daddy and Billy were already sitting at the table when I came downstairs. I pulled out my seat. Betsy's empty chair made me sad all over again.

Dinner was cornbread and beans. Daddy fixed them on the stove. They were okay, but not nearly as good as Mom's used to be. Daddy's cornbread crumbled too much, especially when you tried to spread butter on it. And his beans tasted kind of plain. Mom's had been much better.

Mom had been gone a little over a year now. Didn't seem that long some days, but then on others, it seemed like forever. Sometimes, I couldn't remember what she looked like anymore. I'd get the picture album down from the hutch and stare at her photos to remind me how her face had been. And her eyes. Her smile. I hated that I couldn't remember.

But I still remembered how her cornbread tasted. It was fine.

I missed her. We all did, especially Daddy, more and more these days.

After dinner, Billy and me washed the dishes while Daddy went outside to smoke. When he came back in, we watched the news. Daddy let us watch whatever we wanted to at night, up until our bedtime, but we always had to watch the news first. He said it was important that we knew about the world, and how things really were, especially since we didn't go to school.

Just like every night, the news was more of the same; terrorism, wars, bombings, shootings, people in Washington hollering at each other—and the pedophiles. Always the pedophiles...A teenaged girl had been abducted behind a car wash in Chicago. Another was found dead and naked alongside the riverbank in Ashland, Kentucky. Two little boys were missing in Idaho, and the police said the suspect had a previous record. And our town was mentioned, too. The news lady talked about the twelve little girls who'd gone missing in the last year, and how they'd all been found dead and molested.

*Molested...*it was a scary word.

Daddy said it was all part of the world we lived in now. Things weren't like when he'd been a kid. There were pedophiles everywhere these days. They'd follow you home from school, get you at the church, or crawl through your bedroom window at night. They'd talk to you on the internet—trick you into thinking they were someone else, and then meet up with you. That's why Daddy said none of us were allowed on the computer, and why he didn't let us go to school. Child molesters could be anyone—teachers, priests, doctors, policemen, even parents.

Daddy said it was an urge, a sickness in their brain that made them do those things. He said even if they went to jail or saw a doctor, there weren't no cure. When the urge was on them, there was no helping it. Unless they learned to control it, and even then, there weren't no guarantees.

I went to bed but couldn't sleep. I lay there in the darkness and listened to Billy snoring beneath me. We had bunk beds, and it was a familiar sound—sort of comforting. One of those noises that you hear every night, the ones that tell you everything is okay—your big brother snoring, your little sister in the room across the hall, your Daddy's footsteps as he tiptoes down the hall in the middle of the night.

But tonight, there was just Billy. Daddy wouldn't be tiptoeing down the hall. He'd left just as soon as we went to bed. I heard the car pull out of the driveway. He was gone, out to fulfill his urges. He'd told me and Billy that he'd always had them, but he'd been able to control them until Mom died. After she was gone, they'd gotten stronger. He knew the urges were wrong, but he had to do what he had to do.

It's almost midnight now, and I still can't sleep. Daddy's not back yet.

Tomorrow, another little girl will be missing.
But at least it won't be Betsy.
Betsy is buried in the ground, safe from Daddy's urges.

STORY NOTES

The idea for this story took root during a conversation with my wife. We were discussing how, when I was a kid, my parents let me ride my bike all over town and stay gone all day, coming home only for dinner. Back then, they didn't worry about some nut abducting me. It saddens me that things have changed. I want our son to enjoy the same freedoms I had as a boy, but I also want to protect him from the bad people out there. Burying Betsy *grew out of that. At first, the father was just burying his daughter to keep her safe, but halfway through the first draft, the twist suggested itself to me and the story became something quite different from its original premise.*

THE TIES THAT BIND

"I wonder what time it is."

"Time for you to die."

"Stop that." Philip got up from his bedside chair. The alarm clock in the bedroom broke during the struggle. The power was still on—although sporadic. He walked into the kitchen, glanced at the microwave clock, and saw that it was after midnight.

Outside, the distant sound of far-away thunder rolled across the sky.

Champ brushed up against his leg. Philip bent down and scratched the dog's back end. Champ wagged his tail in delight. Then Philip readjusted the wet handkerchief tied around his face. It helped block out the smell.

He sighed. "It's very late."

"It is indeed," Denise cackled from the bedroom. *"Too late for you all! Humanity's numbers are dwindling while ours grow. We are more than the stars. More than infinity."*

Philip rubbed his tired eyes. They were out of coffee and tea—almost out of food. He was physically and mentally exhausted, but he couldn't sleep. The couch hurt his back, and the bed—the bed they'd slept in—was out of the question. Denise had been tied to it for almost a week now, and she was leaking.

Slowly, he walked back into the bedroom. Champ trotted after him, stopping at the bedroom door. He refused to enter the room. Instead, he stood at the door and growled.

Denise was strapped spread-eagled to the bed frame with bungee and extension cords. More cords bound her torso to the mattress. There was a horrible bite mark on her arm. It was black around the edges, and oozed a stinking, yellowish-brown fluid. The bite was what had killed her—one of the neighborhood kids, dead but hungry. Philip had destroyed the zombie with a garden hoe to the back of its head, but that changed nothing. Infection set in. Within days, Denise was dead, as well.

"Getting a good look?" the zombie rasped.

Philip stared at her. Denise's bathrobe was stained and crusty. Her abdomen had distended and then burst, and her bowels had evacuated. Her white cheeks were sunken, and her eyes looked hollow.

Despite all of this, she was still the most beautiful woman he'd ever seen.

"Why did this have to happen?" he asked. "Why to us? We were happy, weren't we?"

The zombie groaned. *"I've told you. I have your wife's memories and your wife's body, but I am not your wife."*

"No," Philip shook his head. "You are. To me you still are. If Denise's memories of us together still exist, then she still exists. What are we, if not memories? You are my wife, Denise, and I still love you."

A worm wriggled out of the corner of Denise's left eye. Philip tried to ignore it.

"You know what I miss the most? The little things. Watching a movie together or taking a walk. Talking—not like we're doing now, but really talking to each other. You know? Holding your hand. Watching you while you sleep."

He leaned forward.

"What are you doing?" Denise snarled.

"Holding your hand, the way I used to."

Her left hand fluttered against the bedpost, tied right at the wrist and again at the elbow. He took her hand in his. The skin was cold and clammy, but still felt like Denise. If he closed his eyes, he could picture them walking around the lake together, hand in hand, just like this.

He squeezed.

Denise squeezed back. Hard. Philip's knuckles popped. Her laughter sounded like rustling leaves. Champ howled.

Philip gasped. "You're hurting me."

Denise began to sing. *"I wanna hold your haaand. I wanna hold your hand."*

"Stop it!" Philip yanked his hand free and backed away from the bed.

"Come on, darling," Denise tittered. *"You remember the words, don't you?"*

Philip rubbed his fingers. They felt greasy. His pulse was racing, and he fought to keep his emotions in check. A tear rolled down his face.

"Why are you doing this? Tell me, Denise. Why? Can't things be the way they were?"

"Why are you holding me like this," the zombie countered. *"Keeping me here? Why not just let me go?"*

"Because we made a promise," he whispered. "Till death do us part? That was our vow. But not even death kept us apart. You died—when that kid bit you on the arm, you got sick and you died. But you're still here. You're still with me."

He went to the kitchen and selected the biggest knife in the drawer. Then he fed Champ for the last time, a mixture of dog food and rat poison. Champ gulped it down, wagging his tail. Philip returned to the bedroom and sat down in the chair again. He ran the blade across his wrists, and then slashed his own throat.

Philip died with their wedding vow on his lips.

His soul departed—

—and a Siqqusim took its place.

The thing inside Philip sat up, examined his body, and then looked at Denise. It freed her corpse, and they began to hunt, free, unchained, and together in death—never to part.

STORY NOTES

This story is a permutation of an earlier story that only appeared in the ultra-rare, thirty-two copy edition of The Rising: Selected Scenes From the End of the World. *It takes place in the same world as my novels* The Rising *and* City of the Dead, *in which a race of demonic beings known as Siqqusim possess the bodies of the dead, reanimating them as zombies. As I write this, it is currently in production as a short, independent film.*

THE BLACK WAVE

October 26, 1944

The water was so beautiful.

Blue.

Despite everything, the gentle rhythm of the white, foam-topped waves almost lulled him to sleep. Farther down, blue gave way to gray and green, and then black. The depths went on forever. Brady trailed his fingers through the water. The sea was surprisingly warm, but it still felt good on his sunburned skin. He closed his eyes and thought of Rachel; tried to block out all other thoughts and sounds—just the roaring waves and visions of Rachel. He opened his eyes again. The sun reflected off the ocean's surface, shimmering like a swarm of fireflies back home in Indiana.

Then a severed head floated by and reminded Brady of where he was.

Roberts wouldn't stop screaming. Something had ruptured inside his throat, and blood trickled from the corner of his mouth, but he kept on with it. Brady wished Roberts would just pass out.

There were eight of them in the lifeboat. Brady and Roberts, both boatswain's mates; Selman, the radioman, badly burned from an explosion and now slipping in and out of consciousness; Wachowski, the loudmouthed signalman; Brewer, another burly boatswain's mate, fond of getting in fights during shore leave; Chief Petty Officer

Michaels, missing three fingers on his right hand and a chunk of his right ear, his face bloody and pale. There was also a wounded, unconscious man who none of them knew, dressed in the tattered remnants of civilian clothes; and the body of Senior Chief Carter. He'd passed away ten minutes after they pulled him into the boat. When they'd hoisted him aboard, burned flesh sloughed off his arms like banana peels. His left ass cheek was missing.

Their ship, the *USS Brennan*, a destroyer escort, had been part of a task force cruising to the Philippine island of Leyte. None of the enlisted men were sure what the mission entailed, but there were shipboard rumors that one of the vessels in the task force was carrying a new weapon that could decimate the Japanese fleet. Sadly, they'd never had the chance to find out if it was true.

When general quarters sounded, Brady was lying in his rack, staring at a picture of Rachel. They'd grown up together, gone to school together. Brady missed her, and lately, her letters had been shorter and less frequent. That bothered him. He needed to get home. Needed to make sure she still loved him. She was the reason he stayed alive. He wanted to get married. Settle down with her. Have kids. Forget this war and everything he'd seen. Spend the rest of his life lost in her eyes.

"This is not a drill, this is not a drill. General quarters, general quarters. All hands man your battle stations."

"Shit."

The alarm wailed again. The berthing area bustled with activity. Sailors rushed to get dressed. Brady climbed out of the rack, pulled on his boondockers, and raced up the ladder to his battle station on the 40mm gun. He pulled on his helmet and glanced around anxiously. Petty Officer Second Class Leffler was there, smoking a cigarette and scowling at the ocean. His face was lathered with shaving cream. Roberts stood next to him, rubbing the rosary he wore beneath his dungarees.

"What the hell is going on?"

Roberts shrugged. "I don't know. I had mid-watch. I

was sleeping when general quarters sounded."

Leffler blew smoke from his nose. "A man can't even shave in peace. Damn Japs..."

Brady held his breath and tried not to be scared. He scanned the empty horizon. An electronic squawk echoed across the deck and then the Captain's voice came over the speakers. His voice was stern and calm.

"This is the Captain speaking. May I have your attention, please? A large Japanese force is approximately ten miles away and approaching our position rapidly. It's...not good, gents. We can't outrun them, and we're already in reach of their guns. We've drawn a bad lot, men. We have no choice but to stand and fight. Prepare battle stations. Be ready. Be brave."

The Japanese began firing their big guns before their armada was even visible. The blasts echoed across the ocean; the whistling shells sounded like runaway trains bareling overhead. Huge plumes of water shot into the sky and drifted back down, hissing and turning to steam. Then the Japanese warships appeared. At first, they looked like tiny, black dots. As they drew closer, it was clear to all onboard the *Brennan* that the enemy armada outnumbered the small, American fleet.

A second volley of shells rained down on the American ships, quickly reducing most of them to nothing more than twisted, broken scraps of metal. The *Brennan* fared no better than her sisters. She was designed only to provide protection for the escort carriers, and not equipped for a major surface battle. The men onboard could only wait and pray—or curse. They couldn't return fire because the Japanese were still out of range.

A loud explosion rocked the ship, sending Brady toppling to the deck. When he looked up, Leffler's head was missing. Incredibly, the man remained standing, his hands clutching the 40mm. Blood and shaving cream dripped down his shoulders. The shaving cream had turned pink. Roberts screamed. His clothing, hands, and face were covered with bits of Leffler.

The *Brennan* took another direct hit and the bow lurched out of the water. It crashed back down again, showering them with saltwater. Smoke filled the air. The noise was incredible—simultaneous explosions, gunfire, shouted commands, and men screaming.

Jesus, Brady thought, *I'm going to die here. Didn't think that would actually happen. Not to me. I'll never see Rachel again.*

He smelled something cooking. Meat. Despite his fear, Brady's mouth watered. He wondered why the cooks were frying hamburgers in the galley during battle. Did they think their shipmates would be hungry? Then a sailor stumbled out of the smoke. When Brady saw him, he retched. It wasn't burgers cooking. It was his fellow shipmates. The man's skin had been burned so badly that it slipped off his body as he wandered by. Brady had a horrible image of a picnic back home—Rachel pulling the skin off a piece of chicken. The man's charred muscles and tendons still smoked. He creaked as he walked, like old leather. His mouth was open but he made no sound. Another sailor ran past them, shrieking unintelligibly. His arms were missing and blood pumped from the holes. His eyes and tongue were blackened tissue. His teeth seemed very white in contrast.

The deck tilted and the ship groaned. Over the explosions and shouts, Brady heard the order to abandon ship. He grabbed Roberts and shook him.

"Come on. Forget about Leffler. He's dead. We've got to go!"

Roberts shrugged him off and responded with another scream. His eyes were wide, his pupils dilated. Seizing his friend's arm, Brady dragged him forward along the crosswalk. The *Brennan* rocked again, listing to port. Both men bounced against the railing and had Brady not been hanging on to him, Roberts would have plummeted over the side. He never stopped screaming. The stench of cooked meat grew stronger, but many of the screams had stopped.

After reaching the main deck, they made their way to

the starboard side and joined the other sailors lining up for the life rafts. Brady helped Roberts jump onboard a raft, followed by Wachowski and Brewer, who'd carried the injured Selman. The civilian who none of them knew clambered into the raft next, followed by Chief Petty Officer Michaels.

"Nobody else on this side," Wachowski said, staring at the empty deck.

Despite his injuries, Chief Michaels retained command, and ordered them to cast off. They plucked Senior Chief Carter out of the water and then paddled away from the sinking ship. Carter moaned and asked for someone named Lisa. The others urged him to rest, and continued rowing. Oil fires covered the ocean's surface, adding to the smoke and confusion. A whirlpool churned around the wreckage, sucking in some of their more unfortunate shipmates. Brady saw two rafts and a dozen men get pulled beneath the waves. Soon, the *Brennan* slipped beneath the waters as well. All that remained was a slowly-spreading oil slick, black as midnight.

It's all gone, Brady thought. *The ship, my letters from home, my photographs, my clothes, my books, and my Dad's gold pocket watch that his Dad gave to him. All my money. Rachel's picture…Everything – my whole world.*

Now, nearly a half hour later, they rode the waves and watched debris and corpses float by. Carter had died with Lisa's name on his lips. Brady wondered if Carter was the lucky one. All of them felt miserable, even those who were uninjured. Already the hot sun blistered their exposed skin, and dried salt caked their lips and the corners of their eyes. The wind scraped them like sandpaper.

And Roberts was still screaming.

"How long can he keep that up, you think?" Wachowski asked the others. "Hell, Selman's all burned up and the Chief's got his fingers and ear blown off, and they ain't making as much noise."

"Leave him alone," Brady warned. "He saw…"

Brady trailed off, unable to complete the sentence. He

shuddered. Little fragments of Leffler's exploded head had dried on Roberts's dungarees.

Selman woke briefly and made a croaking noise. He asked for water, but they didn't have any to give him. Moaning, Selman closed his eyes again. His body shuddered and his breathing grew shallow.

"Help's gotta come soon," Brady said. "I'm sure we got a distress call out."

"Don't be so certain." Chief Michaels gritted his chattering teeth. He was in shock, but still aware enough to maintain command. "Selman was a radioman. The radio shack was one of the first parts of the ship to get hit."

Nobody replied.

Wachowski removed his boondockers and slipped his feet into the water. He sighed. "That feels good."

Brewer tapped his shoulder. "Put your boots back on, recruit."

"But my feet hurt."

"You won't have feet, you don't put your shoes back on."

"What are you talking about?"

Brewer smiled. "Sharks can see the whites of your feet."

Wachowski drew his feet back up onto the ramp.

"I hate the fucking ocean," he muttered.

"Then why did you join the navy?" Brady asked.

Wachowski shrugged. "I don't know. They said I'd get to see the world."

Brewer laughed. "You wanted to see the world, you could have gone in one of the other branches. We're all on a world tour right now. Europe. The Pacific. Fun and fucking games."

Brady glanced back at the spot where the *Brennan* had been. The ocean's surface was calm again. No bubbles or whirlpools. The current had dissipated the oil fires. There was no sign of the other ships from their task force, either. Brady wondered if they'd all shared the same fate.

Other life rafts drifted by, but most of them were out of hailing distance. The survivors signaled each other and then continued scanning the ocean and sky, looking for their rescuers. The Japanese fleet drew closer as well; slow and cautious, making sure American air support wouldn't arrive. The men on the lifeboats watched the enemy approach.

"Think they'll pick us off," Brady asked, "or pick us up?"

Chief Michaels pushed himself up into a sitting position, wincing in pain as he did. "They'll pull us out of the water. Take us prisoner, I imagine."

*Prisoners of war...*The phrase ran through Brady's mind. It felt unreal.

Roberts began a fresh round of screaming.

"What happens then?" Brady asked.

The Chief lay back down. "Torture, probably. Any of you men armed?"

They shook their heads.

"Damn," the Chief muttered. "Well, they'll launch small boats to retrieve us soon. Can't out-row them, I guess. Tell you something. If capture looks imminent, I'm going over the side and taking a deep breath underwater. I'd advise you all to do the same. Better that than what they'll do to you."

The civilian giggled. All of them turned to the wounded stranger. He hadn't said a word the entire time they'd been in the water, and they'd almost forgotten about him.

"What's so funny?" Brewer snarled.

The man spoke quietly and with obvious effort. They had to lean close to hear him over Roberts' screams. Chief Michaels sat back up again, raised his wounded hand and cupped the mangled tissue of his missing ear.

"No need for the Chief's dramatics," the man said. "I can assure you that there's a good possibility the Japanese will never reach us."

"Why's that?" the Chief asked, groaning from the effort to hold himself upright.

"Because of our cargo."

Scowling, Brewer slid closer to the stranger. "Who the

hell are you, anyway? I never saw you before today."

The man wheezed, and blood trickled from the corner of his mouth. "I'm a..."

He broke into a fit of violent coughing. Blood sprayed the deck. Grimacing, the man grabbed his side.

"Think...one of my ribs must have...pierced a lung."

Wachowski prodded. "You didn't answer his question, mister. You with Special Forces or something? Military intelligence?"

The man's crimson lips pulled back in a tight smile. "Black Lodge."

The other sailors frowned.

"Black Lodge," Brewer repeated. "Never heard of it."

"Nor would you. We're beyond classified."

"I've heard of you," Chief Michaels said. "Special operations of some kind. Deal with weird phenomena."

The man's eyebrows arched in surprise. "I'm impressed, Chief. You know more than...ninety-nine percent of your...countrymen."

Chief Michaels shrugged. "To tell the truth, I thought you guys didn't exist. Figured it was all bullshit. Propaganda."

The man's eyelids fluttered. "You have...no idea..."

His eyes rolled up in his head, flashing white. His body went limp and he slumped forward. More blood leaked from his mouth. Brewer leaned forward and checked his pulse.

"He dead?" Wachowski leaned closer in morbid fascination.

Brewer shook his head. "No, just passed out. He's in pretty bad shape, though."

"I wonder what he meant." Brady glanced out at the ocean again. "He said something about our cargo."

The Japanese ships drew closer, and the American life rafts continued drifting aimlessly. The sky was clear, save for the sun and seagulls. The birds circled the lifeboats, squawking and anxious for a meal. There were no clouds and no planes. The horizons were empty as well, except for the enemy vessels. No land. No American forces. Just endless water…

And the waves—always the waves, carrying the dead.

* * *

"A steak," Wachowski said. "A thick, juicy New York strip, done rare. With a baked potato."

The others nodded in appreciation.

"Good call," Brewer groaned. "Now I'm hungry. But for me, it would be a cold beer." He glanced up at the sun. "Ice fucking cold. And then some pussy."

"What about you, Roberts?" Brady softly nudged him with his elbow. "What's the first thing you want when we get rescued?"

Roberts screamed.

"Jesus Christ, would you shut him up?" Wachowski leapt up from his seat and charged towards the screaming man. Brady balled his fists and stood up to meet him, wobbling a bit, both from the rocking boat and the stiffness in his joints.

"Out of the way, Brady, or I'll feed you to the sharks."

"Sit down, Wachowski."

Brewer stood slowly. "Or what, recruit? You may be able to kick Wachowski's fat ass, but you're damn sure gonna have a harder time with mine."

"All of you knock it off!" The Chief slammed his wounded hand down in anger and then cried out in anguish. Fresh blood flowed from his stumps. His face was covered in sweat, and his forehead had turned bright red in the sun.

Selman moaned in the silence that followed.

"Now look what you made me do." Chief Michaels sounded close to tears.

Brady sat down again. "Apologies, sir."

"Don't call me sir," the Chief grunted, squirming in pain. "I work for a living."

"You okay, Chief?"

"No, Wachowski, I am not okay. And you three aren't making it any easier. Listen to me. Emotions run strong in situations like this. You can't leave them unchecked, or we'll be murdering each other. You want to fight, then remember who the enemy is. Worry about them."

He nodded in the direction of the Japanese vessels.

Roberts kept screaming.

"Or them." Chief Michaels waved over the bow with his good hand. Shark fins cut the surface like knives through butter.

They tried to row away from the approaching enemy, but the current was too strong. After a few yards, the waves tossed them right back again. Helpless, they floated, watching the sharks and the Japanese ships circle closer. Brady wondered which would get them first.

Chief Michaels continued; his voice strained with the effort. "We need to work together. That's the only way we're going to survive. No matter what happens."

The man from Black Lodge stirred again and began to applaud. The sailors stared at him, incredulous and bewildered. Nobody spoke, and even Roberts paused before continuing with his screaming.

"Bravo, Chief…Bravo."

He spoke haltingly, and each time he breathed in, his expression showed pain.

Selman coughed up blood.

"Marvelous…speech," the civilian continued. "You should be…commended."

"Glad you liked it," the Chief moaned.

"I did…indeed."

Chief Michaels waved his fingerless hand. "You'll understand if I don't join in the applause."

The stranger smiled with cracked lips. "How long… was I out?"

"Not long enough," Wachowski said. "Go back to sleep. We ain't rescued yet."

"I'm surprised you did sleep," Brewer told the man. "What with Roberts screaming and all."

"He's…only doing…what we'll all be doing…soon enough."

"There you go talking crazy again."

Frowning, Brewer prodded the wounded agent with the tip of his boot. Wincing, the stranger bit his lip, but did not cry out.

"Who are you, really?" Brewer demanded. "What do you know? Might as well tell us. The Japs will make you tell them when we're picked up."

"I…told you. I'm with Black…Lodge. The task force was…ferrying a new weapon we…developed. We…grew it in…"

He leaned forward and vomited blood onto the deck. Brewer stepped back in disgust. Trembling, the stranger threw up again. This time the blood was dark, almost black. He collapsed as his stomach heaved a third time, convulsing in his own gore.

"He's in shock," the Chief shouted. "Help him!"

Brewer laid a tentative hand on the wounded man's chest. Another gout of blood erupted from the agent's mouth, splattering them both. With one hand, the agent reached out and clutched Brewer's muscular arm.

"We…grew…"

He released the boatswain's mate and his arm flopped back to the deck. He stiffened and then lay still. His eyes stared directly into the sun. He did not blink.

Brewer checked his pulse, and then leaned close to see if he was breathing.

"He's dead."

"Toss him over," the Chief said, his voice weaker than before. "But check him for identification first. We'll need to notify somebody—if we ever get the chance."

"We don't even know his name," Brady whispered. "Who was his family? Did he have anyone at home?"

Again, he thought of Rachel. He'd give anything to see her now, to kiss her with his blistered lips, to feel her fingers on his raw, red skin.

"Nothing," Brewer said, finishing with his search.

Selman moaned something unintelligible, and then rolled over onto his side. Roberts screamed.

"Doesn't matter now," Wachowski muttered. "He's dead, Senior Chief Carter is dead. Selman's gonna die soon, too, if we don't get help."

One hundred yards away, the men on another lifeboat shouted, splashing at the water with their oars. A sleek, dark shape disappeared beneath the boat. The fin resurfaced on the other side. More sharks circled closer.

"We all are," the Chief said. "We all are..."

Roberts continued screaming, drowning out the ocean's roar.

* * *

They saw the black wave a few minutes later.

Roberts was still screaming, and even Brady was losing patience with his friend. The Chief had directed them to throw Senior Chief Carter's corpse into the ocean along with the Black Lodge agent's body, because the seagulls were darting down from the sky and pecking at them. Both bodies floated away on the current. The shrieking birds landed on them almost immediately. They perched on their chests and faces and began feeding—riding their own grisly lifeboats. Survivors from the other rafts did the same with their dead, hoping to pacify the sharks long enough to coast out of range.

Done with the gruesome task, Wachowski and Brewer joked about tossing Roberts over the side as well, just to shut him up. Brady knew it was just gallows humor, their way of dealing with all that had happened, but the callous remark still angered him. He opened his mouth and started to say something, but then he saw it—a black wave, moving against the current. It was the same size as the other waves, but it rolled in the opposite direction. The sun did not reflect off its surface.

None of his fellow survivors had noticed it. The Chief was almost unconscious. Brewer and Wachowski were needling each other about what they'd do to each other's sister when they were rescued. Selman was thrashing on the deck and babbling; white flecks of spittle caked his burned face. And Roberts…

Maybe Roberts did notice the wave, because he stopped screaming.

"Thank God," Wachowski said. "We ought to gag him before he starts again."

Brady barely heard him. His gaze was fixated on the black wave. A shark fin crested the water about ten feet away from it. As he watched, the wave changed direction in mid-course, swerving directly for the predator. It crashed over the shark and the fin disappeared. The wave grew in size.

They heard shouting from one of the other lifeboats. Brady glanced in that direction, assuming the men onboard had witnessed the same thing. Instead, he was surprised to see them pointing at the Japanese ships. The enemy had launched several smaller boats. They sped towards the life rafts.

"Shit!" Brewer gripped the side of the boat. "They're coming. Fucking Japs. What do we do, Chief?"

"Pray. We pray, son."

"Umm, fellas?" Brady pointed at the black wave. It had changed course again, swerving towards one of the American rafts. The men onboard hadn't noticed it. Their attention was focused on their pursuers.

"You hallucinating?" Wachowski asked, without looking. "Seeing mermaids? You've been out here in the sun too long, Brady. Eyes aft. We've got trouble."

"We've got trouble forward too, you fat fuck. Look!"

Growling, Wachowski turned to where Brady was pointing. Immediately, his jaw went slack.

"The fuck is that?"

The Japanese fired several warning shots, letting their captives know they were armed. At the same time, the black wave surged over an American lifeboat, swamping the men onboard. Brady saw several of them try to leap aside, but the black water sucked them into the wave's mass. Both raft and crew vanished, just like the shark. And again, the wave seemed to swell. It changed course once more, flowing smoothly against the tide.

"I did not just see that," Wachowski breathed. "How can it do that?"

All of them fixed their attention on the wave now, the enemy forgotten. Chief Michaels propped himself up with his good hand and stared in disbelief. The Japanese noticed the wave too. They slowed their approach, and as their engines idled down, Brady heard them jabbering at each other.

"They don't know what it is either," he said. "Maybe it's that weapon the Black Lodge man was talking about."

"Then why did it just kill our guys?" Wachowski asked.

"We don't know that it did. It hit them, and then when it moved on, they were gone. We didn't see their bodies."

The big man's sunburned face turned from red to purple. "We didn't see the fucking raft either, Brady. It ate them!"

"It didn't—"

A shriek cut him off. The black wave turned again, once more rolling in the opposite direction of the other waves, and flooded the American raft closest to them. Brady recognized several of the sailors onboard; he'd seen their faces every day—in the galley, on the bridge, in their berthing areas. He didn't know any of their names but he recognized them just the same. They were brothers. He'd served with them.

Somehow, the fact that he didn't know their names made their deaths that much worse.

This time, the attack was close enough to make out details. The wave quivered as it crashed over them, shimmering and flowing. It absorbed the sailors, along with the boat; drew them into its mass and instantly converted them into more dark water. And then they were gone. Washed away.

"Row," Chief Michaels shouted. "Row, row, row...Get

us out of here!"

He clutched an oar with his one good hand, reopening the wounds around his severed fingers. His blood pooled on the deck. Brewer and Brady grabbed two more oars and plunged them into the water. Wachowski just stared.

The wave swelled, paused, and then turned towards them. It swept over the two corpses they'd just thrown into the water, disturbing the seagulls' banquet. The birds took flight, soaring into the air. The wave crested, and tendrils of black water shot up after them, liquefying the fleeing birds in mid-air.

"Oh God…" Brady held his breath.

The wave picked up speed. Roberts started screaming again, and this time, the others joined him.

"Faster," Brewer shouted. "Wachowski, grab an oar and row, goddamn it!"

Blubbering, Wachowski ran to the bow. The raft rocked, leaning to starboard. Seawater rushed into the boat.

"Sit down before you capsize us," Brewer yelled. "Chief, what can we do?"

Chief Michaels didn't answer. Blood loss had finally caught up with him. He slumped over, unconscious. The oar slipped from his hands and floated away. Brewer leaned out over the water and grabbed for the oar as Wachowski cowered at the very front of the lifeboat. The craft tilted farther, spilling Brewer into the ocean. Soundless, the wave rushed towards him. Brewer bobbed up and down on the tide. He opened his mouth to scream and then the black water engulfed him.

Gone.

Brady sobbed. Wachowski joined Roberts in another round of screaming. Chief Michaels and Selman remained mercifully still. The wave made a wide arc, scooped up another shark, and then charged.

A gunshot rang out, echoing across the water. Several more rounds followed. The Japanese small boats had crept closer and opened fire.

"Well," Wachowski said with a half-laugh, half-cry. "It

must not be theirs, either."

Bullets slammed into the wave, spraying droplets of black water into the air, but they had no effect. The wave paused, and then churned towards this new threat. The Japanese continued firing, but as the wave bore down on them, they gunned their engines and fled for the safety of their fleet. The boats skipped across the ocean, bobbing up and down in the surf. The wave picked up speed. It swallowed the first boat whole, and then made quick work of the others. Its size increased again, and by the time the last boat was obliterated, the wave was nearly thirty feet high. Without pausing, it stormed after the bigger Japanese ships.

"Now's our chance," Brady said. "Wachowski, help me row!"

"It's no use. You saw how fast it is."

Roberts's voice finally gave out. He kept screaming, but the only sound he made was a harsh wheeze.

Brady rowed harder. "Help me!"

Wachowski wiped his nose with the back of his hand, and then grabbed the spare oar. It was slick with Chief Michaels's blood, but he didn't seem to notice. He paused, watching as the black wave decimated the Japanese fleet. The water crashed into the side of a large frigate, turning steel to liquid in a heartbeat. The ship tilted, and the wave flowed up onto the deck.

"It's getting bigger," Wachowski gasped. "The more it eats, the bigger it gets."

"So row!"

"We've got to be faster, Brady."

He dropped the oar, bent over, and grabbed the Chief's shoulders. Grunting, Wachowski picked up the Chief's limp form and dragged him to the side.

"What are you doing?"

"Making us faster."

"Wachowski, don't—"

There was a splash. Grinning, Wachowski turned to Selman.

"You too. Sorry about this. Hopefully, you'll sleep right

through it."

Brady gritted his teeth. Tears rolled down his raw cheeks. Wachowski was right. It didn't make it any easier, but he was right. Brady thought about survival; thought about Rachel. He'd do anything to get home safely. He stared straight ahead as Wachowski lifted Selman's body and carried him to the side. There was a second splash, and Wachowski breathed a heavy sigh. Wood clattered against metal as he retrieved the oar. Brady continued looking forward, not wanting to see the bodies floating on the tide. Roberts suddenly grew quiet, and there was a third splash. Frowning, Brady heard Wachowski come up behind him.

"Got to be faster," the fat man whispered.

Brady turned just as Wachowski swung. There was a tremendous, hot pain as the oar slammed into the side of his face. Brady crumpled. Warmth ran down his cheek and ear. His vision blurred.

"Faster..."

Brady felt rough hands on him and then he was falling. He heard another splash, but he didn't care. He was suddenly surrounded with a wonderful cool wetness, and nothing else mattered. Brady took a deep breath and held it. Then he closed his eyes and thought of Rachel.

As he sank beneath the waves, he heard Wachowski screaming louder than Roberts had been.

* * *

Brady opened his eyes. Above him, he saw the dim, shadowy outline of the lifeboat's hull. Below him were the ocean depths. They seemed to go on forever.

The water was so beautiful.

Blue.

Then it turned black.

STORY NOTES

This was written for a themed-anthology of weird war stories. I've been on lifeboats during my time in the Navy, and let me tell you, it ain't no picnic.

I guess some comparisons to Stephen King's The Raft *are unavoidable, although it didn't occur to me until halfway through the final draft. I hadn't read that story since high school, but in retrospect, it obviously influenced me. In any case, though the monsters are similar, the stories are quite different.*

This story also introduces another big player in my underlying mythos – Black Lodge. We don't know much about them yet, other than that they are a top-secret paramilitary organization that deals with supernatural events. You'll see them again soon. Actually – you've been seeing them since the beginning.

You just didn't know it…

TAKE THE LONG WAY HOME

For my parents, Lloyd and Shannon Keene…

I kept my eyes shut after the blast. My head was throbbing and blood filled my mouth. Wincing at the taste, I explored with my tongue and found that I'd bitten the inside of my cheek—probably on impact.

"Steve?"

Charlie. It sounded like he was in pain.

"Steve, you okay?"

I opened my eyes and blinked, staring at the dent my head had made in the dashboard. I spat, bright red, and then spat again. There were chunks of broken glass in my lap, and I wondered where they'd come from. Then it all came rushing back to me.

"Yeah," I groaned. "I'm okay. How about you?"

Charlie coughed. "Got the wind knocked out of me, but I'm all right. What the hell happened?"

I didn't answer, because the answer was obvious. We'd wrecked. It had all happened so suddenly. We'd just gotten out of work, and were crawling north on Interstate 83 during Baltimore's evening rush hour. Hector was behind the wheel, cursing in Spanish because we'd just been funneled from four lanes down to two, and wondering why they couldn't do road construction at night, after the rush hour was over. I rode shotgun, staring out the window at nothing and everything, watching the trees and buildings and road signs flash by, and half-listening to NPR's *All Things*

Considered. Even though it was Hector's van, we took turns with the radio each day. He liked the Spanish station, I preferred classic rock, and Craig and Charlie both liked National Public Radio. But Craig and Charlie weren't listening to the radio. They were in the backseat, arguing over the Ravens' chances of making the Super Bowl this year, which according to Charlie were great, and according to Craig were slim to none and slim had just left town.

I'd opened my mouth to warn Hector that the yuppie idiot driving the Volvo in front of us was gabbing on his cell phone and not paying attention to the road—but I never got the chance.

Because of that weird fucking blast.

It wasn't an explosion. Didn't sound like that at all. What it sounded like was a trumpet. The world's biggest trumpet, blaring a single, concussive, ear-splitting note. I felt it in my chest when it went off, the impact vibrating my ribs. I hadn't seen any smoke or fire. No mushroom clouds on the horizon. No airplanes slamming into buildings or box trucks blowing up on the median strip. None of the usual things you think of these days when you hear a blast.

It must have startled Hector. He jumped in his seat and jerked the steering wheel hard. At the same time, the Volvo darted in front of a flatbed truck loaded down with huge steel pipes for a construction site. The truck swerved into our lane to avoid the Volvo, and we sideswiped a concrete construction barrier. The van came to a sudden, jarring stop. My teeth ground together. The air bags deployed on impact. I'd blacked out for a minute or two.

And now here we were.

I spat blood again.

Charlie moaned in the back seat. "This is fucked up."

I didn't respond. Each time I talked, I swallowed more blood. My stomach felt queasy. Unfastening my seatbelt, I brushed fragments of glass from my hair and lap, and turned towards Hector. My mouth fell open and blood dribbled down my chin.

"Oh fuck..."

There was a pipe jutting from his head. His eyes, nose, and mouth were gone, just eradicated, replaced with a twelve-inch round length of steel pipe. My gaze followed the pipe's trajectory: from the ruined thing that used to be Hector's face to the windshield, over the hood, and into the back of the flatbed truck. An old elementary school rhyme ran through my head: *Through the teeth and over the gums, look out stomach – here it comes.* My mind then changed it to: *Through the windshield and past your gums, look out Hector – here it comes.* I gave a nervous little laugh. The sound scared me.

"Steve?" Charlie's voice was concerned. It must have scared him, too.

Sour bile rose in my throat, and my stomach lurched. I touched Hector's bloody shoulder and gave him a gentle shake. It was a stupid thing to do, but the mind is funny that way in times of crisis. Hector didn't move. His arms hung limp. There was an ugly splotch on his wrist where the airbag had burned him.

"Is he okay?" Charlie asked.

"Take a look. What do you think?"

Somewhere behind us, a car horn blared, loud and obnoxious. I checked Hector's pulse, but there was none. I'd expected as much, but I went through the motions anyway. My own heartbeat quickened. I couldn't put my fingers under his nose to determine if he was breathing, because he didn't have a nose anymore. He had a pipe. And besides, he wasn't breathing anyway.

Abruptly, the car horn died.

"He's gone." The words caught in my throat. The whole situation seemed surreal.

"Jesus Christ." Charlie undid his seatbelt and leaned forward, pressing on my seat. "We've got to do CPR on him or something! Use your cell phone. Call 911, man."

"I don't think that's going to help him, Charlie. He's dead."

"But– "

"He's fucking dead, man! He's got no face."

"Well, how could this happen? I mean, we were only doing what, forty-five miles an hour? Maybe? The airbags deployed."

"Yeah. But he's got a pipe sticking out of his head. It punched right through the air bag and into his head. His face is gone."

Charlie's response was a choked half-sob, half-sigh.

"Are you hurt?" I asked.

"I don't think so." He rustled around in the backseat and then paused. "Where's Craig?"

"He's not back there?" I whipped around, and immediately wished that I hadn't. The muscles in my neck and shoulders screamed.

"Do you see him back here, Steve?"

"Check the cargo space behind you."

"I did. I'm telling you, man. He's not in here!"

My eyes darted around the van's interior, trying to confirm this new bit of information. There were no Craig-sized holes in the side door or back windshield. The roof and floor were intact. The doors were closed. But there was no sign of Craig.

"Shit." I pressed my face into my palms, trying to hold back the sudden and severe headache blossoming behind my eyes. "He must have been thrown from the vehicle. Come on. We've got to find him."

Charlie blinked, and I noticed that his pupils were dilated. They looked like two black blobs of India ink. He grabbed my arm. His hands were sweaty.

"Steve, the only hole is the one in the windshield. Where the pipe is. He couldn't have been thrown out."

I shook him off and opened the passenger door. Hot steam rose from the engine, smearing the windows, and I breathed in a lungful. I stumbled out onto the highway, coughing and gagging.

Charlie followed. He leaned against the side of the van, his eyes wide and dazed. "We were only doing forty-five. We were only doing forty-fucking-five."

I got the impression that he was repeating the mantra in

an effort to bring back Hector and Craig, as if verifying the safety of our speed would rewind the past two minutes. I reached for him. The ground seemed to spin and I fought to keep my balance. My legs suddenly felt like they were made of rubber. My ears rang, and I started sweating. I could feel it pouring off my forehead and pooling beneath my arms. Charlie said something, but it sounded like he was talking from the end of a very long tunnel. My vision dimmed.

Shock, I thought. *You're going into shock. It's okay, Steve-O. You were just banged around in an automobile accident, and one of your co-workers has been killed – he has a pipe in his face – and another one is missing. You're allowed to go into shock if you want to. Nobody will mind. Go right ahead. Hector will still be dead when you wake up.*

I tried to speak. "Charlie –"

"Yeah?"

The road fell out from under me, and I dropped. Then God turned off the lights, and I blacked out again. I'm not sure how long I was out. Probably only a few seconds, but it seemed like hours.

When I opened my eyes, the first thing I was aware of was being thirsty. My mouth was dry, my tongue swollen. The second thing was that Charlie and two strangers were leaning over me. One was a black man in a neatly pressed white shirt and tie with a cross on it. I remember noticing his attire right away—end of the workday and this guy's shirt still looked freshly ironed. Pants creased. Tie smooth, unwrinkled. He looked *crisp.* His wiry goatee and mustache were peppered with silver hairs, and when he smiled his teeth gleamed white. The other man was an overweight white guy in a yellow hardhat and flannel shirt. Underneath the flannel was a stained wife-beater T-shirt, stretched over his prodigious belly. His nose and ruddy face were lined with the red veins of advanced alcoholism. His armpits reeked, and thick beads of sweat rolled off his cheeks.

All three of them leaned close, staring at me in concern.

I could smell the horseradish from the sandwich Charlie had eaten for lunch.

"What?" I smacked my lips together, trying to work up enough spit to talk. My mouth felt like cotton.

"You okay?" Charlie's brow creased.

I nodded, so that I wouldn't have to talk. My hands hurt and I raised my palms to investigate. They were bleeding, cut by the small stones in the asphalt.

"Just lie still, buddy," the guy wearing the hardhat said. "I called 911 on my cell phone. Cops and an ambulance are on the way."

I turned back to Charlie. "Craig?"

He shook his head. "I can't find him. And nobody saw him get thrown from the vehicle, either."

I thought about this, turning it over in my mind. It didn't make sense. Where had he gone? Craig couldn't have just wandered away—Charlie had remained conscious immediately after the crash, and I'd only been out for a few seconds. We would have known if Craig had climbed from the van. He hadn't. And he wasn't inside the van either.

So where the hell was he?

Charlie glanced around, looking nervous and frightened. I wondered if there was something he wasn't telling me.

I struggled to sit up, but the black man pushed me back down. His touch was light, but powerful. It felt like all the strength in the world was in those warm hands. A small jolt of static electricity shot from his fingertips to my chest.

"Easy now." His voice was like flowing water. "Just rest until the paramedics get here."

My head still throbbed, but my saliva was working again and I managed to speak. "You are?"

He smiled. "Gabriel. Or Gabe. Whichever you prefer. I caught you as you fell."

"Not quick enough, though," the man in the hardhat grunted. "You scraped your hands."

I tried to sit up again, but Gabriel gently forced me back down.

"Just lie still."

"I'm okay," I insisted. "We need to find our friend. And our other co-worker, Hector, he's..."

I trailed off, unwilling to finish the sentence. Could Hector really be dead? It just didn't seem possible. Earlier in the day, Charlie and I had stood in his cubicle, laughing over a dirty cartoon Hector downloaded off the Internet. In it, the cast of *Family Guy* was having sex with *The Simpsons*. We hadn't shown it to Craig, of course. He was our friend, but he was also a born-again Christian, and we didn't want to offend him. Craig wasn't preachy. In fact, he didn't bring God up unless somebody asked him directly. He respected our views (I was Jewish and Charlie was agnostic; said he couldn't worship a God who'd condemn him to Hell just for being gay).

We'd laughed over the cartoon. Next weekend, the four of us were going to Lake Redman to do some fishing. Hector had just bought a new bass boat with his bonus. So how could Hector be dead now? And where the hell was Craig? Maybe he'd hit his head and had amnesia or something. Wandered away from the wreck.

The man in the yellow hardhat stared off into the distance. "Wonder what's taking them so long?"

"They'll be busy today," Gabriel said. "This is just the beginning."

Charlie nodded. "You heard the blast, too? Think it was terrorists?"

Gabriel didn't respond.

"Ask me, it didn't sound like no explosion," the guy in the hardhat said. "Sounded more like—well, a trumpet. Fucking weird shit."

Gabriel's smile was tight-lipped and sad. I wondered what he was thinking. Groaning, I grabbed his wrist and removed his hand from my chest. Then I sat up and spat more blood onto the pavement.

"You should rest," Gabriel said again, rising to his feet. "You're going to need it before this day is through, Steven, and I will be very busy with other things. I won't be able to catch you again if you fall."

"What?"

I wondered how he knew my name. Before I could ask, my attention was drawn to the crowd. They were all around us, people from all walks of life. Bankers, customer service representatives, cabbies, stockbrokers, IT techs, secretaries, construction workers, janitors, telemarketers, forklift drivers, systems analysts, machine operators, and soccer moms, all stranded together in the middle of the interstate during Wednesday afternoon's rush hour. We saw each other every day, drove past one another, competed against each other for lane supremacy, shouted at each other and flashed obscene finger gestures when we lost. But none of us had ever truly met, until now. It was like some bizarre version of *The Breakfast Club*.

Charlie gave me his sweaty hand and pulled me to my feet. He squeezed, forgetting about my cut palms.

"Ouch." Wincing, I pulled my hand away.

He wiped my blood on his slacks. "Sorry, dude."

"That's okay. Listen, did you tell that guy my name?"

"Who?" Charlie looked confused.

"The black guy. Gabriel."

Charlie shook his head. Then he turned away and said, "God—look at this."

I glanced around, stunned by the magnitude of it all. Ours wasn't the only wreck on the highway. Remember when you were a kid, and you got out all of your Hot Wheels and Matchbox cars and made one giant traffic accident? That's what the interstate looked like. Vehicles were piled up in both directions as far as the eye could see. Some were just minor fender-benders. Other cars had been totaled. The occupants, those who were mobile at least, milled around on the median strip and weaved between the wreckage, looking as stunned as I felt. Some exchanged insurance information. Others held cell phones to their ears. Many more simply stared in shared disbelief. I wondered how many were in shock.

Charlie, the guy in the hardhat and I were standing in

front of the Timonium exit. The on and off ramps were choked with snarled traffic, too. A thick forest spread out beyond the southbound lane. To our right was a steep embankment. There was a chain link fence at the bottom that surrounded a trucking company. Frantic employees ran around in the parking lot, looking as confused as we were.

A pretty redhead took a step towards us. She swallowed, made a choking noise, and then took off her shoes. I noticed that one of her heels was broken. She looked at us and said, "It's like the end of the world."

We nodded. Charlie coughed.

Then she padded away.

In the distance, a lone siren wailed.

"Sounds like the ambulance," Charlie said.

The guy in the hardhat grunted. "Guess that other fella was right. They're gonna be busy."

The siren faded. Then another one took its place.

It was mid-August and the late afternoon sun beat down on the blacktop, yet I suddenly felt very cold. Shivering, I gently rubbed my arms with my sore, bloody hands.

* * *

We stood there, not knowing what to do next. Charlie and I called out for Craig, but he didn't answer. In truth, I hadn't expected him to. I glanced back at the van once, looked at Hector, and then forced myself not to look anymore.

The guy in the hardhat said nothing. I think he was too shocked to speak. He stood there and watched the employees in the parking lot of the trucking company below.

The breeze kicked up. A traffic helicopter hovered overhead, surveying the damage. Then it flew farther up the highway. Some of the crowd waved their arms and hollered at it, but the chopper didn't return.

Another young woman stumbled toward us through the wreckage. She only wore one shoe. Her other foot was bare, and her nylons were torn. Her blonde hair was mussed. Tears and mascara streamed down her face along with blood from her nose.

"My baby," she sobbed. "Please, somebody help me. I can't find my baby!"

Charlie stepped forward and gently put his hands on her shoulders. "Shhhh. It'll be okay."

"Okay? My baby is missing! She's not in the car."

"Where's your vehicle?" Charlie asked, trying to calm her. "Take us to your car, and we'll help you find your daughter."

She pointed. One car behind us—an undamaged, neon green Volkswagen Jetta. There was an infant's car seat in the back. It was empty. Just like Craig's seat had been. That was when I felt the first pangs of real fear.

"Her name is Britney," the woman wailed. "I can't find her."

"My wife's missing," a man shouted from the opposite lane. "Has anybody seen her?"

"What's she look like?" someone else hollered.

"Brunette. Freckles. She's pregnant! We were on our way to the hospital for a check-up."

Several people clustered around him, while Charlie led the crying woman back to her car.

I thought about my own wife, Terri. No doubt the pile-up had already made the local news. She'd be worried, wondering if I was okay. I pulled out my cell phone and dialed the house. After a minute, I got a recording telling me that all lines were busy and to try my call again. Sighing in frustration, I stuffed the phone back into my pocket.

The guy in the hardhat stuck out his hand. I held up my bleeding palms and shrugged. "Sorry. Don't want to bleed on you."

"Appreciate that," he laughed. "Frank Wieczynski."

"Steve Leiberman. Nice to meet you."

He nodded. "Yeah, you too. Shame it isn't under better circumstances."

"Ain't that the truth." Cringing, I pulled a piece of gravel from my hand and smoothed a flap of loose skin over the cut. My mouth had finally quit bleeding. "Thanks for your help back there, Frank. I appreciate it. I guess it was shock or something that made me pass out like that."

He shrugged. "Don't mention it. To be honest, I didn't do much. Just called 911 as soon as the pile-up started. That's all. It was that other guy, Gabriel. He's the one you should thank. I saw him catch you when you fell. Moved like greased lightning. One second you were falling, and the next he was there, keeping you from cracking your head open on the highway."

I searched the gathering crowd, looking for Gabriel so that I could thank him, but he was gone.

"Where'd he go?" I asked.

Frank took off his hardhat and scratched his balding, sunburned head. "Don't know. He was just here a second ago."

I scanned the crowd some more, but there was no sign of him. "It's like he vanished."

"Seems to be a lot of that going on," Frank said. "Couple of other people are missing, too. Your friend over there, the one helping that blonde—he said one of your other friends was missing? That who you two were hollering for earlier?"

I nodded. "Craig. He's got to be around here somewhere, though."

The yuppie from the Volvo, the one who'd been paying more attention to his cell phone than the road and had caused the truck to swerve into our lane, climbed out of his car and slammed the door. His face was like a storm cloud. Running a hand through his perfectly coifed hair, he surveyed the damage to his rear bumper, muttered something under his breath, and then glared at me. His tie fluttered in the wind. Then he turned his attention to our van, and caught sight of Hector's body. He flinched. The color drained out of his face, but he still looked angry.

"That guy still alive?" He walked over to Frank and me, one hand massaging his neck. "Because if so, then he'd better have a damn good lawyer. I think my spine is hurt."

"He's dead," I told him. "So you'll probably have to sue somebody else."

"Dead?"

"Yeah. In case you didn't notice, he's got a twelve-inch pipe sticking through his fucking face."

The Volvo driver suddenly forgot all about his supposedly injured back. "Jesus Christ. This is bullshit. I'm supposed to be in York by six. I've got a meeting."

Dismissing him with a wave of my hand, I turned back to Frank. "Is your cell phone working?"

He nodded. "Yeah. Signal was fine when I called 911. The woman said she was dispatching units right away. Sounded like she was in a hurry. Frazzled. I'll bet other people were calling about this, too."

"Maybe," I agreed. "I hate to ask, but can I borrow your phone? Mine's not working, and I'd like to call my wife. Let her know that I'm okay."

"Sure." Frank handed me his cell phone. "I'd call my old lady, but she left me two years ago."

He launched into the story, but I tuned him out, made sure I had four bars on the display, and then dialed Terri. This time there was no recording. Just silence. Dead air. I waited, but there was no dial tone or ring.

"I think your cell is out of service, too." I handed the phone back to Frank.

"That's weird." He glanced at the network bars. "It worked before. Looks like I've got a signal, too."

"Maybe they're jammed up or something. Like what happened on September 11th, when everybody was trying to call home at the same time."

"Could be. If that's so, then this is even bigger than we think. That explosion was the damnedest thing. Couldn't tell where it came from exactly, but it must have been close. And I still say it sounded like a trumpet."

Before I could reply, somebody screamed nearby us. I couldn't tell if it was a man or a woman. It was just a high-pitched, drawn out wail that went on and on, and then finally faded after what seemed an eternity. A dog barked.

Then another person called out, wondering where Thomas had gone. Thomas didn't answer. A small child began to cry for her mother.

Frank looked scared. "This is getting bad."

"Thomas? Thomas, you get back here, right now! Where are you?"

"Mommy? MOMMY! Where's my mommy?"

"Thomas! You quit scaring me right now. Come back."

"Motherfucker..." The guy from the Volvo threw his cell phone down, smashing it on the pavement. The broken casing slid under a nearby car. "God damn piece of shit. I've got a meeting, goddamn it!"

"That guy is losing it," I whispered to Frank.

Volvo kicked his front tire.

Frank eyed him warily. "Yeah, we'd better keep an eye on him till the cops show up."

I turned back to Charlie and the young blonde woman. She was in hysterics, crawling underneath her car and scratching at the pavement, and all the while shrieking for her missing baby. Her skirt was soiled with dirt and grease. Charlie knelt beside her, his expression a mixture of sadness and bewilderment. He looked to me for help, motioning me over.

"Leiberman," Frank grunted. "You Jewish?"

I nodded. "That's right."

"I got a friend that's a Jew. Nice guy. We play cards sometimes."

I'd heard this reaction before, many times, in fact. I guess it's that way for lots of people—white, Anglo-Saxon protestants assuring them that they have a friend who's black or Muslim or gay or Jewish, and they're okay with it. I do know it's that way for Charlie, living as a gay man in corporate America. I've watched him go through it time and time again, usually at company functions or Christmas parties, when one of our co-workers has had too much to drink and has to prove how evolved he is by assuring Charlie that even though he's straight, he has a lot of respect for Charlie admitting that he's gay. Either that, or they feel the need to list their gay friends. I never understood the reaction, but then again, I'm not a WASP.

I wasn't dogmatic about my faith. I was Jewish by birth, rather than belief. Most of the time, I wasn't even sure if I believed in God. To be honest, the only time I really talked to Him was when I wanted something. Mine was a faith of convenience. But my parents were devout. And I'd experienced just as much intolerance from them as I had from other religions and races. More, even. Terri was a Christian—a Lutheran, just like her parents. We'd met in college. When I told my parents we were going to get married, they threw a fit, forbidding me to marry her and threatening to disown me if I went through with it. I just laughed and explained that I was an adult now, and while I loved and respected them, I could make my own decisions. Then, when they saw that I was serious, they pestered me about what faith our children would be raised in. It didn't matter to me, but my parents worried that their grandchildren wouldn't be real Jews, since Judaism is traditionally passed down through the mother's lineage. I wondered aloud if they'd love their grandchildren any less if they happened to be raised Lutheran. They didn't have an answer. I'd thought that would be the end of it. Figured they'd come to accept Terri as their daughter-in-law once we were married. But they didn't. My parents were just getting warmed up.

After the wedding, they demanded that a mezuzah be placed on the door of our house, to mark Jewish territory. Terri balked and told my mother exactly what she thought of the idea. Needless to say, relations with my family were strained from then on. I'd overheard them in private a few times, referring to Terri as a shikse. It's a term that's usually used jokingly, made popular by an old *Seinfeld* episode, but in Terri's case, they didn't mean it as a compliment.

After two years, Terri and I found out that we couldn't have children. Turned out I was sterile. Terri didn't want to adopt, and the whole point became moot anyway. Eventually, my parents dropped it.

But my heritage and our marriage didn't cause problems with just my side of the family. Terri's parents got in on the act as well, worrying about my immortal soul. Every chance they got, they'd witness to me about the glory of Christ. About how I had to be born again and needed to believe he was the Son of God, that he'd died on the cross for me. And how I should ask him to come into my heart and forgive my sins, number one of which was being born into Judaism rather than Christianity. It was very important to them that I believed Jesus was the messiah. We'd had several arguments about it. At least they'd never accused me of killing their Savior. But they never missed a chance to let me know about the day when Christ would return to earth and take the faithful home. According to them, Jews—even devout ones—weren't allowed on that ride. They called it the Rapture. I'd asked Craig about it once, when we were out at a bar, and he told me that not all Christians believed in the Rapture. According to him, it wasn't even mentioned in the Bible.

Another shrieking siren brought me back to the present. Frank put his hardhat back on and stared off into the distance again. I wondered about Frank's comment. Was he secretly anti-Semitic and trying to cover it up? No, I decided. I was on edge and overreacting. It was this situation. We were standing in the midst of a massive traffic jam. Dozens of people were injured and dozens more were apparently missing. This was not a normal, everyday commute. Frank was just as scared and freaked out as I was, and he was simply trying to make conversation by telling me about his Jewish friend. I let it go, and walked towards Charlie and the woman.

"I'll see if I can find someone with a cell phone that works," Frank called after me. "If I find one, I'll let you know."

"Sounds good."

"Hey," the guy from the Volvo shouted. "Where the hell do you think you're going?"

I stopped, turned and fought to keep the annoyance out of my voice.

"To help my friend and this woman. Her daughter is missing."

"Bullshit. You're not leaving the scene. You guys rear-ended me. I don't even have your insurance information yet. Just stay put until the cops get here."

"For fuck's sake," I sputtered. "Leave the scene? Take a look around you, dickhead. The entire interstate is one big scene. Where would I go?"

I turned my back on him and walked towards Charlie and the hysterical mother.

"Hey!" Volvo's shout was hoarse and shaky. "Don't you walk away from me. I said get back here, goddamn it."

"Fuck you," I called over my shoulder, and then punctuated it with, "Jackass."

His footsteps pounded across the asphalt. Before I could turn to face him, Charlie was at my side, his fists clenched. Several onlookers watched us warily. A few of them looked excited. Here was something to take their minds off their troubles: fellow commuters getting in a fistfight.

"Get out of my way," Volvo growled.

"Not another step, buddy." Charlie's expression was grim. Anger smoldered in his eyes.

Volvo stopped in his tracks, shaking with rage. "You guys fucking rear-ended me. I've got witnesses."

"Look," I shouted. "I don't know what your malfunction is, but in case you haven't noticed, you're not the only one in trouble here. Seriously. Take a good look around, man. Something's happened. Something is wrong. People are dead—and others are missing. Now, I'm sorry we hit you, but maybe you should have been paying attention to the road instead of your fucking cell phone!"

"You—"

Charlie stepped between us, and drew himself up to his full height. He jabbed a finger at the yuppie's chest. "That woman's baby is missing. We're going to help her find it. When we're done, if you still want to tangle, then I'll be glad to kick your ass. But if you don't back down right now, so help me God, I'll fucking kill you."

"You won't do shit."

Charlie smiled. "Try me."

Volvo's fists were clenched so tight that his knuckles had turned white. But he backed off.

"You just want to bang her," he accused Charlie from a safe distance. "Play Good Samaritan and then screw her later on tonight."

Charlie blew him a mock kiss. "Actually, you're more my type. What are you doing later on, after they clean up this mess and tow away the cars?"

Volvo's ears turned deep red, but he walked away. We watched him go as he shuffled towards his car, casting wary glances at us over his shoulder. The sun glinted off his Rolex watch.

"Too bad he's such a dick," Charlie said. "He's kind of cute."

I chuckled. "No accounting for taste."

The young mother crawled through the weeds and trash at the side of the road. "Britney? Baby?"

Charlie and I hurried to her side.

"We've got to find Britney," she sobbed. "Her car seat is empty. Where's my baby?"

"Don't worry," Charlie soothed. "We'll find her."

She tried to speak, but her words dissolved into tears. Her nose was still bleeding.

"Hey, Steve!"

I turned to see Frank running towards us.

"Sit down here," Charlie coaxed the woman, easing her onto the grass. "We'll find your daughter. She's got to be close by."

"Do you think so?"

"Sure." He smiled reassuringly. "With everything that's going on, we weren't properly introduced earlier. What's your name?"

"St-Stephanie." She wiped her bloody nose with the back of her hand.

"All right, Stephanie. My name's Charlie and this is Steve. We're going to help you look for Britney, okay?"

She sniffed and nodded.

Frank came up to us, panting and out of breath.

"You manage to get a hold of anybody?" I asked him.

"Cell phones are all on the fritz now, but I talked to a trucker in that rig over there. Nice guy. He's got a CB that's working. Said there's some weird shit going on."

Several other people converged on our location and began helping to search for baby Britney. Stephanie seemed to regain her resolve.

"My husband's missing, too," one woman sobbed, touching Stephanie's hand. "We were on the tour bus over there on the other side of the highway, on our way back from Atlantic City. I was asleep, and when I woke up after the crash, he was gone."

"Maybe he's helping someone else," Charlie suggested.

The woman nodded. "I guess that's possible." She sounded like she was trying to convince herself.

I pulled Frank aside. "What kind of weird shit did the trucker say is happening?"

"People are missing."

I snorted. "Yeah, I know that."

"But it's not just here: it's happening all around Baltimore; hospitals, schools, offices—everywhere. All of the highways look like this, and the drivers or passengers from some of the cars are missing. Four planes have already crashed at BWI and they've had a few more reporting that their pilot or co-pilot vanished in mid-air. A runaway train smashed into another one downtown."

I rubbed my aching head. "Let me guess. The conductor vanished?"

He nodded. "And it seems like everybody all over the city heard that trumpet sound, or whatever the hell it was."

"I don't believe it." I shook my head, stunned at how fast the paranoia and rumors had spread. It was the same way on September 11th, when people reported that planes were heading for Baltimore's Trade Center and the Aberdeen army base and Three Mile Island and Peachbottom nuclear power plants just over the border in Pennsylvania, and that the government had forced down a hijacked airliner over Canadian airspace—and of course none of it had turned out to be true. Now it was happening again.

"Listen," Frank said, "I'm just telling you what the trucker told me. You said it yourself, Steve: your friend's missing. And that woman's baby is missing, too. So are a lot of other folks."

I lowered my voice, making sure the others couldn't hear. "Her baby is either trapped in the wreckage or lying along the side of the road. Craig too, for that matter."

Frank stared into my eyes. "Do you really believe that?"

I opened my mouth to reply, and found that I couldn't, because deep down inside the answer was no. No, I didn't really believe that. As impossible as it all seemed, Frank was right. People were missing. Lots of people. All I had to do was listen, and I could hear their loved ones calling out for them, desperately searching through the snarled lanes of traffic.

Again I thought of Terri. There was a lump in my throat. "I need to get home."

Frank nodded. "We all do. Don't think we'll be going anywhere for a while, though. Not until they get a fleet of tow trucks in here and clear away some of these wrecked cars."

I glanced around for Charlie, and found him in a thin stand of trees alongside the highway, looking for Stephanie's baby. I walked towards him, and Frank followed along behind me. Charlie looked up as we approached. His face was covered with sweat, and a mosquito was biting his ear. He didn't seem to notice.

"What's up?" he asked.

Frank pointed at Charlie's feet. "Well, for starters, you're standing in a patch of poison ivy."

Charlie jumped out of the undergrowth, cursing. I reached out and swatted the mosquito away.

"Thanks." He rubbed his ear.

"Listen," I said, "I need to get home. I have to make sure Terri's okay."

"Terri?" He looked surprised. "Why wouldn't she be okay? She wasn't traveling in this. She's safe at home."

"At the very least, she'll be worried. You saw the traffic helicopter earlier. I'm sure this has made the news already. But it's more than that. Frank here overheard some things on a trucker's CB radio."

"What things?"

"Something's going on, Charlie. People have vanished into thin air, just like Craig."

He didn't reply. His Adam's apple bobbed up and down.

"Charlie—"

"I know," he interrupted me. "Just don't want to think about it. This kind of shit doesn't happen in real life."

Another scream interrupted him.

Charlie looked back out to the road. "But it *is* happening, isn't it? People are missing. Gone. Like they've been abducted by aliens or something."

Frank pulled a red bandana from his back pocket, removed his hardhat and mopped his brow.

"Steve," Charlie continued, his voice barely a whisper, "Craig disappeared before we crashed."

"What?"

He sighed. "I didn't tell you before because it sounded crazy. Shit, I didn't believe it myself. Thought maybe I banged my head in the crash or something. Got mixed up. Hallucinated. But that's not what happened. He disappeared in mid-fucking-sentence, dude. I saw it happen. He was there, and then we heard that blast, and he was gone. Then we wrecked, and after that I was confused, and then you woke up and—what the hell is going on?"

I shook my head. "I don't know, man. But right now, I need to get home to Terri. I can't explain it, but I've got a bad feeling. Come with me?"

Charlie, Hector, Craig and I carpooled because we all lived in the same town, Shrewsbury, which was just across the border in Pennsylvania. Charlie was single and rented a tiny efficiency apartment over the hardware store on Main

Street. Terri and I owned a house just a few blocks away, and both Hector and Craig had lived on the outskirts of town in the new development that had gone in after the Wal-Mart. The town of Shrewsbury was basically just a bed-and-breakfast for people like us, people who were born and raised in Maryland and worked in Baltimore, but had moved out of the state to get away from the higher taxes.

"Come on," I urged. "Please? Let's go home."

Charlie pointed at the people combing the road for Stephanie's daughter. "But what about her baby?"

"There's nothing we can do." I hated how callous I sounded, but my mind was made up. "Let's face it—they're not going to find anything. Britney is gone."

"They might," he insisted. "She could have been thrown from the car."

"Stephanie's car isn't even damaged," I said. "Her daughter is among the missing. We can't help her. Maybe when the cops get here, they can do something."

"If it's as bad as I think it is," Frank added, "then I imagine the National Guard is probably out in force. Maybe we should wait for them to show up."

"And do what?" I asked. "If it really is that bad, their hands are full. If people are disappearing, if planes and trains are crashing like you say they are, then the National Guard are going to be doing more than clearing traffic jams. There's liable to be riots, looting—all kinds of shit."

Frank wrung his bandana out and shoved it back in his pocket. "Yeah, I guess you're right. Hadn't thought of that."

Another scream rang out, followed by a horn.

"So where do you guys live?" Frank asked, shuffling his feet.

"Shrewsbury," Charlie told him. "Just off Exit One on the Pennsylvania side."

"I'm pretty close to you," Frank said. "Parkton—last exit in Maryland."

"That's where the Park-and-Ride is, right?" Charlie asked.

"Yeah. Listen, you guys care if I tag along with you?"

I shrugged. "Sure. There's safety in numbers."

"Safety?" Charlie cocked his head. "Safe from what?"

Instead of replying, I checked my cell phone. There was still no service, but the clock was working. It was 5:30 p.m.

"Britney!" Stephanie screamed from the tall grass. "Where are you, baby?"

Britney didn't answer.

None of the missing did.

* * *

Twenty minutes later, after weaving our way through the snarled traffic, we reached Exit 18—Warren Road and Cockeysville. Those were twenty minutes of dazed and hysterical commuters, wrecked vehicles, and mangled, bloody bodies. Twenty minutes of despair and hopelessness that grew with each tortured cry. Twenty minutes of diesel fumes and burning rubber. Twenty minutes that seemed like an eternity.

We stopped to rest and took seats on the guardrail, right beneath the exit sign. Frank breathed heavily, gasping for air, and the veins stood out in his face. He looked like he was ready to have a heart attack. All three of us were drenched with sweat, and Charlie and I both had dark circles under the arms of our dress shirts.

"Whew," Frank panted. "Talk about taking the long way home."

"I'm still not sure we should be doing this," Charlie grumbled.

"Both of us got banged up when Hector hit the construction barrier. Should we be walking this far? I don't know about you, Steve, but my head hurts. What if we've got concussions or something?"

I cracked my neck to get rid of the stiffness. "I don't care. Only thing I want to do now is get home to Terri."

There was a stone quarry to our right, nestled in the shallow valley below. One of the facility's buildings was on fire. Orange flames flickered across the rooftop, and thick, black smoke poured from the doors and windows, drifting up the hill and billowing over the highway. Workers scurried around the building like panicking ants. A few more employees lay on the ground, unmoving. There were no fire trucks or ambulances in sight. We'd only seen one state police cruiser since the Timonium exit, and it was deserted, parked along the side of the road. I'd wondered if the officer disappeared with the rest or had abandoned the vehicle afterward.

My headache grew worse.

"You guys got any aspirin?"

They both shook their heads.

"I'd kill for a beer right now," Frank said.

I wondered about the bars. Would they be jam-packed tonight, filled to overflowing as word of the disaster spread and people's loved ones didn't come home? Would people flock to them, seeking comfort in the presence of others? Or would they all go to church or temple instead? Personally, I'd always thought that there wasn't much difference between a tavern and a place of worship.

Frank watched the flames spread in the quarry. A second building caught fire.

"Where are the authorities?" he asked. "Why aren't they doing something? That whole place is gonna be toast. And it looks like they've got injured."

Charlie took off his shoe and shook a stone out. "Busy elsewhere, I guess."

"They can't all be elsewhere," Frank said. "Some of them should have responded to the fire by now. At least an ambulance."

"Maybe they can't get through," I said.

Charlie frowned. "Like we said earlier, maybe they're shorthanded. Or some of them might have disappeared, too."

I considered this. There was no rhyme or reason to the missing people, nothing to indicate why they'd been taken. From what we'd seen, it affected all races, genders and age groups. The only thing I'd noticed was that we hadn't seen a single infant. Just lots of empty car seats. Were all of the babies missing? I wondered if this could be the glorious Rapture that Terri and her parents had talked about, but decided against it. I'd seen several priests, nuns and preachers among the survivors, and a dozen occupied vehicles with Jesus bumper stickers and license plates. Plenty of Christians were left behind. And Craig was a Christian too, and hadn't necessarily believed in the Rapture, yet he was missing along with the rest. The only common denominator was that everybody had vanished at the same time, immediately after that bizarre blast—except for the black guy, Gabriel. He'd vanished later, after helping me. He'd told me something, just before he disappeared. I tried to remember what it was but the words wouldn't come. Trying to figure it out made my head hurt, so I stopped.

"Maybe it really was a terrorist attack," Charlie said. "Maybe they got their hands on some kind of black ops weapon."

"It isn't that," Frank replied.

"How do you know?"

Frank shrugged. "I don't. I'd just rather not think about the possibility, is all."

"So what is it then?"

"It just is what it is."

A disheveled man wandered towards us. He reeked, the stench reminding me of a litter box. The crotch of his trousers had a wet splotch where he'd pissed himself. There was a long, bloody gash on his forehead.

"Excuse me." His eyes looked dazed. "Do you guys have the time?"

I checked my cell phone. "Almost six."

"Thanks. How about a cigarette? Got one of those?"

All three of us shook our heads.

The man lowered his voice to a conspiratorial whisper. "Need a smoke. I keep thinking that maybe I should find an unguarded gas station and steal some cigarettes. But I've never done anything like that before."

"I wouldn't try it," Charlie said. "The police are probably out by now, patrolling for that kind of thing. I'm sure things will be back to normal by tomorrow."

"Normal?" The man blinked at him. "I guess you guys haven't heard."

I looked up, holding my breath to avoid breathing in his stink.

"Heard what?"

"Alien abduction," he gasped. "Everybody's talking about it. All these folks that are missing? They were abducted by aliens. You know—the Grays, like you see on TV? The ones they talk about late at night on the radio? We're under attack!"

"Get the fuck outta here." Frank spat on the pavement. "Little gray men, my ass."

"I'm serious," the man insisted. "This is happening all over the world, not just here. New York, Washington, London, Moscow, Budapest, Jerusalem—you name it. I heard they even got the President and some of his cabinet. Disappeared right out of the White House. That's why he hasn't addressed the nation. Famous people, too. You guys know that rapper, Prosper Johnson?"

Frank shook his head. Charlie and I nodded. Terri and I had seen him in concert the first year we were dating, back when we still did fun things like that (these days, as we got a little older, we were happy to stay home and play a game of *Uno*).

"Well," the man continued, "you know how he was up for the Nobel Peace Prize, on account of stopping the violence in L.A., right? He was giving a speech on TV. All the cable news stations were carrying it. He vanished live, on camera."

"Seriously?" Charlie asked.

The man raised his right hand. "Swear to God. Disappeared in mid fucking sentence. Fucking aliens beamed him up or something, just like everybody else. People are going nuts. Everything's in chaos."

"Alien abduction," Charlie said. "You really believe that?"

"You got a better explanation?"

None of us did, and the man stumbled away. We watched him stop and bum a cigarette off another man, and tell him the same story.

"So," Charlie said. "Prosper Johnson is among the missing. That's too bad."

"I hate that rap shit," Frank muttered. "Bunch a black guys singing about how much money they got, and how many bitches they got and this gun and that gun."

Charlie threw a pebble over the guardrail. "It's not just 'black guys'. There are plenty of white rappers."

"What's your point?"

"Well, no offense, Frank, but that's kind of a racist statement."

Frank scowled. "How is that racist?"

"You're implying that all black people rap. That's like saying all Asians are good at math, or that all gay men watch *Will and Grace*. It's a stereotype. I'm gay, and I hate that fucking show."

"I ain't a racist."

"You work in construction, right?"

Frank nodded.

"You mean to tell me you and your buddies never stood around on the site and told jokes about queers?"

"Don't start with that politically-correct bullshit. Talk about stereotypes—you think all construction workers stand around and make fun of gay people and whistle at women? You think we're all just a bunch of ignorant, uneducated rednecks?"

Charlie opened his mouth to respond, but Frank cut him off and continued.

"You ever tell a Polack joke?"

Charlie shrugged, then reluctantly nodded.

"So I could call you a racist, too, then. You're making a joke—a stereotype—about how stupid my ancestors are supposed to be. Well, I ain't stupid and I ain't a racist. All I did was state a fact. Most rappers are black. That's where it started, right?"

Charlie turned to me and changed the subject. "How far is it to Shrewsbury, you think?"

I took my tie off and wrapped it around my head for a sweatband. "About thirty more miles."

"And how far have we gone?"

"One mile."

"Shit." He stood up. "At this rate, it'll be morning before we get home. We'd better keep moving."

I tried calling Terri again, but there was still no service, not even when we passed directly beneath a cell phone tower.

We stayed on the side of the road, trying to keep a steady pace. The tension eased between Charlie and Frank. We made small talk. Frank talked about his job, and we told him about ours. Then we came to a bridge. The guardrail forced us into traffic, and we walked between the cars. People leaned back in their seats with the windows rolled down, or lounged on the hoods. Some asked for news, or for help finding a companion, but we had time for neither.

As we passed the Shawan Road exit, I looked to my right at the shopping center, light rail station, hotel and convention center. People milled about in the parking lots. Cars moved on the streets, albeit slowly. The traffic lights at the bottom of the exit ramp still worked and, for the most part, drivers obeyed them. On the surface, things looked surprisingly normal, but I knew it was an illusion. I wondered how many people had vanished in the darkness of the movie theatre, or from the swimming pool at the hotel, or sitting on the train. Did their loved ones even know they were missing yet? Did they expect them to come home tonight?

Footsteps thudded on the macadam ahead of us. We looked up as a guy in a charcoal-colored business suit ran past us, shouting at the top of his lungs to nobody in particular that the stock market had crashed. His tie fluttered behind him as he dashed by. He skidded in the gravel, almost losing his balance. Then, without even glancing at Frank, Charlie or myself, he vaulted over the guardrail and slid down the embankment. A cloud of dust marked his passage.

We passed by a Cadillac with its driver's door hanging open. The keys dangled from the ignition, and were turned to the accessory option. The radio was on, tuned to the news, and sure enough, the stock market had crashed, just like the man had been shouting. I wondered if this was his car. A cell phone lay on the passenger seat. The floor was littered with fast food bags and Styrofoam coffee cups.

"Should we take the car?" Charlie asked.

I stared at him in disbelief. "This isn't Thunderdome, man. Stealing cars is still against the law."

"Well it ain't like whoever left it here needs it. Maybe the driver vanished."

"That's not the point."

Charlie glanced up the highway. "We've got a long walk home, Steve. We'd be there in an hour with the Caddy."

"No." Frank stepped forward. "Much as I hate to say it—believe me, my feet hurt already—but a car will just slow us down. Look how congested things are. Traffic's not moving."

We listened to the frantic reporter for a minute. The news was bad, getting worse by the second, and the reporter's voice kept breaking. The world's financial markets were in an uproar. Millions were reported missing, including politicians, C.E.O.s, world leaders, religious figures and celebrities. They'd vanished from their homes, their cars and their places of business. According to NASA, a Russian cosmonaut had even gone missing off the International Space Station, leaving one countryman and an American astronaut behind. Planes fell from the sky. Trains crashed. The highways were deathtraps. A nuclear reactor at a power plant in China was reportedly in meltdown. Fires and rioting had broken out in just about every major city on Earth, and there were dozens of reports of authorities shooting looters and declaring martial law amidst the unrest. Religious fighting swept through Asia and the Middle East, with the worst of it centered in Israel. All of this within a few hours. I wondered how much worse things would get before it was over.

Charlie gave one last, lingering look at the Cadillac, and then we continued on, trying to ignore the screams and plaintive calls for loved ones from those left behind. I saw surreal signs of the missing as well: an abandoned baby doll in the middle lane, an empty wheelchair, a pair of empty shoes, a castaway purse, and a cluster of roadside construction vehicles—steamroller, bulldozer, and dump trucks. Judging by the path of destruction, it looked like the steamroller had kept going after its operator disappeared, flattening orange traffic cones and toolboxes.

A few minutes later, we came across a tractor-trailer. The seal on the back door had been broken and a gang of youths was looting it, hauling away televisions and DVD players. Most of the teens were armed. Stranded motorists minded their own business, pretending they didn't see it happening. Charlie, Frank and I did the same. There were no cops around. Not even the distant sound of sirens. The last thing we needed right now was more trouble, and besides, stopping would just slow us down even more and impede me getting home to Terri. So they were stealing electronics. It wasn't our problem. It was somebody else's.

The construction ended after Shawan Road and the lanes expanded again, making it easier for us to navigate. Traffic was less snarled here, and although there were still plenty of wrecked cars with missing, injured, or dead occupants, many more had driven on. Several passed slowly by us, and Frank choked on the exhaust fumes.

"Maybe it's clearing up," Charlie said.

I nodded, doubtful.

Charlie grabbed my arm. "Let's go back and get the Caddy. There's no sense walking anymore. Traffic's moving."

"We're not stealing a car," I said. "That would make us no better than those kids ripping off that home electronics rig."

The driver of an ice delivery van was handing out his

melting inventory for free to passersby. We stopped and got a bag, and sucked on ice cubes as we walked. It started to get dark about 6:30 p.m., and though the sun was still clinging to the horizon, the air grew chilly. More cars passed us, but nobody offered a ride. We saw other people walking, too.

"Maybe we should have waited with our vehicles after all," Frank said. "Charlie's right. Looks like things are starting to move again."

I shook my head. "It'll be hours—maybe even morning—before they get this mess sorted out. They're moving, but I bet it gets blocked up again around the turn. I'm going on. If we can hitch a ride later on, then that's all the better, but I'm not stealing a car."

Down in the valley, on the north side of the highway, a church burned. It looked deserted.

Charlie asked, "I wonder if Stephanie ever found Britney?"

"I doubt it," Frank said. "I think there's a lot of people who aren't coming home tonight."

"Maybe not," I said, "but I am."

Charlie and Frank stopped, and looked back the way we'd come.

I thought about Terri, and how we'd parted that morning. It wasn't bad, not at all. No fighting or arguing or anything. It just wasn't—special. The same daily routine we'd both grown used to. The alarm went off at five. I got up. She hit snooze. I took a shower while she hit snooze two more times. Then I tickled her to get her moving. While she showered, I made a pot of coffee—always something good, Columbian or Kenyan, usually. We'd never been big breakfast eaters, so we sat in the living room and watched the news and drank our coffee. We didn't say much. We never did. Neither one of us were what you'd call morning people, and conversation wasn't first on our list until the caffeine kicked in. Then Hector pulled up out front and honked the horn. I gave Terri a quick kiss on the lips, and told her I loved her, and hurried for the door. She'd told me she loved me and that it was my turn to cook dinner when I got home, and then shut the door behind me. In a few minutes she'd start work as well. Luckily for Terri, she worked from our home.

Typical suburban morning, and I'd gotten the chance to tell her I loved her. But I hadn't really said it. I'd mouthed the words, and I'd meant them, of course, but that's all they were—perfunctory words, just like the kiss and the coffee and the snooze button on the alarm clock. They were ritual. I needed to tell her from my heart, to say more than just "I love you." I needed to hold her in my arms and make sure she understood me; that she knew I really meant it, and wasn't just going through the motions. Needed her to know I was okay.

Needed to know that she was okay.

"Steve?" Charlie interrupted my thoughts. "What about Hector's body? Are we doing the right thing, leaving him behind like that?"

I turned. "Look, if you guys want to go back, I understand. But I've got to get home to Terri."

I kept walking. After a moment, they followed me.

* * *

We reached the overpass for Thornton Mill Road by 8:00 p.m., and that was when things started to get worse. The interstate crossed over Western Run Creek. Darkness had fallen by then, throwing everything into shadow. As we tromped over the bridge, I heard the creek trickling below us, but couldn't see it. The sound was eerie. Ghostly, as if the creek had vanished too and its spirit was haunting this place. Traffic was blocked again. A tanker truck lay on its side in front of the overpass. Those with four-wheel drive vehicles and motorcycles went around it, driving up over the embankment and onto the road above. Others parked their cars and milled about, exchanging gossip and small talk. I noticed that nobody was getting too close to the wrecked tanker, and when I saw the Hazmat markings on its side, and the dark stains where liquid had spilled out onto the road, I understood why.

Away from the wreckage, someone had started a bonfire in a rusty fifty-five gallon drum and several people were gathered around it, warming themselves by the fire. Many of them stared upward, and when we got closer, we did the same.

A man hung from the overpass, the rope around his neck twisting slowly in the night breeze. A piece of cardboard had been stapled to his chest, the words CHILD MOLESTER scrawled on it with black magic marker in big block letters. His face looked strange in the flickering firelight. Weird shadows danced across his skin. His bowels had let go, and shit had rolled down his legs and splattered onto the pavement beneath him. The crowd kept its distance from this, too.

Charlie made a noise like someone had punched him in the stomach. He turned his head and threw up all over the road.

Frank said, "What the fuck happened here?"

Cautiously, we approached the group gathered around the fire. They eyed us suspiciously. One of them, an older Hispanic man with a silver beard, nodded.

"How you doing?"

"As good as can be expected," Frank said. "We walked from Timonium. You folks care if we rest here for a minute?"

"Help yourself."

The man moved aside, and the others followed his lead, making room for us. They seemed to relax a bit. They were a weird assortment, business suits and blue jeans, silk and denim, gold jewelry and dirty flannel.

"I'm Tony," the guy with the silver beard said. "Was on my way to work when it happened. Guess I'll have to use a sick day. I work nights at the McCormick plant."

I introduced Charlie, Frank and myself. Nods were exchanged, but nobody shook hands or traded business cards.

Tony studied us. "You guys walked all the way from Timonium?"

"Yeah." I nodded. "Traffic's at a standstill down there."

"It's not moving too quickly here, either," a middle-aged black woman noted. "Not with that overturned truck blocking the road."

"Yeah," Frank said, "but at least it's still moving here. The four-wheel drives and the motorcycles are getting through. Down there, the only thing moving is the wind."

"Lots of accidents?" Tony asked.

I warmed my hands over the open flames. "Yeah, a bunch of wrecks and lots of people hurt or dead. How about here?"

"Here, too. Lots of dead—and even more missing."

"Do they know what caused it?" Frank rubbed the back of his neck.

"So far, we've heard everything from terrorists to aliens. Somebody even said it was some kind of hallucinogen, sprayed through the air by a crop duster or something."

Tony looked up at the moon. I noticed his eyes avoided the hanging man.

"There's all kinds of rumors and speculation," he said, "but no real news. We had our car radios on for a while, but none of us wanted to kill our batteries or run out of gas. Last we heard, nobody knew the cause. Only thing we know for sure is that everybody heard that trumpet noise."

"Us, too," I confirmed.

The black woman laughed, but there was no humor in it. "They heard it around the world. Toronto, Los Angeles, Paris, Beijing—and soon as it happened, millions of people vanished in an instant."

Frank stepped back from the fire and mopped his brow. "What's the government doing about it?"

Tony snorted. "Right now? Nothing."

"But they've got to do something," Frank said. "The Department of Homeland Security and FEMA—that's what they're for. At the very least, they should mobilize the National Guard. What the hell's the President doing? Hiding on Air Force One again while everything turns to shit?"

"No," Tony whispered. "The President's among the missing."

I shook my head. The guy we'd encountered earlier, the one who'd pissed himself, had been right after all. I wondered if he'd been right about the gray aliens part, too.

Conversation died after that. One man produced a bottle of diet soda, and another had a whiskey flask. Both were passed around, along with cigarettes. The group drank and smoked in silence.

Finally, Charlie broke the quiet. "So, anybody want to tell us what happened to the guy hanging from the noose?"

The group shifted uneasily. Charlie pointed but none of them would look directly at the swinging corpse. Nobody answered him, so Charlie tried again.

"He's like the proverbial elephant in the corner, isn't he? Aren't any of you going to tell us what happened?"

They glanced at one another.

"Skinheads," Tony said. "A gang of skinheads; six of them. There was a little girl. Both her parents were missing. That guy—" he cocked a thumb at the swinging dead man, "tried to coax her inside his car. A lot of us saw it, and it was clear that the girl didn't know him. She started yelling and ran away. So we all confronted him. He denied it at first, but the girl swore she didn't know him, and that he'd shown her his 'wee wee.' That was all it took. Before we could do anything about it, the skinheads jumped him."

The black woman pulled her hands back from the fire. "Beat the hell out of him is what they did."

"Yeah," Tony agreed. "They did that, too. Then they put that sign on him and strung him up. After that, they torched his car."

He pointed to the far lane and, sure enough, there was a burned out steel shell sitting on four heat-warped tires.

Charlie shuddered. "And you people just let them?"

"Hey," Tony said, "there were seven of them."

"I thought you said there were six?"

"Six. Seven. What's the difference? They all had guns. A few of us tried calling the cops, but our cell phones aren't working. And besides…"

"What?"

Tony shrugged. "The guy deserved it. I mean, think about what he did. He was going to kidnap and rape a little girl who'd lost her parents. He'd have probably killed her after he was done. You see it every day on the news."

Charlie looked around. "Where's the little girl? Is she okay?"

The black woman pointed. "She's asleep in the back of that van over there. She's safe. We're watching over her, until . . ."

"Until what?"

She stared Charlie in the eyes. "Until things get back to normal. Until someone comes along and tells us what to do."

Frank took a sip of whiskey as it passed by him. He closed his eyes and a look of sheer bliss crossed his face.

"Besides," Tony said, "better him than us, right? They were skinheads. They could just have easily turned on us."

"That's right," the black woman agreed.

"So where are these skinheads now?" I asked.

The black woman pointed up the highway. "They moved on when it was over. Good riddance, if you ask me."

"Guess they didn't want to hang around." Tony smiled at his own gallows humor.

"I don't believe this shit," Charlie said. "Skinheads, my ass."

Tony's smile turned to a frown. "What? Are you calling me a liar?"

I took Charlie by the arm. "Come on. Let it alone."

"Fuck that! They—"

"I mean it, Charlie." I squeezed his arm hard, insisting. "Let's go."

"But—"

I thanked the group gathered around the fire. "Appreciate your help. We need to get moving."

They nodded in understanding, but several of them, Tony and the black woman included, glared at Charlie. He let me lead him away. A moment later, Frank followed us.

"Where you guys heading, anyway?" Tony called out.

"Pennsylvania," I said, without looking back.

"What's in Pennsylvania?"

"My wife."

"What else?"

"That's what we intend to find out."

Frank, Charlie and I continued on side by side, and when we passed under the body, and heard the rope creaking, none of us glanced upward.

There was no time to hang around, after all.

* * *

We didn't talk for a long time as all of us were out of breath. My thoughts were on Terri. Random images, really. When we met in college. Our first date. First argument. First time we made love. Our wedding day, and when we moved into the house. I missed her.

Frank finally broke the silence. "Anybody know a good joke?"

"How's this?" Charlie said. "A Jew, a Polack, and a homo are walking down the middle of the interstate at night..."

Frank and I both grinned.

"What's the punch-line?" I asked.

Charlie shrugged. "I don't know. Guess we'll find out soon enough."

Half a mile later, we came across the Soapbox Man, as Charlie called him. Wild-eyed and frothing, his clothes and hair in disarray, he'd climbed atop the hood of an abandoned car and was preaching the Gospel to all who would listen. Surprisingly, he'd attracted a small crowd. They passed a bottle of wine around and listened, staring at him with rapt attention, their eyes shining in the darkness, their mouths glistening wet.

"It's the end times," he hissed. "The angel has played the trumpet and the seven seals will be opened! Blood. Fire.

Disease. And another angel will appear, the angel of death, and he shall ride a pale horse."

We crept past, trying to avoid making eye contact with the crazed preacher.

"This is your fault," the man roared, jabbing a finger at the crowd. "You have brought this upon yourselves, because you had ears but did not hear. You had eyes but did not see. You denied God, and put other gods before Him. Now He has called His faithful home, and has left me behind to warn you of what will come. You removed Him from your schools and courtrooms and allowed sodomites to marry and babies to be killed in their wombs. Now you will pay the price for your sins. This is the start of the long, dark night."

"Fucking nutcase," Frank grumbled. "As if things weren't bad enough."

After we'd safely made it past the group and were out of earshot, we picked up our pace again.

"Think that's true?" Charlie asked.

Frank snorted. "What? That God took everybody away because of abortion and gay marriage?"

"Well…yeah."

"Fucking bullshit," Frank said. "I've got an easier time believing in little gray men, and I don't believe that either."

I grinned. "I take it you're not religious?"

Frank scowled. "Used to be, until my wife left. Came home from work one day and she'd cleaned the house out. Left me a dinner plate, fork and spoon. And the lawnmower. Come to find out she'd been cheating on me for the last six months. Ended up moving in with the guy, and left me holding the mortgage. We got divorced. I filed for bankruptcy while she got remarried."

Charlie whistled. "Damn. That sucks, man."

"Yeah, it does. After that, I just quit believing. Seemed easier that way. I mean, you take a look around and all you see are wars and famine and people dying of cancer and little kids getting snatched by sick fucks like the guy back at the bridge. There's just too much heartache and pain.

Where's the love? God's supposed to be love, right? I don't think He exists. Think we're all walking around trying to live our lives according to a book that was pieced together when dinosaurs still roamed the earth."

"So you're an atheist?" I asked.

"Yep," Frank said. "And probably going straight to Hell for it. Heh—I don't believe in God but I still believe in Hell. Ain't that funny?"

Charlie and I agreed that it was.

"How about you guys?" Frank asked. "You atheists?"

"I'm agnostic, I guess," Charlie answered. "I believe in something. I just don't know what. Certainly not the Christian God. His believers say that He hates me. I've heard that all my life. Supposedly, He nuked an entire city just because of people like me. So fuck that—I ain't following. But I do think there's something out there. Something that maybe we're not meant to understand. I believe in ghosts and stuff like that, so I guess that's proof of an afterlife."

Frank nodded. "But not a Heaven?"

"No," Charlie said. "At least, not the way you mean. No clouds and people with wings on their backs, flying around and playing the harp. If you want to see that, there's a gay bar in York I can take you to."

Frank started laughing and Charlie joined him. They both stopped, clutching their bellies and slapping each other on the shoulder. Despite my eagerness to get home, I was glad for the break, and even happier to see that the tension between the two was easing.

When they'd gotten their breath back, we started down the road again.

"How about you, Steve?" Frank asked. "What do you believe?"

"I don't know. I was born and raised Jewish. My wife and her parents are born-again Christians. I don't know what that makes me. I guess I don't really believe in anything, other than that I wish everybody could get along."

Charlie nodded. "I can't remember who said it, but there's a quote that goes, 'There's enough religion in the world to make people hate one another, but not enough to make them love one another.'"

"I agree with that," Frank said.

We walked on in silence. A group of crows were gathered along the side of the road, picking at a corpse. In the darkness, I couldn't tell if it was a man or a woman, or what had killed it. Stranded motorists ignored the birds. One of the scavengers took flight with something pink hanging from its beak.

A murder, I thought. *A group of crows is called a murder.*

"But what if they're right?" Charlie asked again. "The Soapbox Man and his crowd. What if this really was the Rapture or the Second Coming or whatever they call it?"

Frank shrugged. "If that's true, then God called everybody home and we don't get to go."

"Sure we do," I said. "We're walking home right now."

"Yeah," Frank replied. "But to get to the home they're talking about, we'd have an awful long way to walk."

I sighed. "Seems to me like we have a long walk ahead of us either way."

"Yeah," Frank agreed. "Wish we'd have brought along some of that whiskey those people back at the fire gave us."

"I've got a new joke," Charlie said. "A Jew, a Polack, and a homo are walking to Heaven, pissed off that God left them behind..."

"What's the punch line?" Frank asked.

"I don't know." Charlie smiled. "Like I said earlier, we'll just have to wait and see."

Charlie's words ran through my mind. Home. Heaven. They were pretty much the same thing, as far as I was concerned. Christians said that when they died, they went home to be with the Lord. They called Heaven home. My heaven was home, too—at home with my wife. I'd walk all night to be with her again, if I had to. And if God really had called His children home and took them all to Heaven, then I'd walk there to find her, too.

In either case, it was a long way to walk.

* * *

We reached Exit 24—Butler and Sparks—around 8:40 p.m. The suburbs and industrial parks had given way to woodlands and farms. Lots of cars traveled past us now, both on-road and off. Those with four-wheel drive raced through the fields and pastures, short-cutting around the slow-moving traffic. Some without four-wheel drive tried it too, and wound up stuck in the mud. We had to raise our voices over the spinning tires and blaring horns as they splattered each other's windshields with mud.

We stuck close to the guardrail as the traffic passed. Frank and Charlie looked as tired as I felt. The cold air raised gooseflesh on my sweaty skin. The muscles in my legs ached and my feet had blisters on them. When I stumbled, Charlie caught me.

"We should rest again," he suggested.

I shook my head. "Can't. Need to get home to Terri."

"You sound like a broken record, dude. You're not going to do Terri any good if you end up lying alongside the highway, dying from exhaustion."

"He's right," Frank panted. "I ain't as young as you guys. I need another break."

Reluctantly, I allowed Charlie to guide me over to the guardrail. We sat down on it. Another vehicle passed by. The woman behind the wheel looked shell-shocked. She stared straight ahead, her eyes not seeing.

A guy in a mud-splattered olive trench coat approached us. He didn't seem wary or afraid. His head was shaved, but long, wispy sideburns framed his leering face. The right lens in his glasses was cracked in a spider-web pattern. He smelled like booze.

"Hi." He smiled. "My name's Carlton. What's yours?"

I returned his smile, still unsure of his motives.

"I'm Steve. This is Charlie and Frank."

"Nice to meet you."

"I take it you got stranded, too?"

He ignored my question. "The mall is menstruating."

"What?"

More cars filed past us.

"The mall, down in Hunt Valley? It's menstruating. A great ocean floods forth."

"Uh, you mean...bleeding?"

Carlton nodded vigorously. "Really. It is. Just like in the Bible. 'And behold, the malls shall menstruate.' The Book of Meat, chapter twelve; verse two."

Frank groaned under his breath. Carlton didn't seem to notice.

"There's cheese in his head," our new friend continued. "Fishy-fleshed cheese, just like they said there'd be."

"That's nice," I said, giving Frank and Charlie a nervous glance.

First it was the Soapbox Man, shouting and preaching from the hood of his car. Now this. I wondered just how many people had gone insane in the immediate aftermath of the disappearances.

"Are you folks going home?" Carlton asked, smoothing the wrinkles from his trench coat.

Charlie and Frank remained speechless, and I hesitated. Clearly, the guy was drunk or insane—or both. The last thing I wanted was a crazy person following us home. But before I could distract him, Frank spoke up.

"Yeah, we're just trying to get home. Gotta be moving on now, actually."

Carlton glanced down the highway, staring into the darkness. Then he looked back at us and smiled. His eyes seemed to twinkle.

"You can't go home. The others went home. He called them home. But not us. We've been left behind."

I shivered in the darkness. Beside me, I felt Charlie do the same. Could it be a coincidence that we'd just had this conversation, or was something else at work?

Frank cleared his throat. "It was nice talking to you, Carlton."

Carlton shuffled away from us, then turned around. "This is level six, if you come through the Labyrinth. Level six. Soon, if we stay here, we'll all have to wear the mark. If we want to buy anything, we'll have to wear it. The number is six six six. That's the number of the Beast. We'll wear it, and then we'll get really painful sores, and the seas will turn to blood, just like the mall did."

None of us responded. What do you say to something like that?

"I'm getting out," he said. "I know a doorway."

He walked on, and we watched him go. He stopped farther up the road and talked to a group of migrant workers sitting in the back of a stalled pick-up truck. As we listened to their conversation, it became clear to us that none of the men spoke English, but that was okay, because we weren't sure that Carlton did either.

Another helicopter hovered overhead, low enough to stir up roadside litter and other debris. Hamburger wrappers, cigarette butts, newspapers and plastic cups swirled in a funnel cloud. People on the ground waved their arms and shouted for help, but the chopper flew on. The crowd cursed the pilot.

Charlie took a deep breath and exhaled. "I've been thinking."

"What about?" I turned to him.

"That guy back there at the Thornton Mill Road overpass."

"Tony? The one at the fire?"

"Yeah, him. I think he was lying about the skinheads. I mean, I've got no love for skinheads, don't get me wrong. But it seems like anytime we need a cultural boogeyman in this country, we lay it on a group like that. Skinheads. Muslim terrorists. Satanic daycare instructors. Republicans."

"What's your point?" Frank asked.

"What if it wasn't skinheads that hanged that guy? What if it was Tony and the other people that were there?"

I rubbed my tired eyes. "Come on, Charlie. You saw them. Most of that group were business people, just like us. Regular people. They're not going to resort to vigilante justice."

"Why not? Things have gotten real weird real quick. The mob rules, man. People have vanished, authorities aren't around, the survivors are scared, and nobody knows what's going on. Sounds like a recipe for disaster to me."

A black Labrador scampered by, its nose to the ground. When Charlie called out to it, the dog ran away, tail tucked between its legs. It must have belonged to somebody because it had a bright red collar around its neck, complete with dog tags. Whimpering, it disappeared.

"I'm starting to think it's true." Frank scratched the back of his neck.

"What?" Charlie asked. "That regular, everyday people hung that guy?"

"No. That aliens abducted everybody. It sounds silly, but could that actually happen?"

"There's no such things as aliens," I said. "It's just another bullshit rumor. They don't exist."

Frank gazed up at the stars. "Just like God..."

"So what's your theory, Steve?" Charlie asked. "We've seen a lot more since it first happened. Where do you think Craig and all these other people went?"

We watched as a Lexus, its speakers rattling with a thudding bass line, swerved to avoid a pedestrian. The driver blew his horn. The man in the road shook his fist and shouted curses.

"I don't know," I admitted, after the car had passed. "But it's not fucking aliens and it's not the Rapture. There has to be a reasonable explanation for what's happened."

"Maybe the scientists did something," Frank said.

"Which scientists?" Charlie asked.

Frank shrugged. "I don't know. Any of them. Maybe there was some kind of accident."

I considered the possibility—a malfunction while experimenting with stealth technology or particle acceleration or teleportation. There was supposed to be a government laboratory somewhere in Pennsylvania that fooled with stuff like that, but those options didn't seem any more plausible than an invisible alien fleet abducting everybody. Not to me, at least.

We shielded our eyes against another pair of approaching headlights—the car was hugging the shoulder, rather than creeping along with the rest of the traffic. The car's horn blared, loud and insistent. All three of us jumped up from our seat, and I almost fell over the guardrail and down the embankment. The horn grew deafening.

"Look out!" Frank shouted.

A black Volvo bore down on us, tires crunching in the gravel along the side of the road. It swerved away at the last second, weaving back into traffic.

Charlie gasped. "That motherfucker..."

Our friend, the yuppie from earlier in the day, rolled down his passenger-side window and flipped us his middle finger as he rolled past.

"Hey," he laughed. "Your friend's still back there in Timonium with a pipe through his head!"

"It's him," Charlie shouted, pointing. "The guy from the crash. The one that wanted to sue us!"

"You guys need a ride?"

The Volvo inched forward, moving farther away from us.

I swallowed. "Are you serious?"

"No." The yuppie laughed. "Fuck you."

Then he swerved back onto the shoulder and raced up the highway, scattering other pedestrians out of his way.

"He needs his ass kicked," Frank sputtered. "Son of a bitch, driving up on us like that. He could have killed somebody."

Both of them shook their middle fingers at the receding taillights. Then the Volvo vanished into the darkness.

"Nothing we can do about it now." I started walking again. "Let's move on."

Groaning with exaggerated effort, Charlie trailed along after me. Frank stood still, staring back the way we'd come. I followed his gaze.

The horizon was on fire. Baltimore's after-dark neon shimmer had been replaced with a hazy, red glow. Smoke curled into the night sky, blacker than the darkness around it.

"My God," I whispered. "What is it?"

"The city's on fire," Frank said. "The whole thing."

"Shit."

"Yeah."

Charlie cleared his throat. "I guess that answers our questions about how busy the authorities are."

We stared in disbelief, watching the glow expand. Baltimore was burning, the entire city engulfed in flames. I wondered if the astronauts on the space station could see it, and if so, what else they were witnessing down here on Earth. The ones who were still onboard the space station, that was. I thought of the news report we'd heard earlier. NASA had claimed that one of them had vanished.

In the woods beyond the exit ramp, somebody screamed. Human or animal—I couldn't tell which, but the sound was like nails on a chalkboard. I fought to keep from screaming myself, and whispered Terri's name.

"Let's get out of here," I said.

We walked on. A blister broke on the bottom of my heel, and I felt my sock grow wet. I winced, trying to ignore the pain.

"You okay?" Charlie asked, concerned.

I nodded. "Blister. I'll be fine."

"I've said it before," Frank panted, "and I'll say it again: I'd kill for a cold beer right about now. Boy, would that taste good."

"I'd settle for a cell phone that worked," I said.

"I'd like an airplane," Charlie quipped. "Or even a taxi. My feet hurt."

"Mine, too," Frank agreed. "Haven't walked this much since I was in the Army."

"What'd you do in the Army?" I asked, trying to get my thoughts off Terri.

"Construction," he grunted. "Story of my life. I did four years and then got out. Wish I'd stayed in, though. Could have retired with a full pension at forty. Shit, there wasn't anything going on at the time. Vietnam was over, and Desert Storm was a decade away. But I was stupid, I guess. The old lady wanted to get married, so I got out. Kick myself in the ass for it now, especially after we got divorced. But I was a stupid kid."

"We were all stupid kids once," I said.

"Yeah, and if we only knew then what we know now, right? If I'd re-upped and taken that early retirement, I could've been at home today, instead of walking down this fucking highway in the dark and listening to crazy people talk about God and aliens and bleeding shopping malls."

Charlie and I both laughed, and Frank continued.

"Don't know why I'm so damn eager to get home, anyway. It's not like there's a beautiful woman waiting on me. You're lucky there, Steve."

"I know it," I said. "That's what's keeping my feet moving right now."

"So you live alone?" Charlie asked Frank. "No kids or anything?"

He shook his head sadly. "Nope. Not even a dog. I had some fish, but the little fuckers kept dying on me. I'd buy one, put him in the tank, and a week later he's floating upside down. My ex and I got divorced before we could have any kids. I don't know. It never bothered me much, but the older I get—I would have liked to have a son."

"You still can. You're not that old."

Before Frank could reply, a deer ran across the highway and leaped over the guardrail. We stumbled to a halt, and Charlie gave a surprised little yelp. The doe dashed away across the field, her white tail flashing in the moonlight, before disappearing into a line of trees.

"My heart's racing," Charlie gasped. "Fucking thing scared the shit out of me."

A thought occurred to me. "I wonder if any animals have vanished, too."

Frank and Charlie stared at me as if I were as crazy as Carlton and the Soapbox Man.

"Whatever it is that's happened," I said, "why should it

just be limited to us humans? Doesn't make sense."

"We saw that dog a few minutes ago," Frank reminded me. "And there's been plenty of dead animals alongside the road."

"Not road kill. I'm serious. Maybe some of the animals have disappeared. Maybe there's empty kennels and cages at the zoo right now."

Charlie shrugged. "It's something to consider, I guess."

We'd walked another two miles before we heard the voices. As we pressed on through the darkness, they grew louder. There was a large group of people ahead, judging by the sound. We rounded a curve and saw taillights in the distance. Traffic had stopped again, and I wondered what was causing the backup this time. As we got closer, we saw that at least a hundred people stood in the road. Then we smelled something burning: an acrid stench that made my eyes water.

Volvo's car lay on its roof in the middle of the highway, stretched across the median strip and one northbound lane. It was on fire. Smoke poured from the interior, and we heard a high-pitched whining sound. It took me a moment to realize what it was.

Screaming. From inside the car.

Volvo screaming.

A hand flailed from the driver's side window. The bubbling flesh sloughed off as it waved desperately, but I recognized the expensive Rolex around the charred wrist. The wind picked up, and I smelled roasting meat.

"Jesus..." Coughing, I turned away. He may have been a yuppie asshole, but he hadn't deserved this.

A trucker with a small fire extinguisher sprayed foam all over the blackened frame, but it was too late.

Charlie bent over and puked on his shoes. As much as he'd thrown up today, I was amazed that he had anything left inside him. Then I ran to the side of the road and did the same.

Three more cars had been involved in the accident. One was smashed into the guardrail, blocking the other northbound lane. The second was on its side in the southbound lane. The third was spread out all over the highway. Shattered glass and pieces of steel and fiberglass littered the pavement. The smell of gasoline mixed with the stench of burned flesh.

Frank muttered something, but it was lost beneath the noise of the crowd.

"What'd you say?" I asked.

"There's one more person who ain't going home tonight."

I checked my watch. 9:30 p.m. sharp. On a normal night, Terri and I would have finished dinner, talked about our days, and would now be climbing into bed together. We'd be reading books, or watching television, or making love. An hour from now, we'd go to sleep.

On a normal night.

Which this wasn't.

I needed to get home to her. Needed to feel her in my arms, to smell her hair and breathe in her scent and tell her that I loved her. It was very important that I tell her. I said it several times a day, but after years of marriage I didn't really think about it anymore—didn't consider the truth behind the words. Saying "I love you" had become a habit. I needed to let her know that it did still mean something to me, and that I did still love her. I loved her so much it hurt. Something swelled up inside my chest.

"Come on," I said. "We're halfway home."

"Wait," Charlie called, pointing back the way we'd come. "Look at that."

Red lights flashed at the bottom of the hill and slowly came towards us. An ambulance. When the driver turned on the siren my spirits soared.

But they plummeted again when we saw what happened next.

The crowd surged towards the ambulance, swarming it from all sides. They clawed at the doors, crying out for help, begging for medical assistance. The driver laid on the horn and the siren wailed, but the mob kept coming. The ambulance slowed to a crawl, and continued rolling forward, tires crunching a discarded soda can. When it became clear that the paramedics had no intention of stopping, the throng grew angry and then violent. They stood in front of the vehicle, blocking the lanes and preventing it from moving forward. Some people pounded on the windows and several jumped onto the hood, hammering at the windshield with their fists. Another guy climbed up on the roof and jumped up and down. Inside, the eyes of the driver and passenger grew wide. They laid on the horn again as the ambulance rocked back and forth.

"I don't believe this shit," Frank said. "They're gonna tip it over."

"They can't," Charlie said. "They wouldn't."

And then they did. A few unlucky people were crushed beneath the ambulance as the rest of the mob pushed it over onto its side, their shrieks lost beneath the roar of the crowd. One man clambered onto the still-rocking vehicle's side and danced. Enraged rioters smashed the driver's window and pulled the screaming paramedic from his seat. Blood streamed from a gash on his forehead. Struggling, he called out for help, and then disappeared in a swarm of clubs and fists. Flesh struck flesh. The sound of the blows was sickening.

I watched, unable to tear my eyes away. It was horrifying but I had to see.

"We should do something," Charlie whispered. "That poor man."

Frank shook his head. "You kidding? I ain't going down there. Fucking suicide."

The second paramedic was pulled from the vehicle and thrown onto the road. The rioters began kicking him. I heard his bones snap and, despite my shock, was surprised how loud the noise of breaking ribs actually was. He coughed blood, tried to cry out, and then a boot connected with his mouth, shredding his lips. His teeth flew from his mouth like popcorn from an open popper. The injured man raised his arms to cover his head, and the crowd fell on him.

Another rioter dashed forward with a bottle in his hand. A burning rag was stuffed into the neck, and I smelled gasoline.

"Get the fuck back," Frank warned us.

We retreated a few steps. There was a whoosh, and then the ambulance burst into flames. The rioters cheered. Then, looking for a new source on which to focus their rage, the crowd turned on each other. It looked like the world's biggest mosh pit. People fell, pushed or punched, and were then stomped on by those still standing, or weaving around and over and under the parked cars. Windshields and teeth shattered. Tires and stomachs ruptured. Oil and blood flowed. A gunshot rang out, followed by another.

Then, as one, the rioters surged towards us, a single entity composed of fists and angry faces and makeshift weapons.

"Let's go." I grabbed Charlie's arm.

He stumbled forward, his gaze locked on the crowd. "This can't be happening. Society doesn't behave like this."

"What planet you been living on?" Frank snorted, breaking into a trot. "This is exactly how society behaves. Always has."

The violence drew closer.

"Always will," Frank continued. "Especially now. You said it yourself. It wasn't the skinheads that hung that child molester. It was everyday people—people like this."

"Come on," I urged them both.

Exhausted, we ran.

* * *

An unmoving, naked woman was sprawled out on her back in the middle of the highway at Exit 25. There were twigs and leaves in her hair and gravel embedded in her face. I assumed she had been raped. She was definitely dead. I'd never seen so much blood. Her throat was cut, her nipples, nose and ears sliced off, and her eyes gouged out. She was young and, despite the horrific mutilation, she was beautiful—even in death.

Frank and I both tried our cell phones again, but there was still no service. Meanwhile, after he'd thrown up again, Charlie stripped off his shirt and laid it over the dead woman's face. Then he stood up again, and tucked his undershirt into his pants.

"What are you doing?" I asked.

"Covering her up," he replied. "It seems wrong, leaving her out here like this. Don't want the animals getting at her."

Frank grunted. "Looks like they already did."

I stared at the young woman's body, her upper half now concealed beneath Charlie's shirt. There was a dark purple bruise on her blood-caked thigh, next to a small tattoo of a dolphin jumping through a peace symbol. More blood pooled between her legs. She'd been somebody's daughter, maybe someone's girlfriend or fiancée. She'd been alive. Had hopes and dreams. Now she was fodder. Road kill. Another unlucky casualty, left behind in the dark and never going home again. I wondered who was waiting for her at home. Was there somebody who missed her, or had they disappeared?

Unable to tear my eyes away, I glanced at the damage between her legs. The space between them was no longer recognizable as a part of human anatomy, and I quickly turned my head.

Frank was right. The animals were on the loose tonight, hunting in packs.

I thought of Terri, home alone and probably scared to death.

"I'm coming, honey," I whispered. "Just a little while longer and I'll be home."

Charlie looked at me. "You say something?"

"Nothing. Just tired."

We walked on. A burning car lit the highway. We made sure to give it a wide berth.

An hour later, we saw flames burning several miles ahead of us. It looked like the entire horizon was on fire, just like the other horizon behind us where the city still burned.

Frank pointed. "What the hell's that?"

"I don't know," I said, shrugging. "Forest fire, maybe? That's Exit 26, and there's nothing around there but fields and woods."

As we got closer, we realized that we'd have to walk around, because Exit 26 was gone. The off-ramp, highway and fields on both sides had been obliterated in a plane crash. A section of fuselage jutted up from the mud, its sides scorched and blackened. Smoking wreckage and bodies were scattered throughout the area; it was like walking into a slaughterhouse. The stench of burning jet fuel and oil and flesh grew thick as we approached it.

Frank gaped. "My God…"

Charlie coughed. "Wonder what brought it down?"

"Maybe the pilot disappeared," I said. "And the co-pilot."

"Don't they got those auto-pilot things?" Frank wheezed.

My eyes began to sting. I breathed through my mouth to avoid the smell.

"Sure." I wiped the water from my eyes. "But you've still got to have somebody to land the plane."

We cut through the woods, avoiding the sections that were on fire, and came out onto Old York Road, which ran alongside the interstate from Harrisburg to Baltimore. The road was quiet and deserted, free of abandoned or wrecked cars. It was darker here. No houses, businesses or even a traffic light. An owl called out from a tree limb, and a rabbit darted through the undergrowth along the bank. Somewhere in the night, a dog howled. The surrounding forest blocked out the moonlight and the glow from the fires on the nearby highway, but we could still smell the smoke and I wondered if the stench had gotten into our clothes. Then I noticed that the wind had changed direction and was blowing it through the trees. We started down the road and rounded a curve.

"Shit," Frank said. "We should have walked this way to begin with, instead of sticking to 83. There's no traffic at all."

Charlie stopped and pointed. "Except for him."

A county police car sat on the side of the road, the driver's door hanging open. A young, baby-faced cop sat behind the wheel, his head in his hands. He looked up as we approached. His eyes were bloodshot and his face pale.

"Let me guess," he sighed. "You called 911 and nobody answered."

His voice sounded tired. Hollow. Beaten.

"No," Charlie answered. "We were just—"

"Because nobody's at the call center," the cop interrupted. "Some of them went missing, and the others went home soon after. We were routing calls through Baltimore, but then that call center went off-line, too. We don't even have a dispatcher answering the switchboard tonight. Cheryl and Maggie were supposed to start their shift at six and neither one of them came in. I can't get in touch with anybody."

We nodded in commiseration, unsure of how to respond.

Something squelched under my foot. I looked down and saw that I was standing in a puddle of vomit. Now I knew why the cop had his door open. I stepped back and wiped my heel on the grass.

Charlie cleared his throat. "You don't have a partner?"

The cop's voice was monotone. "No, I'm all alone out here. All alone…"

"Seems to be a lot of that tonight," Frank said.

The cop ignored the comment. "You guys come from the interstate?"

"From the plane crash?" Frank pointed back the way we'd come.

The cop nodded.

"Yeah, we cut around it," Frank said. "The fire's spreading, though. Any idea when the firemen will get there?"

"I was the only person to respond," the cop said. "Nobody else showed up. No fire departments. No EMTs or NTSB investigators. Or the TSA. No Feds. Just me. Where the hell is everybody? Even with dispatch out, you'd think they'd be patrolling."

"That's what we've been wondering," I told him. "It's like this everywhere."

"Any of you guys got a cell phone? I thought about calling some of the other officers, but I don't have a phone and the pay phones aren't working. Nobody is answering their radios, except for Simmons and all he did was scream."

I shook my head. "Cell phones are out, too. I've been trying to call my wife."

A tear ran down his cheek, and his face crumbled. "There were parts of people hanging in the trees...intestines and stuff. I stepped on somebody's face. It was lying in the mud. Just their face—I don't know where the rest of them was."

He reached in the glove compartment, pulled out a tissue, and blew his nose.

"There was a little girl, lying on the ground. I—I thought she was alive. I grabbed her arm, to pull her up, and it...came off."

"It'll be okay," Charlie said.

"Her fucking arm came off in my fucking hands!"

Charlie stepped closer. "Listen, I know you've had a hell of an evening. We all have. But there's nothing you can do for them now."

The cop frowned. "Yeah, I know. I drove over here to escape the smell. It's in my clothes and my hair. Can't get away from it. I've just been sitting here, waiting. Not sure what to do next."

Charlie held his hands out, pleading. "Could you give us a ride? We're trying to get home. Just over the border."

"Yeah," Frank said. "We've been walking all night. A ride would be great. We'd appreciate the hell out of it."

The distraught man buried his face in his hands again

and shook his head.

"I can't. Not until somebody else shows up. I'm all that's left. You see?"

Frank tried again. "But nobody is going to show up. They'd have been here by now. It's like this everywhere. You said so yourself. Nobody is answering the emergency calls."

"All the more reason then." The officer blew his nose again, and then sat up straight. "It's my job. To serve and protect."

"We'll pay you," I offered in desperation, pulling out my wallet. I opened it, and a picture of Terri smiled at me from behind the plastic sleeve. "I've got sixty bucks."

"Sorry, guys," the cop said. "Really, I am. I'd like to help you. But I can't. I've got to stay."

Charlie and Frank both checked their pockets. I stared at Terri's picture.

"I've got forty," Charlie said. "Frank?"

"Thirty-seven. How about it, Officer? That's almost one hundred and forty bucks."

"And," I added, "I can write you a check for more when we get there."

He paused, and I thought that maybe we'd convinced him. But then he sighed.

"I'm sorry. I'm just going to stay here."

"But why?" I asked, frustrated.

"I'm afraid to go back out there. Afraid of what I'll see. Good luck. Hope you make it home safe."

We didn't argue with him. Instead, we started off again. I cast one glance over my shoulder and he was still sitting there, slumped behind the wheel and crying. His sobs echoed through the night.

It was a lonely sound.

I knew how he felt. I'd missed my wife during the entire journey, but at that moment, it became a solid, tangible thing, swelling deep inside my gut and threatening to explode. My eyes started watering again, and this time it had nothing to do with smoke or fumes. My lips felt numb.

"Thanks, guys," I said, my voice cracking.

Charlie tilted his head from side to side, cracking his neck. "For what?"

"For coming along with me. For not letting me do this alone."

"Safety in numbers, remember?" Charlie winked. "And besides, this is just an extension of our carpool."

"And I needed the exercise." Frank grinned. "Doctor's always on me to do more walking. Well, he got his fucking wish."

His laughter was infectious. We walked together, side by side down the center of the road, and when the darkness swallowed us up, we didn't notice.

* * *

We reached Hereford, which would have been Exit 27 had we stayed on the interstate. It was a small town, no industries or shopping centers, and only a single bar. The streets were empty, no traffic or pedestrians. Televisions flickered in the windows of some of the homes, but many more were dark and lifeless. Everything looked yellow in the sodium lights that lined the sidewalk.

"I don't know about you guys," Frank wheezed, "but I need something to drink."

His face was as pale as cottage cheese, and his clothing was completely drenched with sweat.

"You okay?" I asked, concerned. "You don't look so good."

"Don't feel so good, either, to be honest. I'm too old for this shit."

"We can stop," I offered. "Take a break?"

Frank shook his head stubbornly. "I'll be okay soon as we find something to drink. I've never gone this long without a beer. Must be withdrawal."

He smiled, trying to laugh it off, but I could see that he was serious.

"Yeah," Charlie agreed. "I'm thirsty, too. Don't know

about a beer, but I'd kill for a bottle of water right now."

The Exxon gas station and convenience store was still open, so we stopped there. A bell rang as we walked through the door and the lights were on inside, but there was nobody behind the counter.

Charlie cupped his hands around his mouth. "Hello?"

The fluorescent lights hummed softly in the silence. In the back room, the air compressor kicked on, making sure the soda and milk aisle stayed refrigerated.

"Hey," Charlie yelled again. "Anybody home? You got customers!"

"It's deserted," Frank said. "Maybe the clerk vanished with everyone else."

Something didn't feel right to me, but I couldn't put my finger on it. The compressor suddenly shut itself off. My ears rang in the silence. I sniffed the air and caught a faint trace of cordite.

"Doesn't look like they have a public restroom," Frank observed.

"Maybe they're in the back, using the crapper."

"Screw it," Charlie said. "Let's just take what we need and go."

I started to protest, but he cut me off.

"We'll leave our money on the counter, Steve. That way we're not stealing."

Frank frowned. "It smells like gun smoke in here, don't it?"

I nodded. "I smelled it, too, but I thought it was just me."

Charlie headed down one of the aisles and grabbed a bag of potato chips.

"Hello," I called out. "Anybody here?"

A low moan answered me. We glanced at each other, surprised.

"Behind the counter," Frank whispered.

We ran to the register, and looked over the counter. A Filipino man lay on the floor. He'd been shot in the chest. Blood leaked from the corner of his mouth and pooled beneath him on the tiles. His eyes were open, staring at us in alarm. He coughed, spraying the lottery ticket machine with tiny flecks of red.

"Charlie," I shouted, leaping over the counter. "Call 911. Frank—check in the back room. See if you can find blankets or something."

The manager (he had a name tag that said his name was LOPEZ and he was the MANAGER) looked up at me and tried to speak. More blood spilled from his lips. He was obviously in shock. His skin had the color of paste and was cold and clammy to the touch.

"Shhh," I quieted him. "Don't move. We're gonna help you."

Lopez the manager raised his head and whispered into my ear, spattering my shoulder with blood.

"Maraming salamat…kaibigan."

I didn't understand, but I smiled, trying to look confident and reassuring and feeling anything but.

"Fuck!" Charlie yelled. "Steve, 911 isn't answering!"

"Keep trying. This guy's lost a lot of blood. We've got to get him help, fast!"

"I'm trying." Charlie hung up the store phone. "It's just like that cop said. Nobody's there."

I slapped my head, frustrated. In my panic, I'd forgotten about that. Then a thought occurred to me.

"Do you think you could make it back to that cop?" I asked Charlie.

"Maraming salamat," the man on the floor repeated.

"What'd he say?" Charlie asked me.

"I don't know. Did you—"

Thunder crashed, cutting me off. Then it roared again. On the floor, Lopez flinched and squeezed my hand. His expression was terrified.

That's not thunder, I thought. *Somebody's shooting…*

A third gunshot rang out, echoing through the store. I felt the concussion vibrating in my chest. My ears felt like they'd suddenly closed up. Charlie and I both jumped and the manager began to whimper.

"The back room," Charlie whispered.

My ears were still ringing and I had to strain to hear him.

"What do we do?" Charlie asked.

I jumped up. "Frank? FRANK!"

He hollered back. His voice sounded weak, and in pain. "Steve…Charlie…Run!"

Before we could do anything, the door to the back room flew open and two skinheads stormed out. Both wore tight blue jeans, black combat boots and leather jackets with patches sewn on the front that said, "Eastern Hammer." My stomach fluttered. The Eastern Hammer skinheads were notorious in the mid-Atlantic portion of the East Coast, especially in Pennsylvania and Maryland. Their headquarters was supposedly in nearby Red Lion. They'd been accused of and—in some cases—tried and convicted of a number of hate crimes, including murder. Supposedly, they were linked to the Sons of the Constitution militia group that was based down south.

I thought back to the Thornton Mill Road overpass. It seemed like years ago, but it had only been a few hours. The child molester, swinging from a noose, his shit splattered all over the highway. Skinheads, they'd told us. Skinheads had killed him. Charlie had been skeptical. I wondered what he thought now. I risked a glance in his direction. His eyes were wide. Then I looked back at the two youths. The tall one had a forehead like a caveman, his brow protruding a half-inch from the rest of his face. The shorter of the two had a long, pink scar on his right cheek and clutched a still-smoking pistol in his hand.

"Get down, motherfuckers," the taller one shouted. "On the floor, right now!"

"We don't want any trouble," Charlie said. "We were just—"

"Fucking do it," the other one, Scar-face, spat, motioning with the gun. "If I have to say it again, I will waste your ass."

I held my hands out in front of me, and noticed Lopez

the manager's blood was all over them. I must have stepped in it, too, because the soles of my shoes seemed stuck to the floor.

"Steve..."

"Are you fucking deaf?" Scar-face glared at Charlie. "I told you to—"

Charlie ducked, sprinting for the door. The skinhead fired as the door swung open. Charlie darted through. Glass shattered. The door buzzer rang, almost drowned out by the gunshot. And then Charlie sped across the parking lot and was gone—vanished into the night.

The tall one nodded at his companion. "Go get the fucker, Skink."

So Scar-face had a name.

"He ain't gonna do shit, Al," Skink said. "Cops are busy elsewhere."

Skink and Al. Even their names seemed surreal.

The tall one, Al, spit on the floor. "I said go after him, goddamn it!"

"What about this guy?" Skink pointed at me.

Al smiled. "I'll take care of him."

Cursing, Skink ran after Charlie, his boots crunching on the fragments of broken glass.

Al glowered at me. "Come out from around there, shithead. Slowly."

"Look," I said. "We don't—"

"SHUT THE FUCK UP AND MOVE!"

Too afraid to open my mouth, I did as he said, stepping over the manager's body and almost slipping in his blood. Lopez's eyes were open, but I couldn't tell if he was still alive. I wondered what had happened to Frank and feared the worst. I crept out from behind the counter, my hands still in the air, and left bloody footprints on the floor.

Well, I thought, *I guess that guy Tony was right and Charlie was wrong. There really are murderous skinheads running around tonight.*

I wondered if these were the same ones who'd apparently hung the child molester from the overpass. The one in front of me, Al, was young—maybe in his early twenties. He looked nervous, but angry. His sloped brow creased in frustration.

The thug studied my face. "You got one ugly fucking nose, you know that?"

"S-so?" I cringed at the tremor in my voice. I sounded anything but brave.

"Jews got noses like that." He cocked his head. "You a kike?"

"No," I lied. My voice was steadier this time. My fear was slowly being replaced with anger. Believe it or not, this was the first time in my life that someone had ever called me a kike to my face. I didn't like how it felt.

"What's your name?" Al demanded.

"Steve." I took another step towards him. "What's yours? I mean, I know your name is Al, but what's the rest?"

I realized I was babbling, but couldn't seem to stop. My voice rose in pitch.

He reached inside his coat and pulled out a knife. "Don't you worry about my fucking name. I'm asking the questions. Get over here."

I glanced around for a weapon, for anything to defend myself with. The cash register, the lottery and credit card machines, a display rack of candy bars. Nothing.

"Hey," Al snarled. "I see you. You're checking out the register. You *are* a fucking Jew, ain't you? Worrying about the money."

I inched closer. "You shot the manager."

"No, I didn't. Skink did."

"How about our friend? He went in the back. Did you kill him, too?"

Al grew angrier. "I'll cut your fucking throat if you don't move faster and do what the fuck I tell you."

"You'll do no such thing," said a man's voice from behind me.

I froze. So did the skinhead. He stared over my shoulder, his eyes narrowing. I thought I recognized the voice. It sounded vaguely familiar. The temperature inside the store suddenly dropped. I saw my breath in the air, drifting like fog. In the back, near the pet food section, the fluorescent bulbs exploded. The rest of the lights grew brighter. I heard the electricity surging through them. The hair on my arms and head stood up and static crackled across my skin.

"He is one of God's chosen," said the voice. "One of the one hundred and forty-four thousand spoken of by John the Apostle in the Book of Revelation. He is a saint of the tribulation, and he has many miles to go before he dies. It will not be by your hand, Albert Nicholas."

Al was visibly startled. "How the fuck do you know my name?"

"I know everything."

I wondered who the new arrival was, and if they were friend or foe, and what the hell they were talking about. What was it he'd said about me? I was a saint of what? I focused on the voice, trying desperately to figure out where I'd heard it before. But I didn't dare turn around.

"Get your ass in here, nigger," the skinhead snarled. "Or I'll cut you, too."

"Cut me?" My savior, who judging by the skinhead's reaction was black, laughed. "Think again, Son of Cain. Not with that you won't."

"What? You don't believe me, fucker? Look at the size of this blade."

The skinhead glanced at his knife. I did, too.

We both screamed at the same time.

His weapon was no longer a knife. Instead, he now clutched a live, thrashing snake. It was about twelve inches long and had brown and yellow scales and beady black eyes. Its tongue flicked across his knuckles and the tail coiled around his wrist. The creature's head weaved from side to side and then darted downward. It sank its fangs into the flesh between Al's thumb and index finger.

"Fuck!" Shrieking, Al ripped the serpent loose and flung it across the store.

I watched it twist and sail through the air and crash into

a junk food display, sending bags of potato chips flying. When I looked back at Al, I screamed again.

Al was gone. A white, crystalline statue stared back at me instead, a statue that looked an awful lot like him. Powdery residue fell from its shoulders.

"No harm shall come to you," the voice whispered behind me, and I finally recognized it. Gabriel, the black guy from the crash site. The one wearing the tie with a cross on it who'd caught me when I passed out.

I spun around. The store was empty. Gabriel was nowhere to be seen.

"I know it's you," I called. "Gabriel? Are you following us?"

Silence.

"Gabriel? Thanks for the help. That's twice today."

The temperature inside the store returned to normal. I jumped when the compressor switched itself back on.

"Come on out, man."

Gabriel didn't reply. Outside, through the broken glass in the door, I saw a lone car cruising slowly up the street. One of its headlights was out.

"This Phantom Stranger shit is getting old, Gabriel."

I turned back to the statue of Al. Hesitantly I reached out and touched the coarse, white substance. Then I brought my fingertips to my mouth and tasted.

Salt. The skinhead had been turned into a pillar of salt.

"Holy shit..."

I backed away from the statue. Salt granules crunched beneath my feet. I checked the aisles, but they were empty. There was no sign of Gabriel—if he'd even been here. I felt a little part of my mind slip away and tried to get a grip. Last thing I needed to do now was lose it. I had to get home to Terri. What had just happened couldn't have happened. Knives didn't turn into snakes and skinheads definitely didn't turn into pillars of salt.

And half the human race didn't vanish in the blink of an eye, either...

Looking around the store, I saw the snake's tail disappearing beneath the coolers, and I decided that it was all very real after all.

Biblical, in fact.

I checked on the manager, but he had no pulse. His skin was cold. His eyes stared sightlessly. I reached out to close them, but couldn't bring myself to touch them. Eventually, I closed my own eyes and just did it.

Then I remembered Frank.

"Fuck!"

Being confronted by Al and Skink, Charlie's fleeing, and everything else that had happened after it had made me forget all about Frank. I cursed my stupidity. He'd called out after the gunshots. Was he okay?

I ran into the back room and found him lying dead on a stack of skids. His glassy eyes gazed at the ceiling and a thin line of blood trickled from his open mouth. There was more blood on his shirt; so much, in fact, that I couldn't figure out where he'd been shot.

"I'm sorry, Frank. I am so sorry, man."

He hadn't deserved this. He was a good guy. He'd joked and laughed for most of our walk, even though he seemed sad underneath it all. Well, of course he'd seemed sad. Still carrying a torch for his ex-wife—it was apparent to strangers like us even if he was oblivious to it himself. No kids or even a beloved pet waiting at home. The only thing Frank looked forward to was the next beer. And now he wouldn't even have that. Even though I'd only known him for an evening, it felt like I'd lost a good friend. I tried to remember things about him, and was surprised by how little I actually knew. I had to think about it for a minute before I could even remember his last name. Some eulogy. It wasn't fair, Frank dying like this, gunned down so senselessly by two racist scumbags. All he'd wanted to do was go home.

Maybe now he had.

Frank's blood was on my hands, literally and figuratively. I reached out to shut his eyes, swallowing the same revulsion I'd felt when doing the same for Lopez.

After closing Frank's eyes, I pulled out my cell phone

and attempted to call 911 again. At the very least I should report what had happened. But in truth, after what the cop had told us, I didn't even expect to get a signal, so imagine my surprise when I saw that the phone showed five bars.

Immediately, I forgot about calling the authorities, and instead dialed home. The phone rang, and it was the sweetest sound I've ever heard.

"Yes! Come on, Terri. Pick up. Oh, pick it up."

It rang again.

"Come on, sweetie, be home."

A third ring. A fourth.

"Pick up, pick up, pick up..."

Five more rings.

"Answer the goddamn phone!"

It rang three more times before our answering machine finally picked up. I listened to my own voice telling me that Steve and Terri weren't home right now and to leave a message at the beep.

"Terri, it's me. I'm okay. If you're there, pick up the phone! Something's happened, and Craig is missing and people are dead, but I'm okay. Are you there? Terri? Pick up! Pi—"

The machine beeped again, indicating that it was done recording. A recorded voice told me that the mailbox was full.

"Goddamn it!"

I threw the cell phone across the room, and stalked back out to the front of the store. On my way out, I noticed a small, wooden plaque hanging on the wall, discreetly hidden from the view of customers. I studied it. It was some kind of poem, one I wasn't familiar with, obviously of Christian origin. It was called 'Footprints' and was attributed to an unknown author.

One night, the poem began, *a man had a dream. He dreamed he was walking along the beach with the Lord. Across the sky flashed scenes from his life. For each scene, he noticed two sets of footprints in the sand; one belonging to him, and the other to the Lord. When the last scene of his life flashed before him, he looked back at the footprints in the sand. He noticed that many times along the path of his life there was only one set of footprints. He also noticed that it happened at the very lowest and saddest times in his life. This really bothered him, and he questioned the Lord about it. "Lord, you said that once I decided to follow you, you'd walk with me all the way. But I have noticed that during the most troublesome times in my life, there is only one set of footprints. I don't understand why, when I needed you most, you would leave me." The Lord replied, "My son, my precious child, I love you and I would never leave you. During your times of trial and suffering, when you see only one set of footprints, it was then that I carried you."*

I repeated the last line out loud, and then I started shaking. My hands curled into fists. Enraged, I ripped the plaque from the wall and threw it across the store.

"Fuck you," I shouted. "Are you walking with me now? Are you carrying me? Why did you do this to us? What's the point? Were you really behind it? So this is the Rapture, huh? You called your followers home and left us sinners behind. Why? Because Charlie was gay? Because I'm a Jew? Because Frank didn't believe in you anymore? Bastard!"

I waited for a divine lightning bolt to come down and strike me, but it didn't. There was no thunder. The lights didn't even flicker.

"I'll walk my path alone," I whispered, thinking of Gabriel.

It had gotten darker outside—which seemed impossible given what time of night it was. I walked out of the store, and looked around for Charlie, Skink or the mysterious Gabriel, but there was no sign of them. I hoped that Charlie was okay, that he'd gotten away or had enough sense to hide. Maybe he'd find some help, find the cop, and come back. Maybe not. It didn't matter. He was my friend, but I couldn't wait for him. Not anymore.

Craig was missing, along with several million other people. Hector and Frank were dead; Frank gunned down by skinheads and Hector with a pipe through his face. Charlie was gone, and Skink was still on the loose. And if all of this wasn't enough, a weird black guy was following me up the highway, changing knives into snakes and skinheads into pillars of salt.

And Terri wasn't answering the phone.

I headed north, sticking to the side of the road. I'd gone about a half-mile when I found Charlie. He was lying in a ditch. He'd been shot twice, in the stomach and the lower back. Despite his wounds, he was still alive. Nearby, in the driveway of a darkened house, stood another pillar of salt. Skink.

"Hey." Charlie coughed, grimacing. "What took you so long?"

"Jesus Christ." I knelt beside him, staring at the damage. "Don't try to move, man."

He grinned. "Couldn't move if I wanted to. I can't feel anything below my neck. Kind of glad for that, to be honest."

He started to cry. I patted him.

"Oh Charlie..."

"Can't feel a thing."

"What happened?"

He stopped crying and coughed again. His chest rattled and black fluid leaked from the corners of his mouth.

"That fucker came after me. Figured I'd run this way and lose him, then double around back and check on you and Frank. How is he?"

I shook my head.

"Damn," Charlie croaked. "He turned out to be an okay guy. I liked him."

"Charlie, what happened to the skinhead? Did you see? Was it Gabriel?"

His eyes clouded. "Who?"

"Gabriel. The guy from the wreck. The one who caught me."

Charlie smiled. If he heard my question, he gave no indication. Instead, he reached out and clasped my hand.

"Got a joke for you. A Jew, a Polack, and a homo are on their way home. Who gets there first?"

I squeezed his hand. "Charlie, don't. Listen to me, man. I'm gonna get help."

"Go find Terri, man. Get home."

"I can't just leave you here."

"Bet I get home before you do."

His chest rose then fell. It did not rise again.

I cried then, shuddering as huge, overwhelming sobs wracked my body. I leaned over and touched my forehead to my friend's. I cried for Charlie and for Frank, for Hector and Craig and everybody else. I cried for Terri. I cried for myself.

I shuffled north again, still crying. I kept to the side of the road, walking through fields and yards rather than on the pavement itself. When I looked down, I realized I was trekking through mud. I glanced behind me.

There was one set of footprints in the mud. Mine.

I walked on, alone.

* * *

I continued up York Road for a few miles until the darkness and the silence got to be too much for me. By then, the fires from the plane crash had faded beyond the horizon. Eventually, I cut across the fields and back onto the interstate. There was a steep hill ahead of me, and my leg muscles cramped as I climbed it. Still I pressed forward, gritting my teeth and trying to ignore the pain. It wasn't until I'd reached the top that I realized I was crying again. I wiped my nose on my sleeve, and blinked the tears away.

Another cramp shot up my leg, paralyzing it. Screaming, I collapsed to my knees in the middle of the road. Sharp pebbles jabbed through my pants and I reopened the cuts on my hand, but I didn't care. I knelt there, my blood and tears flowing freely.

I didn't notice the station wagon until it was right behind me. I looked up and shielded my eyes from the headlights' glare. The motor purred softly. The vehicle rolled to a stop just a few feet away. I heard the whir of a power window being lowered.

"Are you okay, son?"

I stood up, wiped my eyes, and approached the driver's side door.

A bald man, probably in his late fifties or early sixties, leaned out the window and smiled at me.

"Are you all right?" he asked again. "Do you need help?"

"I—I need a ride. I'm trying to get home to my wife."

"Where do you live?"

"Shrewsbury. It's the first exit in Pennsylvania."

Smiling, he motioned to the passenger door. "Certainly. I pass it every day. Hop in. I'm going as far as Harrisburg."

I rounded the vehicle and opened the door. For a brief second, I had misgivings. After everything else I'd been through tonight, and some of the people I'd met, I wondered if it was smart to climb in a car with a stranger. But the pain in my legs came back, and I thought again of Terri and my unanswered phone call. I got inside, pulled the door shut, and settled into the seat.

The man put the car in gear and pulled away. "Lucky for you I wasn't speeding. I might have run right over you. What were you doing in the middle of the highway?"

I swallowed, trying to catch my breath. "It's been a rough evening."

"Yes." He nodded, staring at the road. "It has indeed."

I covered my mouth with my hand and coughed. My throat felt like it had been rubbed with sandpaper, but the pain in my legs was dissipating now that I was sitting down.

"Are you thirsty?" he asked, sipping from a plastic travel mug.

I nodded.

"There's a small cooler behind you. I keep drinks in the car so I don't have to stop. Saves me money and time. Help yourself. There should be some bottles of water inside, or soda if you prefer."

"Thanks." I turned and found the cooler, and got a bottle out. The water was ice cold and refreshing, and soothed my raw throat. "I really appreciate this."

"My pleasure." He stuck out his right hand. "Reverend Phillip Brady."

"Steve Leiberman. Thanks again, Reverend. Can I offer you some gas money or something?"

"You can offer it, but I won't accept. It's really no problem. I'm going right by your exit. I volunteer in one of the soup kitchens down in Baltimore, and commute from Harrisburg. I come this way every day."

I whistled in appreciation. "That's a long drive."

"It's what the Lord wants."

"What God wants, God gets?"

He frowned slightly. "That's not quite how I'd put it, but I suppose so. It's what God expects of me."

I laughed, long and hard. The preacher looked shocked, and immediately, I felt embarrassed and worried that I'd offended him.

"Sorry, Reverend. I'm not laughing at you. It's just, with all that's happened today, all the disappearances, I was pretty much convinced that the Rapture had occurred. Seriously. If you could have seen some of the things I've seen tonight...I was really starting to get scared. But now, after meeting you, I know otherwise. It's not the Rapture. Whatever it was that happened today, whatever took all those people, it wasn't that."

"Actually, I think it *was* the Rapture."

"But you're still here and you're a man of God. Look, I'm Jewish and I don't pretend to understand the whole thing, but my wife and her parents were Christian, too. I thought that when the Rapture occurred, all the Christians were called up to Heaven or something? That's what my in-laws always said."

"Not at all. In fact, I imagine that this Sunday the churches around the world will be filled to capacity. We'll see more people in church than ever before."

"But that doesn't make sense."

"Being a Christian isn't enough. There are still plenty of

believers who've been left behind. Just like myself."

I shook my head. "I don't understand."

"How about a quick lesson?"

"Okay." I glanced out the window and saw the exit for Gunpowder Falls flash past. Had I been on foot, it would have taken me another hour to reach it. Instead, it had taken five minutes. The last thing I wanted was a sermon, but I'd sit through one if it got me home to Terri sooner.

Reverend Brady took another sip from his travel mug. "'For the Lord himself will come down from Heaven, with a loud command, with the voice of the archangel and with the trumpet call of God, and we who are still alive will be caught up together in the clouds to meet the Lord in the air. And so we will be with the Lord forever.'"

I didn't respond. I wanted answers, not Bible quotes.

"Sorry," the Reverend apologized, as if reading my mind. "That's from Thessalonians. Talking about a great event. The Rapture is that event—God's calling up millions of His believers to Heaven. It's a prelude to the Second Coming of Christ, when Jesus comes back to rule over all. I'm sure that, like everyone else, you heard the trumpet blast?"

I nodded. "That's really what it was?"

"In First Corinthians, the apostle Paul states that in the twinkling of an eye, the last trumpet will sound and the believers in Christ will be called home. That's what happened today. Those who were born again, meaning they'd accepted Christ as their Lord and Savior, disappeared."

"Where did they go?"

"Heaven."

"But not you. And I saw others today, too: priests and nuns and people with those stupid Jesus-fish bumper stickers. We saw a guy preaching on the hood of his car, right in the middle of the interstate. If God took all of his followers home, why did He leave people like you behind? Aren't you pissed off about it?"

"No, I'm not angry." Reverend Brady smiled sadly. "But you're absolutely right. I am still here. It's my fault. And that breaks my heart, because I know what's coming next. I know what the next seven years will bring."

"I still don't understand. If this is the Rapture, then why aren't you among the missing?"

"Because I lacked belief. One of the most famous verses in the Bible is, 'For God so loved the world, that He gave His only begotten Son; that whosever believes in Him shall not perish, but have eternal life.' Jesus died for our sins, but in the last few years, I've lost touch with Him."

"You didn't believe?"

"No," he whispered. "I didn't. When you're a pastor, whether you want to or not, you become the clearinghouse for your congregation's gossip. Every single day, I'd overhear the worst—their darkest secrets, the things they didn't think anybody else knew. I was exposed to their most base, animalistic natures. Adultery. Abuse. Drug addiction and alcoholism. Gambling. Theft and deception. One of our lay speakers embezzled over thirty-thousand dollars from his employer. Our secretary poisoned her neighbor's dog because it wouldn't stop barking. Our youth pastor was engaging in a sexual relationship with his own fourteen-year old daughter."

"And they told you all this?"

He shrugged. "Sometimes. Often I'd hear it from others. But sometimes they'd tell me themselves. Unlike the Catholic Church we don't require confession, but they'd confess to me anyway, looking for guidance. Looking for somebody to assure them it was okay, that God still loved them. And I'd do that. I'd remind them that God forgives all, and they'd promise me they'd do right from now on—and then two months later they'd be right back at it again."

He sighed. The radio played softly. In the soft glow of the dashboard lights, he looked older than I had assumed he was.

"I grew resentful. Not only of them, but of God, too. How was I supposed to be a shepherd, how could I guide them and teach them to live as the Lord wanted, when they filled me with such revulsion? I hated them for it and, eventually, I began to hate God as well. I was just going through the motions. But my congregation was still counting on me. Not all of them were bad people and I couldn't let them down. So I stood up there in the pulpit every Sunday, and I preached the good news, told them about the Lord, and lent them the power of my belief. And all the while, deep down inside, I lacked the faith of my convictions. I didn't believe."

"And here you are," I finished for him.

"Yes, indeed. Here I am. Left behind. God help me—help us all."

"We'll survive," I said. "We'll pick up the pieces, dust ourselves off and move on. We always do. Look at everything the human race has been through. We always bounce back."

He shook his head. "Not this time. The next seven years will quite literally be hell on earth. War. Famine. Earthquakes. Disease. Total chaos."

"Don't we have that now?"

"No, Steve. This is just the beginning. We have those things now, but they pale in comparison to what's coming. This will be a tough time for the tribulation saints."

I gasped.

"What's wrong?" he asked.

"I—something you said just made me think. I heard something similar earlier today."

"How so?"

I told him about all that had transpired. Even with the disappearances, I didn't expect him to believe me when I got to Gabriel and the skinheads turning into salt. But when I'd finished, he simply nodded his head.

"You've been chosen."

I snorted, trying to keep the sarcasm out of my voice. "Chosen for what?"

"Don't scoff. A dynamic new leader is about to arise. People will see him as a great man. He will fix everything, stop the lawlessness and chaos and usher in an era of peace."

"But you said it would be Hell on earth. Wars and famine and all that."

"It's a false peace, and he's anything but a great man. The Bible calls this man Antichrist. He's a descendent of those who destroyed the temple in Jerusalem in 70 A.D. But who he really is, is Satan. The Antichrist will enjoy world-wide popularity. People will love him like no other world leader they've ever known."

"Who is he?"

"I don't know. He has yet to reveal himself. But I'm sure he's already active. We've probably watched him in action for years, and loved him without knowing his true identity. Soon, most likely within a few weeks, he will set up a new one-world government in response to today's events. He'll even bring peace to Israel with the signing of a seven-year agreement."

"Never happen," I said. "There will never be peace in Israel, especially now. And what does this have to do with me anyway? You said I was chosen."

"The signing of the agreement kicks off a seven-year period called the tribulation, and those who receive Jesus as their Lord and Savior after the Rapture are called tribulation saints. Many of them will be Jews, just like you. Revelation talks about the 144,000 Jewish witnesses. These witnesses, the tribulation saints, will be protected supernaturally from the horrors to come. Much like you were today, with your guardian. What did you say his name was?"

"Gabriel," I whispered. He'd mentioned something about the 144,000 as well, when Al the skinhead held me at knifepoint.

"Gabriel the Protector. You do know Gabriel was an angel of the Lord?"

"No," I said. "But I do now."

I tried to get my head around it. I was chosen simply for being Jewish? I didn't even practice my own faith, let alone know the Christian Bible. It seemed unfair. If this were true, and I was beginning to believe it was, why should I get special protection while others suffered?

We passed the exit for Parkton, and I thought of Charlie. What had he done to deserve all that had happened tonight? He was just trying to get home—same with Frank and Hector and everyone else.

"Why?" I asked. "Why would God do this? He's supposed to be a loving God."

"Yes," Brady said, "but he is also a just God. A comedian who I enjoy once said that the God of the Bible had a split personality. In the New Testament, He is a God of love, promising forgiveness to everyone; but in the Old Testament, He is a God of wrath, demanding sacrifices and punishing those who displease him. People often forget that he is both."

I considered telling the preacher just what I thought of that, what I thought of his God—of any deity that would do this to its people. But I kept my mouth shut and watched the mile markers rush by. This man could deliver me almost to my doorstep, so the last thing I wanted to do was offend him. If I did, I'd find myself walking again.

We passed the weigh station at Exit 36, and crossed over the state line. There were three small crosses off the shoulder, set up in remembrance of three teenagers who'd died there months ago in a drunken driving accident. Looking at them, I shivered.

"Pennsylvania." Reverend Brady smiled. "Won't be long now."

I looked up at the road sign.

YOU ARE NOW LEAVING MARYLAND. WE ENJOYED YOUR VISIT. PLEASE COME AGAIN.

Please come again…

It was a fitting epitaph for the world.

* * *

We drove on in silence, past the deserted Pennsylvania Welcome Center and a few more scattered car wrecks. I watched the sights flick past, numb to the horrors. A farmhouse burned; no firefighters were on site. A decapitated head lay on the median. A teenage graffiti artist had tagged a billboard without fear of retribution or arrest, because the cops were all busy elsewhere. A large, black crow feasted on a dead dog.

The headlights flashed off a road sign: *Shrewsbury – One Mile.*

"You can just drop me off at the exit ramp," I said.

Reverend Brady looked surprised. "Are you sure? It's not a problem to take you to your front door."

"No, that's okay. I'm sure you've got people to get home to as well."

He slowed down as we approached the exit and stopped at the top of the ramp. He checked the rearview mirror to make sure there was no traffic behind us. There wasn't. The highway was a ghost.

I opened the door, and then offered him my hand. "Look. I don't know how to thank you. Are you sure I can't give you some gas money or something?"

"You can thank me by thinking about what I said." He squeezed my hand. "I hope you find what you're looking for when you get home, Steve."

"I appreciate that. Goodbye, Reverend, and good luck."

"I'll pray for you, and for your wife."

"Thanks."

I started to turn away, but then he called out.

"Steve? Don't lose faith. The journey will be hard, but something wonderful is waiting for you at the end."

I nodded, afraid to speak. Despite the kindness he'd shown me, I felt like screaming at him.

The car's window slid closed, and Reverend Brady drove away. I stood there and watched him go until his tail-lights vanished.

"Gabriel?" I said out loud as I walked down the exit ramp. "You still with me?"

There was no answer, but I wasn't really expecting one. If anything, Gabriel had proven himself to be pretty non-communicative.

"So if the preacher was right, if you're some sort of

guardian angel sent to watch over me, then I hope you watched over Terri as well."

In the darkness, a whippoorwill sang out. The grass along the roadside rustled softly in the breeze.

"If not," I said, "there'll be hell to pay."

Then I went home.

* * *

They were looting the Wal-Mart as I walked past. Surprisingly, the whole thing seemed pretty civil. Locals, people I knew and faces I recognized, filed out of the store carrying everything from food to televisions. They pushed shopping carts filled to overflowing with goods. There was no fighting or shoving. It was eerily calm. Neighbors greeted each other, and helped each other load up their cars and trucks. I heard laughter, saw lovers holding hands, children smiling. The scene was polite and friendly, almost festive. A carnival atmosphere where all that was missing was a Ferris wheel and a few cotton candy vendors.

Charlie had been right. We should have taken the abandoned Cadillac when we came across it. Everybody else was doing it, and the Caddy's owner doubtlessly wouldn't have needed it again. Had we commandeered the car, I'd have been home already. We'd all be home. If I'd said yes, Charlie and Frank would still be alive.

There weren't many abandoned cars in town, but there were a lot of dark houses. I wondered how many of their occupants had actually disappeared and how many more were simply hiding inside, hunkered down behind the windowsill, clutching a shotgun in the darkness and waiting for the hordes invading the Wal-Mart to attack.

On one block where the homes were close to one another, a fire had gutted four buildings, stretching from Merle Laughman's antique shop down to Dale Haubner's house. The sidewalks and street were wet and water dripped from the fire hydrant. I assumed that the firefighters here in our community had been less busy than elsewhere. Or maybe they'd just gotten to this one early. Whatever had occurred, they'd managed to save the rest of the block.

The pain in my legs and feet had dissipated during the car ride, and now I had my second wind. The fatigue lessened with each step, and I quickened my pace.

"I'm almost there, Terri. Almost home."

The traffic light blinked yellow at the intersection across from my block. Shattered glass indicated a wreck, but there were no cars in sight. I crossed Main Street, turned right, and walked another few yards.

Then I stood in front of our house. I took a deep breath.

The lights were on and I saw the flickering blue glow of the television from the living room window.

"She's here!"

I ran up the stairs of the front porch and my hands shook as I fumbled for my keys. I unlocked the door and barged into the living room. A frazzled-looking newscaster was on television, reporting on what I already knew. The volume was turned up loud.

Terri's spot on the couch was empty, but the cushion where she sat every evening still held her imprint.

"Terri? Honey? I'm home!"

I turned off the television.

"Terri?"

Silence. I was home, but my wife wasn't. I searched the house, hoping against hope, but I knew what I would find. Or wouldn't find.

Terri was missing.

After twenty minutes, I collapsed onto the bed and cried into her pillow. It smelled like Terri, and I breathed in her fading scent. Soon it would be gone, just like her imprint on the sofa cushion. And then there'd be no trace left.

I prayed. I asked for it to be taken back, that the day be rewound and erased. Prayed for a second chance. I prayed for Charlie and Frank and Craig and Hector and all the others. More than anything, I asked for my wife to be returned to me, or to be allowed to go where she was, and again there was no answer. God was deaf, dumb and blind. I pleaded with Gabriel to show himself, but he didn't. The silence was a solid thing. Downstairs, our grandfather clock ticked off the seconds and each one was excruciating.

I lay there all night and continued to pray. My parents would have been so proud of me. Terri and her parents would have been proud, too, because I finally believed in something. Believed in a force beyond Judaism or Christianity or dogma or faith. Believed in something concrete.

Something real.

I prayed as only a God-fearing man can—because God exists. I know that now. God exists, and I fear Him.

I am afraid.

So I pray. I pray every day now, even as things get worse. The preacher was right. The Rapture was just the beginning. And still I pray. I pray for mercy. Pray for forgiveness.

Pray to go home.

It's such a long way and there are many miles left to go.

STORY NOTES

Take The Long Way Home *was originally written for an anthology called* On A Pale Horse. *The premise was four religious themed, end-of-the-world novellas by four different horror writers – myself, Tim Lebbon, Michael Laimo, and Gord Rollo.*

Each of us began work on our novellas, and everybody agreed that I should write about the Rapture. Why? At the time, there was a very popular Christian horror series written by Tim LaHaye and Jerry Jenkins called Left Behind. *The series spanned twelve-books and a subsequent young adult series before giving birth to its first prequel. That prequel, amusingly enough, was called* The Rising. *My own book,* The Rising, *which caused a minor stir among zombie fans, had been out for about two years at that point. You can imagine the fun that ensued for booksellers. Zombie fans who had read* City of the Dead *and were looking for the previous book picked up something about the Rapture instead, and Christian readers who were expecting more of LaHaye and Jenkins' Biblical adventure got Ob and Frankie and a bunch o' gut-munching zombies.*

I originally wanted to call this story Left Behind. *My attorney said we couldn't be sued for it, and I laughed with glee. But then my wife's more sensible head prevailed, and the title changed to* Take The Long Way Home, *which is also the title of my favorite Supertramp song. I think I like this title better.*

Sadly, despite the best efforts of everyone involved, On A Pale Horse *fell through. Luckily, I owed Necessary Evil Press a novella, and it was published by them as a beautiful little limited edition hardcover.*

The story itself is based on the primarily evangelical interpretation of the Biblical scriptures, specifically the Rapture and how it relates to the Second Coming of Christ. The 144,000 Jews who become Tribulation Saints are a part of this belief.

I was raised by two Irish-American Protestant parents, attended a Methodist church, and was even the president of the church youth group at one point, if you can dig that. My grandparents were Presbyterians, my extended family hardcore Southern Baptists, and I once dated a preacher's daughter. My point is; I was surrounded by religion, specifically Christianity, all through my childhood and teenage years. Readers have commented that my fiction seems to be primarily based on the Christian mythos – well, that's why. Readers have also said that they see a deep schism; that I often depict God as the ultimate bad guy, and I think that's also a fair assumption. I trace that to adulthood. As a young man, I traveled the world and was exposed to many other religions and alternative ways of thinking. I came to realize that what I was brought up to believe wasn't the whole truth, the big picture; and that there were millions of other people whose ideas and faiths were just as valid and deep and personal.

I've gone through phases: occultism, powwow, paganism, Buddhism, atheism, and finally, agnosticism. At forty, I'm no longer sure what I believe, and that bothers me more and more each day. I believe in an afterlife, but I'm not sure that it's Heaven. I believe that there's something more to this world, to this universe, something behind the veil, but I'm not sure that it's

God.

Sometimes, it seems like the more I learn, the less I know.

I do know this. I often feel like Steve does at the end of this story. Sometimes, that kid inside of me, the kid who read Marvel comic books and rode his BMX Mongoose and watched Land of the Lost *and* Six-Million Dollar Man, *and listened to Rush and Ozzy Osbourne – and still made it to church every Sunday, speaks up and lets me know that he's still alive, that this cold, hard, cynical bastard I've become hasn't buried him completely. It is during these times that I remember exactly why I went to church each Sunday.*

Fear.

Fear of getting spanked by my parents for not going; fear of not fitting in with my peers (because back then, most of the cool kids did indeed go to church); and most of all, fear of what God would do to me if I didn't.

Fear of God.

I like to think I'm a new world man. I support gay marriage. I don't think religion should have any place in our schools or government or courts. I think we should reach out to other cultures and ways of life, regardless of whether they believe in our God or their God or any god. In Terminal, *when Tommy O'Brien rants that religion has fucked this planet up since day one, that's Brian Keene talking. It has. Most of the evils perpetrated by mankind aren't the work of the Devil, but can be traced back to religion; all done in God's name.*

I'd like to think I've evolved beyond that.

But then that kid inside of me, the one who made sure he sat still during the sermon and paid attention during Sunday school, speaks up, and reminds me of my fear.

I am afraid of God, and therefore, I believe.

I'm afraid not to.

BUNNIES IN AUGUST

One year later.

* * *

He shouldn't have come here. Not today. Especially not today.

This is where it happened, he thought. *This is where Jack died.*

Gary stood beneath the water tower. It perched atop the tallest hill in town, right between the Methodist church cemetery, and the rear of the tiny, decrepit strip mall (abandoned when Wal-Mart moved in two miles away), and a cornfield. The tower was a massive, looming, blue thing, providing water to the populace below. Every time he saw it, (which was all the time, because it was visible from everywhere in town) Gary was reminded of the Martian tripods from *War of the Worlds*. When Jack was old enough to read the graphic novel adaptation, it had reminded him of the same thing.

"It looks like one of the Martian robots, doesn't it Daddy? Doesn't it? Let's pretend the Martians are invading!"

The first tear welled up. Then another. They built to a crescendo. Surrendering, Gary closed his eyes and wept. A warm summer breeze rustled the treetops above him. His breath caught in his throat. He tried to swallow the lump, and found he couldn't. Sweat beaded his forehead. The heat was stifling. His skin prickled, as if on fire. As if he was burning. The wind brushed against him like caressing flames.

Blinking the tears away, he glanced back up at the water tower and wondered how he could bring it down. He saw it every day—on the drive home, from the grocery store parking lot, the backyard, even his bedroom window—and each time he was reminded of his son. The tower's presence was inescapable. How to erase its existence—and thus, the memories? A chainsaw was out of the question. The supports were made of steel. Explosives maybe? Yeah. Sure. He was a fucking insurance salesman. Where was he going to find explosives?

He hated the water tower. It stood there as an unwanted reminder, a dark monument to Jack.

This was where it happened.

This used to be their playground.

Weekends had always been their time together. During the week, Gary and Susan both worked, he at the insurance office and she from home, typing up tape-recorded court transcripts. Jack had school, fourth grade, where he excelled in English and Social Studies, but struggled with Math and Science. Gary didn't see them much on weeknights, either. He'd had other…obligations.

Leila's face popped into his mind, unbidden. He pushed her away.

Get thee behind me, Satan.

The weekends were magic. Once he'd waded through the mind-numbing tedium of domestic chores; grocery shopping, mowing the lawn, cleaning the gutters, and anything else Susan thought up for him to do while she sat at home all day long; after all that, there was Daddy and Jack time. Father and son time. Quality time.

Jack's first word had been "Da-da."

Gary had loved his son. Loved him so much that it hurt, sometimes. Despite how clichéd it may have sounded to some people, the pain was real. And good. When Jack was little, Gary used to stand over his crib and watch him sleeping. In those moments, Gary's breath hitched up in his chest—a powerful, overwhelming emotional wave. He'd loved Susan like that too, once upon a time, when they'd first been married. Before job-related stress and mortgage payments and their mutual weight gain—and before Susan's little personality quirks, things he'd thought were cute and endearing when he'd first met her, the very things he'd fallen in love with after the initial physical attraction, became annoying rather than charming. They knew everything there was to know about each other, and thus, they knew too much. Boredom set in, and worse, a simmering complacency that hollowed him out inside and left him empty. When Jack came along in their fifth year of marriage, Gary fell in love all over again, and his son had filled that hole.

At least temporarily...

Parental love was one thing. That completed a part of him. But Gary still had unfulfilled needs. Needs that Susan didn't seem inclined to acknowledge, and in truth, needs he wasn't sure she could have satisfied any longer even if she'd shown interest. Not with the distance between them, a gulf that had grown wider after Jack's birth. There were too many sleepless nights and grumpy mornings, too many laconic, grunted conversations in front of the television and not enough talking.

So Gary had gone elsewhere.

To Leila.

A crow called out above him, perched on a tree limb. The sound startled him, bringing Gary back to the present. The bird spread its wings and the branch bent under its wings. The leaves rustled as it took flight. Gary watched it go. His spirits plummeted even further as the bird soared higher.

He stepped out from underneath the water tower's shadow, back into the sunlight, and shivered.

We beat the Martians, Daddy! Me and you, together...

"Oh Jack," he whispered, "I'm so sorry."

Gary felt eyes upon him, a tickling sensation between

his shoulder blades. He glanced around. Through his tears, he noticed a rabbit at the edge of the field, watching him intently.

He sniffed, wiping his nose with the back of his hand.

The rabbit twitched its whiskers and kept staring. Gary felt its black eyes bore into him. He wondered if animals blinked.

The rabbit didn't.

"Scat." Gary stamped his foot. "Go on! Get out of here."

The rabbit scurried into the corn, vanishing as quickly as it had appeared. Gary studied the patch of grass where it had been sitting. The spot was empty, except for a large rock. Was it his imagination, or was the stone's surface red?

Maybe the animal was injured. Or dying.

His mind threatened to dredge up more of the past, and he bit his lip, drawing blood.

Gary checked the time on his cell phone. He'd been gone a long while. Susan would be worried. He shouldn't have left her alone, especially on today, of all days. But she'd insisted that at least one of them should visit Jack's grave. That was what had brought him here in the first place. He'd been drawn to the water tower without even thinking about it. Susan hadn't come with him to the cemetery. Said she couldn't bear it. She'd visited the grave many times over the past year, but not today. It had been left for Gary to do, and so he had.

He pressed a button, unlocking the keypad, and the phone's display lit up. It was just after twelve noon, on August fifteenth. But he'd already known the date.

How could he forget?

He trudged back the way he'd come, wading through the sweltering afternoon haze. Heat waves shimmered in the corners of his vision.

He shouldn't have come here. Not today, on the one year anniversary of his son's death. This was a bad idea. It was bad enough that he could see this stupid water tower everywhere he went. Why come this close to it? What was he hoping to find? To prove?

The wind whispered, *Daddy.*

Gary turned around, and gasped.

Jack stood beneath the water tower, watching him go. The boy was dressed in the same clothes the police had found him in.

Daddy…

His son reached out. Jack was transparent. Gary could see corn stalks on the other side of him.

"No. Not real. You're not real."

La la la la, lemon. La la la la, lullaby…

Gary shivered. Jack's favorite song from *Sesame Street.* He'd sung it all the time. All about the letter "L" and words that began with it; a Bert and Ernie classic from Gary's own childhood.

"You're not there," he told his son.

Gary stuck his pinky fingers in his ears and closed his eyes. When he opened them again, Jack was gone. He'd never been there. It was just the heat, playing tricks on him. He lowered his hands.

Something rustled between the rows of swaying corn.

Gary didn't believe in ghosts. He didn't need to. Memories could haunt a man much more than spirits ever could.

He walked home, passing through the cemetery on the way, and his son's grave.

He stopped at Jack's headstone, knelt in the grass, and wept. He did not see Jack again. He did spot several more rabbits, darting between tombstones, running through the grass. Playing amongst the dead.

He tried to ignore the fact that they all stopped to watch him pass.

* * *

By the time he got home, Gary's melancholy mood had turned into full-fledged depression. He'd been off the medication for months now, ever since he'd stopped seeing the counselor. If he went inside the house, he'd feel even worse.

Susan had been crying all morning, looking at pictures of Jack. He couldn't deal with that right now. Couldn't handle her pain. He was supposed to fix things for them, and this couldn't be fixed. Gary couldn't stand to see her hurting. Had never been able to.

He decided to mow the lawn instead. Even though he dreaded mowing, sometimes it made him feel better—the aroma of fresh cut grass and the neat, symmetrical rows. He went into the garage; made sure the lawnmower had enough oil and gas, and then rolled it out into the yard. It started on the third tug.

Gary pushed the lawnmower up and down the yard and tried not to think. Grasshoppers and crickets jumped out of his way, and yellow dandelions disappeared beneath the blades. He'd completed five rows and was beginning his sixth when he noticed the baby bunny.

Or what was left of it.

The rabbit's upper half crawled through the yard, trailing viscera and blood, grass clippings sticking to its guts. Its lower body was missing, presumably pulped by the lawnmower. Gary's hands slipped off the safety bar, and the lawnmower dutifully turned itself off.

Silence descended, for a brief moment, and then he heard something else.

The baby rabbit made a noise, almost like a scream.

Daddy?

He glanced around, frantic. A few feet away, the grass moved. Something was underneath it, hiding beneath the surface. Gary walked over and bent down, parting the grass. His fingers came away sticky and red. Secreted inside the remains of their warren were four more baby bunnies. The lawnmower had mangled them, and they were dying as he watched. Their black eyes stared at him incriminatingly. The burrow was slick with gore and fur.

Gary turned away. His breakfast sprayed across the lawn.

Despite their injuries, despite missing limbs and dangling intestines, the bunnies continued to thrash, their movements weak and jerky.

"Oh God," he moaned. "Why don't they die? Why don't—"

The half-rabbit dragging itself across the yard squealed again.

"Please," Gary whimpered. "Just die. Don't do this. Not today. It's too much."

Daddy? Daddyyyy? La la la la, lemon. La la la la lullaby…

Gary stumbled to his feet and ran to the driveway. Without thinking, he seized the biggest rock he could find, dashed back to the rabbit hole, and raised the rock over his head.

"I'm sorry."

He flung it down as hard as he could, squashing them. Their tiny bones snapped like twigs underfoot. Swallowing hard, Gary picked the rock back up again, ignoring the sticky, matted blood and fur that now clung to its bottom and sides. He stalked across the yard, tracked down the half-bunny and put it out of its misery, too.

Gasping for breath, he left the rock lay in the grass, concealing the carcass. His bowels clenched; then loosened. Kneeling, he threw up again. When it was over, he washed his hands and face off beneath the outside spigot.

This time, the tears didn't stop.

Gary wailed. One of his neighbors poked their head outside, attracted by the ruckus. When they saw his face, saw the raw emotions etched onto it, they ducked back inside.

Eventually, when he'd gotten himself under control, Gary went inside. He poured a double scotch, and gulped it down. The liquor burned his raw throat. He called out for Susan, but there was no answer. He found her in Jack's bedroom, sitting on their son's bed and holding one of his action figures. Her face was wet and pale. He sat down next to her, put his arm around her, and they cried together for a long time.

* * *

That night, Susan said she'd like to try again; she'd like to have another child. She murmured in his ear that it had been a long time since they'd made love, and apologized for it. Said it was her fault, and she'd like to try and fix things. Make them like they used to be, long ago, when they'd first been married. Every party of Gary stiffened, except for the part of him that could have helped insure that. When she noticed, and asked what was wrong, he told her that he didn't feel good. Too depressed. Susan pulled away. She asked Gary if he still loved her and he lied and said yes. She snuggled closer again, and put her head on his chest.

Gary thought of Leila and tried very hard not to scream. The guilt was a solid thing, and it weighed on him heavier than the thick blankets pulled over his body. He held Susan until she fell asleep and then he slipped out from underneath her. She moaned in her sleep, a sad sound. He went downstairs, turned on the television, and curled into the fetal position on the couch.

He'd never told her about Leila. As far as he knew, Susan had never suspected. At one point, he'd thought the secret might come out. Leila had made threats. She was unhappy. Wanted Gary to leave Susan and be with her. He'd been worried, frantic—unsure of what to do. But then Jack had died and the whole affair had become moot. For the past year, he and Susan had both been overwhelmed with grief. And though Leila was no longer in the picture, and though Gary had tried very hard to be there for his wife and make the marriage work, he couldn't tell Susan now. She was a mother who'd lost her child.

He couldn't hurt her all over again.

Restless, Gary tossed and turned. The couch springs squeaked. Eventually, he needed to pee. Rather than using the upstairs bathroom and risk waking Susan, he went outside, into the backyard. He pushed his robe aside, fumbled with the fly on his pajamas, and unleashed a stream.

And then he froze.

In the darkness, a pair of shiny little eyes stared back at

him. Although he couldn't see the animal itself, Gary knew what it was—the mother rabbit, looking for her dead children.

"I'm sorry," he whispered.

The eyes vanished in the darkness.

He went back inside and lay down on the couch again. Sleep would not come, nor would relief from the pain. It hadn't been this bad in a while, not since the months immediately following Jack's death.

Gary stared at the television without seeing.

It was a long time before he slept.

* * *

That December, when Gary got home from a particularly harrowing day at the office, Susan was in the bedroom, holding the stick from a home pregnancy test. It was the second of the day. She'd taken the first that morning, after he left for work. Both showed positive; a little blue plus sign, simple in its symbolism, yet powerful as well. That tiny plus sign led to joy and happiness—or sometimes—fear and heartbreak.

Susan was ecstatic, and that night, after they'd eaten a romantic, candlelight dinner, and curled up together to watch a movie, and made love, Gary decided that he'd never tell her about Leila. Not now. He couldn't.

After all, he'd lived with the guilt this long.

He could do it for the rest of his life.

* * *

According to the obstetrician, (an asthmatic, paunchy man named Doctor Brice) Susan was due in August, within ten days of the anniversary of Jack's death.

On the way home from Doctor Brice's office, Susan turned to Gary.

"It's a sign."

"What is?"

"My due date. It's like a sign from God."

Gary kept silent. He thought it might be the exact opposite.

* * *

Two years later.

* * *

On the second anniversary of their son's death, with Susan's due date a little more than a week away, they woke up, dressed solemnly, and prepared to visit Jack's grave. Susan had picked a floral arrangement the night before, and both of them had taken the day off work.

Once again, the August heat and humidity were insufferable. Gary waded through the thick miasma on his way to start the car (so that the air conditioner would have time to cool the interior before Susan came out). He slipped behind the wheel, put the key in the ignition, and turned it. The car sputtered and then something exploded. There was a horrible screech, followed by a wet thump. The engine hissed, and a brief gust of steam or smoke billowed from beneath the hood.

Cursing, Gary yanked on the hood release and jumped out of the car. He ran around to the front, popped the hood, and raised it. The stench was awful. He stumbled backward. Something wet and red had splattered all over the engine. Tufts of brown and white fur stuck to the metal. A disembodied foot lay on top of the battery.

A rabbit's foot.

Guess he wasn't so lucky, Gary thought, biting back a giggle. He was horrified, but at the same time, overwhelmed with the bizarre desire to laugh.

The rabbit must have crawled up into the engine block overnight, perhaps seeking warmth or just looking for a place to nest. When Gary had started the car, the animal most likely panicked and scurried for cover, taking a fatal misstep into the whirring fan blades.

He glanced back down at the severed rabbit's foot again.

A bunny. Same day. Just like last year. With the lawn-mower. He'd run over the nest, and then he'd...with the rock...

Susan tapped him on the shoulder and he nearly screamed. When she saw the mess beneath the hood, she almost did the same.

"What happened?"

"A rabbit. It must have crawled inside last night."

She recoiled, one hand covering her mouth. "Oh, that's terrible. The poor thing."

"Yeah. Let me get this cleaned up and then we'll go."

Susan began to sob. Gary went to her, and she sagged against him.

"I'm sorry. It's just..."

"I know," Gary consoled her. "I know."

She pushed away. "I think I'm going to be sick."

"Susan—"

Turning, she waddled as quickly as she could back to the house. Gary followed her, heard her retching in the bathroom, and after a moment's hesitation, knocked gently on the door.

"You okay?"

"No," she choked. "I don't think I can go. You'll go without me?"

"But Susan, I..."

She retched again. Gary closed his eyes.

"Please, Gary? I can't go. Not like this. One of us has to."

"You're right, of course."

Susan heard the reluctance in his voice.

"Please?"

Gary sighed. "Will you be okay?"

The toilet flushed. "Yes. I just need to rest. Remember to take the flowers."

"I will. Susan?"

"What?"

"I'm sorry."

He heard her running water in the sink.

"Don't be sorry," she said. "It's not your fault."

* * *

The graveyard was empty, except for an elderly couple on their way out as Gary arrived. Despite the heat, he'd decided to walk to the cemetery rather than dealing with the mess beneath the hood of his car. By the time he reached Jack's grave he was drenched in sweat, his clothing soaked.

Panting, he knelt in front of the grave. Droplets of perspiration ran into his eyes, stinging them. His vision blurred, and then the tears began. They were false tears, crocodile tears, tears of sweat and exertion, rather than grief. Oh, the grief was there. Gary was overwhelmed with grief. Grief was a big lump that sat in his throat. But still, the real tears would not come.

But the memories did.

When he glanced up at the water tower, the memories came full force.

Grief turned to guilt.

* * *

"I mean it, Gary. I'm telling Susan."

"You'll do no such thing."

Leila's smile was tight-lipped, almost a grimace. "I've got her email address."

Gary paused. Felt fear. "You're lying."

"Try me." Now her smile was genuine again, if cruel. "I looked it up on the internet. From her company's website."

Gary sighed. "Why? Why do this to me?"

"Because I'm sick of your bullshit. You said you loved me. You said you'd leave her—"

"I've told you, it's not that simple. I've got to think about Jack."

"She can't take Jack from you. You're his father. You've got rights."

"I can't take that chance. Damn it, Leila, we've been through this a million times. I love you, but I—"

"You're a fucking liar, Gary! Just stop it. If you loved me, you'd tell her."

"I do love you."

"Then do it. Tell her. If you don't have the balls to, I will."

"Are you threatening me? You gonna blackmail me into continuing this? Is that it?"

"If I have to."

Gary wasn't sure what happened next. They'd been naked, sitting side by side on the blanket, their fluids drying on each other's body, the water tower's shadow protecting them from the warm afternoon sun, hiding their illicit tryst. He wasn't aware that he was straddling Leila until his hands curled around her throat.

Choking, she lashed out at him. Her long, red fingernails raked across his naked chest. Flailing blindly, his hand closed around the rock. He raised it over his head and Leila's eyes grew large.

"Gary..."

The rock smashed into her mouth, cutting off the rest.

He lost all control then, hammering her face and head repeatedly. He blocked out everything; her screams, the frightened birds taking flight, his own nonsensical curses. Everything—until he heard the singing.

"La la la la, lemon. La la la la lullaby..."

Jack. Singing his favorite song.

The boy stepped into the clearing. Believing his father was working that Saturday (because that was the lie Gary had told Susan and Jack so that he could meet up with Leila for an afternoon quickie in the first place—he'd even stayed logged into his computer at work so that if anybody checked, it would look like he was there working), Jack froze in mid-melody, a mixture of puzzlement and terror on his face.

"Daddy?"

"Jack!"

His son turned and ran. Gary sprang to his feet, naked and bloody, and chased after him.

"Jack, stop! Daddy can explain."

"Mommy..."

Unaware that he was still holding the rock, he struck his son in the back of the head.

"I said stop!"

Jack toppled face first into the grass. He did not move. Did not breathe.

When Gary checked his pulse, he had none.

Something inside Gary shut itself off at that moment.

The rest of the memories became a blur. He dressed. Wrapped the blanket around Leila and loaded her into the trunk of the car, which he'd parked behind the abandoned strip mall, just beyond the cemetery and the water tower. Her blood hadn't yet seeped out onto the grass, and he made sure none of her teeth or any shreds of tissue were in sight. He'd thrown her clothes and purse inside the car as well.

Then he picked up the bloody rock, the rock that he'd just bludgeoned his son to death with, and threw it down a nearby rabbit hole.

He drove to the edge of LeHorn's Hollow, where a sinkhole had opened up the summer before, and dumped Leila's body. Gary knew that the local farmers sometimes dumped their dead livestock in the same hole, as did hunters after field dressing wild game. The chances were good that she'd never be found.

He cleaned his hands off in a nearby stream, then got back in the car and drove to the closest convenience store. He bought some cleaning supplies, paid cash, and then found a secluded spot where he could clean out the trunk. Then he returned to the office, unlocked the door, logged himself off the computer, and went home.

The police knocked on the door a few hours later. Three teenaged boys found Jack's body. One of them, Seth Ferguson (who was no stranger to juvenile detention) immediately fell under suspicion. When the police cleared him later that day, they questioned the local registered sex offenders, even though Jack's body had shown no signs of sexual abuse. In the weeks and months that followed, there were no new leads. The case was never solved.

The murder weapon was never found.

* * *

Daddy...

Gary sat up and wiped his eyes. Steadying himself on his son's tombstone, he clambered to his feet. His joints popped. He hadn't aged well in the last two years, and his body was developing the ailments of a man twice his age, arthritis being one of them.

Daddy?

"Oh Jack," Gary whispered. "Why couldn't you have stayed home that day?"

Daddy...

His son's voice grew louder, calling to him, pleading. Sad. Lonely.

Slowly, like a marionette on strings, Gary shuffled towards the water tower.

"Where are you, Jack? Show me. Tell me what I have to do to make it up to you."

Daddy...Daddy...Daddy...

The voice was right next to him. Gary looked around, fully expecting to see his son's ghost, but instead, he spied the rabbits. A dozen or so bunnies formed a loose circle around the water tower. They'd been silent, and had appeared as if from nowhere.

Penning him in.

Daddy. Down here.

Gary looked down at the ground.

Jack's voice echoed from inside a rabbit hole.

The same hole he'd thrown the rock into.

Gary's skin prickled. Despite his fear, he leaned over

and stared into the hole. There was a flurry of movement inside, and then a rabbit darted out and joined the others. Then another. Whimpering, Gary stepped backward. More bunnies poured themselves from the earth, and he felt their eyes on him—accusing.

Condemning.

"What do you want?"

Daddy.

Gary screamed.

* * *

They found him when the sun went down. He'd screamed himself hoarse while pawing at the ground around his son's grave. His fingers were dirty, and several of his fingernails were bloody and ragged, hanging by thin strands of tissue. He babbled about bunnies, but no one could understand him. The police arrived, as did an ambulance.

From the undergrowth, a brown bunny rabbit watched them load Gary into the ambulance.

When he was gone, it hopped away.

STORY NOTES

This story first appeared on the Horror World *website. It takes place in the same town as my novel* Dark Hollow *(as does the end of* Take The Long Way Home*), and alert readers might recognize a few familiar places and people. The water tower exists much as I described it here, but it is far less sinister in real life. My oldest son and I used to play there when he was little. The mishap with the rabbits and the lawnmower is also based on something that happened in real life. I was mowing my lawn and accidentally hit a hidden nest of baby rabbits. It was horrifying and terrible and I felt guilty about it for months afterward. I channeled some of that into the story.*

MIDNIGHT AT THE BODY FARM

For Susan Repasky

The dead outside the body farm's security fence were much more lively than the ones inside the compound. They smelled just as bad, though.

"My God..."

Hector Bolivar took a last sip of cold instant coffee, and watched their efforts.

Both types of dead were dangerous.

The corpses on the body farm didn't move, but they posed a danger through microbes and disease. Following established procedures and wearing the proper protective gear negated these threats, but such protocols offered little protection against the dead outside. The new dead were different. They moved. Bit. Clawed. And while they spread disease like the farm's inhabitants, the more prevalent danger was that they'd eat you long before infection set in.

When the zombies finally tore through the razor wire and made it onto the property, Bolivar ran for the building's exit. He jumped into a battery-powered golf cart, started the engine, and pulled away, heading towards the forest. The body farm's massive acreage held many different kinds of landscape—forests, thickets, grassland, ponds and streams. They'd even built a manmade desert near the rear of the property. But sand dunes would offer little cover. He'd be safer among the trees.

The zombies plodded along in slow pursuit.

Bolivar grinned, despite his terror. As long as he could outrun them, he'd be okay.

Before Hamelin's Revenge—a name the media gave the disease in reference to the rats that had spawned it—eradicated all of mankind's achievements and reduced them to meat, Bolivar had been a leading Forensic Anthropologist and head of the National Institute for Justice's "body farm"—a secure, twenty-acre parcel of land in rural Virginia. The compound's purpose was to advance the study of decomposition on the human body in relation to climate, weather and exposure to the elements. One of three such locations in the country, the Virginia body farm provided every possibility for research—snow, rain, heat, and other conditions. Professionals from the Federal, State, and local levels—criminologists, medical examiners, coroners, pathologists, biological anthropologists, homicide investigators, and even the armed forces—regularly visited the site in the pursuit of science and better law enforcement. They studied how climate, insects, plants, and other factors advanced or slowed decay. The bodies were donated by families, universities, and medical research institutes.

The facility operated with a staff of twenty and usually contained at least two-hundred corpses.

Now it was just Bolivar.

And the corpse count had just doubled.

The cart's top speed was five miles per hour, but it was still faster than his pursuers. The zombies fell far behind as Bolivar drove into the darkness. The moon and stars were hidden behind a thick cover of clouds. The air was hot. Sticky. It felt heavy and charged. Bolivar had no doubt there would be a thunderstorm before morning. The cloying atmosphere made the stench that much worse. In his rush to leave, he'd forgotten his protective gear. He was used to the smell of decomposition, of course, but that didn't make the reeking miasma any more pleasant. Coughing, he breathed through his mouth.

The headlights flashed off a corpse in an advanced stage of decay. It was propped up against a tree. A small red tag fluttered from a stake next to it, denoting how long it had been there, the cause of death, and other factors. The legs had turned to pudding and spread out all over the grass.

Upon reaching the woods, he turned off the cart and walked towards the edge of the forest. The space between the trees was shadowed and silent. Bolivar shivered in the heat. As he crept into the woods, his pulse beat faster. Sweat ran into his eyes and dripped from his nose.

A branch snapped to his left. Bolivar spun around, but couldn't see anything in the darkness. He suppressed the urge to cry out. Instead, he crouched down and waited. More branches snapped. Something rustled nearby. There was a wet, phlegm-filled snort, and then a shape emerged from the shadows.

A deer.

The body farm had wildlife, of course. That was part of the studies. He'd seen deer on the grounds before—had watched them with his colleagues from their office windows.

But as it drew closer, Bolivar saw that this deer was different.

It was dead. Even though he couldn't see it very well, he could smell the rot and hear the flies buzzing around it.

Hamelin's Revenge had jumped species. First the rats, then humans, and now deer.

My God, he thought, *if it manages to infect avian life forms...*

The deer made an awkward lunge for him. Bolivar dodged it easily enough and scampered backward—straight into another congealing corpse. Wetness soaked into his pants and shirt. His hands clawed through something warm with the consistency of tapioca pudding. Bolivar raised his arms to shield himself. Gore dripped from them.

The zombie attacked.

And then the only thing left on the body farm were two types of dead.

STORY NOTES

This story was written for the special lettered edition of Dead Sea, *and takes place in that same world. I got the idea from an old friend of mine, Susan Repasky, who teaches high school chemistry. She sent me an article about a real-life body farm, and attached a note that said, "I bet you can do something with this."*

She was right.

It might also interest you to know that each year, Susan has her classes conduct an experiment based on my story Red Wood *(from* Fear of Gravity*). She's hardcore, man.*

THE GHOSTS OF MONSTERS

The moon peeked down through the treetops.

"That's weird."

"What?"

"The moon is red."

Roy shrugged. "Yeah, I know."

"Wonder what made it do that?" Sally mused. "Pollution, maybe?"

"It's a hunter's moon," he explained. "That's what my daddy and my grandpa used to call it."

"Were they hunters?"

Smiling, Roy nodded. "Best damn hunters you've ever seen."

"How about you? Do you hunt?"

"Sure."

"Ever hunt *here*?"

"In LeHorn's Hollow? Nope, not yet. I usually hunt in Adams County, out by Gettysburg. I need to find a new place, though. There's too much posted property and the game are all skittish."

Roy ducked under a low-hanging branch and then pulled it out of the way until Sally had passed by. Then he performed a mock bow, making a sweeping gesture with his arm.

Sally giggled. "Thank you, sir."

"My pleasure."

They continued down the narrow, winding trail, heading deeper into the forest. The woods were dark and still. There were no birds or insects. Neither one of them minded. That just meant that their impromptu midnight stroll was mosquito-free. Roy gripped the flashlight in one hand, moving the beam back and forth in front of them. An old blanket was tucked into the crook of his arm. His other hand held Sally's. Her long, pink nails grazed against his skin, making him shiver with excitement. The crotch of his jeans seemed to grow smaller—more confining. His erection strained against the zipper.

"This isn't really the hollow," Sally said. "That's miles from here, near that ghost walk where all those people died last year. The real hollow is all burned down now."

"Yeah, but this is still part of the same forest. People call it LeHorn's Hollow, even if the actual hollow isn't there anymore."

"So how come you never hunted here?"

Roy shrugged. "Never had the chance before. I live all the way out in Hanover. I don't get to this side of the county very often."

"So what brought you out this way tonight, then?"

He shrugged. "I don't know. Tired of drinking at the same old bar, I guess. Needed a change of scenery. Figured I'd see how things looked out this way."

Sally gave her hips a little shake. "And have you liked what you've seen?"

"So far."

"Me, too. I'm glad you decided to have a drink in my regular bar."

"You go there often?"

"Every Friday night. You come back next week, and I'll be waiting. Maybe we can do this again."

"Well, we didn't do anything yet."

"The night is young."

Roy smiled. His erection grew harder.

"So, are you married?" he asked.

"Nope."

"Boyfriend?"

She shook her head. "Nah. Only men in my life are my father and my two brothers. You'd like them. They're big hunters, too."

"Oh, yeah?"

"Yeah. Every year, they take a week off work for deer season and go up to Potter County."

Roy paused, let go of her hand, and lit a cigarette. He offered Sally one, but she declined.

"Don't worry," he said. "I've got some of those Listerine thingies in my pocket."

She took his hand again and squeezed. "I don't mind. And besides, those things burn if you—"

"What?"

She seemed flustered. "If you put one on your tongue, and then go down on somebody, it burns."

Roy's laughter echoed through the darkness. When he shined the flashlight on Sally, she was blushing.

"Don't laugh." She punched his arm playfully.

"Don't worry. I won't put one on my tongue if you don't want me to."

She arched an eyebrow. "Is that a promise of things to come?"

"We'll be doing more than that, soon as we find a good spot."

"I still don't understand why we had to come all the way out here."

"Well, not to be rude, but I don't want to get stuff on my upholstery."

"What kind of stuff?"

Now it was Roy's turn to seem flustered. "You know. Bodily fluids..."

Sally snickered. "You're really something, Roy. I'm glad I met you tonight."

"So am I."

"Still, I don't know why we couldn't have just spread that old blanket out in the cab of your truck."

He swept the flashlight beam in a wide arc, letting it

glide across the dark tree trunks and boulders. "And miss all this ambience?"

"Aren't you afraid of the monsters?" Sally teased.

Roy snorted in derision. "What monsters?"

"Oh, come on. You've never heard all the legends about these woods? The Goat-Man who plays his pipes at night and seduces women? That writer guy from Shrewsbury supposedly went nuts while working on a book about him."

"Adam Senft—the one who escaped from the nuthouse last year and killed those people on the ghost walk?"

"Yeah."

"Well, he was batshit crazy."

"But he wasn't the only one who was supposed to have seen the Goat-Man. And there's more. The black hound dog with red eyes. Balls of light that float around through the forest. Ghosts. Demons. And some people say that the trees move on their own."

"It's all bullshit," Roy said. "There's no such thing as monsters."

"You don't believe any of the stories about this place?"

"Well, I know that a lot of people have died here over the years. But that doesn't mean it was monsters. It was just people acting like people. Human beings are evil enough. We don't have to invent stories about monsters. Why? Don't tell me you believe in that stuff?"

Sally pouted. "I don't know…a little, maybe."

Roy stopped in the middle of the trail, and shined the beam across the ground. He released her hand, sat the flashlight down on a rock, and unfolded the blanket.

"This looks like a good spot."

"You read my mind."

"Come here."

He pulled her close. They kissed, tongues entwining hungrily. Their hands explored each other's bodies. Sally shivered.

"You cold?"

She nodded, nuzzling his chest. "A little. And a little

nervous. I mean, we just met."

"You sure that's all?"

"Well what else would it be?"

"I don't know. Maybe you're afraid of the Goat-Man."

She hugged him tighter. "You've got to admit, it is a little creepy out here at night."

"Don't worry," he said. "There are no monsters in LeHorn's Hollow."

Then he pulled out the knife and stabbed her in the neck. He let her body sag onto the blanket, and watched it jerking and twitching. Sally's eyes were wide. She clawed at the hilt jutting from her throat, and made faint gobbling noises. Her hands grew slick with her own blood. Roy could no longer contain his excitement. He pulled down his zipper and let his erection bob in the cool night air.

"No monsters," he repeated. "Just hunters, like me. The monsters are all ghosts now. I'm the real thing."

STORY NOTES

This was written for the special lettered edition of Ghost Walk. *It takes place in LeHorn's Hollow – the spooky setting for* Ghost Walk, Dark Hollow *(also published as* The Rutting Season*) and* "Red Wood". *This story occurs sometime after the events of* Ghost Walk. *I think it has a real Richard Laymon and Ed Gorman vibe to it, which pleases me to no end.*

TEQUILA'S SUNRISE
(A Fable)

Tequila has no history; there are no anecdotes confirming its birth. This is how it's been since the beginning of time, for tequila is a gift from the gods and they don't tend to offer fables when bestowing favors. That is the job of mortals, the children of panic and tradition.
—Alvaro Mutis

Where shall I go?
Where shall I go?
The road of the god of duality.
Is your house in the place of the fleshless?
Perchance inside heaven?
Or here on earth only?
—Traditional Aztec funeral chant

To open doors, one must first know how to find them.
—Daemonolateria

Once upon a time, which is how most fables begin, there was a land known as Oaxaca. The people who lived in Oaxaca called themselves the Tenochas, but history would call them the Aztecs. Oaxaca was a deadly place, a country full of extremes—in its people, creatures, and the landscape itself. Although it offered much beauty and wonder, there were myriad dangers lurking there as well.

Atop one of Oaxaca's snow-covered, treeless mountains, a thousand feet above the sea and overlooking a wide, fertile valley, sat the city of Monte Alban. It was a large city (though not the biggest) and many people lived there. In the morning, the sun glinted off the frescoed temples and buildings in its plaza. At night, the moon reflected on its ceremonial pools.

Before the Spaniards arrived in Oaxaca, a young boy named Chalco could often be found on Monte Alban's expansive ball courts playing tlachtli and patolli with his friends. But when Cortes's army landed on their shores, Lord Moctezuma issued a war summons. The invaders' intentions were unclear. They said they came in peace, but they brought a new god and drove the people of Oaxaca before them like cattle.

Most of the able-bodied men in Monte Alban answered Moctezuma's call to arms, and traveled to the capital city of Tenochtitlan. Chalco and the other boys had to assume their place and were now responsible for farming, hunting, and all the other tasks. There was no more time for play or fun—only for the everyday drudgery of life. Childhood ended early and there was no time to miss it or weep for its passing. There were no more games and no more play, and the ball courts sat empty and silent, their stones dusty.

Some people said it was the end of the world.

Perhaps they were right.

* * *

The day Chalco met the worm began like any other.

It began in darkness.

* * *

Before dawn, the call to rise echoed across the city, as it

did every day. Inside the pyramid temples, the priests blew conch shell trumpets while their acolytes beat on wooden drums. The noise disturbed the birds roosting on the temple peaks. Shrieking, they flew into the sky, adding to the cacophony. The music throbbed through the streets and alleys, waking the residents.

Chalco stared up at the thatched roof of his family's adobe hut and rubbed sleep dust from the corners of his eyes. He was still tired. After working in the fields all day long, he'd gone to bed late the night before. Today would offer a welcome change. He planned on going hunting.

His clan's larder grew empty.

The drumming continued and the trumpets sounded again. Around him, Chalco's mother, sisters, and younger brother stirred. The adobe had two rooms, partitioned down the middle. On one side were the sleeping quarters. The other side held the kitchen and dining area.

As Chalco stumbled out of bed, his mother tended to the fire, which they'd banked the night before. Kneeling, she blew it back to life. Was it his imagination or did she look older today than she had in recent months? Her once black hair was now streaked with white. She didn't smile very much anymore, and there were lines on her face. He knew that she missed his father.

Chalco missed him, too. He wondered if they'd see him again.

Outside, the trumpets sounded one more time—wailing long and mournfully before they faded. Somewhere, in a nearby hut, a baby cried.

Yawning, Chalco got dressed. He passed his otterskin maxtli between his legs, and then cinched it around his waist. The two ends of the loincloth hanging down in the front and back were embellished with intricate designs of an eagle and a jaguar—the totems of his clan. He pulled a mantle of woven cloth over his left shoulder, and then slipped into his deerskin sandals. His feet had gotten bigger, and his toes felt cramped inside them. Soon, it would be time for a new pair.

At five feet five inches, Chalco was considered tall for his people. His father often joked that perhaps he was really the son of the cannibal giants rumored to live in the Northern caves. But he also said that Chalco's size was a blessing, especially when it came to work. His broad head and thick neck were good for carrying baskets, and his long, muscular arms and wide feet aided him both in the field and on the hunt. Chalco did not mind his size. He knew it gave him an advantage over the other boys. The only thing he did not like was his coarse, dark hair. Currently, the thick bangs hung over his almond-shaped eyes and got in his way. He had to constantly flip his hair away from his face. Despite the annoyance, Chalco was reluctant to cut it. He wanted a long, braided ponytail like many of the older men had. He'd noticed that women seemed to fancy them.

The fire's glow filled the hut. The warmth felt good. Dressed for the day, Chalco turned to his little brother. He was still in bed, blinking, half-awake.

"Quintox, get up."

The younger boy shook his head. "I am still tired, Chalco."

"Did you not rest well?" Chalco knew that Quintox missed their father and uncles, and wondered if it was affecting his sleep.

"I had a strange dream."

Chalco sat on the edge of the bed and patted his head. "What was it?"

"I shouldn't say." Quintox frowned. "It might be wrong to tell."

"Then whisper if you are ashamed, so that our sisters won't hear."

Quintox lowered his voice. His eyes were wide. His bottom lip trembled.

"I dreamed that Cortes was really Quetzalcoatl."

Chalco stiffened. He glanced around quickly, making sure the rest of the family hadn't heard his brother's blasphemy. Such talk could lead to only one thing—Quintox being sacrificed to Tlaloc, the rain god who required children several times a year as tribute. Although the priests also gathered children's tears in a ceremonial bowl as an offering, that would not be Quintox's fate. Not for blasphemy. He would shed blood rather than tears. To compare Quetzalcoatl, the Plumed Serpent, greatest of all the gods, to Cortes, the leader of the Spanish invaders, was unforgivable.

"Stop that right now. I mean it. No more of this talk."

"But Chalco, the priests say that this is the year Quetzalcoatl is supposed to return. Remember? He promised that he would come back and deliver us. He would usher in a new era of peace and prosperity. 'Look to the east', they say. If this is the end of the world, then surely he must come."

The boy recited it from memory. The prophecy was ingrained in them all from the time they learned to speak and read. Chalco knew it well. In Tenochtitlan's grandest place of worship—a temple devoted to Tonatiuh, the sun god—there was a gigantic stone monolith, eighteen feet in diameter and carved from a single, black volcanic rock. It was a calendar. According to the calendar, Quetzalcoatl would return this year to save his faithful servants. He would sail across the ocean from parts unknown and arrive on Oaxaca's eastern shore. After he'd driven their enemies from the land, one hundred years of peace would follow.

So far, none of this had come to pass. Instead of Quetzalcoatl, it had been Cortes and his armies who landed on the eastern shore. They'd carved a swath through the country as they pressed farther inland, claiming to come in peace even while people died. It was a bad omen.

Although he would never admit it out loud, Chalco often wondered if Quetzalcoatl would ever return. Maybe the priests were wrong. Or maybe…maybe the plumed serpent didn't even exist. Maybe none of the gods did. Perhaps the gods were just stories. It wasn't the first time he'd considered this, and it filled him with dread. In the light of day, he was sure the gods existed, and fearful they would exact revenge for his doubt.

"Chalco," Quintox asked. "What are you thinking?"

"Nothing." Ashamed by his thoughts, Chalco pulled the covers off his little brother and boxed the boy's ears. "Enough talk. The sun will be up before you are. Get dressed. And don't speak of this anymore."

When Quintox was ready, they kissed their mother goodbye and walked down the street to the communal bathhouse. The huts were separated—one for men and one for women. The boys took their place in line and slowly shuffled forward. Once inside, they undressed and then bathed, using sticky soap made from tree sap. Morose slaves poured water over heated rocks and the room filled with steam. As they cleaned themselves, the boys listened to the older men gossip—merchants, craftsmen, medicine doctors, priests, the elderly or infirm, and others who had been excused from Moctezuma's call to arms.

The talk was mixed; much of it was dire. A black pheasant had been spotted the day before, lurking in the brush near the temple of Huehueteotl. A prisoner of war, condemned to sacrifice, briefly lived after his head was cut from his body. His legs and arms had flopped and jittered while the priest held his severed head aloft. Then his decapitated body tried to run away. Another priest who'd been carrying a stone tray laden with palpitating human hearts had been wounded by a jaguar. The beast leapt from the shadows and mauled the unfortunate victim, and then snatched the offerings from the tray before vanishing. A two-headed calf was born in the night. It cried out like a human and then died. A metalworker came in contact with his wife's menstrual blood—always an invitation to disaster. Bad tidings, all.

To make matters worse, these things happened in the midst of an invasion. The Spanish continued with their conquest, and the talk and rumors soon turned to that. It was said they brought their own slaves with them—people with skin as black as coal. The men in the steam room wondered what kind of people these obsidian slaves were. They seemed fierce and proud. Could they not rise up against their captors and break their bonds?

When they'd finished bathing, the boys got dressed again and hurried home for a breakfast of tortillas, beans, and warm goat's milk. In contrast to the gossip of the bathhouse, Chalco's family ate in silence. His mother admonished one of his sisters to chew with her mouth closed. Quintox asked for more beans. But other than that, they were quiet. Their mood mirrored the oppressive atmosphere that seemed to hang over all of Monte Alban.

After breakfast was finished, his mother and sisters cleaned the clay bowls while Chalco drew his brother aside.

"I must go hunting today. We need more meat." Quintox grew excited. "Can I come with you? Please? Before he left, Father said that I am old enough to start learning how to hunt."

"And you are." Chalco smiled. "Soon, I'll teach you as Father taught me. But not today. There is too much to be done. Mother needs help in the fields—you have a strong back, just like I do. Just like all the men in our clan. You will be more help to us there."

Quintox's expression soured. He looked at the ground and pouted.

"But I don't want to farm. Farming isn't noble or exciting. I want to hunt—to help."

"Listen." Chalco squeezed his shoulder. "It's war time. We each have to do our part. That is the way it has always been. Remember what we've been taught. Nobody is more important than another, except for Lord Moctezuma and the priests. By helping our mother in the fields you are helping us all. That is a very noble thing, Quintox—the noblest thing of all. Honor our clan. And don't worry. There will be many more days to go hunting, and much game to kill. You'll get your chance."

"Promise?"

"I promise."

Quintox smiled. "I want to grow up just like you. I want to make our father proud, the way you do."

"Oh, you do, Quintox. You really do. You make our entire clan very proud."

And he did. Chalco had very recently begun to take an interest in girls, particularly Yamesha, the jewel-cutter's daughter. He hoped that when the time came, their families might arrange a marriage for them. If so, he hoped that his first child would be a son—and that the boy would be just like his little brother.

Grinning, he gently boxed Quintox's ears. The younger boy pushed him away. Laughing, they punched one another until their mother spoke up. Her voice was stern and tired.

"Go on now, both of you. Enough talking. You can do that at dinnertime. To the fields with you, Quintox. The sun is coming up. It will be hot in a few hours. It is better to work now, while the air is still cool."

"Are you not coming, Mother?" Quintox asked.

"I will join you shortly. First, I must stop by the temple and offer prayers for your father and uncles. Chalco, your sisters have prepared a lunch for you to take on the hunt. Don't forget it."

"Thank you, Mother. I won't."

She kissed them both and then left the hut. Quintox and his sisters departed for the fields. Alone in the dwelling, Chalco gathered his weapons. He strapped a deer hide sheath to his waist and thrust his stone knife into it. Then he collected his bow and strapped a quiver of arrows over his back. Finally, he slung a wicker basket over his other shoulder. Inside were tortillas, wrapped in leaves to keep them fresh, along with two small limes and a water skin sealed with beeswax. The skin was filled with pulque, a slightly alcoholic drink made from agave. Chalco preferred water. He hated the bitter taste of pulque. But it would give him stamina later, and water was too precious to spare. Rain had been scarce this season and water was being rationed.

Chalco departed. The first rays of dawn shone across the sky. With many of the men off to war, the streets were quieter than normal. But in the silence, Chalco heard things he didn't normally pay attention to. Birds chirped from the rooftops, having returned to their roosts once the morning trumpets faded. A goat snorted as Chalco passed by a trough. A baby wailed from a nearby hut. In one of the temples, the first sacrifice of the day screamed. Several small children chased each other in the street, shrieking in delight. The cries intermingled, becoming indistinguishable from one another—screams or laughter, they sounded the same.

Chalco admired one of the pyramids as he passed by. He wished, not for the first time, that he could build something like it. How grand would that be, to honor the gods and his clan in such a manner? But his skills lay elsewhere, like his father and his father before him. He was a hunter and a farmer—and a warrior. His hands were made for soil and blood, rather than stone and brick. Still, he'd always been enamored with Monte Alban's artisans and craftsmen. The city's architecture was marvelous. Chalco hoped that one day soon he might travel to the capital, and gaze upon Tenochtitlan's fountains and streets. He'd heard so many wonderful stories about the city. They had running water there. The temples were supposed to be the grandest in all of Oaxaca. He longed to traverse the canals, visit the great houses full of books, to touch the golden Codex wheel, and see Lord Moctezuma's procession as they passed by adorned with bells and jewels and brightly colored feathers. It was said that dancers went before him, casting flower petals on the ground.

Chalco shuddered, wondering what would happen to all of Tenochtitlan's wonders if they fell into the invaders' hands. Would Monte Alban be next? If so, what would happen to his family? To his little brother? To Yamesha?

The thought made his stomach hurt.

Around the next corner, he passed an old woman pushing a cart piled high with woven fabrics. The old woman did not smile.

He knew how she felt.

Gripping his bow tightly, Chalco clenched his teeth and walked on. He passed by a row of stone monuments—a throne symbolizing Moctezuma's rule, and several giant heads representing the previous rulers. Slaves scrubbed bird droppings from the carvings. They hummed as they worked. The tune was sad.

When he arrived at the marketplace, the city came to life, bustling with sound and activity. Voices cried out between the stalls, bartering and selling, and alternately praising or beseeching Yacatecuhtli, the god of merchants. The market thrummed with smells and sights. There was livestock and wild game: rabbits, lizards, serpents, quail, partridges, turkeys, pigeons, parrots, and goats—some alive and others freshly killed. He ignored these, thankful as always that he came from a clan of hunters. There was no need to spend money on such things when you could kill it yourself.

Flipping his bangs away from his eyes, Chalco passed by a row of apothecaries. In front of the structures, merchants sold medicinal herbs and roots, as well as charms and totems. There was a barbershop, a rug-maker, and a metalworker. On a small platform, sullen slaves—mostly the children of other slaves or prisoners of war from beyond Oaxaca's borders—were sold like livestock. Sometimes, Chalco felt sorry for the slaves. But they were necessary.

Prostitutes preened in a side-alley, ready to start another day. With so many of the men gone, their business was down. Craftsmen shouted, hawking their various wares and services. There were stalls of cotton, thread, sandals, animal skins, blankets, dyes, pottery, ceramic dolls, trinkets, amulets, rope, bricks and mortar, oils, paints, charcoal, beads, paper, tobacco, salt, gold, silver, precious stones like jade and amber, feathers and quetzal plumes, earrings and nose ornaments, weapons, tackle, wicker baskets, and even lumber (imported since Monte Alban had sparse woodlands).

Chalco's mouth watered as he passed by maize, beans, maguey, peppers, cereals, squash, sweet potatoes, pumpkins, tomatoes, nuts, and chocolate. If the hunt was bountiful, he would sell some wild game on his return and buy some chocolate for his mother and siblings. That would make them happy. For the first time since his departure, Chalco smiled.

He reached the outskirts of the city and passed through the fields. Clan members and slaves worked alongside each other, tending rows of maize and beans, and gathering tree sap to make rubber and soap. An apiary buzzed with honeybees. Smoke curled from a burning sewage pit.

A group of warriors—left behind to guard Monte Alban when the rest of the men had gone—wound their way along a narrow trail, traveling down into the valley below. Chalco wondered where they were going, but didn't ask. Their faces were grim, their bodies painted.

After slinging his bow with gut-thread and readjusting his quiver and basket, Chalco headed farther up the mountain. It was easy travel at first. He stuck to the well-trod footpath, avoiding the prickly cacti. Soon, the city's noise faded and the sounds of nature took over—the screech of a hawk far overhead (out of range of his arrows), the whisper of a spider clambering over a rock, a bush rustling in an all-too-brief gust of wind. He saw no other people and no game, either. The countryside was deserted. The hot sun climbed higher into the sky and no further breezes were forthcoming. Chalco started to sweat. Thin beads of perspiration dripped from his forehead and upper lip.

The steep, winding trail grew narrower, and then vanished altogether. Chalco pressed on, watching where he stepped, alert for snakes and scorpions. Both could penetrate the soles of his sandals. There was still no movement. He found some rabbit tracks in the dirt, but they were at least two days old. A sidewinder track followed after them. He wasn't the only predator looking for game. He hoped the serpent had better luck than him. The bow grew slippery in his sweaty hands. He spotted a brown lizard sunning itself on a flat stone, but it was too small to bother with—nothing more than a mouthful. It skittered away as he walked by.

Pausing, Chalco knelt in the dirt and rooted through his basket. He pulled out the water skin, unsealed the beeswax with his thumbnail, and took a long drink of pulque, grimacing at the taste. Then he sealed it back up and pulled a lime from the basket. Continuing on his way, he bit a hole in the fruit, relishing the tangy peel. He sucked the juice out as he walked. Sweat ran into his eyes.

Even this far from Monte Alban, the mountain still seemed deserted. It was as if all the wildlife had fled from the advancing Spaniards. Boredom set in and instead of watching for game, Chalco daydreamed. He thought of his friends. He remembered their days spent playing tlachtli, or gathering in the main plaza to watch prisoners of war be sacrificed, or joining in the great feasts. He missed his friends. They rarely saw each other these days. Like him, their fathers had all gone to Tenochtitlan and the boys were left to provide for their clans. The only time he really got to see his friends anymore was at temple, and then they couldn't speak freely.

His thoughts turned to Yamesha, and his stomach fluttered.

More sweat stung his eyes, but now it wasn't just from the heat. He hated the way Yamesha made him feel, but at the same time, it excited him. On the rare occasions that he got to talk with her, Chalco's mouth refused to work. He tried hard to think of something clever or funny to say. Instead, he said nothing. When she looked at him, he looked away. When she smiled at him, he frowned. Yet she was never far from his thoughts. She was intoxicating—and terrifying. The worst part was that he didn't understand why. What made the jeweler's daughter so different than the other women in his life? His sisters didn't have that effect on him. Neither did his mother or aunts. Why should it be otherwise with Yamesha? Why should he grow his hair long just to impress her? It made no sense.

Despite his conflicted emotions, Chalco really did want to marry her. At fourteen, he wasn't old enough yet. Men from the clans could marry at twenty and the women at sixteen. But with all of the recent changes in Monte Alban, perhaps the priests would ease that restriction. After all, if, in his father's absence, Chalco was now the head of his clan, why could he not enjoy all the benefits of adulthood? Couldn't he and Yamesha perform the right of Tilmantli, just like any other young couple? They were of different clans and different blood, as required by law. That was enough. He pictured himself going before the clan council and seeking permission from the old woman matchmaker. His father was there, celebrating victory over the invaders. His mother was smiling again, as were his sisters. So was Quintox.

I want to be just like you…

Lost in his fantasies, Chalco didn't see the pheasant lurking inside a nearby thicket. Startled by his approach, the bird burst from the shrubs, squawking with fright. Its wings beat the air in an explosion of multi-colored feathers.

Startled, Chalco jumped backward, dropping his bow. His heart beat faster. As the pheasant flew away, he scrambled to retrieve the weapon. He notched an arrow with trembling hands and tried to aim, but the bird was already out of range.

"Gods damn the fowl!"

Chalco shivered, and then wondered why. It was the middle of the day. The sun was at its peak. He should be sweltering in the heat. Instead, his sweat had dried on his skin.

He glanced around, stunned. There were no familiar landmarks, no rockslides or canyons or caves that he recognized. Lost inside his head, thoughts consumed with Yamesha, he had wandered farther up the mountain than he'd ever been before. But how? Had he really been daydreaming that long? It didn't feel like it. He pushed his hair back and looked up at the sun again. It was in the midday position. Impossible. How could he have wandered for so long, without falling into a chasm or tripping over a stone? How had he made it so far without coming to harm? Surely, the gods had watched over him.

Had they guided him here, as well?

His shock gave way to curiosity. An overwhelming sense of adventure stirred inside him. If the gods had indeed guided him here, he reasoned, there must be a purpose behind it. He decided to explore farther. If anything, perhaps the wildlife would be more plentiful here. As long as he didn't kill anything too heavy—like a wolf or a deer—he shouldn't have trouble hauling it back to Monte Alban.

* * *

After washing down his lunch with a sip of pulque, Chalco pressed on. Slinging his bow over his back, he scaled a small cliff, his agile fingers expertly finding the right cracks. He jumped over a deep crevice. A jaguar's skeleton lay at the bottom, bleached bones pointing towards the mountaintop. He paid his clan's totem animal a silent tribute.

The air grew colder, the vegetation more sparse. Soon, his sandals crunched over a thin layer of snow. There were tracks in the frost—rabbit, coyote, and deer. Unslinging the bow again, he notched an arrow, proceeding up the mountain with caution, his senses alert for any movement or sound.

He clambered up onto a small jumble of boulders and paused, staring back down at the city, and the valley far below it. A shimmering haze seemed to hang over Monte Alban. The buildings and pyramids seemed so small from this height, like tiny replicas rather than real structures.

"It is beautiful," he whispered.

"Yes, it is."

Chalco screamed.

"Oh, stop that," the voice said. "You'll scare everything away and have to return home empty-handed tonight."

Chalco whirled around. He was alone, yet the speaker sounded like they were right beside him. It was a male voice, deep and calm, almost hypnotic. He scanned the mountainside. There was nothing to hide behind. The nearest boulder was too far away, and the only plants were a few thin, scraggly pines and a single agave plant. He was momentarily surprised to see an agave growing this far up the mountain, but before he could consider it further, the voice spoke again.

"Look again, Chalco. Look at your home."

"W-who are you? Where are you?"

"I am one of the first. I am everywhere and in between. I am here with you."

Chalco turned around in a circle, trying to find the source. The voice sounded like it was coming from four different directions at once.

"Y-you speak Nahuatl?" he asked.

"No," the voice said. "You hear Nahuatl. I speak the language of my kind."

"Are y-you a…god?"

Chalco's voice was barely a whisper. In contrast, the other speaker laughed loudly. The sound boomed across the mountain, echoing off the rocks. Chalco began to tremble. Unable to hold the bow steady, he slung it over his back and drew his knife. Then he dropped into a defensive stance and held the weapon in front of him. This was no god. Surely it was a demon, or perhaps one of the giants his father spoke of. It would try to eat him if he didn't fight it off. But where was it?

The laughter faded. Silence returned.

"Please," Chalco cried. "Please, demon. I have done nothing to you. If I am trespassing in your domain, then I am sorry. I was merely hunting and then—"

"Do not be afraid. I am no demon. Your first guess was right—although it is such a small word. Although I am not a god in the true sense, your kind considers me a deity of sorts. I am a messenger."

"W-what is your name? Who are you? Why can I not see you?"

"I have many names. The Burning Bush. The Hand That Writes. The Watchman. The Guardian. The Sleepwalker. The Doorman. The Gatekeeper. But none of these are my secret name. I cannot tell you my real name. It is not for you to know. Names have power. Your people call me Huitzilopochtli. You may call me that as well, if you like."

Gasping, Chalco dropped the knife and fell to his knees. A sharp stone cut into his flesh, but he did not cry out. Instead, he bit his lip, lowered his eyes, and begged forgiveness. Huitzilopochtli, the guardian spirit of his people, the messenger of the gods, the Hummingbird Wizard, second only to Great Quetzalcoatl himself! It was Huitzilopochtli who had guided the Tenochas before they settled in Oaxaca. Back then, they'd been nothing more than a wandering tribe of mongrels, the cast-offs and misfits of all the other regional tribes. They roamed the wilderness, lurking at the edges of other civilizations until they were chased away. They were a demoralized, decadent people.

Then Huitzilopochtli appeared and blessed them with advice and wisdom. He told them to continue wandering. They were to be fierce but cautious, avoiding combat whenever possible, but not shrinking from their enemies either. He told them to send scouts ahead. The pioneers planted maize along the way. When the harvest was ready, they settled that area and then sent more pioneers ahead to the next location. As they traveled, Huitzilopochtli admonished them to keep him with them at all times, carrying him before them like a banner. Sacrifices were to be made in his honor, as he was a messenger for the gods and deserved tribute. The priests fed him on still-beating human hearts. The Tenochas complied with all of his demands, and within a few generations, they ruled over all of Oaxaca, vanquishing the other tribes in the region. No longer demoralized, they were lords of the world.

Sadly, as time passed, the priests forgot about Huitzilopochtli. After all, he was merely a messenger of the gods, rather than one of the gods himself. Instead, they worshipped Quetzalcoatl and the rest of their pantheon. Chalco's generation was unsure what Huitzilopochtli even looked like. Chalco had always assumed that he was a hummingbird of some kind. He did so now, as well, and glanced up at the sky, looking for birds. It was empty.

"You must turn your eyes to the ground."

"But where, lord? I do not see—"

"Here. On the agave."

Chalco crept closer to the plant. There, on one of the fronds, was a tiny, segmented worm no longer than his thumb and thinner than his arrow shafts. It had a black head and a pale, white body. Two pinprick eyes stared up at him.

"Oh..." Chalco whispered.

The worm winked.

Chalco's hands went numb. His ears rang. He thought that he might pass out.

"You...you're a worm."

"I am many things. And yes, right now I am a worm. Though it is not how I prefer to look. I have taken the form of an agave worm because I am in hiding and because the agave is linked to what must transpire today. Behemoth and his kind would find the irony amusing."

"Who?"

"Never mind. Your people don't have a name for Behemoth in your pantheon. He is one of the Thirteen, those who are neither gods nor demons and yet are mistaken for both by humanity. You worship them without understanding what they are. They, along with the Creator, are all that is left of the universe before this one. Behemoth takes the form of a Great Worm."

"Please," Chalco whispered. "I don't understand."

"Of course you don't. Humankind isn't meant to understand, for that knowledge has been denied you. Indeed, the Creator denied you knowledge of many things. Some of it is for your own good. The rest...well, I think it was terribly unfair, what happened in the Garden."

"We have gardens in Monte Alban."

"Yes, you do indeed. But those are not the Garden I speak of. Never mind. Again, it's not from your pantheon, and yet, it affects your people just the same. You should know about it. After all, Quetzalcoatl, the Plumed Serpent, is part of your belief structure, as he is to all other peoples, as well. Why not the Garden?"

"Quetzalcoatl..." Chalco's eyes grew wide. "Great Huitzilopochtli, I am sorry that I did not recognize you. I will give you the heart from my breast if it eases the insult. But I must know—are you here to herald Quetzalcoatl's return? The priests say that this is the time."

"Arise, young Chalco. Yes, it has been many years since your people have paid me tribute, but I do not require your heart. There will be time for that later. Indeed, if your people are not saved, there will be no further sacrifices to anyone."

Chalco stumbled to his feet. "Then it is true! Quetzalcoatl is about to uphold his covenant? He's returning to save us all? You have come to deliver the message."

"No, I'm afraid not. Quetzalcoatl will not return, at least, not in that form. Every time he does, you people nail him to a cross or burn him at the stake or shoot him in the chest or...well, that hasn't happened yet. It happens later. But you see what I mean? No matter what form or name he takes—Quetzalcoatl, Jesus of Nazareth, Adonis, Mohammad, Buddha, Divimoss, Kurt Cobain, Prosper Johnson, Benj—"

"I have never heard of these gods."

"Do not interrupt me again."

"I beg your forgiveness, lord."

"You have not heard of them," the worm said, "and yet you have, for they are all one and the same. They are but different incarnations of the same being."

Chalco waited until he was sure the worm was done speaking. "So Quetzalcoatl has different names?"

"Correct. So do many others. Tonatiuh, the sun god, is known as Ra to the Egyptians, and although you both believe him to have different responsibilities and worship him in different ways, he remains the same deity. Your rain god, Tlaloc, is called Cthulhu, Leviathan, Dagon, and many other things by different peoples. Huehueteotl is called Api by the Sumerians. Your Lord of the Dead, Mictlatechuhtli, is really Ob, Lord of the Siqqusim. Those last three aren't even gods, not in the true sense. They are also of the Thirteen. But regardless of their origins, be they god or devil, of this plane or another, to know their real names gives you power over them. Thus, that knowledge has also been denied you and will be until science replaces magic and you lose the ability to bind them."

"And Quetzalcoatl—or whatever his true name is—will not save us? He will not return to vanquish our enemies?"

"No."

"But he promised. The priests have said so. He promised to return."

"He has made that promise repeatedly throughout history. On this world and others. But it will not happen. It never does."

Chalco's heart sank. "Then it is true. This is indeed the end of the world."

"Not necessarily. Quetzalcoatl will not save your people. *You* will."

"M-me?"

"Indeed. That is why I am here, Chalco. Things are dire. Hernan Cortes's conquest is destroying your land. He does not serve your king. He serves Charles, the King of Spain—and his God. And though all worship stems from the same Creator, you people get so caught up in names that you think you serve different gods. That is what King Charles and Cortes believe. They believe that they are doing the work of the Creator, but they are wrong. Cortes does not care about your people. He is here for new lands and new riches, and death follows with him."

Chalco shuddered.

"Let me tell you of the future," the worm continued, "and how it will be if Cortes is not stopped. He brings with him a disease called smallpox, against which your people have no defense. This disease will race to Tenochtitlan and decimate the capital. Many will die from it, including your father—but not before he returns to infect you all. Your brother, Quintox, will be the first to die in Monte Alban, followed by Yamesha. Soon, everyone you love will be dead."

"Please...no."

"That's just the beginning. Those who die will be the lucky ones. The invaders will enslave your people and slaughter your priests. They will melt down all of your gold and mint it into coins so that King Charles can pay off his war debt. Your homes and temples will be torn down so that the Spanish can build churches and mansions in their place. What they don't destroy will be converted. Their holy men will destroy your codex and calendars. They will burn your books. Most importantly, they will teach you only of their God, and deny you access to your own gods—even though all stem from the same source...the Creator."

"Then we are lost."

"No. This can not be allowed to occur. So, as I have in the past, I am going to aid your people. I will impart a gift. And I have chosen you, Chalco, to receive that gift. I will give you a key to unlock the doors of human perception and visit unseen worlds. You will eventually gain all of the knowledge that has been forbidden to your kind, and thus, gain understanding. You will slay Cortes before he ever arrives and lead your people to triumph."

"I do not understand, lord. Why me? I am no one important. My clansmen are nothing but farmers and hunters."

"Have your priests taught you of how I appeared to your people and guided them?"

"Yes."

"I remember it well. Your people came down from the cold mountain wastes, searching for a hospitable land to call their own. Often they starved or died from exposure to the elements. Sometimes they had to fight other tribes for passage. But when they settled on the shores of Lake Texcoco in the Valley of Anahuac and began to farm, I was there waiting. I advised them to send settlers out to find more land. One of those explorers was your direct ancestor."

Chalco felt a sudden, immense pride at this revelation.

"While searching for a good location, your ancestor encountered a Toltec tribe and became involved in their affairs. Since he was only one man, they welcomed him. Your ancestor aided the Toltecs in a war against yet another tribe. He fought well and showed great valor. He slew many and turned the battle's tide. As thanks, the Toltec chieftain offered him a boon. Your ancestor asked for one of the chieftain's daughters. She was very fair, with hair like golden flax and eyes of blue. No one in these lands had ever seen a woman like her. It was whispered that she was of the gods. Perhaps this was true. Regardless, the Toltec chieftain granted the request, impressed as he was with your ancestor's contributions."

Nodding, Chalco picked up his knife and sheathed it.

"After the boon was fulfilled," the worm continued, "your ancestor returned to his encampment with the girl in tow. But rather than marrying her, he returned to his crops and once they were planted, he sacrificed the girl. He flayed her skin and draped it over himself so that the maize might receive a blessing. He hoped the harvest would be bountiful by the time the rest of your people arrived. When the Toltecs learned of this, they attacked your ancestor. He slew them all, just as he had slain their enemies, and then used their blood to irrigate his crops. The maize grew strong, thus, your people grew strong. Two hundred years later, you rule over all. Your vast empire is one of the greatest this world has ever known. But within a generation, all of that will end because of Cortes. Your people will be reduced once again to a tribe of starving mongrels. That is why I come to you. Like your ancestor, *you* will save your people."

Chalco bowed again. "I am honored, Lord. But how will I do this? I am just one, and nothing special. Will you bestow powers upon me?"

"No. As I said, I will give you a gift and teach you to open doors. With this, you will receive knowledge, which is the greatest power of all."

"But how, lord?"

"Look inside your water skin."

Chalco did as commanded. He unsealed the beeswax and pulled off the cap. Then he sniffed the contents. His nose twitched and his eyes watered. He peered inside the skin. It was filled with a yellow-brown liquid the color of ginger root.

"What happened to the pulque?"

"This is pulque, but it has been transformed into something more powerful—the drink of the gods. This is my gift. It is called tequila. One sip and you will unlock the doors of perception. Try it."

Hesitant, Chalco drank from the skin. He coughed. The strange liquid tasted like wood smoke and burned his throat. His stomach lurched. Gagging, he reached in his basket and pulled out his last lime. He sucked on it to rid his mouth of the taste.

"It is bitter," the worm agreed. "But the lime should help. Salt would also cut the bite."

Chalco started to reply, but found that he couldn't. His tongue felt thick and swollen, and his lips were numb. It was difficult to breathe. His throat was still on fire.

"With that taste, the knowledge of how to transform pulque into this drink is passed unto your people. It stems from the agave plant. Even now, the idea takes seed in the mind of one of your clansmen. But their salvation—indeed, your entire civilization's future—lies with you. Now, take a second sip."

Chalco closed his eyes and did as commanded. He pursed his lips. The liquid's kick was still strong, but he immediately followed it with the lime. His throat felt warm, but not fiery like before. His stomach muscles clenched. Slowly, Chalco opened his eyes…

…and stared.

A doorway floated in the air above him, hovering just off the ground. The lime fell from his gaping mouth. Chalco reached out with one trembling hand to touch the door, but then yanked it away.

"What…?"

"Behold. Through that door lies the Labyrinth, a dimensional shortcut between worlds, universes, and realities. This is how my kind travels from world to world, plane to plane, back and forth through time and space."

Chalco stumbled forward, walking in a wide circle around the door. There was nothing behind it—just more mountain. He completed the circle, and stared.

"But where is it?"

The worm chuckled. "Very good, Chalco. Where indeed? The door is suspended right in front of you, is it not? And yet, it isn't. The Labyrinth is nowhere and everywhere all at once. It is the in-between—the black space amidst the stars, the backdoor of reality. What you view as a doorway, is really just an extension of the Labyrinth on this level. It is indeed an entrance—and exit, but it doesn't truly exist here. The doors of the Labyrinth merely connect to various levels."

"Levels?"

"Planes of existence. Different worlds and realities."

"Why couldn't I see the door before?"

"Because your eyes were not open. Normally, the only time your kind see the Labyrinth is when their spirit has departed their body. There are some among you—a select few—who know how to open the doorways and can traverse its passageways while they are still alive. But they have sacrificed much for that knowledge. I am bestowing the ability upon you so that you may save your people."

"I feel dizzy, lord."

"That is the drink. One does not sup as the gods do without feeling the effects. Are you ready for the final sip?"

Chalco's voice trembled. "What will happen?"

"With the third taste, you will be ready. You will go through the door and travel the Labyrinth. At the far end of the hallway is another door. You will open it, and find yourself on the beach at the time of Cortes's arrival. The doorway will remain stationary behind you. The invaders will not be able to see it. It is only for your eyes. Hide in the foliage near the surf. Have your bow at the ready. Slay Cortes as he sets foot on your soil, and then return through the Labyrinth, taking the same path you took before."

Chalco picked the lime back up again, brushed the dirt off, and sucked on the fruit while he listened.

"The death of Cortes will set into motion a chain of events on this level, culminating in your people's eventual domination of the world. But be wary, Chalco. You must not be distracted. The drink of the gods sharpens your senses, but you must also maintain your wits. Although you might be tempted to travel other passageways or step through other doors, do not. Some entrances do not have exits, and not all doorways are meant to be opened. Too much knowledge is never a good thing. Stray not from the path. When you enter, go straight to the end of the passageway. After you have killed Cortes, return the way you came. Do you understand?"

Chalco nodded. Despite the lime, his mouth felt parched. His ears rang.

"Good." The worm crawled to the edge of the agave.

"Then partake of the third sip and throw open the doors of perception."

Chalco drained the skin, and sat it next to the agave. There was only a small bit of liquid left inside. This time, he didn't need the lime. He dropped the half-eaten fruit onto the ground and wiped his mouth with the back of his hand. The tequila coursed through his body. The air seemed to thrum with energy. The hovering doorway shimmered. Overhead, an eagle cried out. Chalco took a deep breath and cast one last glance back at the worm. Then he pushed the door open, revealing a long stone corridor.

Chalco stepped inside.

There was a flash of white light. Immediately, the eagle's cries ceased. Chalco glanced behind him. The door was closed. There was no sign of the mountain, the agave, or the worm. They lay on the other side of the exit. He turned around. The corridor seemed to stretch into infinity. He couldn't see the end. It was brightly lit, but there were no candles or torches. The illumination had no source. The gray stone walls were featureless, the ceiling high. There were no windows, but both sides of the hallway were lined with hundreds of closed doors. He wondered what was behind them all. More mountaintops, perhaps? Other worlds?

Admiring the masonry, Chalco touched the wall with his fingers, and then jerked them away with a gasp. The surface was cold. There was no moisture, no condensation. No texture, either—not even a crack or pit. The icy surface felt smooth. He sucked his fingertips. They were red, as if burned.

"This is not stone. It is something else."

He didn't know how he knew that, but he did. Perhaps it was the tequila. He felt it inside him. What was it Huitzilopochtli had said? The doors to reality would be thrown open and Chalco would receive knowledge. Maybe that was how he knew that the walls weren't made of stone. But if so, then why didn't he recognize the mysterious substance? Was it beyond his human reckoning? Or had the drink's effects not yet been fully realized? It didn't matter. He was experiencing something that no Tenochan had ever beheld. The Labyrinth was the path to glory.

"Oh, Quintox," he whispered. "If only you could be here with me now, brother. You would be proud indeed."

He noticed that despite the length of the hall and the ceiling's height, his voice did not echo. The sound was muted. Chalco fumbled for his knife. Clutching it in one fist, he crept down the passageway. After he'd taken thirty steps, he turned around to make sure the exit was still there. It was. The door remained shut, but visible. Heart pounding, he continued on his way.

He counted the closed doors as he walked by them—twelve, then twenty-four, then sixty. The corridor was obviously longer than it looked—an optical illusion of some sort, like the mirages that appeared in the desert. His father had told him all about those. A thirsty man would see water on the horizon, but when he reached it, he'd find only sand.

Occasionally, Chalco passed other corridors, intersecting with or branching off from the main hallway. He hesitated at each one, listening, but they were as silent as the rest of the Labyrinth. They, too, seemed endless—straight lines into infinity. He wondered where they went, but did not explore them, remembering Huitzilopochtli's warning.

He stared ahead. When he squinted, he thought he could see the end of the hall. Despite the passageway's deceptive length, he was gaining ground.

* * *

Chalco was filled with an immense sense of pride as he continued on. Such a boon! *He* had been chosen by the gods. Him. Chalco. The gods had selected him and nobody else—not the priests or medicine men or the seasoned, battle-scarred warriors. He had never felt more alert and aware than he did at that moment. He wondered if it was another effect of the tequila or just the atmosphere of this place in general. He thought of Quintox again. What would his family say if they could see him now? How joyous they would be, knowing that he'd been chosen by the gods to save them. When he triumphantly returned to Monte Alban, things would be different. His father and the other men could come home. Quintox would be prouder of him than ever before. And Yamesha—her clan would certainly approve of their marriage. The priests would honor him as they did the gods. Lord Moctezuma would call upon him, or invite him to the capital. All of Oaxaca would sing his praises and his face would be forever memorialized in stone. Perhaps a village would be named after him, or maybe even a city. Songs would recount how the gods blessed him with power and how he slew Cortes and stopped the invasion. Books would be written about his exploits. He would get his own Codex in the Great Temple. It would be grand!

Lost in thought, Chalco giggled. The sound of his own laughter startled him from the daydream. He halted. The corridor continued on uninterrupted, with no end in sight.

Was that possible? Surely he had traveled forward. The

end—another doorway—should be visible. He looked back the way he'd come. The hallway stretched in that direction as well, and he could no longer see the exit. The door he'd come in through was missing. Where had it gone? Had he traveled that far in such a short time? His stomach sank, and he felt a twinge of panic. Chalco squeezed the hilt of his knife until his knuckles turned white. Had he somehow taken a wrong turn while he was daydreaming, gotten disoriented and wandered off down a side passage?

"Great Huitzilopochtli," he prayed, "hear my call. Guide me, for I am lost. I did not heed your warnings or think of my people. Instead, I thought only of myself. Pride has led me astray."

Silence. The guardian spirit was not coming. Not as a worm. Not as a Hummingbird Wizard. Not at all. Chalco had never felt so afraid or alone. Dropping to his knees, he sheathed his knife and beat the floor with his fists, moaning in frustration. Like the walls, the floor was cold. He leaned back, resting against a closed door, and considered what to do next—turn back and search for the way he'd come in, or keep moving forward, hoping that he'd come to the right doorway?

He sat there, leaning against the closed door, for a very long time before he heard the water.

It was coming from the other side of the door; the steady, monotonous roar of the ocean. Chalco had heard it once before in his life, when he'd accompanied his father and uncles to a religious celebration in a seaside village on Oaxaca's western shore. He'd been very young at the time, but he'd never forgotten the sound. Sometimes when he slept, he dreamed about it.

Chalco closed his eyes, put his ear to the door, and listened. It was definitely the ocean. He heard waves crashing and seabirds cawing out. His hopes rose. Maybe this was the door to the beach after all.

Jumping to his feet, Chalco opened the door and looked out into a sea. It wasn't Oaxaca's eastern shore. He wasn't even sure it was Oaxaca. The doorway hovered on the surface of the ocean. There was no land, only water. The sun hung in the sky, reflecting off the sea. Seagulls circled, hunting for fish. Chalco shielded his eyes against the glare and watched them. He smelled salt and brine. Foam-topped waves crested against the doorframe but did not splash into the corridor, prevented from entering by some kind of barrier he couldn't see. Chalco wondered if the same invisible wall would prevent him from crossing the threshold. Experimenting, he stuck his foot through the doorway. The surf lapped at his foot. The water was cold. Slowly, Chalco pulled his foot back into the corridor and grinned.

No, this wasn't the right door. This wasn't his world, or at least the part of his world he was looking for. But wherever it was, it *was* beautiful.

And then something erupted from the water. Two long, greenish-gray tentacles, each one as thick as his waist and covered with puckering suckers, thrust towards the door, grasping for him. He glimpsed a massive, shadowed bulk just beneath the surface, and then two more tendrils burst forth.

Screaming, Chalco backed against the far wall. The tentacles pushed through the open doorway and slithered across the floor. Chalco yanked his knife free of its sheath and stabbed one of the appendages as it slid across his foot. The stone blade sank into the flesh. Hot, black ichor squirted from the wound, staining his hand and splashing across the walls and floor. On the other side of the doorway came a great splash and the tentacles retreated.

Chalco barely had time to free his knife. The monster vanished beneath the surface. Chalco slammed the door shut, and the corridor was silent once more. Steam rose from the monster's spilled blood.

When he'd stopped trembling, Chalco cleaned his hands and blade with his loincloth. Feeling helpless and unsure of what to do next, he decided to try another door.

Perhaps he'd find the right one by chance. After all, the previous exit had opened into the ocean. Maybe the next door would lead to the beach.

He put his ear to another door and listened. This time, there were no birds or waves. Just silence. Knife in hand, Chalco opened it. Inside was a small metal room. A group of people were huddled against the walls—several men, a few women, and a young boy about the same age as Quintox. When he studied the boy, Chalco was overwhelmed with a sense of familiarity—as if he'd known him before. But that was impossible. More likely the child simply reminded him of his little brother. Their clothes were strange. One of them seemed to be injured. He was lying in the corner, covered in blood. His face was pale and waxy. Another man brandished a weapon of some kind. Chalco didn't know what type, but assumed it was deadly, based on the fearful reactions of the others in the room every time the object was pointed at them.

None of them noticed Chalco, so he eavesdropped on their conversation.

"He's not breathing, Tommy. He hasn't been for a while. I'm sorry, but it's true. Your friend is gone. He's dead. Look at him, son."

"Shut the hell up, you old fart. Just shut the fuck up right now!"

Their speech was as odd as their garments and surroundings, but Chalco could understand it—another effect of the drink, he assumed. He was fascinated by everything in the odd metal room, but this was obviously not his destination, so he reluctantly shut the door and tried another.

The third door opened into nothingness. A black void yawned before him, filled with pinpricks of light. After a moment, Chalco realized it was the night sky, as seen from high above the Earth. He'd heard the priests talk of such things. They said that the lights in the sky at night were the eyes of the gods. The door had apparently opened into a place amidst those eyes.

Stars, he thought. *I know now that these are called stars. Oh, this drink—this tequila—is wonderful. I'm learning so many things. When I get back to Monte Alban, I must explain this all without being labeled a heretic.*

Awestruck, he tried to find a horizon or an end to the gulf, but its boundaries were limitless. He admired the simple beauty. Knowing now that the stars weren't eyes, but suns, made them even more impressive. In the center of the darkness was a scarlet moon, slightly bigger than the one he was used to. It was an amazing sight.

And then the moon blinked.

It drifted towards him, crossing the unimaginable distance in seconds. A second moon soared into sight. The moons *were* eyes. They had no body or face. Just two huge orbs floating in the darkness. They stared at him with penetrating glares. It felt like his soul was being examined. Chalco slammed the door and the feeling disappeared.

Once he'd recovered from his fright, he tried again. The next door opened into a subterranean cavern lit by some sort of phosphorescent lichen. The rough walls were hewn, rather than naturally formed. A pile of bones lay near the door. He couldn't tell what sort of animal they'd once belonged to. A great, smokeless forge burned in the distance. A line of pig-faced creatures lurched past, lumbering into a nearby tunnel. They had tusks and snouts and their language consisted of squeals and grunts (but again he could understand it). Despite the deformities, the pig-things walked upright like men and carried tools and weapons with them. One of them gnawed on a human forearm, stripping the meat from the bone. Their stench was incredible. Their sound was worse.

One of them stopped suddenly and raised its snout. Thick mucous dripped from the creature's nostrils. Snuffling, it turned towards him. Chalco quickly closed the door, overcome with revulsion.

He continued on. Each door was like a window on the worlds, each scene more wondrous or terrifying than the previous.

He saw a great city with tall, silver spires and men made of shiny metal rather than flesh.

He glimpsed another city built out of pure light.

He watched the dead get up and walk again, hunting

the living for nourishment, tearing them apart with their hands and teeth.

He laughed at a silent clown whose face was painted white. The clown tried juggling three yellow balls, but kept dropping them.

He shrank away from a roaring lizard taller than the biggest temple in Monte Alban, its mouth lined with razor-sharp teeth longer than a warrior's spear. It stood over the bloody, torn corpse another, long-necked lizard.

He spied on a young, obsidian-skinned couple as they made love in the reeds along a stream bank.

He faced a tribe of creatures that were more goat than men, gathered next to a roaring campfire. Nearby them were wicker cages stuffed with terrified human women. The goat men danced in a circle around the fire and then rutted with their female captives.

He shielded his eyes from a great ball of fire that produced a mushroom-shaped cloud.

He thrilled as an armored fighter battled with a ferocious man-serpent.

He laughed in amazement at a massive creature the size of his adobe, with long, floppy ears and a trunk for a nose. The beast trampled through a steaming jungle.

He cowered at the sight of a man-sized being with gray skin, enormous black eyes, and only a slit for a mouth.

He marveled over the eruption of a great volcano that spewed molten rock and clouds of ash into the sky.

He gasped at chariots that moved without the benefit of livestock to pull them—on the ground, in the sky, and even into that black space above the Earth.

He saw births and deaths, armies clashing on a dozen battlefields, people laughing and crying. He could not know the names for all that he saw, or understand them entirely, but he knew them all the same. With each new world, he felt his consciousness expand. There would be so much knowledge to share when he made it back home.

Finally, he found what he assumed was the right door. It opened onto a beach of white sand. The sun was shining.

Vegetation waved in the breeze. Rolling waves crashed onto the shore. Far out to sea, Chalco spotted an armada of ships.

"This must be it! Huitzilopochtli be praised."

He leapt through the door and onto the beach. The sun-baked sand was hot beneath his soles. It shifted beneath him as he walked. He tasted salt in the air and heard birds calling out above him. A small crab scuttled away. Washed up seashells glittered in the surf.

The heat plastered his bangs to his forehead. He flipped his hair out of the way and searched for a good place to hide, somewhere that would conceal him from the ships yet offer a good vantage point and a clear shot once Cortes came ashore. He spotted a copse of trees surrounded by dunes farther up the beach, and headed for them, walking backwards, using his bow to smooth out his footprints in the sand so that nobody would see them. He looked up once, making sure that the door was still hovering above the beach.

As he concealed himself, Chalco noticed something etched in one of the tree trunks, high off the ground, certainly out of reach of a full-grown man. They were letters or glyphs of some kind, carved deep into the wood. The edges were splintered and ragged, as if claws had been used rather than a blade. The strange symbols were in another language, but the tequila gave him understanding of what they said—if not their meaning.

CROATOAN

Was it a name? A place? A tribe of people? He didn't know, despite the drink's influence. It sounded…unclean.

Ominous.

In the distance, three small boats cast off from the larger ships. Their flags fluttered in the wind. Men sat perched in them, watching the shoreline. Kneeling in the sand, Chalco strung his bow and notched an arrow, waiting.

The breeze died down and the birds grew silent. Even the ocean seemed still.

And then, something snuffled behind him.

Screeching, the birds took flight, fleeing the area.

Still crouching, Chalco whirled around, pointing his arrow in the direction of the noise. Several yards away, a terrible creature rose from behind a shifting dune. It was almost three times his height, and covered with white, matted fur. The thing was broad-shouldered and barrel-chested, and its powerful arms hung down to its knees. Talon-tipped fingers clenched and unclenched. The monster's face was almost human, except for a wide mouth filled with gleaming fangs, and two black, brooding eyes above a flat nose. Seeing Chalco, it snorted in surprise. Chalco was reminded of a cat. The thing's ears looked feline, pointed and twitching. A monstrous phallus swung between its legs.

Chalco's heart beat. Once. Twice.

The creature charged.

Chalco let his arrow fly.

The thing grunted as the arrow plunged into its chest. The shaft protruded from its breast, the white fur turning crimson around the wound. The monster never slowed. It snapped the shaft with one hand and lunged for him.

Biting his lip, Chalco notched another arrow and let loose. The beast snatched it from the air and tossed it aside.

Chalco leapt to his feet and ran. Behind him, he heard trees snapping as the creature gave chase. The sand shook with each loping stride the monster took. Its growls echoed across the beach.

It can't see the doorway, Chalco thought as he fled. *Only I can. If I make it back into the Labyrinth, it won't be able to follow.*

The beast closed the gap between them. Chalco heard its harsh breathing. Its stink fouled the air. Flinging his bow aside, he pounded across the sand, forcing his legs to go faster. His lungs burned. The wind howled in his ears—or maybe it was just his pursuer.

Chalco dived headfirst through the floating doorway. He landed in the corridor, banging his head on the stone that wasn't stone. He rolled across the floor, coming to rest against the wall. Rubbing his head, Chalco drew his knife.

Outside, on the beach, the growls changed to laughter.

Animals don't laugh. That thing is intelligent.

As he watched, it headed straight for the doorway.

It can't see me. It can't...

The monster plunged an enormous, fur-covered hand through the open door, grasping at him. Screaming, Chalco slashed at it with his knife. The hand withdrew, and then reached for him again. The blade bit deeper. Blood spattered the floor. Enraged, the beast pulled away again.

Chalco held his breath.

The monster slammed against the doorframe, heaving its bulk through the opening. The door seemed to shimmer and stretch to accommodate the creature's size. One hand thrust through, then an arm, then another. The entrance grew wider as the beast's head followed.

Chalco took advantage of the arduous progress to escape. He slid out of the monster's reach and sprinted down the hallway, ignoring all of the other doors. His feet pounded in silence. His breath stiffened in his throat.

Behind him, the monster raged. Then it spoke for the first time. Its cadence was slow and halting. The rough, guttural sound terrified Chalco as much as the beast itself did.

"You...not...escape...Meeble."

Chalco turned left down a side passage and kept running, not looking back. Closed doors flashed by on both sides, each one of them an invitation to more terror. Who knew what lurked behind them? Wisdom was a curse. He wanted to go home, wanted to go back to being a boy.

Wanted to forget.

He ran for a very long time, and the beast—Meeble—pursued him. Usually, it was far behind, but several times it nearly caught him.

Finally, Chalco came to a dead end. A double door, larger than the others, stood before him. He wondered what new horror waited on the other side. Behind him, around the corner, he heard the monster catching up. It snorted like a bull. Its breathing sounded like a geyser.

Closing his eyes, Chalco opened the door and stepped

through. Wind brushed against his face. He opened his eyes, but it was too late.

He fell into darkness…

…and did not stop.

* * *

Back on the mountaintop, the doorway flickered and then vanished. Still perched on the agave plant and still in the form of a worm, Huitzilopochtli hung his head and cried. He had failed. Humanity was not ready for the knowledge tequila provided. Perhaps they never would be. They were too prideful, too worldly—too human.

He'd deceived his masters. Slipped away and hid inside this form, hoping to tip the scales in humanity's favor—turn the tide of infinity. But he had failed. Soon, he would be found out. He could not hide forever, not even outside the Labyrinth.

As the sun began to set, Huitzilopochtli inched his way down the agave and onto the ground. The soil was cooler now. He crawled across it. A shadow fell over him. He had time to look up and then the bird plunged toward him.

Wriggling beside the agave to avoid the flashing beak, he fell into Chalco's discarded water skin, which had a few drops of tequila in the bottom. The worm struggled, and then became still.

Night descended. The wildlife returned to the mountain, and in Monte Alban, Quintox waited for Chalco to return home.

He never did.

But eventually, their father and uncles returned to Monte Alban. Death came with them. The worm's prophecy came to pass.

And the doors were closed to humanity.

* * *

And that is why to this day, some people believe in the

legend of tequila. They believe that tequila is a gift of the gods. That it will grant knowledge of the universe and open the doors of perception. And they also believe that eating the worm will allow them to visit an unseen world.

But they never do.

Instead they fall.

STORY NOTES

When you write for a living, you usually write every day. And while you (hopefully) never lose that sense of magic and wonder, it is easy to become bogged down in the process. There are deadlines and publisher demands. Editors and readers are eager to suggest what you should really be writing, especially if you want to get paid. And if your mortgage payment relies on that next sale, you tend to at least consider their suggestions. If you're not careful, crafting stories can become more like work and less like fun.

So it's always a treat when you get to try something different and explore new literary horizons. Just like in a relationship, experimentation can reinvigorate a writer's muse.

That's what this story was to me. An experiment – and great fun, as well. After reading Jack Ketchum's masterful fable, The Transformed Mouse, *I fell in love with fables all over again and wondered if there were any new ones to tell.*

Luckily, I was thinking about this while drinking a bottle of tequila.

Tequila has no concrete history. There are a number of different theories as to how it came to be. If you don't believe me, check the internet. Tequila and mezcal experts argue over the drink's origins, what actually constitutes the drink, where the worm came from, etc. As an enthusiast, this seems like a shame to me. And since nobody can apparently agree on its true origin, I figured I'd make one up. Thus, I wrote a fable detailing how the "drink of the gods" came to be, incorporating much of its trappings and mystique. It's fiction, of course. Historians might point out things I got wrong. I suggest they have a shot and shut the fuck up. It's my mythos and I can do what I want with it.

Indeed...my mythos—the ongoing Labyrinth saga, about which much was revealed here. The second half of this story is certainly not for the uninitiated. It is decidedly mythos heavy. There are references to various novels and stories, characters and villains. If you are indeed new to this, an explanation is in order. The Labyrinth is a dimensional shortcut between worlds, universes, and realities, and is only accessible to those who know how to open the doors. Glimpses of this mythos wind through everything I've ever written. Every novel, every novella, and every short story contains a hint of it. Yet, I've purposely tried to keep those links vague, so that new readers can also enjoy the stories and books. You shouldn't have to read Terminal *to understand* Ghoul, *or* The Rising *to enjoy* Kill Whitey. *And yet, for the hardcore fans, the folks who read everything I write, the mythos is there—and they love it. Indeed, they want more, as evidenced by the preponderance of threads on my message board in which people ask for more.*

This was my gift to them. It's a love letter to one of my favorite vices (tequila) and a thank you to some of my favorite people (my readers).

THE WAITING IS THE HARDEST PART

The sun went down on Platt Street but the dead did not sleep. Danny heard them outside—shouting, hunting, killing other people. People like him and his mother.

He called the dead "monster-people."

Danny didn't know how many days they'd been hiding in the attic. His step-father, Rick, was still gone. Danny and his mother barricaded the attic door and waited for somebody to come help them—the police, Mr. DeSantos from next door, anybody. Mommy was hoping Rick would come back. Danny hoped for his real Daddy, who lived in West Virginia with Danny's stepmother, Carrie.

They waited, but nobody came.

Until now.

"Dannnnyyyyy..."

It was Tommy Padrone, one of the older kids from up the street. Danny figured he must be one of the monster-people. Otherwise, he wouldn't be outside shouting. He'd have been attacked and killed by now...or eaten. Shouting attracted attention and attention got you killed. Danny tried to ignore the faint cries. This wasn't the first time he'd heard one of the monster-people outside. Usually they kept going, but a few times it had sounded like they were trying to get inside.

The attic was hot and stuffy, but at least it didn't stink like raw meat the way the rest of the house did. A few flies crawled over the surface of the attic window, but there weren't nearly as many as there were downstairs. Danny wished he had something to do. He was bored, and most of his stuff was downstairs. Two weeks ago, they'd a yard sale and cleaned the attic out. It was almost empty now, except for Rick's bowling ball and some of Danny's old baby toys that he didn't play with anymore, and what they'd grabbed when they retreated to the attic—bedding, clothes, water bottles and food. And the flies.

And his mother.

She coughed. Her whole body shook. Every time this happened, Danny got more and more afraid. She'd gotten sick before everyone who died started turning into monster-people. That was why Rick wasn't here with them. He'd gone out to buy some medicine, making Mommy promise that if she didn't feel better tomorrow, she'd go to the doctor. Except that never happened. And Rick never came home. And Mommy never got better.

When she'd settled down again, he reached out and touched her forehead. She felt hot and slick. Her eyes stayed shut.

"Mommy?" His voice was barely a whisper.

She didn't respond. Didn't move. Her bathrobe was plastered to her body with sweat, and there were dark circles under her eyes. Her skin was pale.

"Danny…anybody in there?"

Ignoring Tommy, he closed his eyes and thought about his Daddy. Danny missed him. Rick had forgotten his cell phone when he went out. Danny wanted to use it to call his Daddy, but he couldn't figure out how to make it work and Mommy was too sick to show him. Danny thought about the last time he'd seen his father and tried to tune out the other sounds—his mother's moans, Tommy's shouts, the buzzing flies.

Eventually, it was quiet again.

Until something creaked downstairs.

Danny sat up and opened his eyes, listening.

The noise came again. The stairs, leading up from the first floor. They creaked when somebody walked on them. And somebody was walking on them now. Tommy?

"Hello? Danny? Tammy?"

No, not Tommy. Tommy Padrone didn't call Danny's mother by her first name. It was his stepfather. It was Rick.

Danny almost called out, but then he smelled something bad, like the inside of a garbage can. It was how monster-people smelled. That meant Rick wasn't his stepfather anymore. He was one of them now.

"Guess who? I know you're here somewhere. Come on out. Everything's gonna be okay."

"Go away," Danny shouted. "Leave us alone!"

"Got you, fucker." The monster-person laughed. *"Hiding in the attic?"*

Regretting the outburst, Danny scuttled backwards towards his mother. She slept soundly, still not moving despite the noise. Rick hammered at the door, rattling it in its frame. The barricade shook. It wouldn't hold for long. The thing on the other side of the door was determined.

"It'll be okay, Mommy." Danny kissed her forehead. She tasted sour.

The blows on the door continued. Wood splintered. A hole appeared in the door's center, and a hand thrust through the opening, grasping at the lock. Danny glanced around the attic, looking for something to protect his mother with. Spotting Rick's bowling ball, he picked it up with both hands, grunting at the effort. It was heavy, and he wasn't sure he could move it. But then he looked back at his mother and found his strength.

The door crashed inward and Rick stumbled through the opening, falling onto the stairs. Shards of wood had pierced his skin, and his fists were bloody and battered. He brushed aside debris and tottered to his feet, then looked up at Danny and smiled. Some of his teeth were missing. His eyes were black.

Then he saw what Danny had in his hands, and those

black eyes went wide.

Danny dropped the bowling ball on his head. There was a terrible, wet smack, followed by a loud crack. Blood splattered all over the stairs, and Danny cringed, trying not to cry. Rick slumped to the floor again. The bowling ball rolled through the gaping doorframe.

Rick didn't get back up. This time he was *dead* dead.

Later, Danny dragged the body out of the way and barricaded the door again. He used plywood from the attic to patch the hole in the door, and a hammer and nails his mother had left behind when they first went upstairs. He tried to do a better job this time, but it was hard work and left him tired. He took a nap when he was finished.

After he woke up, he was surprised to see that his mother was awake, too. She asked him if his stepfather had arrived yet. Danny lied to her. Then his mother showed him how to work Rick's cell phone, and went back to sleep again.

He called his father. His spirits soared when he heard his father's voice, and plummeted a second later when he realized it was just a recording.

"Hi, this is Jim Thurmond. I'm not available right now, so leave a message."

"Daddy, I'm scared. I'm in the attic. I 'membered your phone number but I couldn't make Rick's cell phone work right. Mommy was asleep for a long time but then she woke up and made it work for me. Now she's asleep again. She's been sleeping since…since they got Rick."

Danny paused, blinking away tears.

"I'm scared, Daddy. I know we shouldn't leave the attic, but Mommy's sick and I don't know how to make her better. I hear things outside the house. Sometimes they just go by and other times I think they're trying to get in."

He thought about Rick. He couldn't tell Daddy that he'd killed his stepfather, even if his stepfather was one of the monster-people. If he did tell, he might get in trouble. So he lied.

"I think Rick is with them. Daddy, you promised to call

me! I'm scared and I don't know what to do..."

The cell phone beeped. Danny didn't know if it was still working or not, but he continued, begging and pleading for his father to come save him. The cell phone beeped again and the light went out. He threw the phone across the room and sobbed. Then he snuggled up against his sleeping mother and wiped his eyes and nose on her robe. Her chest rose and fell with each breath, and Danny closed his eyes...

...until her chest stopped moving.

He waited.

Waited for Mommy to wake up.

Waited for Daddy to rescue him.

Waited.

STORY NOTES

This story appeared in the collector's edition of The Rising: Selected Scenes From The End Of The World. *It features Danny Thurmond (from* The Rising *and* City of the Dead*) and takes place during the early chapters of* The Rising.

THIS IS NOT AN EXIT

"You ever kill anyone?"

He licks his lips when he asks me, and I can tell by his expression that he doesn't really want to know. His eyes dart around the hotel bar before coming back to me. No matter what I say, my answer will barely register with him. The question is perfunctory. He desires the act of confession. He's killed, and it's eating at him. It weighs on him. He needs to tell.

"What?" I pretend to be shocked by the question.

The young man is maybe twenty-one or two. Still learning his limits when it comes to alcohol. His slurred words are barely noticeable, but the empty beer bottles in front of him reveal everything. He leans closer, nearly falling off his stool.

"Have you ever killed someone?"

This is his conversation starter. A chance to unburden. Or to brag. This is a beginning.

An entrance.

I close entrances.

The first person I ever killed was named Lawrence. I've killed so many people over the years that they blur together—a nameless, faceless conglomerate. But I remember Lawrence. Pale and pasty. Hair on his knuckles. Rheumy eyes. He drove a red Chrysler mini-van and the glove compartment was full of Steely Dan cassettes and porn.

Lawrence cried when I cut the sigils into his skin. Mucous bubbled out of his nose and ran into his mouth. Disgusting back then, but oddly amusing now. It brings a smile to my face, like thoughts of a childhood friend or first love.

In the years since, I've streamlined my efforts. I no longer bother with sigils or ceremony. I no longer speak the words of closing. The mere act of killing accomplishes my work. Spilling blood closes the doors. I don't need the rest of the trappings. Indeed, I prefer to act quickly these days. A shot in the dark. A knife to the back. Burn them as they sleep. Over and done. No muss. No fuss. Move on up the highway to the next exit. There are miles to go and doors to close before I rest, and I am getting older. Robert Frost took the road less traveled, but I take all roads. Speed and efficiency are the key. I didn't know that, back when I killed Lawrence.

I know it now.

I am swift. My avatar is a hummingbird. Metaphorically speaking, I move through the night at eighty miles per second, traveling from blossom to blossom, taking their nectar and then moving on.

I tell the young man none of this. Instead, I say, "No, I've never killed anyone."

"I have. A few years ago."

I sip my scotch and dab my lips with the napkin. When I respond, I try not to sound disinterested.

"Really?"

"Yeah." He nods. "Seriously. I'm not bullshitting you."

I say nothing, waiting, hoping he'll unburden himself soon so that I can go to my room and sleep. Dawn is coming and I must be on my way.

He signals for another round. We sit in silence until the bartender brings our drinks. The man glances at my half-full glass of scotch and I smile. He sets the drinks down and helps another customer. The young man picks up his beer and drinks half the bottle. I watch his throat work. He puts the bottle down and wipes the condensation on his jeans.

"My girlfriend's name was Janey," he says. "I was eighteen. She was fourteen. I mean, that's only four year's difference, but people acted like I was a fucking child molester or something. I wasn't, dog. I knew Janey since we were little kids. Our parents took us to the same church and shit. We were in love. Her old man freaked when he found out we were doing it. Somehow—I don't know how—he got the password to Janey's MySpace page and he read our messages. He told her she wasn't allowed to see me anymore. Then he called my folks and said if I tried to contact Janey again, he'd call the cops and have me arrested as a pedophile. He actually called me that—like I was one of those sick fucks Chris Hansen busts on that show. You know?"

I don't. The only television programming I watch is PBS, and only when the hotel I'm staying in offers it. But I nod just the same, encouraging him to continue. I hope he'll hurry up. I am bored.

"Well, Janey sent me a text message the next day. Her dad found out and he smacked the shit out of her. So I went over there and knocked on the door, and when he answered, I told him I wanted to talk. He was mad. So mad that he was fucking shaking, yo. But he let me in. Said we were gonna have this out once and for all, and then he never wanted to see me again. He made Janey stay upstairs in her room. I heard her and her mother arguing. I asked if I could get a glass of water and he said yeah. So when he went into the kitchen to get it, I followed him. They must have just gone grocery shopping, because there were a bunch of empty plastic bags lying on the counter. I picked up two—double-bagged, like they do for heavy stuff, you know? There was a little bit of blood inside, probably from steak or hamburger or something. I remember that. And while her dad's back was still turned, I slipped those bags over his head and smothered the motherfucker."

There is no regret in his voice as he says this. There is only grim satisfaction. His smile is a death mask. He takes another sip of beer and then continues.

"Upstairs, Janey and her mom were still hollering at each other, so I grabbed a knife from the drawer and tiptoed out of the kitchen. Janey's little brother, Mikey, was standing there. He screamed, so I stabbed him, just to shut him up." He chuckles, but there is no humor in it. "Yeah, I shut him the fuck up, all right. I remember when I pulled the knife out, blood just started gushing. It was hot and sticky, you know?"

I do indeed. I know all too well what another's blood feels like on your hands. How it smells. How it steams on cold nights and turns black when spilled on asphalt. How it dries on your flesh like mud, and can be peeled away like dead skin.

I tell him none of this. Instead, I finish my scotch and reach for the second glass. I hold it in my hands, not drinking.

"How did that make you feel?" I ask.

He blinks, as if he'd forgotten I was there.

"W-what?"

"Killing your girlfriend's brother. How did you feel about it?"

He shrugs. "I don't know. I didn't really feel anything at the time, except maybe scared. Janey's mom heard him scream. By the time Mikey hit the floor, she was running down the stairs, hollering at Janey to call 911. So I chased her down and shut her ass up, too. I didn't really think about it. I just did it. The news said I stabbed her mom forty-seven times, but I didn't count."

I arch my eyebrows, bemused. Forty-seven is a powerful number. It has meaning in certain occult circles, but I doubt he is aware of the significance.

"I went into Janey's room. She was hiding in the closet. Crying and shit. I told her we could be together now. We could leave, before anybody figured out what had happened. Take her parents car and just fucking drive, dog. Just hit the road and see where it took us. Go live somewhere else. Together."

I know where that road leads, but I don't tell him that, either.

"But Janey...she...she wouldn't stop hitting me. I

slapped back and the knife..."

A shadow of genuine emotion—the first I've seen him express—flashes his face. I raise my glass and drain it. Then I set it on the bar and slide two twenty-dollar bills beneath it.

"I've got the tab." I rise from the stool.

"Yo!" He grabs my arm, and I allow him to pull me close. "You gonna call the cops? You gonna tell somebody?"

I smile. "No. Your secret is safe with me."

"Bullshit. You're gonna go outside and call someone."

I grab his hand and squeeze. Hard. He flinches. My face is stone as I step away.

"I'll do no such thing," I say. "I have heard your tale and it means nothing to me. Do you think yourself some great murderer? You're not. You're an amateur."

"Fuck you."

"On the contrary. Fuck you. You play at being a killer, but have you murdered anyone since your girlfriend?"

"No."

"Well, there you go. If you really want to transcend, you'll go out tonight and continue your spree."

"You're crazy."

"No. I am the last sane individual in the world."

I leave him sitting there and walk away. I leave the hotel bar and instead of returning to my room, I sit on the smoker's bench outside and keep careful watch on the lobby through the big glass doors. Out on the highway, miles from here, a big rig's air brakes moan. They sound like a ghost.

I only kill out of necessity. I only do what needs to be done. There are doors in our world, and things can come through them. What is an entrance, but an exit? I shut those doors. I close exits.

Eventually, I see him stumble through the lobby, heading for the elevators. He is far too inebriated to notice me reenter the hotel. He just leans against the wall, waiting for the doors to open. I smile and nod at the desk clerk. The doors slide open. He steps inside, staring at his feet. I join him.

The doors close.

"What floor?" he asks, still looking at his shoes.

I do not answer.

He looks up and I cut his throat before he can scream. It is a practiced stroke. Perfunctory. Clinical. But I grin as I do it, and my heart beats faster than it has in many years.

I am breaking my rules, just this once. I am killing not out of necessity, but out of justice. Out of mercy. This is about putting down a rabid animal.

This is not an exit.

But I am.

STORY NOTES

This is a sequel to a short story called "I Am An Exit" *(which appeared in* Fear of Gravity*). Readers have often asked me for a follow-up to "I Am An Exit", so I wrote one. It tells you a little bit more about The Exit (as I've come to call the serial killer) – but not so much as to reveal everything about him. So who is he? Why is he killing people at highway exits? Well, I know, but I ain't telling. Not yet. You'll see him again in a forthcoming novel. Maybe the rest of his secrets will be revealed there. In fact, I'm sure they will.*

TAKE ME TO THE RIVER

I'm so fucking thirsty. Just can't seem to get enough water, which is funny, considering what's happened. Kelly said it was magic; that was the only explanation for the weather. Black magic. Maybe he was right. I mean, talk about a shitty forecast! Today, chance of rain one hundred percent with showers overnight and into tomorrow; more of the same for the rest of the week, the month—for your entire fucking life.

I saw bits and pieces on the news, but not much. The power went out pretty quick in these parts. But what I did see was horrifying. Cities flooded and people drowning, and then the cities were gone, buried beneath the waves, all within a matter of a week. Hell, entire countries got swallowed up. I'm living in the middle of Ohio and it's beachfront property now.

Yeah, a storm that powerful, and the fact that it hasn't stopped yet—that's got to be magic, I guess. Kelly knew what time it was.

Of course, Kelly also dropped acid every goddamn day, so maybe he didn't know.

I don't know, you know?

It itches, this white stuff that's growing on me. Itches so bad it burns. But when I try to scratch it, something happens. The stuff does something weird. Not sure how to describe it. Calming, maybe? The fungus whispers in my brain, speaking to me.

Soft…soft…

That's what it whispers. The words are wet. Cool. Soothing. They sound like my voice, but I know it's not me that's thinking it. It's the fungus. It looks like bleached peach fuzz.

I noticed it growing on me two days ago, right after Kelly died. God, I don't want to think about that. Something that looked like a cross between a human and a Great White shark came and bit him in half. One minute, we were shooting birds, and the next, something jumped out of the water and Kelly's lower half was standing next to me, gray and purple guts spilling out over his legs. His upper half was gone, and the thing that did it splashed back into the water. I caught a glimpse of its eyes before it vanished beneath the waves. They weren't black, like a shark's. They looked human. Intelligent.

I was splattered with Kelly's blood. Screaming, I watched his lower half totter forward. The choppy surf tossed his legs and guts around. A seagull darted down from the sky and flew away with a strand of Kelly hanging from its beak. I'm not sure what. His intestine, maybe? It looked like a purple and red worm.

I ran back inside, ripped off my clothes, and washed up. And that's when I noticed the fungus. There was a small patch sprouting between my toes. The White Fuzz. That's what we'd heard other survivors call it. It's like a case of athlete's foot from hell.

I'd seen it before I got it myself. The shit began sprouting up all over town about two weeks after the rains started. After everything went to hell. It was growing on things—buildings that were still above water, and people. Before the river covered Main Street, I saw a Mitsubishi flower delivery van with this shit growing all over the side of it. Saw a bird—it had thin white strands growing between his feathers. The bird didn't fly, didn't move, not even after I shot it. It just sat on a phone wire, getting drenched. And there was a guy, too, on the roof of the movie theatre. The shit had grown over his flesh and his clothes. Covered him almost completely. His eyes were still visible, but that was all. They were like two round dots of black ink, staring out of a white, hairy human-shaped mound. He just stood there in the rain, his arms stretched upward to the sky, like some sort of weird tree, soaking up the water. The white fuzz absorbed the raindrops as they fell on him, and I swear, I heard it growing. It sounded like a bowl of Rice Krispies in milk.

The man kept saying, "Soft." His voice was barely a whisper.

Every time he opened his mouth, I saw that the stuff was inside of him, too, and when I shot him, instead of blood, more strands of white fuzz poked out.

He didn't fall over after I shot him, and that's when I realized that he'd taken root. The fuzz had sent out little tendrils, anchoring him to the roof. It's like he was turning into something else. I don't know what.

I don't fucking know much of anything anymore.

All I do know is that this itching is driving me crazy! I want to scratch at it, dig my fingernails into my skin and just scratch until I bleed.

Soft…soft…

There. That's better. Didn't even have to scratch.

Like I said, I didn't see much of what happened elsewhere, but here, it was fucked up. It started raining one day, around six o'clock in the morning—and just didn't stop. The power went out, and soon after, the looting began (that's how Kelly and I got all that cool stuff). The governor mobilized the National Guard, but that didn't last too long. By then, most of those soldier dudes had seen the writing on the wall. They deserted, taking their families and heading for higher ground.

The Ohio River flooded its banks and just kept right on flowing. It took out the farmlands on the outskirts of the city and then it washed over the rest, flooding the downtown district. By that time, Kelly and I had set up shop in the Sheraton's penthouse suite, so we were safe and dry. At night, we'd get stoned and listen to the rain. In the morning, we'd do more of the same. Until we ran out of weed and acid.

Thirsty. No more bottled water left, either. I drank it all. Hell, there's nothing left. All that shit we ganked during the looting; the televisions and compact discs and food and guns, all of it is gone now, taken by those fucking bikers.

I hid inside the shower when they raided the building this morning. Pulled the shower curtain closed and held my breath. I guess with all the water outside, they didn't much feel like checking the bathtub. I stayed in there while they cleaned us out. The urge to scratch got really strong, but the voice inside my head calmed me down and kept me from blowing my hiding place.

Soft…soft…

Shut the fuck up and get out of my head!

The bikers loaded up their motorboats and sped off downstream—down Main Street.

And here I am.

I hope one of those shark things eats the fucking bikers.

Soft…soft…

Shit. Can't write. Can't even think. It's this fucking stuff. Will finish later.

So thirsty…

* * *

Later. I must have slept all day. Feels like I hibernated or something. It's nighttime now. The moon is out, but I can barely see it through the cloud cover. It should be full tonight, if the calendar is right, but there's just a sickly yellow glow in the sky.

Soft…soft…

It's still raining. Didn't really expect anything different, I guess. Sometimes I think the constant sound of falling rain will drive me insane. It never fucking stops, man! The drops just beat against the window constantly.

I'm still thirsty. My mouth feels like cotton, and my arms and legs are numb. My head hurts. Like I'm hung over.

Soft...soft...

Shut up.

Sof–

I said shut the hell up!

There's a big white patch of fuzz on my stomach. I touched it. It's soft and cool, like moss. Soon as I probed it, the itching started again, and then it burned.

I thought about getting a knife, and trying to cut it off me, but if I do that, I'm gonna lose some serious skin. Don't know if I'm strong enough to go through that. I already feel like shit. If I operate, there's a chance that I could pass out and die from blood loss.

I could shoot myself. I mean, who am I kidding? I've seen what this shit does. It grows right overtop of you, turns you into some kind of white, fuzzy plant-zombie. Yeah, maybe sucking on the end of that pistol—

Soft...soft...

—is the easy way out. But every time I reach for the pistol, the fungus starts burning again.

So I'm pretty much fucked.

Soft...soft...

But now it doesn't seem to itch anymore, so that's okay.

Soft...soft...

Wish I could figure out what it wants. It's driving me crazy. Chattering in my head every few seconds. Just repeating that word over and over again.

I'm so fucking thirsty!

Soft...soft...

Is that it? It needs water?

SOFT...SOFT...

That's it, isn't it? You need water? Well fuck you, fungus. You can't have any. There's a whole river right outside the door, but you're not—

What's it doing now?

It...

I can feel...*soft*...feel it inside my...*soft*...head, doing something...*soft*...going to...*soft*...go outside...*soft*...for a while...*soft*...and look at...*soft*...the moon...*soft*...and... *soft*...stand...*soft*...by the...*soft*...by the...*soft*...banks of the river.

No! What am I saying? Look at this—it's even showing up in my writing. I didn't write that. This white fuzz did. There is no riverbank. The water is all the way—

SOFT...SOFT...SOFT...SOFT...

Oh...

Oh, that's nice. That feels better. Much better. Going to go outside now and stand next to the river. I like the water. The water is nice. The water is...

It's soft.

Soft.

Soft...

STORY NOTES

This story is based on events from my novel The Conqueror Worms *and first appeared in the lettered edition of that book. If you haven't read the novel, this tale might not make much sense to you. There's not a lot of room here to tell you what happens. Suffice to say, ninety-percent of the Earth is flooded and the rains don't stop. The survivors face a variety of dangers, including giant worms and something that may or may not be Cthulhu. The white fungus was briefly touched upon in the novel, and given the spotlight in this story.*

AN APPOINTMENT KEPT

The man approached the jailer's house. It was a red and brown brick structure built onto the side of the prison. The man knocked on the door and waited, softly whistling a tune.

Sundown had come and gone. The sky was violet—not quite full dark yet. A full, yellow moon dominated the horizon. In the jailer's yard, a brass urn spit sparks into the gloom, disturbing a hovering cloud of mosquitoes. The man watched it sputter and smiled. The urn had been lit early that morning, informing Monroe's citizens that a trial would be held. The defendants were a farmer charged with non-payment of taxes, a woman accused of prostitution, a man charged with theft, and a woman accused of witchcraft. The latter was the more common crime.

There was a lot of witchcraft in Monroe these days.

Even though the urn was now extinguished, thick curls of resin-smoke still drifted up from the bowl. The visitor breathed in the aroma, patiently smoothed his tie, and then knocked again. Around back, in the cells beyond the prison yard, prisoners mumbled. The man stopped whistling and listened. A woman, the same one tried for witchcraft earlier in the day, sobbed from above him. She was jailed at the top of the house, separate from the other prisoners.

The door bolt clicked as it was drawn back. There was a pause, and then a black woman opened the door. The man smiled at her. The woman's eyes went wide and she gasped, her hands fluttering to her chest.

The man's smile faded. "I am not here for you, good mother. I seek an audience with Mr. Bullock."

The woman bowed and mumbled a good evening. Her bottom lip trembled.

"Sorry, sir," she apologized, eyes cast to the floor. "I mistook you for—another."

"Indeed? Which other? There are dark men about these days. Do I resemble one of them?"

"No, sir. Begging your pardon. You reminded me of someone I saw one night when I was a little girl. Back home."

"Do tell?"

"I was young when they took me from Africa. But I'll never forget. My father called to him one night, and he came to our fire to grant my father a boon. But you could not be him, lest you hadn't aged."

"They say that everyone has a doppelganger. Do you believe this to be so?"

The woman was too nervous to respond. Something in the stranger's demeanor terrified her. The man's smile returned. He swept past her and into the foyer. The woman scurried off.

The jailer's assistant, Matthew Bullock, sat in front of the fireplace in the next room, blowing hard on the orange coals. He was dressed in a dirty, stained tunic and pants—both of which were two sizes too small—and his hair was sweaty and unkempt. Several days' worth of beard clung to his face. There were food crumbs in the whiskers. He seemed morose, and did not look up when the visitor entered.

Patiently waiting to be addressed, the man glanced around the room. A lantern glowed softly on the mantle. An oil painting of a ship at sea hung on one bare wall. A round wooden table and a few battered chairs sat in the center of the room. They were all oak, because the jailer couldn't afford to have mahogany transported all the way from South

America.

"Look here," Bullock muttered, "If you come to speak with the jailer, then I'm afraid you're out of luck."

"Indeed? And why is that?"

"Because Mr. Grant ain't here right now. He's away over to the Miller's house for a visit. Gone to hear Miss Tessa play the organ."

Bullock still did not look up or rise to meet his caller. Instead, he leaned forward and blew on the coals again. They flared. Then Bullock pulled an iron brand out of the fire and began filing it, removing the rough edges and flecks of dead skin that were stuck to the sides.

On the ball of Bullock's thumb was a lump of scar tissue, a brand—T, for thief. It stood out in the firelight as he filed the edges of the hot branding iron.

"I am not here for your master," the visitor said.

"Well, I ain't got no time to talk. I'm about my tasks, as you can see. Mr. Grant bid me to finish these brands for court tomorrow. Been a busy week. So I'll bid you good night."

The man made no move to leave.

Ignoring the visitor, Bullock placed the brand back in the center of the coals, then withdrew it and pressed it down on a leather pad. There was a soft hiss as it burned a perfect T into the leather. Bullock eyed the mark with satisfaction, and then set the iron aside.

"Perfect."

"Not nearly as perfect as the brand you wear," the visitor said. "You are marked. Identifiable to those who know where to look, despite whatever lengths you go through to hide it."

"You mean this?" Bullock held up his branded thumb and shrugged. "I thought I'd bid you a good night, but since you asked—it ain't so bad, being an indentured servant. Fair and square, you know? I pleaded benefit of clergy and was shown mercy. They sentenced me to serve Mr. Grant. Could be worse. I could have hanged."

"Indeed." The man's dark eyes twinkled in the firelight.

"You could have."

Bullock stood up. "So you ain't here for Mr. Grant. Who you here for, then? Have you come to claim the body of Myers? If so, I hope you brought along a bag of lavender or flower petals, because he's starting to stink something awful. Even with the gallows a mile away, you can smell him. Been hanging there for two days. The birds have been picking at him. Taking off with the choice bits. Ghastly affair. It's making the other prisoners restless."

"I did indeed have an appointment with him, but I am not here for Stephen Myers body. I have no claim to that."

Bullock walked to the window and looked out into the darkness. "I ain't surprised. Don't imagine anyone will claim his corpse. He was a wicked man, that one. If ever a man deserved to be condemned, it was him. All those children they found butchered out in the hollow near his place…"

"You sound surprised."

"Well, sure. Good man like Stephen Myers, capable of such horrible crimes. Wouldn't you be surprised?"

"Not if I were you. After all, you knew the real Myers."

Bullock whirled around, his face flushed with anger. "What's that supposed to mean?"

"When they arrested Myers, his tongue had been cut out. The magistrate opined that it had something to do with the rituals he was performing; some form of self-mutilation. But it wasn't. It was to keep him from talking. Stephen Myers was illiterate. He couldn't read or write, other than to sign his name. He had no way of communicating when he was sentenced."

"He didn't need to communicate. His handiwork spoke for itself—the way he butchered those innocents. Nothing he'd have said could have saved him from the gallows."

"While Myers was in his cell," the visitor interrupted, "the cabinetmaker arrived to measure him, just like he does with all of the condemned, and then built him a pine casket. The coffin was kept in Myer's cell with him until the day of his hanging. He wept over it. Both he and the box were loaded onto a horse-drawn cart and taken to the gallows. The fear in his eyes was beautiful to behold."

"Sure it was." Bullock looked uneasy. "Myers knew what waited him at the end of that ride."

"Ah, but there is the rub. It wasn't Stephen Myers who swung from that rope, and that is why I am here tonight."

"You saying we hung the wrong man?" Bullock moved towards the fireplace. "That's a serious accusation, fellow. You'd best take that up with Mr. Grant."

"I'm saying that he wasn't himself. You threw a rope around your neck. The cart pulled away, and you choked to death. You defecated in your pants."

"I...I don't..."

"You used an old, reliable rope to help make it quicker. Am I right?"

"What?"

"Why did you do that? Because you didn't want the rope to kink up and twist. Why do that for a child murderer? You rubbed pig fat into the rope so the knot would slide easier; the death would be quicker."

"You're insane, fellow. You keep talking like I hung myself."

"You did, Stephen. In a manner of speaking."

Bullock reached for the branding iron. "My name is Matthew Bullock."

The visitor laughed. "No, your name is Stephen Myers. You butchered those children in accordance with the old laws, the laws you gleaned from books of old. When the rituals were finished, you gained the power to hide yourself inside the body of this jailer's assistant. You condemned another man to death and hid inside his body. You killed yourself so that you could live."

Bullock moved quickly. He thrust the still-hot brand at the visitor's face. The man easily sidestepped the assault, and waved his hand. The brand turned into a serpent. The creature sank its fangs into Bullock's left hand. It drew back for another strike. Shrieking, Bullock dropped the writhing snake to the floor.

"We had an agreement, Mr. Myers; a binding contract. I did not forget our arrangement. I never do. When your time was up, you sought to break our agreement. Imagine my surprise when I arrived at the gallows to keep our appointment, to claim your soul, and instead found someone else's inside your body."

Whimpering, Bullock backed against the fireplace. He held his hands up, pleading. His left hand had already swollen up to twice its size. Black venom bubbled beneath the skin.

"God save me," he cried.

"He won't."

The coals in the fireplace flickered; then flared up. The flames roared.

Bullock screamed.

The dark man laughed.

Outside, the prisoners fell silent. Later, the black woman, who'd been cowering under her bed since the stranger's arrival, would creep downstairs and find no trace of Mr. Bullock.

The visitor exited the jailer's house. He resumed whistling his mournful tune. Monroe's streets were deserted. The silent homes were all shuttered for the evening. The only sign of life was the bawdy laughter drifting from the taverns and coffeehouses, as men played dominoes and cards and dice. He walked on. The sky grew black in his wake. Trees and grass withered as he passed. A bird fell dead from her nest; the eggs she'd guarded turning black. Dogs howled, scampering beneath beds and tables, cowering in fear. Babies cried in their cribs. Children moaned in their sleep.

Smiling, the man disappeared into the night. He had other appointments to keep.

STORY NOTES

Richard Chizmar and Thomas Monteleone called me one evening, around 6pm, and said, "We're putting together an anthology and we need a new story from you. We'll pay you top dollar."

I agreed, and then asked them when the story was due.

Rich said, "Tomorrow morning. Six o'clock, sharp."

I assumed they'd both been drinking, but they were serious.

Writing is a cruel and savage business.

Anyway, I wrote this story overnight – a little twist on the old selling-your-soul-to-the-devil tale.

STONE TEARS

For Jamie LaChance...

Something splashed in the water hard enough to rock the small boat. Nelson LeHorn reached out and grabbed the sides of the craft. His knuckles turned white.

"Don't let it spook you," Hodgson said. "Probably just a channel cat."

"I ain't spooked. Just surprised me, is all."

"They get big in here. Heard tell of ones on the bottom that are longer than a man. I'd love to catch me one of them. Bet they put up one hell of a fight."

Nelson didn't respond. He stared out over the dark river, watching the moonlight reflect off the waves. Behind them, the launch near Wrightsville faded into the gloom. The lights of Columbia and Marietta twinkled on the far side of the shore. For the most part, the Susquehanna flowed quietly. The silence was broken only by the swells lapping gently against Hodgson's boat, and the droning hum of the small motor, as Hodgson guided them towards their destination.

A bat darted overhead, catching their attention. It was followed a moment later by the shadow of a hawk.

Nelson knew it was an omen.

He just didn't know what it meant.

Nelson LeHorn had never been much of a water person. He'd taken his family to Ocean City, Maryland once, when the kids were young. Matty, Claudia and Gina had loved it.

They'd have stayed in the ocean for the entire weekend, if he and Patricia had let them. But Nelson was wary of so much water. That wide, unbroken expanse made him uneasy for reasons he couldn't explain. He much preferred the small fishing pond on his farm, and the thin stream that ran through his property.

It occurred to him that his dislike of water was funny, in a way, since water had been involved in his introduction to Hodgson, who now ferried him across the river.

Ten years before, when Richard Nixon was still in office and American troops were still in Vietnam, Hodgson and some other employees of the Gladstone Pulpwood Company had been clearing trees on Nelson's property. Crops were bad that year, on account of too much rain. To make some extra money, Nelson sold off some timber. He had plenty. His farm was surrounded by acres of forest and deep, dark hollows.

Hodgson had been cutting through the trunk of an old, gnarled sycamore when the chainsaw hit the knot. Suddenly, it snapped back and caught him in the chest and shoulder, slicing through his shirt and deep into his flesh. Nelson, who had been working in the barn at the time, was alerted by the shouts of Hodgson's co-workers. When he arrived on the scene, the man was lying on the forest floor, unconscious and in shock. Hodgson bled profusely, but the ground around him was nearly dry, as if the forest's roots were sucking it up. Still, Nelson knew that if they didn't stop the bleeding, Hodgson would never live long enough to make it to the hospital. He'd told the co-workers to apply pressure to the wound as best they could, and then dashed back to the house.

The Gladstone employees must have figured he was going to call 911, which he did, but they were surprised when Nelson returned a few minutes later with a piece of paper, a pen, and an old, brown book called *The Long Lost Friend: A Collection of Mysterious and Invaluable Arts and Remedies For Man As Well As Animals* by John George Hohman. Hohman had written the book in 1820. It was a curious mix of German and Hebrew mysticism, Dutch herbal recipes, and Egyptian lore collectively known in the Central Pennsylvanian region as powwow. Hohman was considered a powwow magician.

So was Nelson LeHorn, as his father was before him, and his grandfather and great-grandfather, as well.

Nelson knelt beside the injured man and referred to the book. Then he wrote the name of the four principal waters of the whole world—Pison, Gihon, Hiddekel, and Perath—on the sheet of paper. While the men watched in bewilderment, he placed the paper on the wound. He then whispered, "Blessed wound, blessed hour, blessed be the day on which Jesus Christ was born, in the name."

And just like that, the bleeding stopped.

Hodgson's co-workers were amazed. Many of them had, of course, heard of powwow magic, given its long-standing connection with the region's folklore. But this was the first time any of them had actually seen its methods in action. Nelson modestly brushed aside their questions and comments, and urged them to get Hodgson up to the house before the ambulance arrived.

That was how they'd met. Hodgson got worker's compensation and disability from the accident, and rather than going back to cutting trees, he bought a small place in Wrightsville along the river and spent his days fishing from his little bass boat.

And once a year, indebted to the man who had saved his life, he ferried Nelson out to the middle of the Susquehanna River, and landed on the shore of Walnut Island.

"Pretty out tonight," Nelson said.

"Yeah," Hodgson agreed. "It is. Wife's probably pissed as shit at me right about now. Nice night, like tonight, and I'm out here, instead of back home. Especially with them saying who shot J.R. on *Dallas* tonight. You ever watch that show?"

"Can't say that I have. I read, mostly. My family's been bugging me for that cable television. Imagine—paying for TV. Dumbest thing I've ever heard of. What's next?"

"I hear you. I wouldn't have fooled with it at all, but the wife made me get it. Twenty bucks a month! But we get fifteen channels. She loves her shows. Likes me to rub her feet while we watch them, which is why she'll be pissed that I'm out here."

"I'm sorry about that. Like I've told you before, you shouldn't feel obliged. What I done for you, I'd do for anybody. If these yearly trips make trouble for you at home, I won't ask no more. It's just that you're the only fella I know with a boat—only one I trust, anyway."

"Oh, don't worry about it. To be honest, I like to get away once in a while. And she's used to it by now. Alls I got to do is show her my scar and remind her of what you did for me, and she gets over it quick. But she thinks it's pretty odd that you go night fishing every year on this day. I don't tell her what we really do out here, of course—I don't tell no one, just like you asked."

"I appreciate it. More than you know."

"Least I can do. I've got to wonder though, if you don't mind me asking—what's your wife think about it?"

Nelson frowned. "Patricia? She's fine with it. Why wouldn't she be?"

"Don't know. Figured maybe she wasn't privy to all the powwow stuff."

"She knows it well. Even helps me with it sometimes. Her Daddy practiced powwow, same as mine. And she knows what today's date is, too, and why it's so important to me."

"Why is it so important?" Hodgson asked. "I mean, I know you can't tell me what you get up to out there on Walnut Island, and I'm not sure that I even want to know. But I always wondered about the date? Is it one of them equinoxes or something?"

Nelson was quiet for a moment. He watched another bat dive down towards the water, snatch a lightning bug in mid-air, and then flit away towards shore. Another omen, and still, he couldn't divine any meaning from it. When he looked back at Hodgson, Nelson sighed.

"I don't reckon it will hurt to be straight with you. You've done right by me over the years. Not to mention you've brought me out here each year, and never asked why."

Hodgson nodded, encouraging his passenger to continue. His expression was eager.

Nelson pointed at Walnut Island, looming out of the darkness.

"You ever hear of the petroglyphs out here?"

"No, can't say that I have. What's that—some kind of oil drilling place?"

Nelson laughed. "How in the world did you come up with that?"

"Petro. Ain't that what the Brits call gasoline?"

Nelson, who had never been out of the tri-State area in his life, and whose knowledge of the United Kingdom's modern culture was limited to Margaret Thatcher, the occasional British sitcom on PBS, and a band that his son, Matty, listened to (Deaf Leopards or something like that) had no idea, but he didn't admit it to Hodgson.

"Petroglyphs," he repeated. "They're pictures and symbols carved into the rocks out here. Some of them were made by the Indians."

"Which ones?"

"Take your pick. The Susquehannocks, of course. The Iroquois. The Algonkians. There's a bunch that were carved by white men, too—sort of like Civil War-era graffiti. Some were made by prehistoric man, long before the Indians came. And a few are even older than that."

"How can they be older than prehistoric man?"

Nelson ignored the question. "There used to be a lot more of them out here. But back in the Thirties, when they built the Holtwood and Safe Harbor dams, a lot of the petroglyphs ended up underwater. Some archeologist folks managed to save a few. Dug them out with a big pneumatic rock drill and put them on display at the Pennsylvania Historical Museum. But to see the rest, you've got to put on a diving suit and swim around down there with those big catfish you mentioned earlier."

Hodgson shuddered.

"The only ones left above water," Nelson continued, "are on Big Indian Rock, Little Indian Rock, and Walnut Island. And since the County Historical Society, the Museum Commission, and the State don't like folks traipsing around on the islands, I have you bring me out here at night."

"Could we get arrested for it?"

"I don't know. Reckon we'd get fined, at least."

Hodgson paused, seeming to consider this. "So, every year, you come out here to look at some rocks?"

"Sort of. There's one petroglyph in particular that I come to see."

Hodgson stroked his mustache. "Well, I don't guess it's any weirder than the Arabs making their pilgrimage to Mecca or all that carrying on the Baptists do."

Nelson smiled. "It's something I have to do. That's why Patricia don't get mad at me. Cause she understands."

"So her daddy practiced powwow just like yours did, huh?"

"Both her parents did. They were both great healers."

"Yours, too?"

Nelson shook his head. "No. Just my father. My mother went away when I was younger. Daddy caught her with another man, and there was hell to pay. My father had a wicked temper."

"That so?"

"Yep. He worked powerful powwow, though. Hexed the river witch over in Marietta once, after he found out she'd put a blight on our cattle. Hexed a man who he caught stealing from our root cellar one year, too. Fella went blind and deaf."

Hodgson grinned, bemused. "Sounds like your Daddy wasn't one to piss off."

"No, he wasn't."

"And he really did all of that? Actually hexed people?"

"Sure."

"And it really works?"

"It worked on you well enough, didn't it?"

Hodgson shrugged. "I reckon that's true. But that was healing. Hexing is something different, right?"

"It all comes from the same source. And it don't matter who you are and which kind of powwow you practice—sometimes, you're called upon to do the other. That's one of the prices."

His companion nodded, but Nelson could tell from Hodgson's expression that he didn't really understand, and was just humoring him.

They fell silent again as they approached Walnut Island. Lightning bugs twinkled on the shore. When they were close enough, Hodgson shut off the engine, and the silence deepened. Using an oar, he guided them in the rest of the way. The bottom of the boat scraped along the rocks. He hopped out and dragged it up onto the bank.

"I'll wait here for you, like always."

Nelson shook his hand. "Appreciate it. I'll be back soon as I can."

"Take your time. It's a nice night. I don't mind waiting."

Nelson took off his orange life vest, and pulled a small, plastic bag from the boat. It rustled, catching Hodgson's attention.

"What you got there?" he asked. "Magic stuff?"

Winking, Nelson wagged his finger at the man. "A magus don't ever reveal his secrets."

He removed his orange life vest, grabbed the flashlight from the boat and then headed off into the island's interior. An empty beer can, a torn pair of women's panties, and the burned-out remains of a campfire told him that someone else had been there recently. Frowning, Nelson continued onward. Birds rustled nearby, disturbed by his intrusion. The lightning bugs disappeared as he approached. Somewhere in the darkness, an owl hooted. Otherwise, the island was silent. Lifeless.

The gentle breeze cooled the sweat on his neck. The plastic bag slapped against his thigh with each step. The flashlight beam bobbed up and down.

Walnut Island was small, little more than a large outcropping of bedrock covered with sparse trees and vegetation, and he didn't have to go far before encountering the petroglyphs. Some were clearly recognizable—animal tracks, birds, deer, bear, foxes, snakes, trees, and human faces. Some depicted scenes of everyday life—a hunter with a bow, a mother with her baby, a group attending to a field of corn. There were abstract designs—spirals and geometric shapes. Others were of more mysterious figures—birdmen, goat-men, reptile-men, a giant serpent (that many, including Nelson, thought depicted Old Scratch—a legendary water snake rumored to haunt the Susquehanna River), and a snail-like creature with a headdress. There was a smattering of what looked like Chinese, Hittite, and Cypriot characters. He'd seen those before but hadn't mentioned them to Hodgson. No sense in confusing the man. Nelson knew better than to argue with the popular conception that Columbus had been the first non-Indian in America.

Amidst all of these petroglyphs was a smattering of modern graffiti. Its presence angered Nelson. There were declarations of love, crude little hearts, names, dates, and genitalia, not to mention the numerous pentagrams and swastikas, all carved by stoned teenagers who hadn't the slightest understanding of the latter two symbols' true meanings or power.

He passed by all of the petroglyphs with barely a cursory glance. He was seeking another.

In the center of the island was a huge slab of rock. The flashlight beam trailed over it as he neared the spot, illuminating a life-sized petroglyph of a woman. The figure was about five and a half feet tall, naked, and incredibly lifelike and detailed. Her hair, facial features, and even the blemishes on her skin had all been painstakingly recreated. Unlike the other carvings, erosion and vandalism had not faded or damaged the petroglyph.

Nelson cleared his throat.

"Hello, Mom. Happy birthday."

Nelson opened the plastic bag and took out a bouquet of fresh flowers—tulips, roses, petunias, Queen Anne's Lace, and daisies. All of them had been grown on his farm, and all of them had been picked by his hand that morning. He talked to the carving for twenty minutes, telling her what her grandchildren had accomplished in the last year, and of how much he missed her. He repeated his annual promise that some day, he'd figure out a way to bring her back again. Then he leaned over, kissed the rock on the cheek, and said goodbye.

As he made his way back to Hodgson's boat, rainwater leaked from the corners of the petroglyph's stone eyes.

STORY NOTES

Regular readers will note that this is not the first appearance of Nelson LeHorn. He first appeared in my novel Dark Hollow *(also published as* The Rutting Season*). This story takes place a few short years before the events that occur to him in that book. Hopefully, it gave you a little more insight into his character and his motivations.*

The Susquehanna River petroglyphs are real, as are Walnut Island, Big Indian Rock and Little Indian Rock. I was unaware of them until several years ago, when a local reader mentioned them in a post on my message board. Since then, I've become fascinated with them. Some replicas of the carvings are on display at the Indian Steps Museum, located in Airville. If you're ever in the area, the museum is worth visiting. Much like the characters in this book, I have undertaken a midnight journey to see the real, remaining petroglyphs. They are, quite simply, awe-inspiring, even despite the ravages of time, nature and human vandalism. To the best of my knowledge, however, there is no life-sized carving of a human female.

If you're interested, there are also two very good books examining the petroglyphs. The first one is Petroglyphs in the Susquehanna River near Safe Harbor, Pennsylvania *by Donald A. Cadzow. As the title suggests, it is dry, academic read-*

ing – especially for the novice. But that doesn't make the material it presents any less fascinating. The second book is Indians in Pennsylvania *by Paul A. W. Wallace. Both books were published by the Pennsylvania Historical and Museum Commission, and are (as of this writing) still in print and available at various locations, including online.*

STORY NOTES

This time, you get the story notes before the story, rather than after. "Gratefully Dead" *was written for an anthology called* Dead Cats Bouncing. *The anthology's title was a bit misleading. The deceased feline in question is actually a singular character named – appropriately enough – Dead Cat. Dead Cat was created by Gerard Houarner and Gak. Centuries ago, he lived in an Egyptian cattery, but when his master died, Dead Cat got mummified right alongside him. Now he wanders the Earth, looking for a home. He also has a funny way of speaking, as you'll soon find out. Dead Cat appeared in a chapbook by Gerard and Gak. It was a success, and they invited other authors to write a story featuring their creation.*

This was mine.

GRATEFULLY DEAD

I Dead Cat.

Still dead.

Dead not better.

Dead boring.

Dead sucks.

* * *

Hunt. Eat. Nap. Walk.

Yadda-Yadda-Yadda.

Hunt mice. Rats. Birds. Snakes.

Too slow. Bandages get caught on things.

Body not quick now.

Prey smell dead cat coming.

Catch them sleeping. Surprise.

Go for young, old and crippled.

Then eat.

Eat no good.

Eat meat. Spit back up.

No taste.

No need.

No hunger.

Boring.

Sleep.

Take nap. Nice cat nap.

Dream black dreams…

Cattery. Falling.

Fall long, long time. No bounce.

Dream of Hell.

Cat naps not nice.

Wake. Walk.

Always walking.

Dodge cars. Run from dogs and little humans.

Little humans have sticks and cans. Tie cans to tail.

Keep walking.

Dead sucks.

* * *

Want peace.

No more living. No more dead.

Just peace.

* * *

See people on picture box.

Sign behind people.

GREEPEACE

Peace. They help.

Walk through city. Find building with same sign.

Go inside.

Stinks. Worse than cattery.

Patchouli oil. Incense. Sweat.

Marijuana.

That why they called 'Green' Peace?

Lots of humans. Loud. Agitated.

Want to blow up animal testing lab.

All talking. Don't notice me.

Spit up hairball. Clear throat.

Noticed.

Gasps. Screams.

Silence.

Then all talk at once.

Seize dead cat. Poke stiff joints. Unwrap bandages.

"Here is another victim of the evil cosmetics company fascists!"

No. Here victim of pilgrims.

Humans don't listen.

Call other humans. PETA

Hmmmm.

People Eating Tasty Animals?

Not good. That doesn't work at all.

Dreadlocks man shouting into phone. "Joint effort!"

Not liking this. Bandages half gone.

Squirm.

Somebody playing Grateful Dead on squawk box.

Out of here! NOW!

Hiss. Spit. Scratch. Claw.

Escape.

Grateful.

* * *

Walk on.

Church.

Temple for new God.

No more Bast or Set.

New age. New God.

This God not say "eat sand."

Find Priest.

Priest go in small booth.

Follow. Leap onto bench. Window opens.

"How long has it been since your last confession?"

"Never."

"I see. Well, I'll help you in any way I can. What is it that you seek, my son?"

"Peace."

"Ahhh. Peace can only be found through our Lord and Savior, Jesus Christ. But first you'll need to confess your sins."

"Eat sand."

Priest laughs.

"No, I'm afraid that's not a part of it. The Lord said 'This is my body that has been shed for you. Eat this in remembrance of me'."

"Then peace?"

"It's the start, my son. Yes."

Crawl through window. Priest screams.

Eat body. Full. Spit back up.

Still no peace.

* * *

Walk on.

Bad neighborhood.

Dark. Noisy. Dirty. Smelly.

Hopeless.

Worse than cattery. Worse than Hell.

Worse than GREENPEACE.

Men on street. Bad men.

Trade green paper for white powder.

Man stuffs green paper in pocket.

"A'ight, yo. Peace out!"

Walks away.

'Peace out.' Follow him to peace?

Man walks down street. Pants drag on ground.

Follow along curb.

Car drives by. Low. Flashy.

Thunder trapped in squawk box.

Headache, even through bandages.

Window rolls down.

"Yo, T-Bone!"

Peace out man turns.

"What'chu want?"

"You be working our corner!"

More thunder. Louder. Different.

Peace out man falls.

Doesn't bounce.

Drops boom stick.

Boom stick goes down sewer grate.

"Punk dropped his piece."

Peace? Does boom stick bring peace?

Car drives away.

Follow boom stick down hole.

* * *

Sewer. Smelly. Humid.

Always night.

Follow piece but no peace.

Walk long time. Tunnels. Twisting. Fetid.

Lose piece. Find croc.

Pale. Bloated. Blind.

"Want peace."

"Then you must seek the magic man of the mountains. Only he can give you eternal rest."

Walk on.

* * *

Leave city. No peace.

Walk long time.

Hills. Woods. Towns. Villages.

Valleys. Mountains.

Peak.

Find magic man.

Magic man has familiar. Cat like me.

But not like me too.

Cat alive, not dead. Black. Fat. Old.

"What do you seek, reanimated one?"

"Peace."

"Do you mean life, my friend?"

"Eat sand."

"Oblivion then."

Not speak. Nod. Good word. Oblivion.

"There is a way. I can help you. But it will cost you."

"Name price."

"Your name is the price."

"Don't have name. Just dead cat."

"Nonsense. All things have names. Names are power."

Remember things people called me. 'Here Kitty-kitty.' 'Scat.' 'Moth-eaten old thing.'

No good.

"Don't know name."

"Then you must find it. Discover your name and bring it back to me. Then, I will help you find the peace you so desperately crave."

* * *

Walk on.

Back down peak. Mountains. Valleys.

Towns. Villages.

Back to woods.

Crying.

So is another.

Stop walking.

Part bushes.

Small human. Boy. Crying.

Watch.

He doesn't have sticks. He doesn't have cans.

He has bruises.

Cuts. Scrapes. Twisted. Broken.

Bloody. Pale.

Creep out into clearing. Bushes rustle.

Boy looks up.

Doesn't scream. Doesn't gasp. Doesn't wrinkle nose.

Smiles.

"Cool! Come here kitty."

Sticks out hand. Glide to him.

Boy pets and scratches. Behind ears. Good spot.

Real good.

"Nelson and his gang chased me into the woods. They live in my neighborhood. They're always picking on me. I don't really have any friends. We just moved here a few months ago."

He talks. He rubs. He pets.

Feel weird. Funny. Strange.

Insides vibrating. Walk in tiny circles, round and round boy's hand.

"Anyway, today they chased me in here. I climbed a tree so they couldn't find me, but after they left, I fell. It was a long way down."

Fell. Long way. Know something about that.

Boy didn't bounce.

Whole body vibrating now.

Purring. This what it's like to purr.

This works. This works real good.

"I don't think I can go home now, can I?"

Nudge boy's hand. Purr.

Boy sniffles. Wipes eyes. Smiles.

"Would you like to be my friend?"

That works real good too.

"I'll have to give you a name."

Purr. Purr. Puuuuuuurrrrrrrr.

"I'll call you McGwire. You know, like the baseball player."

Have sudden urge for ball of string.

"C'mon, McGwire. Let's go play!"

Not crazy about name. Could get used to it though.

Found name at least.

Found peace.

Dead good.

Dead peaceful.

THE SIQQUSIM WHO STOLE CHRISTMAS

Ob entered the fat man's body at thirty-thousand feet. After taking control of the corpse, he glanced over the side of the craft. A snow-covered landscape zipped by far below. The wind howled in his ears as he passed through a cloud. The dampness chilled him.

It was nighttime. Stars cast their cold, lonely lights from far above. Ob hated each and every one of them.

The Lord of the Siqqusim stared at his reflection in the vehicle's polished silver handrails. Outwardly, the man's body wasn't much. A long, white beard, bordering on unkempt, dangled from a face whose centerpiece was a bulbous red nose. The fat man was adorned in a red suit, matching the color of his nose, like the garb of a jester or clown. He smelled faintly of gingerbread. Ob scanned the body's memories, picking through the brain like it was a filing cabinet, searching for clues to this new host's identity.

The fat man had died of an aneurism. He'd been—

Ob's laughter was louder than the roaring wind. Had the rest of the Thirteen been present, they'd have shared in his amusement.

This host body had suffered an impossible aneurism—

impossible since the fat man was supposed to be immortal. He was one of the old gods, known to various tribes as Santa Claus, Kris Kringle, the Dark Elf, Father Christmas and other, long-forgotten names. He was not able to die, and yet he had—the victim of a slow, eons-long spiritual rot. Ob had seen it before, in Rome and Greece and elsewhere.

Santa Claus had died from the cancer of non-belief.

All gods existed on belief. It was their power. Their food. The more people that believed in them, the stronger they became. But when they lost favor with their devout followers, when people stopped believing in them and began worshipping other deities, the gods grew weaker. If it continued long enough, the gods could die. It had happened to Zeus. To Odin. To countless others, both remembered and forgotten. History was written in the blood of forgotten pantheons. They'd been replaced with new gods. Shinier gods. Gods of medicine and science and peace.

Of course, humanity hadn't realized that Claus was a god. They just thought of him as some kindly old legend, a story to tell children. A benevolent figurehead. A marketing icon. Which was fine, since millennia ago, he'd been that very thing—a god of production and commerce. Claus had transformed over time, altering his identity and duties to suit the ever-changing demands of his fickle believers. All gods did so, when required. They had no choice. Beholden to the whims of the faithful, even the gods had to adapt or die.

Ob and the rest of the Thirteen were not gods, and thus, they had no such weaknesses. The Thirteen scoffed at the inferior beings—gods, angels, demons, devils. All of them were amateurs. They were mere children, battling for scraps from the Creator's table, fighting for the right to be chained to the desires of humanity, sentenced to obey their believer's prayers, for to do so was to reward their faith. Rewarding humanity's faith kept the belief strong—and thus, kept the gods strong.

Ob longed for the day when he could destroy them all.

He would kick the Creator from the throne and ascend for himself.

But not yet.

One planet, one reality, at a time. Ob and his fellow Siqqusim had just finished with another Earth, slaughtering the last of the humans and making a mockery with their corpses. While his brothers, Ab and Api, took over, Ob had led the Siqqusim into the Great Labyrinth between worlds, moving on to this level of existence.

Finished with Claus's memories, Ob looked around the sled. It was piled high with colorfully-wrapped boxes and bags. The vast storage space behind the seat was much bigger inside than it appeared from the outside. Ob knew that if he dived into that mound of presents, he could burrow all night and still not reach the bottom. Leather reins lay in his lap. Ob picked them up and sleighbells jingled. The reins were tied to nine mangy familiars. Each had taken the earthly form of a reindeer. The familiar at the head of the procession was smaller than the others, but its nose glowed scarlet with arcane energies.

Ob experimented with the reins. The familiars obeyed his commands, unaware that their master no longer inhabited this obese shell. Ob directed them to land. They dropped out of the sky and soared above a village in the Lapland province of Finland. The sled drifted to a halt in the deep snow. Other than the sleigh's jingling bells, the town was silent. The streets were deserted and the villagers were most likely asleep. Smoke curled from a few chimneys. Many doors and windows were adorned with Christmas decorations. Icicles hung from roofs and gutters.

Ob climbed out of the sled and approached the reindeer. They stomped their hooves and pawed the snow, sensing that something was wrong, but unaware of what it was. Their master smelled different. His aura had vanished.

"Well," Ob said, *"ho, ho, ho and all that. Names have power, so let's get down to the act of naming."* He pointed at each as he spoke. *"Rudolph, Dasher, Dancer, Prancer, Vixen, Comet, Cupid, Donner and Blitzen. Now…do you know who I am?"*

The familiars glanced at each other, snorting in fear.

"I'm the reason for the season." Ob licked his lips. *"Meet the new boss, same as the old boss."*

His teeth flashed in the darkness.

* * *

Alvar Pokka slept next to his hearth. The embers glowed softly. The warmth eased his aching joints, stiff with arthritis. He was eighty-two years old and had lived in Lapland all of his life. Until that night, Alvar had thought he knew everything there was to know about the region's flora and fauna. But the sound that woke him was like nothing he'd ever heard.

Alvar hadn't known that reindeer could scream.

He crept to the window. The fire's warmth seemed to vanish. Alvar peered out the frosted glass and gasped. Santa Claus was slaughtering his reindeer. One by one, he tore out their throats with his hands and teeth. His white beard had turned crimson, dripping gore. The dead animals dropped to the frozen ground. Steam rose from their corpses.

Then they got up again and prowled through the snow-filled streets.

Soon, Alvar's shrieks mingled with the rest of the villagers' screams.

* * *

Tony Genova bolted upright in his bed, wondering if he'd screamed out loud. His heart hammered in his chest, and his ears rang. He glanced around the dimly lit room. His long-time associate, the severely overweight Vince Napoli, sat in a chair, eating junk food and watching television. Vince turned when Tony cleared his throat.

"Sorry," Vince said. "Did the TV wake you up?"

Tony shook his head, waiting for his racing pulse to slow down. He slid out from under the covers, fully dressed, and put his feet on the floor. A log on the fireplace popped, sending a shower of sparks drifting up into the chimney. He smoothed his tie and noticed that his hand was trembling.

"Jeez, Tony! You're sweating like a pig. You okay?"

Tony nodded. "I'm fine. Just had a bad dream is all."

"It's that shit they fed us for dinner," Vince mused, his eyes not leaving the television. "You should have brought some stuff from the States, like I did. Sleep like a baby."

"No thanks. We're in fucking Finland—I want to eat like they do. You go to Italy, you eat Doritos?"

Vince nodded.

"Okay," Tony rolled his eyes. "Maybe you do. But other people don't. People go to Italy, they want to eat Italian food. Same thing here."

Vince didn't reply. Secretly, Tony thought he might be right. The village only had one place to eat—a rustic tavern with a few elderly patrons. Tony and Vince didn't speak the language, and their translator, a young man named Tjers, had met with an unfortunate accident after offering Tony a blow job, so they'd had to muddle through the menu. Tony ended up getting a boiled sheep's head on a plate. It stared at him with big mournful eyes while he ate it. What kind of country was this where they left the eyes in your fucking dinner? And who the hell ate sheep *heads*, anyway?

Tony sighed. What was supposed to be a simple job had turned into a cluster-fuck. It had seemed so straightforward. Travel from the United States to the Savukoski county of Lapland, Finland, which was right on the border with Russia. Meet up with Tjers. Wait for Otar, who was based in Murmansk Oblast, to cross the border, and then make the exchange—money and heroin for a dozen vials of black-market Soviet-era anthrax—a weaponized strain that their employer, Mr. Marano of the Marano crime family, was anxious to obtain. Once the exchange had been made, Otar would fuck off back to Russia, and Tony and Vince were supposed to cross the Korvatunturi mountains, meet up with their transport, and deliver the anthrax back to the

States.

Now they were holed up in a converted bedroom in the tavern's attic. Tjers was dead and buried in the snow, and Otar hadn't shown. They had no one to guide them over the mountain path, and it looked like they were going home empty-handed—if they made it home at all. Their employer was going to be pissed. He didn't like mishaps or mistakes. Their asses were grass and Marano was the lawnmower, unless Tony figured out how to salvage this whole mess.

Merry fucking Christmas.

On the television, cartoon characters jabbered in Finnish.

"All things considered," Tony muttered, "I'd rather be in fucking Pittsburgh."

"What was the dream about?" Vince asked.

Tony watched his obese partner shovel three double-stuffed Oreo cookies into his mouth at once, and sighed again.

"We were sitting in this little cafe in Atlantic City, waiting for Frankie Spicolli to show up. Then a bunch of crab-things straight out of a bad Sci-Fi Channel movie showed up and started killing people. They looked like a cross between a crab, lobster and scorpion."

"Then what happened?"

Tony got out of bed and stretched. Then he smoothed his suit.

"Something about a fucking hurricane or some shit. I don't remember. What the hell are you watching?"

Vince shrugged. "I don't know. It ain't in English. Pretty good, though. Kind of reminds me of Thomas the Tank Engine, except it's got chicks in it. Look at the tits on her!"

"Very nice."

"I was hoping they'd show that Rudolph cartoon."

"The one with the Bumble?"

Vince's eyes lit up. "Yeah, that's the one! I always liked Bumble when I was a kid."

Probably cause you're about the same size, Tony thought. Then he said, "I liked Herbie, the elf that wanted to be a dentist. But then they did that stupid fucking sequel, with the Baby fucking New Year. Ruined the whole thing."

Vince turned back to the television. "Seems like there'd be some kind of special program on, what with it being Christmas Eve and all. Santa lives near here, you know?"

"What?"

"Santa Claus," Vince explained. "Everybody knows his reindeer stay in Finland during the year. There aren't any reindeer at the North Pole."

Tony paused before speaking. "Vince, there ain't no fucking reindeer at the North Pole because there ain't no Santa Claus."

"You sound like my folks, back when I was a teenager. They tried to say there weren't no Santa, too."

"You still believe in Santa Claus?"

"Well, sure, Tony. Don't you?"

"No, I don't. And neither does anybody else over the age of nine. And probably not many of them anymore, either. Hard for a kid to believe in Santa when there's people flying airplanes into buildings and shooting up schools. Jesus fucking Christ, Vince. You believe in the Easter Bunny, too?"

"No." Vince sulked. "Everybody knows the Easter Bunny is make believe. But Santa Claus ain't. He's—"

A scream cut him off, followed by more. A gunshot echoed through the darkness.

"The fuck?" Tony grabbed his Sig-Sauer off the pine nightstand.

More screams and gunshots drifted up from the streets below. The gunfire didn't surprise them. Gun ownership was fairly common in this part of the world, at least by European standards. What startled them was the sudden clattering sound on the roof.

"Turn that shit off," Tony whispered. "Let's see what's the matter."

The television screen went black. Vince pulled his Kimber 1911 and heaved his prodigious bulk out of the chair, staring at the ceiling. Meanwhile, Tony crept to the window and peered through the blinds.

"Anything?" Vince asked.

Tony shook his head. "Nothing. Sounds like a—wait a fucking second. What the hell?"

Outside, a reindeer was goring an old man in the stomach. When the animal raised its head, entrails hung from its bloody antlers. Before Tony could react, the noise on the roof grew louder.

"Cops?" Vince said, moving towards the chimney.

"Why the fuck would they be coming through the roof, Vince? No. This is something else."

Something jingled in the night. Tony swore it was...sleigh bells.

There was a rustling noise from the roof. Soot and dirt tumbled down the chimney, sprinkling the fire and filling the air with dust. Vince sneezed and Tony's eyes watered. The fire flared, and then sputtered. More debris fell down the chimney. Then they heard a scraping sound and a huge mound of snow fell onto the fire, extinguishing it. Smoke curled from the fireplace. Vince sneezed again and glanced at Tony.

Tony put his finger to his lips, and then motioned towards the fireplace. The two men tiptoed towards it, standing on either side with their handguns at the ready. A long shadow stretched down from the roof. The sleigh bells rang again. Vince started to speak, but Tony shushed him. More snow fell down the shaft, and then something scuffed against the sides of the chimney. The shadow lengthened. Whoever—whatever—was on the roof was coming down.

Moving as one, Vince and Tony backed away from the fireplace. Standing side by side, they extended their arms and clutched their weapons with both hands, holding the barrels steady. Their fingers rested lightly on the triggers. Neither man flinched. They barely breathed. They stood statue-still, waiting.

A figure crashed into the sodden remains of the fire, knocking burnt logs and ashes aside. Crouching, the intruder surveyed the two and cackled.

Tony had seen some bizarre shit in his time. Back home, he'd seen weird lights at night in the woods of LeHorn's Hollow, which was supposed to be haunted. They'd hovered above the ground, no bigger than softballs, before zooming up into the sky and disappearing. There was other oddness, too. He and Vince used the services of a cannibal who lived in York, Pennsylvania to dispose of bodies when the occasion called for it. They'd once had to steal a diamond that burned your skin like acid if you touched it. Then there were the dreams—dreams he'd never told anyone about, not even Vince. Dreams that he'd lived in other times and places. Other worlds. Fighting weird crab-monsters and all sorts of other creatures.

But the figure that emerged from the fireplace was the strangest fucking thing Tony had ever seen.

It looked like Santa Claus—fat (though not as fat as Vince), red suit and hat, rosy cheeks and a beard. But that was where the similarities ended. This garish figure was better suited for Halloween than Christmas. His skin was pale—almost blue. Blood and gore had matted in the beard, and the rosy glow on his cheeks was more dried blood. Most telling was the gunshot wound in his chest. Tony glanced at it, remembering the shot they'd heard earlier. He'd seen men shot there before—had shot men there before. That wasn't a wound you walked around with, let alone crawl across rooftops and drop down chimneys.

Tony tried to speak and couldn't.

Vince summed it up for him, his voice tinged with unexpected delight.

"Santa Claus!"

"Ho, ho fucking ho. Time to die, humans. My brothers need your bodies."

Vince paled. "Santa doesn't curse."

"I am not Santa. I am Ob the Obot, Lord of the Siqqusim and greatest of the Thirteen! Your time is over. For each of you that we kill, one of my kind will take your place. There are so many of us. More than infinity."

Tony smirked. "Are all of them as fat as you?"

The man in red charged towards them.

Tony squeezed the trigger, aiming for the intruder's belly. His mark was true, but Santa barely slowed. He grunted as the bullet slammed into him and ripped through his back, before hitting the brick wall behind him. Santa grinned and took another step forward.

"Tony, you can't shoot Santa Claus!"

Tony barely heard his partner. The sound of the gunshot filled the room. Instead of responding, he fired again. Whoever this guy was, he was still standing despite two shots to the body. This time, he aimed for the face. Santa's grin vanished in a wet explosion of red.

"Shoot the fucker, Vince!"

Santa tried to speak, but his lower jaw was missing. His tongue flopped uselessly, sliding across his the shattered remnants of his upper teeth. He seized a fireplace poker and swung it at Tony. Tony dodged the blow, raised his pistol, and fired again. This time, he aimed for the fat man's forehead.

He didn't miss.

Santa uttered a short, garbled moan. Then he fell forward, face first onto the floor. His body twitched once and then he was still. Tony put a foot on his back and fired two more rounds into the back of his head at close range. Then he kicked him. Santa didn't move.

Silence returned. The air was thick with wood smoke and gunpowder. Outside, the screaming continued.

"Jesus..." Vince leaned against the wall with one hand, panting. "I told you, Tony! See? There is *so* such a thing as Santa Claus."

"No, Vince. There ain't no fucking Santa Claus."

He prodded the corpse with his shoe.

"At least, not anymore."

Tony popped the magazine from his Sig-Sauer, slid a few more bullets into place, and then slammed it back home. He ran to the window and glanced outside. The slaughter continued in the streets as Santa's dead helpers ran riot. Tony grabbed Vince by the arm.

"Come on. Let's go kill ourselves some zombie reindeer."

STORY NOTES

I originally intended to publish this story as a chapbook and give it away to each person on my message board as a holiday greeting to thank them for their continued support. However, at the time, the community had over 2,000 members, and that plan wasn't very cost effective. This story features three of my most inarguably popular characters—Ob, the body-hopping zombie lord (I told you he'd be back later in the book), and stone-cold killers Tony Genova and Vince Napoli (from Clickers II: The Next Wave *and the short stories* "Crazy For You" *and* "Marriage Causes Cancer In Rats"*). I hope you had as much fun reading it as I had writing it.*

GOLDEN BOY

I shit gold.

It started around the time I hit puberty. I thought there was something wrong with me. Cancer or parasites or something like that, because when I looked down into the bowl, a golden turd was sitting on the bottom. When I wiped, there were gold stains on the toilet paper. Then I flushed and went back to watching cartoons. Ten minutes later, I'd forgotten all about it.

You know how kids are.

But it wasn't just my shit. I pissed gold. (No golden showers jokes, please. I've heard them all before). I started sweating gold. It oozed out of my pores in little droplets, drying on my skin in flakes. It peeled off easily enough. Just like dead skin after a bad case of sunburn. Then my spit and mucous started turning into gold. I'd hock gold nuggets onto the sidewalk. One day, I was picking mulberries from a tree in a pasture. There was a barbed-wire fence beneath the tree, and to reach the higher branches, I stood on the fence. I lost my balance and the barbed wire took three big chunks out of the back of my thigh. My blood was liquid gold. And like I said, this was around puberty, so you can only imagine what my wet dreams were like. Many nights, instead of waking up wet and sticky, I woke up with a hard, metallic mess on my sheets and in my pajamas.

Understand, my bodily fluids weren't just gold colored.

If they had been, things might have turned out differently. But they were actual gold—that precious metal coveted all over the world. Gold—the source of wars and peace, the rise of empires and their eventual collapse, murders and robberies, wealth and poverty, love and hate.

My parents figured it out soon enough. So did the first doctor they took me to. Oh, yeah. That doctor was very interested. He wanted to keep me for observation. Wanted to conduct some more tests. He said all this with his doctor voice but you could see the greed in his eyes.

And he was just the first.

Mom and Dad weren't having any of that. They took me home and told me this was going to be our little secret. I was special. I had a gift from God. A wonderful, magnificent talent—but one that might be misunderstood by others. They wanted to help me avoid that, they said. Didn't want me to be made fun of or taken advantage of. Even now, I honestly think they meant it at the time. They believed that their intentions were for the best. But you know what they say about good intentions. The road to hell is paved with them. That's bullshit, of course.

The road to hell is paved with fucking gold.

My parents started skimming my residue. Mom scraped gold dust from my clothes and the sheets when she did laundry and from the rim of my glass after dinner. One night, they told me I couldn't watch my favorite TV show because I wouldn't eat my broccoli. I cried gold tears. After that, it seemed like they made me cry a lot.

Everywhere I went, I left a trail of gold behind me. My parents collected it, invested it, and soon, we moved to a bigger house in a nicer neighborhood with a better school. Our family of three grew. We had a maid and a cook and groundskeepers.

I hated it, at first. The new house was too big. We'd been a blue-collar family. Now, Mom and Dad didn't work anymore and I suddenly found myself thrown into classrooms with a bunch of snobby rich kids—all because of my gift. I had nothing in common with my classmates. They talked about books and music that I'd never heard of, and argued politics and civic responsibilities and French Impressionism. They idolized Che Guevara and Ayn Rand and Ernest Hemingway. I read comic books and listened to hip-hop and liked Spider-Man.

So I tried to fit in. Nobody wants to be hated. It's human nature—wanting to be liked by your peers. Soon enough, I found a way. I let them in on my little secret. Within a week, I was the most popular kid in school. I had more friends than I knew what to do with. Everybody wanted to be friends with the golden boy. But here's the thing. They didn't want to be friends with me because of who I was. They wanted to be friends with me because of *who* I was. There's a big difference between those two things.

So I had friends. Girlfriends, too.

I remember the first girl I ever loved. She was beautiful. There's nothing as powerful or pure or unstable as first love. I thought about her constantly. Stared at her in class. Dreamed of her at night. And when she returned my interest, my body felt like a coiled spring. It was the happiest day of my life. But she didn't love me for who I was. Like everyone else, she loved me for *who* I was.

So have all the rest. Both ex-wives and the string of long-term girlfriends between them. My happiest relationships are one-night stands. The only women I'm truly comfortable with are the ones I only know for a few brief hours. I never tell them who I am or what I can do. And before you ask, yes, I always wear a condom and no, I can't have children. There are no little golden boys in my future. I don't shoot blanks. I shoot bullets.

I've no shortage of job opportunities. Banks, financial groups, precious metals dealers, jewelers, even several governments. Of course, I don't need to work. I can live off my talent for the rest of my life. So can everyone else around me. But that doesn't stop the employment offers from coming. And they're so insincere and patronizing. So very fucking patronizing. They want to invest in my future. Just like my parents and my friends and my wives, they only want what's best for me. Or so they claim.

But I know what they really want.

And I can't take it anymore.

I'm spent. My gold is tarnished. It's lost its gleam. Its shine. I can see it, and I wonder if others are noticing, too.

Here's what's going to happen. I'm going to put this gun to my head and blow my brains out all over the room, leaving a golden spray pattern on the wall. The medical examiner will pick skull fragments and gold nuggets out of the plaster. The mortician can line his pockets before embalming me. You can sell my remains on eBay, and invest in them, and fight over what's left.

I want to fade away, but gold never fades. This is my gift. This is my legacy. This is my curse.

I have only one thing to leave behind.

You can spend me when I'm gone.

STORY NOTES

I thought this might be a nice way to end things, given the title of this short story collection. The first and last sentences of this story came to me one day, and I liked them so much that I wrote a story to tie them together. Author Kelli Dunlap read this (as she does with all of my stories prior to publication) and said it was a metaphor for my current place in the genre. But Kelli is quite possibly mentally ill, and she says that about all of my work. Plus, I'm fairly certain she was drunk when she read it. Take from "Golden Boy" what you will, but I just think it's a quirky and kind of fun fable. Not a metaphor, and (hopefully) not a prediction of the future.

STORY NOTES

Again, this time you get the story notes at the beginning.

I don't write a lot of poetry – primarily because I'm not very good at it. The vast majority of my poetry ends up sounding like death metal lyrics.

I debated whether or not to include these three poems in this collection. Ultimately, I decided to include them at the end. The first one is a poem that many readers have requested a look at (it's been long out of print). I'm rather fond of the latter two.

Maybe you'll dig them. Maybe you won't. In either case, they won't take up much of your time.

HANGAR 18

It fell from the sky with the sound of thunder
Frozen now in cryogenic slumber
A lost traveler, far from home
Now trapped by Man and all alone
Soldiers and scientists gather around
Not telling the public what they found
Politicians lie and proof we lack
Death at the hands of the Men in Black
Under the desert I silently crept
To see the captive where it slept
Now I must tell of what I've seen
That which lies in Hangar 18

OFF-WHITE KNIGHTS

When we were kids
I was always there for you
That's what you said
When you hurt your knee
And that time in the rainstorm
And when he made you cry

I was there

When we were teens
I was still there for you
That's what you noticed

When we kissed
And that time we went swimming
And when he made you cry

I was there

I said I was your knight in shining armor
You laughed, and said knights weren't bad boys
And I was
So I was your knight in off-white armor

We're older now
But I'm still here for you
That's what you know

When life's too much
And that time on the phone
And when he makes you cry

I am here

I don't get to ride off into the sunset with you on my horse
That's for white knights
The off-white knight goes back into the shadows
With your words still in his ears
And memories in his head
And waits for the next dragon to slay

FOUR YOUNG BLONDES IN A RED MAZDA

You on my ass
Trying to pass
Flicking your hair
Laughing
And talking on your cell phones

I slowed down and
You sped up
And I braked
Stopped
You swerved into the other lane

Waved as you passed
But then I
Gave you the
Finger
Because your youth pisses me off

I sped up again
Cut you off
You got mad
Angry
Flashing your perfectly manicured red fingernails

Let me introduce you
To the guardrail
To your unhappy
Ending
Because this is what awaits you

Ten years ago, I would have happily fucked you
Now, I'm happy to fuck with you

PUBLICATION HISTORY

The following are reprinted with permission:

"The Resurrection And The Life" first published as *The Resurrection And The Life*, Biting Dog Press, 2007.

"Burying Betsy" first appeared as an audio broadcast on DreadCentral.com, 2006.

"The Ties That Bind" first published in *The Little Silver Book of Streetwise Stories*, Borderlands Press, 2008.

"The Black Wave" first published in *A Dark and Deadly Valley*, Silverthought Press, 2007.

"Take The Long Way Home" first published as *Take The Long Way Home*, Necessary Evil Press, 2006.

"Bunnies In August" first published on Horror World.org, 2005.

"Midnight At The Body Farm" first published in *Dead Sea* (lettered edition), Delirium Books, 2007.

"The Ghosts Of Monsters" first published in *Ghost Walk* (lettered edition), Delirium Books, 2008.

"Tequila's Sunrise" first published as *Tequila's Sunrise*, Bloodletting Press, 2006.

"The Waiting Is The Hardest Part" first published in *The Rising: Selected Scenes From the End of the World* (collector's edition), Delirium Books, 2007.

"This Is Not An Exit" first published in *The Little Silver Book of Streetwise Stories*, Borderlands Press, 2008.

"Take Me To The River" first published in *Earthworm Gods* (lettered edition), Delirium Books, 2005.

"An Appointment Kept" first published in *4 Fear of,* Borderlands Press, 2006.

"Stone Tears" first published as *Stone Tears,* Infernal House, 2008.

"Gratefully Dead" first published in *Dead Cats Bouncing,* Necro Publications, 2002.

"The Siqqusim Who Stole Christmas" first published in *The Little Silver Book of Streetwise Stories,* Borderlands Press, 2008.

"Golden Boy" first published in *The Little Silver Book of Streetwise Stories,* Borderlands Press, 2008.

"Hangar 18" first published in *The Golden Age of Flying Saucers,* 1997.

ABOUT THE AUTHOR

BRIAN KEENE is the author of over twenty books, including *Castaways, Ghost Walk, Dark Hollow, Kill Whitey, Fear of Gravity, Dead Sea, Ghoul, The Conqueror Worms* and many more. He also writes for Marvel Comics. In 2009, his novel, *Terminal,* debuted as a stage play and his short story, "The Ties That Bind," debuted as a short, independent film. Several of his short stories have been adapted as graphic novels, and several of his novels and stories have been optioned for film. The winner of two Bram Stoker awards, Keene's work has been praised in such diverse places as *The New York Times,* The History Channel, CNN.com, *Publisher's Weekly, Fangoria Magazine,* and *Rue Morgue Magazine.* Keene lives in Pennsylvania with his wife, son, dog, and cat. You can communicate with him online at www.briankeene.com.

JOIN DELIRIUM'S HORROR BOOK CLUB
Save 40% off all titles
Shop online
Major credit cards accepted
Free book when you join
Discover the future of horror today
www.deliriumbooks.com/bookclub

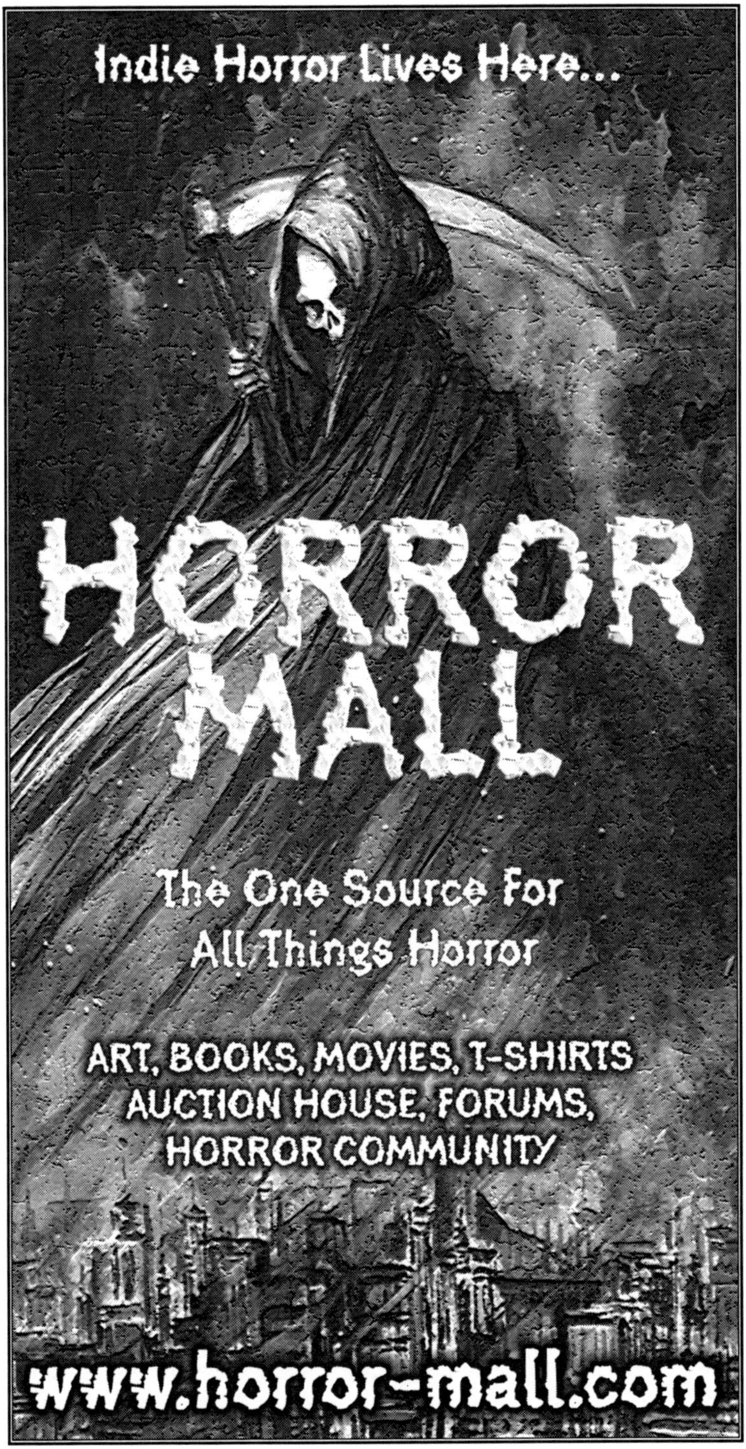

Indie Horror Lives Here...
HORROR MALL
The One Source For
All Things Horror
ART, BOOKS, MOVIES, T-SHIRTS
AUCTION HOUSE, FORUMS,
HORROR COMMUNITY
www.horror-mall.com

LaVergne, TN USA
08 September 2009
157166LV00004B/33/P

9 781934 546109